Thomas E. Lightburn served for twenty-two years in the medical branch of the Royal Navy. He reached the rank of Chief Petty Officer and left the service in 1974. After gaining a Bachelor of Education degree with Honours at Liverpool University, he taught for sixteen years before volunteering for early retirement. He then began writing stories for The Wirral Journal and the Sea Breezes, a nation-wide nautical magazine. He interviewed Ian Fraser, VC, ex Lieutenant RN, and wrote an account of how he and his crew, in a midget submarine, crippled the Japanese cruiser, Takao, in Singapore. Tom lives in Wallasey, pursuing his favourite hobbies of soccer, naval and military history, the theatre, art and travel.

The emblem of the R.N. Patrol Service.

By the same author

The Gates Of Stonehouse
(Vanguard Press)
ISBN 978 1 84386 203 1

Uncommon Valour
(Vanguard Press)
ISBN 978 1 84386 301 4

THE SHIELD AND THE SHARK

Thomas E. Lightburn

THE SHIELD AND THE SHARK

Vanguard Press

VANGUARD PAPERBACK

A CIP catalogue record for this title is available from the British Library

ISBN 978 1 84386 350 2

Vanguard Press is an imprint of Pegasus Elliot MacKenzie Publishers Ltd.
www.pegasuspublishers.com

First Published in 2007

Vanguard Press
Sheraton House Castle Park
Cambridge England

Printed & Bound in Great Britain

DEDICATION

This book is dedicated to my father, Edward Lightburn, Ex Able Seaman, Royal Navy. The men of the MMS 50 and all who served in the Royal Naval Patrol Service during the Second World War.

ACKNOWLEDGEMENT

I would like to express
my sincere thanks to the following people.

Joseph Steele, DSM. Ronald Balshaw, Edward Gooding, John Pue, Marshal Brooks, John Hutchins and Derek Jackson, (Algerines). All served on minesweepers during the Second World War and are members of Wallasey Royal Naval Association. Lieutenant Commander George Storey RN, Retd. James Rankin and Victor Phillips; retired officers of the St John's Ambulance Brigade. Jane Wakenham, Institute of Naval Medicine, Alverstoke. John R. Haley, MA, Dip Gen. Robert Nicholson and Linda Sanderson for their expert computer advice. The staff of Greenwich Library in South London and Earlston Libraries in Wallasey. Mrs Linda Hodgson for reading the manuscript and for her helpful comments. Liverpool Maritime Museum. The Naval Historical Research Association. Brigadier J.F. Rickett, CBE and John Lenaghan for allowing me access to the archives of The Union Jack Club in London, and last but not least, Robin Seymour, ex Royal Marine Commando whose idea inspired this book.

Thomas E. Lightburn. Wallasey 2006

PROLOGUE

'Are you sure you'll know one another, Ted dear?' said Edna, as she helped me on with my heavy blue overcoat. 'And what about that nurse, Susan something or other you told me he married? I wonder if you'll recognise each other, sixty years is a long time.'

The mention of Susan gave me a start; for a fleeting moment an image of a beautiful girl with a flashing smile and soft brown eyes came into my mind. Even now, despite what happened all those years ago, I had never forgotten her.

I gave a short, nervous laugh. 'I expect you're right, love,' I said, 'but I'll remember them all right.'

Over the years, especially on Remembrance Day watching the lines of ex service men and women march past the Cenotaph, I had often wondered what had happened to Harvey and Susan; had he eventually recovered from the injury that threatened to drive them apart? More important, how could I ever forget the man who once saved my life and whose friendship and trust I had betrayed.

I suddenly conjured up a tall, broad shouldered man with clear blue eyes, thick fair hair and a mischievous smile. Over the years I had tried to forget those perilous times Harvey and I shared during the Second World War; now, standing in the hallway, memories of those distant days came flooding back to haunt me again.

'Strange he didn't tell you more about his wife,' said Edna, handing me a small suitcase. 'You did ask him, didn't you?'

'Yes,' I replied, trying to sound casual. 'But he...'

Edna's voice interrupted me. 'You probably wouldn't recognise her anyway. And you've altered quite a bit since the end of the war.'

A glance at the long mirror in the hallway told me she was right. Deep set brown eyes and a dark, foreign-looking, well-lined face stared back at me; a series of double chins hid what was once a firm jaw line and my thick black hair had long since disappeared. In its place, tufts of whiteness bordered a shiny bald head. However, I couldn't help noticing how the shoulders of my once six-foot plus frame sagged; even pulling in my stomach failed to conceal an obvious paunch.

As I continued to stare in the mirror I was overcome with a mixture of fear and apprehension; several questions bounced around my head. Harvey Rawlinson and I hadn't met since him and Susan parted outside the 'Nelson' pub in Gosport on a bitterly cold night in January 1944. What, I wondered, had happened to them since then? And why, after all this time had he suddenly come back into my life; more important, why all the secrecy about Susan?

Whatever the reasons, I would find out during the next twenty-four hours.

The gentle touch of Edna's hands brushing my shoulders interrupted my reverie.

'There,' she said with finality of a judge passing sentence, 'you look as smart as a guardsman. Now remember. When you get to Euston you'll have to ask the way to Waterloo Station.'

With concern etched in her sad, grey eyes, Edna looked at me. In a soft voice she said, 'Are you sure you don't want me to come with you?' Pushing back a strand of grey hair she added, 'that arthritis in your hip isn't getting any better, so do be careful, love.'

'It's no use both of us going to London,' I replied, taking hold of her hand. 'I'll be home in a few days, and I'll, telephone you as soon as I arrive. So don't worry.'

This was a futile thing to say. Of course she would worry. Edna worried when I went down the road for a morning paper; she was a born worrier. That was one of the reasons I still loved her as much as when we were married nearly fifty years ago.

We had met at the Kingsland Dance Hall, Birkenhead shortly after the war. The first thing I noticed was her shoulder-length blonde hair; her blue dress matched the colour of her eyes and she wore black high-heeled shoes. At first she refused to dance with me.

I remember looking down at her and saying, 'Y'know, you're the kind of girl I thought about when I was a POW in Germany.'

That piece of subterfuge did the trick.

'Were you *really* a prisoner of war?' she asked as we danced.

For a few seconds I didn't answer; I casually shrugged my shoulders and grinned. She looked at me questionably and we both suddenly burst out laughing. Twelve months later we were married in Saint James's Church, Birkenhead.

After working for the Mersey Docks and Harbour Board for five years I was promoted to chief clerk. The extra money enabled us to take out a mortgage and move to where we now lived, a pleasant semi in Prenton Road East, Birkenhead.

'I've packed a clean shirt and underwear for you,' said Edna, handing me a small suitcase. 'And a flask of tea and sandwiches.'

I looked down at Edna's ample waistline encased in a red and white polka-dot apron. As soon as I left she would immediately lose herself doing housework as she always did when upset.

Sadly, we had no children; two years after we were married Edna was diagnosed as having cancer and had a hysterectomy. Following a course of radiotherapy, she made a full recovery. For a long time afterwards she was depressed and felt guilty of not being able to give me the son I always wanted. As the years passed, I sometimes felt envious watching the children of relatives and friends grow up; it was even worse for Edna whose sister Agnes had two lovely boys, Harold and Michael. Both were now grown up with families of their own. At Christmas they would come and visit Edna and I. They were very happy occasions but when they had left Edna would sit in silence. Even to this day the sight of a baby in a pram sometimes brings tears to her eyes

However, our love for one another saw us through what was a very difficult period. Now, as she straightened my collar and adjusted my tie, I looked at her and not for the first time, realised how lucky I was.

'Anyway, Agnes is coming to visit you tomorrow,' I replied. 'You two can have a good old natter. You won't even know I'm not here.'

'Don't be silly,' she answered dryly. 'You know I will. Now are you sure you've got your ticket?'

'Yes dear,' I replied with a sigh.

'The train leaves Lime Street at ten eighteen,' answered Edna, carefully removing a spec of dust from my overcoat collar. 'Are you sure you'll be all right, love?'

'Yes, dear,' I repeated, squeezing her hand, 'now stop fussing.'

The sound of the taxi outside the front door drew our attention. A few tears appeared in Edna's eyes and I felt a lump come in my throat.

'Cheerio, love,' I said, placing my free arm around her and giving her a kiss on the lips. 'I'm only going for a couple of days, not a two year commission. I'll be back in no time. Just you see.'

A cold October wind greeted me as I opened the door. The nights were drawing in and Christmas 2005 was just around the corner.

The journey through the Birkenhead Tunnel to Liverpool didn't take long. Lime Street Station had changed dramatically since 1942 when I joined the Royal Navy. Gone was the dark, dismal shed-like structure, the acrid smell of grime, steam and soot. Diesel and electrification had long since arrived and the air tasted fresh and clean.

In front of me was a wide, well-lit concourse with shops, cafés and a bar for a quick pint before catching the train. There was even a replica of a palm tree to put holiday-makers in the mood for exotic destinations.

The train compartment wasn't crowded and I had a small table to myself. I removed my overcoat and settled down.

Trains and coach journeys are great places for thought and reflection, perhaps it's something to do with the rhythm of the engines and the relaxed atmosphere. Shortly after the train pulled out I found myself thinking if it hadn't been for Edna I wouldn't be sitting here.

Early on Saturday evening three days ago we were watching television. Suddenly, Edna placed her knitting in her lap, peered over her rimless spectacles and said, 'Why don't we go to the "Naval Club", love. It'll do us both good to get out for a change. And you never know, I might even win a few bob on the bingo.'

I didn't feel like going but knew she would only nag me if I refused; so I gave in, and off we went.

No sooner had we entered the club than Ronnie Norris shouted across from a table. 'Hey Ted,' he yelled, his red face full of curiosity. 'I see your name's mentioned in this month's *Navy News.*'

This was a monthly newspaper issued in HMS *Nelson,* Portsmouth, especially for the Royal Navy and Marines, past and present. It was distributed around every royal naval and marine reservist club in Great Britain. One column called *Over to You* was devoted to contacting old shipmates.

'What d'ye mean, Ronnie?' I asked, as Edna and I sat down at a table.

'Someone called Harvey Rawlinson has put an advertisement in the paper,' he replied. 'Says he's an old pal of yours from the war. Look, I'll show you.' He then produced a copy of the newspaper from his pocket, opened it up, found the column and passed it to me.

My God! I said to myself, Harvey Rawlinson! It was name I hadn't heard for decades. Then I remembered Susan and suddenly felt my stomach contract.

As I read the section in the paper my hand shook.

Harvey Rawlinson wishes to meet Ted Burnside, his old shipmate between 1943- 44 from the MMS 50. Can be contacted on 020-744-1269.

As my eyes followed the print I felt a shiver run down my spine. The paper shook in my hand; surely I said to myself, he couldn't have found out what happened all those years ago.

'What's the matter, Ted?' I heard Edna say. 'You look as if you've seen a ghost.'

I swallowed hard and handed the newspaper to her, 'In a way I have, love.'

'Harvey Rawlinson,' said Edna after reading the advertisement. 'I remember you mentioning him after you were demobbed. Wasn't the *MMS* 50 a minesweeper you both served on during the war, dear?'

'Yes, it was,' I replied dryly.

'How lovely for you, dear,' said Edna. 'You must telephone him tomorrow.'

Before I forgot I took out my notebook and wrote down Harvey's telephone number.

That evening I made a mess of my Bingo cards; Edna didn't seem to mind though, she won five pounds!

The next morning I decided to ring Harvey.

The voice that answered spoke with a slight Australian accent tinged with a touch of Scouse.

I nervously cleared my throat. 'Hello, Harv,' I said. 'It's me Ted Burnside. I read your add in the paper.'

'Stone the crows!' exclaimed Harvey. 'It's good to hear you, Ted. How the hell are you? How long has it been? Sixty years?'

I breathed a sigh of relief. At least he didn't appear to be angry. Perhaps I was worrying too much.

'Something like that,' I replied. 'But what happened to you and Susan after the war finished?'

Speaking the name of Harvey's wife for the first time in years made me feel uncomfortable. The image of a clearly defined, beautiful face with soft brown eyes suddenly appeared in my mind.

My thoughts were abruptly interrupted by Harvey's voice.

'We emigrated to Oz just after the war.' He paused then added. 'Bloody great place, I can tell yer. Look mate, I'm at a friend's house in Clapham. Can you come down to the Smoke? I'm moving into the "Union Jack Club" tomorrow.' He paused, then, in a faltering voice went on. 'I'd love to see you and talk over old times. Besides, there's…there's something important I want to tell you. What do you say?'

'How is Susan?' I asked, trying to control my emotions. 'Is she with you?'

For a few seconds the line went silent.

'No,' replied Harvey quietly. 'I'll tell you more when we meet. Oh, and don't forget to bring some Identification. D'you still have your discharge papers?'

His question caught me by surprise. I remembered the 'papers' were made of white linen, however, I hadn't seen them for years. 'I'm not sure,' I replied. 'They must be around somewhere. I'll ask Edna. She probably know where they are.'

'Good on yer mate,' answered Harvey. 'You'll need ID to get in the club.'

How ironic, I thought. Harvey would have to choose the 'Union Jack Club' – the place where it all started back in 1943.

Although I hadn't been back there since the war ended, I recalled standing in the foyer by the reception desk, reading a framed history of the club.

Completed in 1907, the imposing, red-bricked, Edwardian building stood in Waterloo Road, a haven for the armed forces during and after both world wars.

The 'U J' was the brainchild of a retired nurse named Ethel McCaul. It was she who, after the Boer War (1899-1902), decided servicemen discharged from the forces, and who had nowhere to go, should have a place where they could get a good meal and a bed. She approached Members of Parliament and a public subscription of £12,751. 3s. 4d was raised to build the club.

I smiled to myself thinking about how much that money would be worth today. (Probably well over a million pounds.) In those days, a breakfast of bacon and eggs, tea and toast in the UJC was less than a shilling. A cabin cost 1/9d a night beer was 9d a pint and you could get your boots cleaned for 2d.

I also remembered my first night in London when a few pals and myself visited 'The Windmill Theatre'. The faces of young men I hadn't seen for years came clearly into my head. Good Lord! I sighed I wonder where they are now?

Once again the sound of Harvey's voice suddenly brought me back to reality.

'Are you still there, Ted?' he asked.

'Yes… Yes I am,' I replied, then with a half-hearted laugh, added, 'heaven's above, Harv, the "The Union Jack Club". It's been a long time since I've been there. But tell me, why all the mystery? What's so important after all these years?'

'I don't want to discuss it over the 'phone, mate,' answered Harvey. As he spoke, his voice dropped as if he thought someone was listening. 'Just do me a favour, and come down. It really is important.'

'All right, but I'll have to check with the missus first,' I replied, then added. 'I have to admit, Harv, you've got me puzzled.'

After a brief consultation with Edna it was agreed I would go to London on the following Monday.

'Those naval discharge papers of yours are in the back of the chest of drawers,' said Edna. 'It's a good job I didn't throw them away like you said when we moved in.'

When I told Harvey I would come to London he sounded quite elated.

'Great!' he replied. 'I can't wait to see you, mate. I'll book you a room and meet you in the lounge about five o'clock.' He then added, 'You know, your voice sounds the same as it did all those years ago. Listening to you brings back a lot of memories.'

Suddenly my heart missed a beat! What memories was he referring, and why all the secrecy?

'Right, Harv,' I replied, trying to sound calm. 'I'll see you there, but I wish you'd tell me what's up.'

For a few seconds Harvey didn't answer. Then, in a subdued voice, replied, 'I'll tell you when I see you. So long Ted.'

The journey to London took almost three hours: much quicker and more comfortable than during the war. Like Lime Street Station, Euston had undergone a dramatic change since 1945. For a while I stood in the huge concourse somewhat bewildered by the bustling crowds. Finally, after following an underground sign, I saw an official-looking man in uniform and asked him how I could obtain a ticket and directions to Waterloo.

'It's been many years since I was last here,' I said, following the official to a machine.

'A single to Waterloo, you say?' he said. 'That'll be one

pound fifty pence. Just follow the signs. You'll want the Northern Line. It's six stops to Waterloo.'

The underground train was crowded but I managed to find a seat. There seemed to be people from all over the world in the compartment. The couple next to me sounded like Germans, while a fair-headed family opposite spoke in the singsong language of Sweden. Further along a family of four from the Orient sat glancing anxiously at the colour-coded tube map overhead on the advertisement boards.

Arriving at Waterloo, I obeyed the voice from the speaker system telling me to '*Mind the Gap',* and stepped carefully onto the platform.

My arthritic hip felt stiff after sitting down for so long. I flexed my right leg a few times and looked around. Masses of people were stood on the station concourse their faces turned upwards, studying the train timetables. Once again I became disorientated and sought help from another official.

'"The Union Jack Club", guv'nor,' he said, pointing towards an exit, 'go down the escalator into Waterloo Road. You can't miss it.'

I followed his instructions and found myself staring across the road at a building that looked nothing like the one I remembered in 1943. In place of the five-storey façade of the UJC stood a tall, glass covered structure that looked like a block of offices.

Buses, taxis and other vehicles poured down the busy road; crowds jostled along pavements making their way in and out of the tube station. I anxiously looked around wondering if I was in the right place. Then I realised where I was standing once housed a hostel. In 1943 this was an extension of the club and was used as an annex. That was now gone and in its place was a large underground tube terminal.

Suddenly, a feeling of panic welled up inside me. Where the hell was I?

In an act of sheer desperation, I asked an elderly man selling copies of the *Evening Standard,* where the club was.

'Over there, me old China,' he said, pointing across the road to a public house. Suddenly I recognised the pub. It was appropriately called 'The Wellington', the place where Susan, Harvey and I had our first drink many years ago.

'It's just on yer right, down Sandell Street,' he said, 'yer can't miss it.'

'But what happened to the one that was over there?' I asked nodding across the road.

'Knocked down years ago,' he replied, handing a newspaper to a customer. 'Built a new one, so they did. Opened in 1975.'

Feeling confused, I thanked him and crossed the road. A bitter gust of wind hit me as I turned into a Sandell Street. On the left side of the street a door led into a section of Waterloo Station. Further down opposite a French wine bar stood a modern building. On either side of the central section, brown-bricked columns studded with darkened windows, towered into the air like skyscrapers. Above the entrance was a small, but obvious sign that read 'The Union Jack Club'.

For a while I stood at the bottom of two flights of steps, straining my neck looking up at a structure that seemed to disappear into the clouds. I then noticed a White Ensign, the flag of the Royal Navy, fluttering from the top of the building. Its movement in the breeze seemed to hypnotize me. Suddenly, I broke out into a cold sweat. Scenes I had long forgotten flashed before me. The sound of bombs exploding echoed around my head; I closed my eyes and saw bits of human flesh flying in the air, ships disintegrating and heard the screams of wounded men.

Quite abruptly the sound of a man's voice brought me back to my senses.

'Are you all right, sir?'

I opened my eyes and saw a tall young man looking down at me. He wore a blue shirt and dark trousers.

'Yes,' I replied, 'I was just catching my breath.'

'I work here. Can I help you sir?' he asked politely.

I took a deep breath and nervously licked my lips. 'Er…no,' I replied. 'Thank you all the same.'

A glance at my wristwatch told me the time was a half past three. In less than two hours I would know the secret behind Harvey's telephone call. Taking a tight hold of my suitcase I began to walk slowly up the steps. As I did so, my mind went back to those dark days before the Second World War…

CHAPTER ONE

Monday, January 1st 1943 was a bitterly cold day. As I closed the door of our small terraced house on Random Street, Birkenhead, the warm atmosphere was a welcome contrast to the sharp, south-easterly wind blowing down the River Mersey.

Mum and dad were busy getting ready for their weekly visit to Aunt Aida and Uncle Bert who lived in Upper Stanhope Street, Liverpool.

'There's chicken pie in the oven for your supper, Ted,' said Mum, putting on her coat.

Mum was a small woman, plump, with dark brown hair always tied in a bun, and soft, kind hazel eyes. Dad was the strict one; he stood just over six feet with greying black hair, a swarthy, complexion and a small well-waxed military moustache. Dad had been a sergeant in the Cheshire Regiment during the First World War and had been wounded at Gallipolli.

'And don't forget to lock up before you go out,' barked Dad, as though he was on parade. 'And put some coke on the fire,' he added putting on his trilby. 'It'll keep the water hot in the boiler for Mum's washing tomorrow.'

'Keep warm when you leave,' said Mum, 'and don't forget to eat your supper.'

I'll never forget the smile on mum's face as she kissed me on the cheek; it was the last time I saw either of them again.

Much to my surprise there was an air raid that evening. A year previously I had joined the St John's Ambulance Brigade. After attending a series of lectures and doing practical work I became a fully-fledged Cadet. Thankfully, I missed the carnage of the Merseyside May Blitz of 1940. But later, in 1941, the horrific scenes of men, women and children being dragged out of rubble became scenes indelibly etched on my mind. The air raids had suddenly stopped in the later part of 1941. In fact we hadn't had one since November, so hearing the wailing sound of the siren the evening mum and dad left came as a surprise.

Early next morning, the banging on the front door woke me up. I put on my trousers and went downstairs. My heart leapt up when I saw two burly policemen standing outside.

'I'm afraid we've got some bad news for you, son,' said one of them.

'What d'you mean?' I asked, full of apprehension. 'You'd best come inside.'

The policemen entered the hallway and removed their helmets. The taller of the two, a ginger-headed man about forty, frowned and avoided my gaze. His friend, a medium-sized, stocky man took out a notebook. He looked at me with a sombre expression.

'I sorry to tell you, son,' he said with a sigh. 'Your parents were killed during last night's air raid.'

For a second I stood transfixed staring at them. As their words filtered into my head I felt the blood drained from my face.

'Killed!' I heard myself say, 'how could they be? They were just here last night…' my voice tailed off. All at once my mind was in turmoil. I sat down on the sofa, and gazed up at them.

'*They can't be!*' I gasped. 'I…I don't believe it!'

Suddenly I remembered today was my eighteenth birthday. For a while I sat with my head in my hands. My world had fallen apart and I felt numb with grief.

Jack Burnside met Ethel, my mum, at a dance shortly after the end of the First World War and married in 1920. After two miscarriages I was born in January 1924.

Times were hard and work was scarce; dad, who was a joiner by trade, was forced to take work as labourer. Mum took in sowing and together they just about managed to make ends meet. However, there was always food on the table and clothes on my back. Later on when I was ten, I helped out by earning a shilling a week from a newspaper round. I gave mum sixpence and kept the rest for the *Champion,* the *Hotspur* and a bag of 'Everton' toffees.

I attended Saint Hughes' School but left at fourteen before obtaining my School Certificate.

'Best get a job and earn your keep,' Dad had said.

This was during the Depression and I was lucky enough to obtain work at Miller's Saw Mill on the Dock Road. I was tall and strong for my age, but found moving heavy planks of wood around boring. Later, I managed to lie my way into the offices of the Mersey Docks and Harbour Board. I told a pale faced man who interviewed me I had a School Certificate. Perhaps it was my second hand blue, pinstriped suit, white shirt and tie that impressed him; anyway, he didn't ask to see any academic credentials and I got a job as junior clerk working in the freight office.

'I see that bugger Hitler has become Chancellor of Germany,' I recall Dad saying one morning over breakfast. His head was buried behind the *Daily Mirror.* 'Take my advice, son,' he added, 'if ever you have to join up, don't go in the bloody infantry like I did. Nowt but bloody cannon fodder, they are. Learn to swim and join the Navy.'

I was twelve in January 1936, when Hitler occupied the Rhineland. Like the rest of my pals at school (and many adults), I failed to appreciate the significance of this. Nor could I understand the solemnity on people's faces when King Edward VIII abdicated the same year in December. However, I had great fun at the street party when King George VI and Queen Elizabeth were crowned the following May in Westminster Abbey.

Two years later, on 3 September 1939, mum, dad and I crowded around the wireless and listened as Prime Minister Neville Chamberlain announced in a sad, monotone voice that we were at war with Germany.

'Now we'll be for it,' said Dad leaning back in his chair smoking a cigarette, 'the buggers will bomb the livin' daylights out of us. That fascist sod Oswald Mosely said so in the paper yesterday.'

But for a while nothing happened.

'Those politicians are talking through their hats,' commented Mum, one evening. We were sitting around the fire listening to Tommy Handley's *Itma.* 'All they've done is put up those horrible barrage balloons and painted white rings around every lamp and tree.' She paused and gave a soft chuckle. 'The dogs will have a field day. And if you ask me that tape we have to put on the windows is a waste of time. As for the black out, we've seen neither hide nor hair of any German bombers.'

'Nonsense, woman,' replied Dad, flicking cigarette ash into the hearth. 'Winston knows what he talking about. The bugger's will be here, so don't forget to collect those gas masks for you and Ted from the town hall. They used gas against us in the last lot and they'll use it again. Mark my words.'

Winston Churchill was now Prime Minister; his stirring speeches were to galvanise the nation when the Blitz began. But for the time being everything was quiet.

Then, in May 1940 the Nazi hordes spread over Europe and in six weeks Hitler had conquered most of Europe. With the French and remnants of the British Army fighting a rearguard action, over three thousand men of the British Expeditionary Force were evacuated from the beaches of Dunkirk.

The real war was about to begin.

It was Uncle Bert who convinced me to join the St John's Ambulance Brigade. He was a stout, semi-bald man about fifty. He had round, fleshy face and deep set, blue eyes that always seemed to be smiling. By stark contrast, Aunt Aida was a tall, willowing woman with a thin pale face and sad, brown eyes.

'Why don't you join the St John's Ambulance Brigade, Ted?' he said to me one evening. Uncle Bert and Aunt Aida were on one of their usual Saturday visits. 'I've been in it for a few years. Besides teaching you first aid, they hold dances regularly.' He gave me a mischievous grin and dug me in the ribs, 'just the ticket for a young man like you.'

'What about the uniform?' I asked. 'The pale, grey shirt and black beret costs money.'

'Don't worry about that,' he said, taking out a tobacco pouch and filling his pipe. 'I'll help you out there. There's a lad I know who's going in the army. I can get his uniform cheap for you.'

'Pay no attention, Ted,' said Aunt Aida, teacup poised in

hand. 'He only goes there for the cheap beer.'

Uncle Bert was right. The dances held in Bebington Hall, the headquarters of the Birkenhead Branch, were a welcome relief from the weekly lectures – and the beer was only five pence a pint!

The headquarters was a good ten-minute bicycle ride from where I lived. I had the lamp of my bicycle covered in strips of brown paper to reduce the light. One night, as I approached the headquarters, I was challenged by a stern voice barking, '*Who goes there?*'

'It's me, Ted Burnside, you daft bugger,' I replied.

'Well next time, switch on yer lamp,' came the gruff reply of a Home Guard soldier. 'For all I know you could 'ave been a Jerry spy.'

The St John's lecturers were elderly men, many of whom who had seen service in the First World War. 'The most important thing is to stop bleeding and treat for shock,' said one small, grey-haired veteran of the Somme. 'Don't move the injured man unless necessary. In 1916 the trenches and fields were so muddy, many men died through man-handling them across No Man's land.' He paused and told me to come out in front of the class and lie down. Then went on. 'Remember, shock accompanies all injuries.' he said, glancing around. 'And it can kill! When this happens blood drains from the brain and pools in the extremities. So, to combat this, raise the legs up, so.' He then lifted my legs up and placed them under some cushions. 'There,' he added, 'you reverse the flow of blood to the brain and the person's life is saved.'

I attended classes twice a week. In next to no time I became proficient in bandaging arms, applying wooden splints and the use of tourniquets to stop bleeding. I also learnt basic anatomy and physiology.

My newfound skills were to be tested sooner than I thought.

'When you hear the air raid siren,' said the Commandant, a tall, sharp-featured man with a row of faded First World War medal ribbons, 'report here as soon as possible. You have each been given an area to cover. Go there, and with experienced staff you'll be under the supervision of the police.'

Shorty Smith and myself were designated the area around Prenton Park, the home of Tranmere Rovers Football Club.

Shorty was a tall, freckled faced lad with untidy, light brown hair. He lived in the next street to me and we became firm friends.

'Hope the buggers don't bomb Tranmere Rover's soccer ground,' said Shorty. 'Me dad'll go barmy. He's been going there for years and thinks Pongo Waring is greater than Jesus Christ.'

In an air raid later in August the football ground was damaged. Nobody was hurt but all fixtures were cancelled. Shorty told me his dad was drunk for a week!

Between March and April Birkenhead and Wallasey suffered several air raids. The docks were badly damaged and sixty parachute mines were dropped. Like the other St John's people I was called out; but being a junior member often remained at headquarters and manned the telephone. However, between July and August, because of staff shortages this changed.

On these occasions I watched as flashes of gunfire lit up the darkness. Beams of searchlights criss-crossed the night sky probing to find the enemy. Bombs exploding set the skyline of Merseyside ablaze with light; the reflection of yellow flames from the docks, danced like demons in dark waters of the River Mersey.

One night Shorty and I watched as a Junkers 88 plummeted into the Mersey estuary, flames sprouting from both engines.

'Hope the buggers fry,' said Shorty angrily.

There were no survivors; but this was small compensation for the 631 people killed on Merseyside during this period.

On Sunday 2 September 1940 the familiar wail of the air raid siren sounded. It was just after five o'clock evening and I was having my tea.

'Here we go again,' I said to mum, as dad helped me on with my overcoat.

'Just you mind how you go, son,' replied Dad, handing me my first aid bag and gas mask. Mum was sitting opposite dad quietly knitting. As she looked across at me a ball of pink wool fell off her lap, unravelling as it rolled onto the floor.

'This is the third time you've been out in the last seven days, Ted,' she said, concern etched on her face. 'And you have work in the morning. I'm not sure you should be doing so much.'

'We've all got to do our bit, mum,' I replied, giving her a kiss on the forehead. 'Now don't worry.'

As I cycled furiously along the road, I heard the monotonous sound of the de-synchronised engines of the German bombers high above. A fire engine came roaring past, its bells clanging violently. Some of the crew, half dressed in their uniforms, clung desperately to the sides.

By the time I arrived at the headquarters, the *Boom Boom* of gunfire and the shudder of bombs exploding, shook the ground. A necklace of tracer bullets from the Bofor guns in Central Park arched upwards as the barrage became intense.

Across the city the muffled sound of explosions filled the air. The dull drone of the German bombers was a constant counterpoint to the cacophony of the night.

'Come on lads,' cried one of the senior officers. 'Euston Grove's been bombed. The ARP (Air-Raid Patrol) and police are on their way.'

Euston Grove was a small road not far from Birkenhead Park; smoke and flames could be seen in the sky as we approached.

Each of the three houses was a total wreck; the frontal facades had all but disappeared in mounds of rubble; roofs, looking like stateless skeletons hung precariously over naked rooms; torn curtains flapped around shattered windows and floors, torn from what was left of walls lay at angles waiting to collapse. Bits of coloured wallpaper fluttered in the breeze alongside lopsided pictures. Lying amongst the grit, grime and debris, pieces of furniture and children's toys lay broken like the dreams of the people who once had lived there.

Firemen, gripping hoses, their faces streaked with grime and sweat, glowed in the flames as they fought the fires. Dust and smoke hovered in the air like thick fog, and the smell of burning wood stung my nostrils as I shielded my eyes from the blaze.

'Over here, you two!' shouted a policeman.

Shorty and I hurried to the aid of a woman who was sitting on a wall opposite the bombed houses. A policeman sat holding a piece of cloth to her head. Someone had placed a blanket over the woman's shoulders and she was crying.

'We were on our way to the shelter when the bomb hit us,' she sobbed. 'Oh God! My poor daughter Jeanie! Where is she…?'

The woman, her dress torn and ashen face covered in blood, looked at me with desperation. 'Please, please, find her…please,' she cried, reaching out and clutching my arm.

I gently removed the cloth from her head revealing a large gash across her forehead; I quickly applied a pad and bandage. Another woman gave her a cup of tea and a few comforting words.

Suddenly, a voice from across the road yelled. 'Everyone lend a hand! There's somebody trapped down here.'

Shorty stayed with the woman while I joined a party of police, St John's men and ARP. Together we grovelled in the dirt, frantically pulling bits of debris, bricks and wood away.

'Watch that wall!' cried the ARP man over the noise. 'If it falls move away swift-like.'

Policemen kept away a few neighbours who hadn't gone to the air raid shelter. 'There's someone here!' I heard the ARP man yell.

With frenzied haste he pulled away more debris. Very soon I saw a hand and arm. The fingers of the hand were bent and the arm was streaked with blood. As bric-a-brac, masonry and more bricks were removed, the limp figure of a little girl became visible. Both eyes were closed and her face, covered with dust, looked grey and cold. The girl's hair was a tangled mess of grit and grime and what was once a pretty pink dress was a tattered and torn. She looked like a small, ragged doll, limp and lifeless.

A St John's man carefully lifted her from the ground. The devastated expression on his face told its own story. With loving care he gently brushed the dust away from the girl's face and laid her on a stretcher.

Just as the dead girl was about to be covered with a blanket

I heard a scream. The injured woman I had treated earlier rushed across the road. 'Jeanie! Jeanie!' she cried. The note in her voice sounded so grief-stricken it made me wince.

Pulling aside a policeman she bent down and picked up the dead girl. For a while she sat and cradled the child in her arms, sobbing and rocking to and fro. As the All Clear sounded the police and St John's men helped her up; still clutching her daughter, they led her to an ambulance.

I glanced up at Shorty. His freckled face was ashen and streaked with tears. The horrific scene became indelibly etched on my mind. However, it would not be the last time I would witness death and destruction.

The air raids continued throughout 1940; in October 136 people were killed and 167 injured on Merseyside; November was even worse; 180 people lost their lives with 96 injured, and in December over 40 ships were damaged in the various docks.

However, even though there was a small air raid on 24 December, this didn't stop the St John's Ambulance organising a Christmas dance.

The members decorated the hall with flags of the commonwealth. Over the makeshift bar Shorty and I hung pictures of the royal family.

'The King and Queen can gaze down while I get pissed,' quipped Shorty as we stacked crates of Nut Brown Ale and Guinness behind the wooden counter.

'At sixpence a bottle, that shouldn't take long,' I replied with a grin.

The dance was very popular, especially with the local girls. Members of the brigade provided a five-piece band; even mum and dad put in an appearance. I had to laugh when dad almost fell over doing the Palais glide.

'He's no Fred Astaire!' cried Mum, 'but he does his best.'

That night Shorty and I got lucky.

We met two local girls. Mine was a good-looking blonde with a well-developed bust. Her name was Iris and she lived in Oxton, a suburb of Birkenhead. Shorty's girl, Janet, was plump with dark, curly hair and a mole on the left side of her cheek.

'After the dance is over,' said Shorty as we collected a

glass of cider for each girl. 'We'll wheel 'em away to Birkenhead Park.'

'What about the Bofors and barbed wire?' I asked. 'The bloody place is like a fortress.'

'So what?' replied Shorty, passing me the drinks. 'I don't care where we shag 'em.'

Later, lying on a grassy verge with one arm wrapped around Iris, we listened to the sound of bombers overhead. The air raid siren didn't go off, so we knew they were ours.

'I wonder what their target to-night is?' I said, handing Iris a cigarette.

'I don't know what you're worrying about,' replied Iris, cuddling into me. 'You certainly got yours.'

I gave a throaty laugh. 'Judging by the noise your mate and Shorty made,' I said, allowing my free hand to sneak under her sweater and cup her ample breast, 'they did as well.'

The first week in January 1942 was frosty with flurries of snow. Fuel was scarce therefore dad and I often had to go to the gas works and queue for a few bags of coke. We had to balance the heavy bags over the crossbar while pushing our bicycles. It was hard, cold work but kept the fire burning and the water heater on the boil.

'Thank God, the Yanks have come into the war,' I said one evening on our way back from the gasworks.

The Japanese had bombed Pearl Harbour in December and America had declared war on Japan and Germany.

'About soddin' time too, if you ask me,' replied Dad, slightly out of breath as we pushed our bikes uphill. 'It was the same in the last lot. They came in just at the last minute. We never heard the end of it!'

'Well,' I replied as we reached our house. 'We won didn't we?'

The night before mum and dad were due to go to Liverpool to visit Uncle Bert and Aunt Aida was quiet. During the past month the air raids had slackened off and for once the air raid sirens were silent.

Mum was sat by the fire knitting and dad was reading the *Liverpool Echo.*

'Ses here, our lads have captured Tobruk,' mumbled dad from behind his paper, 'and Marlene Dietrich has become an American citizen.'

Mum glanced up from clicking her knitting needles. 'I wonder how many men she had to do for that?' she said.

Dad gave a snort and looked at her. 'Please Ethel. Not in front of Ted.'

'He'll be eighteen next September,' replied Mum, 'and be called up like the rest of them. I'm sure he'll hear worse than that then.'

Dad put down his newspaper. 'Put the kettle on son,' he said, glancing at me. 'On yer eighteenth birthday, I'll take yer down to the "Nag's Head", for a pint.'

Even though I considered I was doing a man's job in the St Johns Ambulance, dad thought I was too young to go into a public house.

I smiled and looked at dad's well-groomed dark brown hair barely visible over his newspaper.

'I'll hold you to that, Dad,' I replied. Then with a grin, added, 'What about going to see Marlene Dietrich in *Destry Rides Again*. It's on in town.'

Mum gave a smirk and poured the tea.

Now, sitting on a chair in the house looking at the two policemen, I realised dad and I would never have that celebratory drink.

CHAPTER TWO

Our house was rented, so a week after the funeral of mum and dad I moved in with Auntie Gladys, mum's cousin.

For the last time I closed the front door of the home I had lived in since I was a boy; it was one of the saddest moments of my life. Auntie Glad informed the landlord and he organised the house clearing.

'Take whatever you want, son,' said the landlord, a small dapper man with a military moustache named Mr Radcliffe. 'Any money I get for the furniture and things, I'll send to your Aunt. She'll keep it for you.'

But other than my personal belongings and a few photographs, there was nothing I wanted. Mum and dad had given me everything while they lived. That, and wonderful memories, were more than enough for me. As I walked away from the house I suddenly realised at the tender age of seventeen I was now an orphan.

Auntie Glad was a fifty-five year old spinster with short, wire wool hair and kindly hazel eyes. She lived in a small terraced house in Singleton Avenue, Birkenhead.

'Now don't you worry about a thing, young Ted,' she said, taking my suitcase and ushering me into a lounge full of bric-a-brac and chintzy covered furniture. 'I've made a pot of tea and there's some apple tarts I baked this morning in the kitchen.'

Auntie Glad did her best to make me feel comfortable, but I missed my parents. As well as several relatives, Shorty and members of the St Johns Ambulance Brigade attended the funeral.

'No need to report for duty at the moment,' said Harry Spencer, the grey-haired commandant. 'Jerry's got cold feet and things are quieting down.'

Nevertheless I kept attending parades just to keep my mind off everything.

'How about checking out Iris and Janet?' said Shorty, one night. 'I hear they often go to that café in Charing Cross.'

'No, ta, mate,' I replied. 'Maybe some other time.'

Even though the air raids stopped, the war carried on.

'I heard on the news that the first American soldiers have arrived in Northern Ireland,' said Albert Jones, a tall, spotty-faced lad from Bebington.

We were sitting around a table at headquarters playing gin rummy.

There was money on the game and all I needed was the Queen of Hearts to complete my hand.

'The judies'll like that, I bet,' replied Shorty, throwing a card away and picking another off the top of the pack.

'And it said in the *Daily Mirror,* the Board of Trade have ordered hem-lines of skirts to go up and turn-ups to go down,' commented Spike Williams, a senior cadet.

With a shake of my head I watched as Spike threw away a queen of hearts and picked up a two of Clubs.

'The Yanks must have heard,' said Shorty, picking up the queen of hearts. 'That's the reason why they're coming.' With a satisfied glance at Spike and me, he placed his cards on the table. 'And that's Gin! You lot owe me a tanner (sixpence) each.'

Meanwhile I kept myself busy at work. Everyone knew what had happened to mum and dad and were very sympathetic.

'Why don't you take a few weeks off, Ted?' said Mr Henshaw, my boss. He was a small, stout man with a bald patch surrounded by a ring of fair, curly hair. 'I know how you feel, son. I lost my lad at Dunkirk. It'll do you good to get away for a while.'

However, I refused. Sitting in Auntie Glad's sitting room wouldn't do me any good. What I really needed was to get away from Merseyside.

In May, Rommel's Afrika Corps drove the Allies back across the Libyan Desert; the Russians attacked German forces at Kharkov and on 25 June the American navy routed the Japanese fleet at Midway. On the same day Major-General Dwight D. Eisenhower, a relatively unknown officer, was given command of all the United Nations forces in Europe; two months later, General Bernard Montgomery was put in charge of the Eighth Army. However, of the 5,000 troops put ashore, half were killed or captured when a raid on Dieppe failed.

'Only a few months to go before the buggers'll 'ave you in the army,' said Shorty, who wasn't due for call up till November. We were in the 'Nag's Head' having a few pints. 'So drink up and enjoy yourself while you can.'

I gave Shorty a Woodbine and lit one for myself. Remembering dad's advice, I replied, 'No bloody foot slogging for me pal. I'm joining the Royal Navy.'

'Girl in every port, eh?' laughed Shorty.

'With a bit of luck,' I replied, downing my pint and pushing the empty glass across the table. 'Now, get 'em in. It's your round.'

By the end of 1942 there was still the occasional air raid, but the main Blitz on Merseyside had come to an end. On 18 September I celebrated my eighteenth birthday in the 'Nag's Head'.

'If you manage to get in the Royal Navy,' said Spike. 'Think of all that rum you'll get.'

Shorty gave a loud laugh and almost choked on his beer. 'From what I hear it's rum, bum and backy in that lot!' he retorted. 'Anyway, Ted,' he added with a grin, 'a fine sailor you'd make, you once told me you're a lousy swimmer.'

The next day the BBC announced the Germans had been routed at Stalingrad. Three weeks later, on 15 November Churchill ordered church bells to be rung throughout the country to celebrate victory at El Alamein; on the same day I received my call-up papers.

As I opened the envelope I closed my eyes and saw a picture of mum and dad smiling. Thank Christ my papers have come, I thought to myself. As a medic I could help save the lives of service men and women. A surge of anger suddenly ran through me. I realised not only did I want to join up, but most of all I wanted revenge.

'Now mind you put on that clean shirt I ironed for you,'

fussed Auntie Glad, brushing my sports jacket. 'Maybe they'll let you join your dad's old regiment, the Lancashire Fusiliers.'

I didn't reply. Instead I kissed her on the cheek.

The recruiting office was a large, smoke-ridden room situated on the ground floor in Birkenhead Town Hall. The place was crowded with young man sitting in rows of wooden chairs. Some were smoking; others read newspapers while one or two sat quietly wondering what fate had in store. Facing everyone was a grey haired sergeant with rows of campaign ribbons that probably dated back to the Boer War. As each man's name was called out they took a seat in front of the sergeant. After filling out a long form they were told to go through a side door.

'That's where they make you piss in a bottle,' whispered a pale-faced youth sitting next to me. 'I know 'cos me mate was 'ere yesterday. There's a quack in a white coat who squeezes your bollocks and asks you to cough.'

'Fuckin' lot of perverts if you ask me,' chimed a lad with ginger hair. 'Pity it ain't a woman doctor. I 'avent 'ad a bit for ages.'

An older man, sitting close by added. 'I hear they also give you some sort of education test, like.'

'That clears me,' replied Ginger. 'I can't add two and two together.'

The sergeant called out my name and I took a seat opposite him.

'Says 'ere,' he rasped, looking at my form, 'you've been in the St John's Ambulance Brigade.' As he glanced at me his left eye twitched. He then added. 'I suppose you'll want to go into the RAMC?' (Royal Army Medical Corps.)

'No sir,' I replied, trying to sound polite. 'I want to join the Royal Navy.'

The sergeant put down the form and twitched at me. 'Oh, you do, eh?' he replied with a smirk while handing me the form. 'Well, we'll see about that. And don't call me "sir"; I'm a *non*-commissioned officer. Take this and report to the doctor through that door.'

Much to my embarrassment both pale-face and Ginger were right. After an extensive medical, I went into another room where another sergeant ordered me to sit and answer questions ranging from simple mathematics to writing a few sentences about myself.

'You've got ten minutes,' he snapped. 'So get a move on.'

I found the questions very easy and finished quickly.

'Right,' growled the sergeant, giving me a suspicious glance. 'Carry on through the side door into the street. You'll be contacted in due course.'

A week later a buff-coloured envelope marked 'War Office', fell through the letterbox.

With shaking hands I tore it open. After a quick read I looked at Auntie Glad with a grin as wide as the Mersey Tunnel.

'I've been accepted for the Royal Navy, Auntie Glad!' I cried, giving her a hug. 'It says I have to report to a Victoria Barracks in Portsmouth in a week's time. Then I go to a hospital called Haslar for training as a sick berth attendant.'

'Put me down. You great oaf,' replied my Aunt, with a smile. 'And what the blazes is a sick berth attendant? And where's this Haslar place?'

'A sick berth attendant is a male nurse,' I replied. 'According to the pamphlet I read, the navy train you well enough to go on ships without a doctor.' I paused and read the letter again. 'I'm not sure where Haslar is. Anyway, they've enclosed a travel warrant. I'm to leave Lime Street on the eight o'clock train for Euston, London. I arrive at one o'clock and go to Waterloo on the underground. I then catch the first available train to Portsmouth and report to the RTO, (Regulating Transport Officer). Oh yes, and I'm to bring a suitcase for my civvies to be returned to you.'

Auntie Glad stood and looked at me with a puzzled expression on her face. 'All that messing about just to join the navy, and the underground too, well I never…' she muttered, turning away. 'I'd best wash up the breakfast things.'

When I told Mr Henshaw, he slapped me on the back and told me to take the rest of the week off.

'With pay, of course,' he grinned. 'And I'll make sure you get a few extra bob, to boot.'

Saying goodbye to Shorty and the lads at St Johns was sad

but at the same time exciting. Everyone shook my hand and wished me well.

'Watch out for them tarts in London,' quipped Spike, with a grin. 'They'll suck you in and blow you out in bubbles, so they will.'

'It's not the London judies he has to worry about,' added Shorty. 'It's those Wrens. I hear they're hot stuff!'

'Look after yourself, Ted,' said the Commandant. 'And don't forget what you have learnt with us.'

The next morning I bid farewell to Aunt Glad.

'Don't forget to write, Ted,' she said, giving me a wet kiss on the check. 'I've packed some Spam sandwiches and a flask of tea in you suitcase.' Then in a fit of tears added 'Your mum and dad would have been so proud…'

Making my way to Woodside to catch the ferryboat across the River Mersey I felt overcome by a deep feeling of sadness. How I wished my parents could have been here to see me off.

On a dank, dark morning, Lime Street Station was crowded with groups of servicemen and women, many wearing greatcoats carrying gas masks in brown canvas satchels. The pungent smell of smoke and the hiss of steam attacked my eyes and nostrils.

Sailors with their distinctive round caps carried kit heavy bags; a splattering of RAF airmen stood around reading newspapers, laughing and smoking; some soldiers from a variety of regiments had rifles slung over their shoulders; a few Wrens, ATS (Auxiliary Territorial Service) and WAAFS (Women's Auxiliary Air Force) mingled with servicemen. Occasionally a muffled voice over the loudspeaker, informed everyone about train arrivals and departures. Dim, yellow lights from the high arched roof cast a pale glow on a scene no doubt being re-enacted in railway stations all over the land.

The journey to London was quite enjoyable. After changing at Crewe, I found myself in a compartment with two sailors and a lad in the RAF. The sailors wore skin-tight jumpers and blue collars scrubbed to hard the colour had faded. With their caps worn flat-a-back (on the backs of their heads) and wide, bell-bottomed trousers, they looked the typical 'jack tars', I had seen on posters.

Cigarettes were passed around, the tobacco smoke adding to the already warm, muggy atmosphere. One of the sailors, a stocky lad with dark, curly hair, produced a deck of cards, and the airman handed around bottles of Nut Brown Ale.

'Brag all right with everyone?' asked the curly-headed sailor.

Everyone nodded in agreement and the RAF lad placed his suitcase on the floor to act as a table.

As the sailor dealt the cards I noticed the name on the sailors' cap tallies simply read *HM SHIPS.*

'Just joining up, eh?' said the airman, glancing at my small suitcase. He had a thin, pale face and brown hair plastered with Brylcreem.

'Yes,' I replied, nodding towards the sailors. 'I'm joining their lot.'

'Which branch?' asked the curly headed sailor who introduced himself as Nobby Clark.

'Medical,' I replied. 'If I pass the course.'

'A poultice-wallopper, eh?' said his mate, a fresh-faced man with black hair parted in the middle. Like Nobby, he spoke with a pronounced Scouse accent and introduced himself as Pincher Martin. 'We 'add a few good docs on board the old *Penelope*, didn't we Nobby?'

'We certainly did, lad,' replied Nobby. Shuffling the pack of cards and dealing three to each of us. 'We're gunnery ratings you see,' he added, pointing to the gold crossed-gun insignia on his left arm. 'I was on the Oerlikon and caught a piece of shrapnel. The killick doc did a bloody good job stitching me, so he did.'

Nobby put down his cards face down and rolled up his sleeve. Above a tattoo of a dancing girl was a large diagonal scar. 'Fifteen big ones the doc put in there,' he said proudly. 'Didn't feel a thing!'

'That's because I gave you my tot,' added Pincher, with a laugh.

'What do those three stripes on your other arm mean?' I asked.

'You get one o' them for every four years service, matey,'

replied Nobby.

'Three badges gold,' said Pincher who wore two stripes, 'too fuckin' old.'

'Pipe down and deal the cards,' replied Nobby with a grin.

'What type of ship was the *Penelope?*' I asked throwing away a ten of diamonds and picking up a six of clubs.

'She's a cruiser, my son,' replied Nobby. 'And a good one at that. Got that many holes in her from Jerry shells, she was nick-named HMS *Pepperpot!*'

I laughed but inwardly envied them. They had seen action – the kind I wanted, and intended to find. 'A killick,' I said, with a half-hearted laugh. 'That's a leading hand isn't it?'

'That's right,' replied Nobby, throwing away a King of Hearts. 'The surgeon lieutenant and an SBA were killed. That just left Dusty Miller. Bloody good doc was Dusty.' He then picked up an Ace of Hearts, lay down his hand and with a satisfied grin, said, 'Brag! I think that pile of pennies is mine.'

My God! I thought as conductor drew back the compartment door and asked for our tickets. Stitching people up! They didn't teach me anything about that in the St John's Ambulance Brigade. Clearly, I had a lot to learn.

By the time we arrived in Euston the windows were steamed up, the card game was well and truly over and I had fallen asleep.

Someone shaking my shoulder woke me up. 'Wakey! Wakey! mate,' I heard a voice cry. 'You can't sleep here.'

The cold air outside soon woke me up. I watched as personnel disgorged from the train and file through the ticket barrier. I shook hands with the RAF lad and wished him good luck.

'If you're bound for Pompey,' said Nobby, hoisting his kit bag on his shoulder. 'You'd best stick with Pincher and me.'

'Thank fuck for that,' I replied looking around. 'This is my first time away from the 'pool and I feel lost already.'

I followed Nobby and Pincher down into the underground. The place was packed with service personnel all of who seemed to be carrying luggage. We crammed into the tube and after several stops arrived at Waterloo.

The time was shortly after one o'clock.

'Come on,' said Pincher, 'we've time for a quick, pint. The train for Pompey doesn't leave for half an hour.'

Of course the bar was crowded.

While Nobby pushed his way through a mob of sailors to get served, I asked Pincher what ship they were on.

'Watch it, Ted, my son,' he replied, touching the side of his nose with his finger. 'Careless talk an' all that.'

'Oh yes,' I replied, shooting a furtive glance around. 'I forgot.'

Pincher grinned and leant close to my ear and whispered, 'Although we're regular navy, we've slapped in a request to be sent to minesweepers – the suicide squad.'

The term 'suicide squad', instantly caught my imagination.

Nobby returned, spilling some of the beer down the side of the glasses.

'Just told his nibs here we 'ope to get on the 'sweepers,' said Pincher, accepting his pint.

'Why did you call them the suicide squad?' I asked, before taking a large gulp of beer.

'I had a mate, Duchy Holland on one of them,' said Nobby. 'Like most of the men on the 'sweepers he was a HO, (Hostilities Only) and used to be a fisherman. He told me after they'd sweep a channel sometimes a mine is missed. Another minesweeper would come along, hit the mine and *Boom* – up it goes – suicide squad you see.'

'Christ almighty!' I exclaimed. 'It sounds bloody dangerous. You must be mad. Why are you volunteering for them?'

They looked at one another and laughed. 'The extra money,' replied Nobby, finishing his pint.

'Extra money!' I exclaimed. 'How much was that?'

'A bob (shilling – twelve pennies, worth about fifty pence in modern currency) a day,' replied Nobby with a grin. 'Now let's bugger off before that train goes.'

By the time we arrived at Portsmouth it was almost dark.

'You'll find the RTO over there,' said Pincher pointing to where a matelot (a naval term, derived from the French, for a sailor) in white gaiters and belt stood outside an office. About twenty bewildered looking men carrying suitcases surrounded him. Many were smoking, the tobacco smoke mingling with streams of vaporised breath in the cold evening air.

Nobby and Pincher took it in turns to shake my hand and wish me good luck. 'Who knows,' he added with a laugh, 'you might end up with our lot.'

Many a true word said in a jest, I said to myself as I watched them disappear.

CHAPTER THREE

'Aye, aye,' cried a voice as I joined the men outside the RTO's office. ''Ere comes another lamb for the slaughter.' The speaker was a tall, thin man wearing a flat cap and dressed in a dirty black overcoat that had seen better days. He spoke with a broad Cockney accent and had a grin as wide as London Bridge.

One or two of the others looked at me and laughed; the rest seemed too preoccupied stamping their feet and blowing into their hands to pay much attention. In one hand the matelot held a clipboard. He had a ruddy complexion and a large dewdrop hung from his nose.

'About bloody time you got 'ere,' he sniffed, glancing at his clipboard. 'You're the last. Burnside, isn't it?'

'Yes,' I replied.

After ticking me off his list he looked at everyone.

'Right, you lot!' he cried. 'There's a lorry outside. Throw your gear inside and climb aboard, and look lively about it.'

As we moved away the dewdrop dropped onto the collar of his greatcoat.

Waiting outside the station was a blue lorry with large 'RN' painted on its side. 'Miserable sod, ain't 'e?' quipped the Cockney, as we clambered on board. 'I 'ear they call 'em 'crushers. I think it's because they always wear those big boots.'

'I bet the buggers never go to sea,' said a lad wearing a Balaclava. 'Me dad was in the last lot and he said they were regular barrack stanchions.'

I later learned the term 'barrack stanchion' referred to men who spent most of their service time in the naval barracks.

Cockney was sitting on the bench next to me. He passed me a Woodbine and a light.

'Me name's Jim Taylor,' he said offering his hand. 'But me mates call me Tinker,' he paused and grinned, 'Tinker, Taylor,

Soldier, Sailor an' all that.'

'Ted Burnside, 'I replied shaking his hand. 'Cheers for the fag.'

'What branch are you joining?' he asked, sending a stream of tobacco smoke in the air. Before I had time to answer, he went on, 'I'm gunna be a sick berth attendant. You see, I worked in Paddington General before I was called up.'

'So am I,' I answered with a grin. 'I was in the St John's Ambulance Brigade. What did you do in the hospital?'

With a cheeky grin, he replied, 'Mortuary attendant – it was a bit of a dead-end job!'

One or two overheard him and joined in our laughter.

The journey didn't take long. A sailor raised the duckboard and a canvas sheet was drawn across the back of the lorry. Consequently we didn't see anything of Portsmouth. Finally, the lorry stopped and a sailor told us to climb out.

Waiting outside was an officer with a swagger stick under his left arm. He stood over six feet and was as broad as a barn door. His blue uniform, with three brass buttons on each sleeve, looked immaculate and his trousers neatly tucked into black gaiters, had creases in them sharp enough to cut meat. A row of campaign medals stretched across his left breast, and from under a peaked cap two sharp eyes observed our every move.

'Right, me beauties!' he snapped. When he spoke his weather-beaten features broke into a smirk. 'My name is Chief Petty Officer Weather. You address me as "sir", This 'ere establishment is Victoria Barracks, and will be yer 'ome for the next three weeks. When you go inside you'll find rows of double bunks. On each one is a mug, eatin' irons and bedding. Grab a bunk and make up yer bed. Then, someone will come and show you where the dining hall is.' He paused, glared around and added, 'any questions?'

'When do we get our duty free ciggies, mate?' asked Tinker.

The chief's eyes became evil looking slits as he moved close to Tinker. 'When I say so,' growled the chief, staring Tinker in the face. 'And I'm no mate of yours. Call me sir, next time you speak to me. Got it?'

Tinker casually shrugged his shoulders, and replied. 'OK… sir.'

Before entering a large red-bricked building I looked across a wide parade ground and saw another one three storeys high. The curtains were drawn and the windows were criss-crossed with tape; those on the ground floor were sandbagged. At the end between the two was a long wooden building I later learnt was the NAAFI (Navy, Army, Air Force Institute).

We were ushered into a spacious room on the ground floor; in the centre was a box coal fire. Its warmth on my face was a welcome relief from the cold wind outside. Hanging from a high ceiling were electric lights that cast a shadowy glow over everything.

Rows of bunk beds and metal lockers stretched down each side of the room, and on either side of the fire stood a well-polished oak table and chairs. Several men in blue overalls sat around writing, smoking or lying on their bunks reading. All looked as if Apache Indians had scalped them.

'Attention when an officer comes into the room!' barked the chief.

Immediately everyone rose to attention, including those on their bunks, who jumped down as if jolted by an electric shock.

The chief glanced around. 'Who's Webb?' he snapped.

A medium sized, muscular lad with fair hair who looked older than the others made a half-hearted gesture with his hand.

'I am, sir,' he answered in a Geordie accent.

'Right,' replied the chief. 'You're senior hand. Make sure this lot settle in then show them where the dining hall is. Understand?'

'Yes, sir,' replied Webb.

'And don't forget,' added the chief, glaring around. 'Call the hands at six thirty.'

He then did a smart about turn and marched out of the room.

'Indeed to goodness!' exploded a lad in a sharp, Welsh accent. 'Is he for real?'

'That's old 'Stormy' Weather', said Webb 'He's our drill instructor. And believe you me, he lives up to his name.'

'How come he put you in charge?' I asked, lighting a cigarette and passing one to Webb.

'I suppose it's because I'm the oldest,' replied Webb. 'I was a Bevan Boy and exempt from call up. Then there was an accident in the pit at Gateshead. Even though I was a trained first aider, there wasn't much I could do. A lot o' me mates were killed, so I left the mine.' He paused and flicked his ash in a round, metal spittoon. 'And would you believe it, me call up papers arrived a week later. Even though me missus was six months gone.' As he spoke his face broke into a worried frown. 'I've not 'eard from her since I arrived 'ere four days ago. By the way, me names. George, but me mates call me Spider.'

'Ted Burnside,' I replied as we shook hands. 'Don't worry, Spider,' I said, throwing my suitcase on a top bunk. 'She'll be OK, just you see. Anyway, thank fuck we've only got three weeks to put up with old Stormy.'

With a sigh Tinker sat down on the bottom bunk. 'Three weeks of square bashing then off to a hospital and all them nurses,' he said. 'I can hardly wait!'

Our class of twenty HO's were a mixed bunch.

There were six would-be cooks, five hoping to train as stewards, three wishing to be stores assistants, and the remaining six, including Spider and me, hoped to be sick berth attendants.

'When do we get our uniforms?' asked a small, skinny lad with a Birmingham. Like the rest of us he was busy making up his bed. Unfortunately, slipping the cover over his mattress was proving too much. A lad with what was once a mop of red, curly hair helped him.

'In a few days,' replied red hair, 'when you've had your haircuts, jabs and been examined by the MO.'

'Bloody hell!' cried little Brum. 'I hate bloomin' needles. I only joined the medics 'cos no other branch would 'ave me.'

While Buck and me were unpacking what few things we had, two lads sauntered up to us. One was built like an all-in wrestler with dark, swarthy features. The other was tall, with fair hair. Both had cigarettes dangling from their mouths like gangsters in a film.

'So you two gunna be medics, eh?' said the swarthy one,

removing his cigarette and flicking ash on my mattress.

Tinker, sensing trouble shot me a warning glance. 'Yeah, so what?' replied Tinker.

The swarthy one grinned and looked at his mate. 'I hear all medics take it up the arse. Isn't that right Harry?'

'That's right, Darky,' replied Harry, stubbing out his cigarette against the side of my bunk. Both he and Darky spoke with broad North Country accents.

Although I hadn't met any homosexuals, I knew about them and what the two men were inferring. I also knew anyone of that sexual persuasion was banned in the navy.

I glanced at Tinker; to my surprise his eyes glared up at Darky, his fists clenched by his sides.

'Did you now?' replied Tinker, gritting his teeth. 'Well, you two must be fuckin' deaf 'cos you heard wrong, see. Anyway, what branch are you two tossers in?'

'Officer stewards,' replied Darky. 'And watch who you're calling tossers.'

'Humf,' muttered Tinker. 'Shit house cleaners, eh?'

Darky didn't reply. Instead he moved closer to Tinker and glowered down at him.

Harry did the same and glared at me. 'And what about you?' he said with a sneer. 'Are you arse too?'

I stared up at him and replied, 'Why don't you two piss off!'

'Why don't you make me?' he replied menacingly.

Just then, Spider came and stood between Darky and me. They were both about the same size and for a moment I thought they would come to blows. At that moment two others joined us. One was a big, strapping lad with black bushy eyebrows and a jaw like a prizefighter. The other was pint-sized and stocky with a round cherubic, choirboy face.

Bushy eyebrows stood close to Darky. 'And what might your problem be then laddie?' he growled. 'It so happens me and my mate are gunna be medics as well. Isn't that right, Buster?'

'Och aye, that's right, Big Mac,' replied Buster, staring up at Darky.

When Big Mac and Buster spoke, their Scottish accents

sounded like a role of drums.

'And so am I,' interjected Spider, flexing his shoulders.

'Now, laddie,' said Big Mac, hands on hips, 'just what was that you said about medics?'

By this time everyone in the mess had stopped what they were doing. Several crowded around our bedside. The place suddenly went quiet and I could feel tension in the air.

Darky's mate, Harry, stared at me and pushed me in the chest with his hand. 'You sound like a Scouser,' he said. 'I hear all you lot in Liverpool are homos, anyway.'

'What about Geordies?' growled Spider.

Harry sneered, and said, 'You're like the Scousers, all as queer as six pound notes.'

His comment made my blood boil. I felt my face redden. Anger rose inside me. I squeezed both fists. A glance at the expression in Spider's eyes told me he felt the same.

I was just about to throw a punch at Harry when to everyone's surprise little Buster suddenly kicked Harry in the genital area. Harry screamed like a stuck pig, folded in two, clutched his balls and fell, writhing in agony on the deck. At the same time Big Mac landed an uppercut on Darky's chin. Darky staggered back and with a startled expression, collapsed like a concertina.

The lads in the mess cheered. Tinker, Spider and me looked at each other in stark amazement. One minute we were about to be flattened by a pair of hard knocks, the next thing we knew our would-be attackers were on the deck – one holding his balls the other staring into space as if felled by an ox.

'Nice one, Lofty,' said Spider slapping Big Mac on the back. 'Those two have been throwing their weight around since they got here. That'll teach 'em.'

'Och away with ye,' said Big Mac wiping his hands down the sides of his trousers. 'Twas nothin.'

Big Mac extended his hand to Spider. 'Me name's Hamish MacDonald, Big Mac to me friends.' As he spoke his chiselled features broke into a grin displaying a row of white teeth. 'I'm from Glasgow. What about you?'

'I'm from Gateshead, Spider Webb's the name.' They

shook hands.

'And I'm Ted Burnside,' I said, 'and this here is Tinker Taylor from the Smoke.'

Big Mac's hand engulfed mine like a boxing glove. 'Glad to meet you,' and added, 'you handle yourself like a boxer.'

'That's because he was the heavy weight champion of the north of Scotland hospitals,' chimed in Buster. 'Unbeaten as well.'

When Big Mac let go of my hand my fingers were numb.

'Were you a doctor, or something?' asked Tinker.

Big Mac threw back his head and gave a loud laugh.

'Och no!' he replied. 'I worked in the dispensary, cleaning up samples of shit and piss.'

'And what did you do in civvy street, Buster?' asked Tinker handing out his cigarettes.

A twinkle came into Buster's eyes and his chubby face wrinkled into a grin. 'Me?' he replied. 'I was a butcher's assistant!'

'Well, Big Mac,' I said, working the circulation back into my hand. 'I don't know what you'll do to the Jerries, but you frighten the fuckin' life out of me.'

Just then Stormy Weather came into the room. He stopped, and with a frown, looked down at Darky and Harry. With Tinker's help, Harry staggered to his feet still clutching his midriff. Big Mac reached down and with a smile, assisted Darky up.

'What the 'ell's going on 'ere Webb?' barked Stormy, shooting a withering glance at Spider. 'You lot should 'ave everything squared away by now.'

The rest of the lads in the room slowly moved away from our bunks and stood silently in groups.

Spider swallowed nervously. 'Oh, er… nothing, sir,' replied Spider, glancing anxiously at Big Mac.

'That's right, sir,' replied Big Mac hurriedly. 'Just showing Darky and 'is mate 'ere a few tips on self-defence, no problem whatsoever. Is there Darky?'

'Er… no, sir,' replied Darky, gingerly rubbing his chin. 'Everything's OK.'

Stormy looked suspiciously around the room. His eyes narrowed at the sight of little Brum who was grinning his head off.

'And what do you find so funny, me laddo?' he snapped.

Brum shrugged his shoulders but couldn't stop grinning. 'Nowt,' he replied.

Stormy moved close to Brum. 'I'll give you something to laugh about, my son.' As he spoke a line of spittle shot from his mouth and splattered onto Brum's face. I watched as it slowly trickled past the side of Brum's nose. Brum winced and was about to wipe it away, when Stormy barked, 'Stand still when I talk to you. Now get your dinner and pipe down.' Stormy lowered his voice into a threatening whisper, and glared at Brum. 'I shall remember you tomorrow on the parade ground, make no mistake.' He then turned on his heels and marched out of the room.

On the way to the dinning hall Spider looked at Brum and said, 'Old Stormy isn't kidding. I have a feeling he has it in for you.'

'Why?' asked Brum innocently, 'what the 'ell have I done?'

Everyone looked at him and burst out laughing. 'Nothin', yet,' replied Spider, 'now shut up and let's get some scran, I'm bloody starvin'.'

The next morning we received a lecture; we had just returned from breakfast and were in the mess having a smoke. Suddenly, the door burst open and in strode a tall, sharp-featured officer with one thin gold ring on his sleeve. Stormy Weather accompanied him.

'Attention in the mess!' barked Stormy, 'and put those cigarettes out.'

Everyone immediately did as he ordered.

The officer placed his hands behind his back, sniffed the air and looked at us.

'My name is Commissioned Gunnery Officer Gray,' he said in a distinct West Country accent. 'I am your divisional officer while you are here. Along with Chief Weather, we intend when you leave here you will be in a fit state to represent His

Majesty's navy.' He paused, removed his hands and walked around glaring at each of us as he did so, and in a stern voice, added, 'if not, you will be swiftly disposed of. Understand?'

Like sheep we nodded, and in unison, answered, 'Yes sir.'

When Stormy and the officer had gone, Brum turned to Big Mac, pursed his lips and said, 'What does he mean by "disposed of", I wonder?'

With a mischievous glint in his eyes, Big Mac shot a glance at Buster and me.

'It means yee'll be keelhauled, laddie!' said Big Mac.

'Oh aye,' replied Brum innocently, 'they still do that then, do they?'

The rest of us glanced at one another and grinned.

'Dolly' Gray, as we called our illustrious DO, (not to his face, I hasten to add) was as good at his word.

The same day a tall, gangly Able Seaman named Bungy Williams, showed us where to do our joining routine. The barracks looked different by daylight; two red-bricked Victorian buildings faced onto a parade ground looked bigger than when we saw it in the dark. On the parade ground, gunnery instructors barked orders at classes doing close order drill. A high, wrought iron gate interlaced with barbed wire surrounded the barracks and close to the main gate was the guardroom. Facing the guardroom was a circular, well-kept lawn. In the middle rose a tall, white flagpole with a yardarm from which rigging angled down into the ground; at the top of the flagpole fluttered the white ensign.

'That!' bellowed a petty officer from the guardroom. 'Is the quarterdeck. Whenever you pass it, you salute. And woe betide any of you who forget.'

Next to the barracks was another slightly smaller building.

'That's the Wrens' training establishment,' said Bungy.

'Och mon,' said Big Mac, rolling his eyes and sniffing the air. 'I can smell all that fanny from here.'

'And that's all you can do, mate,' replied Bungy with a grin. 'As far as you and me are concerned, it's completely off limits.'

During the next three weeks we were transformed from

gawky civilians, to men who doubled marched everywhere. If we didn't, some Chief GI's (Gunnery Instructor) harsh voice would soon order you to do so. Even our vocabulary changed. Toilets were now called 'heads'. Going out into town was 'going ashore' despite the fact we were in barracks. Chocolate and sweets were referred to as 'nutty' and women were colloquially called 'partys'.

Each man was issued with everything from a single-breasted, blue serge uniform, boots and shirts with detachable stiff collars, to a small do-it-yourself kit called a 'housewife'. We were given mackintoshes known as Burberrys, and a greatcoat as heavy as lead. At first none of the peaked caps fitted our heads, but the Wrens in 'slops', (stores, for the use of) giggled and politely informed us we would grow into them.

'Especially after you've been to see our friend Sweeny Todd!'

Leading Seaman Todd was the barrack barber.

As we took it in turns to sit in his chair an impish expression came into his eyes.

'Short back and sides, laddie,' grinned Buster Brown as he sat in a chair. 'And something for the weekend.'

'Oh, a smart arse, eh?' replied Sweeny, switching on his electric clippers. 'We'll soon see about that.'

By the time he finished we looked like plucked chickens, but our caps fitted perfectly.

We were then marched to the sick bay.

As we lined up, hands on hips for our first injection, little Brum murmured, 'I don't think I'm gunna like this.'

Brum was in front of me. His body looked frail and undernourished. As he spoke, I could see fear in his eyes. He winced as the doctor injected each man and began to tremble.

'Ah, you won't feel a thing, Brum,' I said, trying to calm him down. 'It'll be over in a second. Mark my words.'

It was. When Brums' turn came he closed his eyes and as the needle entered his upper arm, his face turned the colour of milk and he fainted. As he collapsed Tinker and I managed to catch him and sit him in a chair.

'Is it over?' gasped Brum, opening his eyes.

'Yes,' I said, suppressing a smile. 'That was the first one. The smallpox vaccination is next.'

'Oh my God,' he whimpered, and promptly fainted again.

'The poor wee man,' said Big Mac. 'Ta think that one day he might have ta give jabs to a whole ship's company.'

'I hope it's a MTB, (motor torpedo boat)' I replied, shaking my head. 'They only have a crew of about six.'

Every morning at six-thirty the strident voice from the Tannoy woke everyone up. ''Eave ho, 'eave ho. Lash up and stow,' echoed around the barracks, 'Hands off cocks and on socks.' The 'lash up and stow', part referred to men sleeping in hammocks. Although we slept in bunks, we were issued with hammocks. One morning a ruddy-faced petty officer showed us how to 'sling' them.

'A 'ammock, if lashed up properly,' said the PO, 'should float and could save yer from drowning.'

Our class were in a cold, damp, drill shed. Outside the harsh cries of CGI's could be heard putting other classes through their paces. Slung between two metal bars hung an open canvas hammock.

'These,' he said indicating to long pieces of strong twine at the end of the hammock, 'are called "nettles". You will notice 'ow each one is attached to by a small ring at one end and to the 'ammock at the other end.' The PO paused and looked at us. 'All right so far?' he asked.

'Aye,' said Big Mac 'But how the hell can you stay in the bloody thing, sir?'

The PO grinned. 'I'm coming to that, so 'old yer horses.' The PO picked up a piece of wood about two feet long from a nearby table. 'This is called a stretcher. It is notched at each end, and can be placed inside the two outside nettles. This keeps yer 'ammock spread out and enables yer to stay in it.' He looked at Big Mac and grinned. 'I 'opes that satisfies you.' He took out a packet of cigarettes and lit up. Most of us followed suite.

The PO carried on. 'Now, from the larger ring-bolt is a lanyard which is, as yer can see, secured to the 'ammock bar. And the same can be seen at the other end of the 'ammock.'

The PO now showed us a length of rope. 'This 'ere is made

of sisal. It's used to lash up yer 'ammock and 'as an eye splice at one end used to pass the first turn through when lashing it up.' He then added, 'When you lash up yer 'ammock, make sure yer bedding is evenly spread inside.' The PO folded the bedding and using one hand he tightly pulled the edges of the hammock together. Using his right hand he passed the lashing over the hammock and brought it under with his left hand. He then hauled it taut (tight) around the hammock. 'This is called a marling hitch,' he said, and slowly repeated each turn until the hammock was firmly tied up. 'You must 'ave seven hitches around the hammock. Now, release the nettles, twist 'em and tuck 'em in so.'

With a satisfied expression he tucked the ends neatly under the previous two turns. 'There,' he said, lifting up the hammock and throwing it towards us, 'Now, one of you try it.'

One by one we tried to 'sling our mick', as it was called. I managed to tie it up but fell out; Buster became entangled with the nettles and almost strangled himself; Big Mac's hammock collapsed and Tinker and Brum gave up in disgust.

'How the fuck did yon Sassenachs beat the Frogs at Trafalgar sleeping in these bloody things!' cried Big Mac kicking the crumpled heap on the floor.

'They used 'em to plug up the holes in the ships,' replied the PO. 'And they did a bloody better job of lashing them up than you.'

'I'll never be able to use one of these fuckin' things,' cried Tinker. 'We'll all 'ave bunks on board ships, won't we? It's all very confusing to me.'

'Not in a corvette or destroyer you won't,' replied the PO. 'So you better get the hang of it. Anyway, remember the old navy saying. *"He who is not confused is not well informed!"* '

After several attempts we finally got the hang of it. Patting my secured hammock, I turned to the PO, and said, 'Are you sure this thing's supposed to float, sir?'

'Aye,' he replied, stubbing his cigarette out with his foot. 'But not with you in it.'

Each morning we wore webbing belts and gaiter and drilled till our feet ached. Then we were issued with rifles and practised close arms drill.

'I'm gunna be a medic, sir,' grumbled Brum, one morning. 'Medics are non-combatants, so I don't want to know about rifles.'

We were lined up in single file. Stormy slowly walked up and put his face close to Brum. Stormy's eyes narrowed and his face became crimson.

'Oh it's you again, is it? You 'orrible little man!' cried Stormy. 'What was that you said?'

Brum's face suddenly turned pale. He looked up at Stormy and muttered, 'Guns, sir, I don't like guns.'

'Oh you don't do you, eh?' replied Stormy, his bated breath blowing into Brum's face. 'Well, you'll like 'em even less by the time I've finished with you.'

For what seemed like an eternity, Stormy made Brum double around the parade ground holding his 303 rifle over his head. In the end, Brum fell against a wall, dropped the rifle and slid down, bathed in sweat, exhausted.

'Take 'im inside,' yelled Stormy, 'men – I've shit 'em!'

Our only respite was found in the NAAFI. This was long, wooden building with a low ceiling and a box coal fire in the centre. There was a bar that not only sold beer and spirits, but also nutty. These last items were rationed and could only be bought by presenting coupons, issued every fortnight on payday. Each evening we would congregate there for a welcome pint of beer, a relaxing smoke and a game of darts.

'Bloody 'ell, mon,' cried Big Mac when we first went there. 'These Players are only sixpence for twenty. In civvy street they're one and two pence.'

The five of us were sitting at a table. Tinker had just bought a round of beer. Vera Lynn, the forces sweetheart with a catch in her voice, was on the wireless singing *We'll Meet Again.* Many of the lads in between sips of beer joined in.

'Bugger the ciggies,' replied Tinker. 'The beer is only a tanner (6d) a pint. With a bit of luck this bleedin' war will last forever!'

Buster Brown's eyes lit up when he opened a small tin of Woodbines.

'Och away wee ye!' he exploded, 'Half a dollar (half-a-crown, worth 2/6d), for this lot. There's a few spivs I know in Glasgow who'd give me a good price for a few dozen o' these.'

'Watch it laddie,' replied Big Mac, passing a packet of Senior Service around. 'You're only allowed a pound of tobacco a month. And if yer caught smuggling any more ashore, it's cells for orders.'

'Just wait till we get on board a ship,' said, Brum, finishing off his pint. 'What with the cheap nutty and rum everyday we'll live like kings.'

'Don't get too carried away, Brum,' I replied. 'We're not allowed rum in hospitals, and certainly not while we're under training.'

'Aye,' replied Big Mac,' that's as maybe. But think o' all them gorgeous nurses to make up fer it.'

'I thought that film we saw on VD might have put you off women for life,' I said giving Big Mac a perfunctory glance. 'When the MO put that syringe thing down the eye of the welt of that man's cock, I'm sure I heard you say you felt sick.'

'Propaganda, mate,' replied Big Mac. 'Those films are all put up jobs to stop you enjoying yersel.'

Tinker, Brum and Buster looked at each other, grinned and shook their heads.

'I bet you ten bob, you're the first one to "catch the boat up",' (a colloquialism for contracting a venereal disease) said Tinker.

'Och away we ye,' replied Big Mac, extending his hand. 'Yer on.'

On a bitterly cold December morning our class was fallen in two deep outside the mess. Men were dressed in their number one uniforms that failed to protect them against the harsh north-westerly wind. The sharp cries of drill instructors rent the air as other classes were put through their paces.

Stormy Weather, his back ramrod stiff, faced us. With his swagger stick firmly tucked under his left arm, he slowly walked along each rank eyeing each man up and down. He didn't miss a thing. Brum stood next to me. Stopping in front of him, the chief reached down and flicked something off Brum's lapel.

'Dust,' he bellowed. 'You're covered in shit, me laddo. Perhaps you'd like another bit of rifle drill, eh?'

'N…no, sir,' replied Brum nervously.

Just then Dolly Gray, our DO arrived. The trousers of his immaculate uniform were neatly tucked in highly polished, black gaiters and the peak of his cap shone like ivory. In one hand he carried a clipboard.

'Stand them at ease, Chief,' he ordered.

'You men have now completed your initial training,' he said, peering at us. 'And will now be posted to begin your professional courses.'

He then read out the names of he cooks and stewards who were to be drafted to HMS *Ceres,* a shore base up north. He went on. 'Those hoping to become sick berth attendants will be sent to the Royal Naval Hospital Haslar. Good luck to you all.'

As the officer then turned away, the chief brought us to attention.

'You would-be pox doctors' clerks,' (naval slang for medics) said the chief, 'are to pack your kit and be outside in one hour. You won't 'ave far to go. Haslar is in Gosport just across the 'arbour.'

'One day I'd love to get that that miserable bastard on the end of a needle,' muttered Brum after we were dismissed. 'I'd make the sod squirm.'

'No chance of that,' replied Tinker. 'That bugger's a barrack stanchion.'

'Och stop complaining,' interrupted Big Mac. 'And just think of them wee lasses in yon hospital just waiting fer us.'

I must say I agreed with him. The thought of seeing a nice pair of legs in black stockings appealed to me.

After the longest three weeks I can remember our square bashing was finally over.

CHAPTER FOUR

I became curious about Haslar, so a week before we were due to leave I borrowed a book from the barrack library about the history of Portsmouth.

We were in the mess after having dinner. It was a cold, miserable night; the curtains were drawn and the air was thick with tobacco smoke. The heat from the coal fire only increased the muggy atmosphere, making me think of warm, wintry nights at home. Nobody had any money for a pint in the NAAFI, so someone started a card school playing for cigarettes. I was lying on my bunk reading.

'Hey!' I cried out to nobody in particular. 'Did you know it was Henry the Seventh's idea to build the Harbour at Pompey in 1496?'

'Was it his idea to build all the pubs as well?' asked Tinker who was playing gin rummy with Big Mac, and a few other trainees.

'Not ta mention the brothels,' added Big Mac.

'Is that all you ever think about,' I replied, shaking my head.

'Och aye,' muttered Big Mac studying the cards in his hand. 'There's na much else ta do around here.'

'According to this book,' I said, glancing at them, 'it was Eleanor of Aquitaine in 1149, who first issued advice to skippers of ships on how to treat sick men on board.'

'I knew a party called Eleanor once in Doncaster,' said Tinker. 'I was caught shagging her one night when her old man came back early from work.'

'What 'appened?' asked Big Mac.

'Nothun' much,' replied Tinker, picking up a fresh set of cards. 'He threw a pound note on the bed, and said, "'ave one on me Jack, she's already been with half the Yanks stationed near here"!'

Everyone looked up from their hand and laughed.

'Apparently,' I went on, ignoring their laughter, 'it were during the wars with the Dutch between 1652 and 1674 that made someone called Doctor Daniel Whistler suggest a hospital was needed for sick sailors.'

'Wasn't he some sort of painter,' muttered Buster, picking a card off the top of the deck.

'That was another feller called Whistler, you ignorant bugger,' said Tinker.

'Too many fuckin' Whistlers, if yer ask me,' mumbled Buster, studying his cards.

'Anyway,' I continued. 'According to this book, a site was chosen in 1745 called Hasler Farm on the Gosport Peninsula.'(Hasl*er*, was later changed to Haslar.)

Big Mac looked from his cards, and with a grin, said, 'Just think, if they 'add kept it as a farm, us lot would be off to the Naval Hospital at Plymouth.'

I lit a cigarette and carried on. 'Finally, in 1746 the foundations of Haslar were laid. It was to be the largest brick building in Europe and took sixteen years to build.'

'Sixteen bloody years!' cried Spider. 'They must 'ave 'add strikes galore in them days.'

'Strong unions, you see, Spider,' replied Brum. 'Strong unions.'

With a sigh I closed the book. 'I give up,' I said. 'It's a waste of time trying to educate you lot.'

'Och now,' said Big Mac, placing his cards on the table, 'that's what me old teacher in Borstal told me!'

That discussion took place a week ago. Now, on a bitterly cold morning in early December 1942, our merry band boarded a lorry bound for the Royal Naval Hospital Haslar.

The book I read informed me the hospital was situated on the tip of the Gosport Peninsula. Cut off from the town of Gosport by Haslar Creek, it fronted onto the Solent.

We drove through a village called Stubbington, and followed the road around to the right. As we approached Haslar's main gate we passed an MTB base called HMS *Hornet.* When the lorry slowed down we caught sight of several motor torpedo boats tied up alongside one another; a few matelots, bareheaded but wearing warm sweaters and sea boots were busy cleaning the decks. Others worked on single-barrelled guns mounted on the sharp bows of the boats. Away to our left was a gigantic structure that arched upwards into the dull, grey sky.

'Bloody hell, lads!' exclaimed cried Tinker. 'Take a gander at that bridge. I bet it gets a bit windy going over that bugger. It certainly is high enough.'

The driver, a petty officer with a red beard, glanced over his shoulder. 'That's why it's called Pneumonia Bridge,' he said with a laugh. 'As you can see, it spans Haslar Creek and leads into Gosport. Believe you me, after a few scoops ashore, the wind up there will soon sober you up. It's a wonder no bugger falls off. Further down, next to *Hornet* is HMS *Dolphin,* the big submarine base.'

The lorry stopped outside a high, wrought iron gate; nearby stood a matelot in white gaiters and belt. Close by was a policeman, who, after a quick glance opened the gate.

'What 'ave yer got fer us t'day, Ginge?' said the policemen in a sharp Hampshire accent.

'Five trainees from Vicky Barracks, Harry,' said Red Beard leaning out of the lorry window, 'staff quarters as usual?'

'Aye,' replied the policeman. 'You know where to go?'

Red Beard nodded and started the engine.

'Christ almighty!' cried Buster, gazing outside the lorry. 'It sure looks big enough.'

'If you remember,' I said, preening forward and looking through the driver's window, 'I told you it was once the largest brick building in Europe.'

Directly ahead rose the imposing frontal façade of a three-storey building. On top of this was a wide pediment with the royal coat of arms cut out of stone. Three square windows looked down from the top floor. Underneath another three tall, arched windows occupied what I thought were two floors. All the windows were criss-crossed with white tape. In the centre of the ground floor was an archway leading into the hospital and on either side smaller windows were sandbagged.

The lorry slowly moved around and came to a halt outside a

long three-storey building. The red brickwork looked newer and was obviously built after those we had seen so far. Next to it ran a line of railings through which I could see the waters of the Solent.

Turning his head slightly, Red Beard said, 'This is the staff quarters. It was built in 1910 and was the lunatic asylum until they moved the nutters to Netley.'

'You've brought us to the right place, then, sir,' retorted Buster. 'A few more head cases won't make any difference.'

Kit bags, suitcases and hammocks were slung outside forming a heap on the ground.

The time was just after eleven o'clock. As we climbed out, the lorry the wind cut right through me, while high above dark clouds threatened snow.

A fat petty officer with a bass-drinkers florid face greeted us; his single-breasted uniform hung was in danger of bursting and his shoes needed cleaning. Suddenly, Victoria Barracks seemed a long way off.

'Welcome to the bone yard,' he said in a slightly high-pitched voice. 'You are now Probationary Sick Berth Attendants. (PSBA's). Pick up your gear and come this way.'

We followed the Fat One through a wide door, along a passageway into a long room. Hammock bars and metal lockers lined each side and in the middle of the room was a stove similar to the one in the barracks.

'Keys in a spare locker,' said the PO. 'Stow your gear away. Sling your hammock and fall in outside at one o'clock, 1300 to you. And by the way, my name's Petty Officer Pinkerton and I am your divisional PO. Any problems don't come and see me, visit the padre. Carry on.'

'When do we get some scran, sir?' asked Brum with a pained expression. 'Me stomach thinks me throats cut.'

Pinkie, as we immediately christened the PO, turned as he reached the door. 'Twelve hundred,' replied Pinkie. 'The dining hall is just down the passageway where you came in. And you only refer to petty officers and chiefs, as sir in basic training. Call me PO. Understand, young man?'

'Oh, yes sir,' replied Brum. 'I…I mean PO.'

‘Will dinner be piped, PO?’ asked Tinker.

‘There’s no pipes in hospitals,’ replied Pinkie. Then with a chubby grin, added, ‘it would disturb the patients.’

As well as the space allotted to ours, there were a dozen or more hammocks slung up next to lockers; clearly we were not the only men under training. As if to confirm this, two ratings wearing greatcoats came into the mess. The tallest of them, a fair-haired man was smoking. The other one was much smaller with dark hair and a pallid complexion.

‘Just arrived, then?’ asked the tallest one. By the side of a long table was a round aluminium gash basin. (Gash is a naval term for rubbish.) With pinpoint accuracy the tallest one flicked his dog end into it.

‘Aye,’ replied Big Mac, ‘and so far, we havna seen one bloody nurse.’

‘There’s only a few of them here,’ said the tallest one. ‘They belong to the QARNNS, (Queen Alexandria’s Naval Nursing Service,) the rest are VAD’s.’

‘VA fuckin D’s!’ cried Big Mac, looking aghast. ‘What the hell are those?’

‘Voluntary Aid Detachment,’ replied the tall one. ‘They are volunteers from the British Red Cross Society;’ the tall one grinned and added, ‘otherwise known as Virgins Awaiting Disaster.’

‘Och, that sounds fine,’ replied Big Mac with a smile. ‘They won’t have ta wait long while I’m around.’

The tallest one introduced himself as Digger Barnes. ‘This little shrimp is Titch Handley.’ We shook hands and told him who we were.

‘The bar is down the corridor,’ said Digger, ‘just past the dining hall. We share it with the trained staff. They’re a good lot, but pay no attention to what they say. Some of them sometimes forget they were once like us.’

Shortly after twelve o’clock about a dozen other lads, all carrying exercise books filed into the mess.

One of them, a tall, gawky lad with freckles threw his exercise book on the table.

‘Thank fuck you lot ’ave arrived,’ he said. I immediately

recognised the voice of a fellow Scouser. 'Now we can start our course proper like.'

A lad with ginger hair chimed in. 'At least Rectum Rosie will be pleased,' he said, lighting a cigarette. 'Now she'll really be able to show us how to give an enema.'

The rest who had just come in laughed. One lad with a narrow face and eyes like a ferret sat down on a chair. He looked at Ginger Hair and in a voice straight from the Welsh valleys, said, 'That's right, boyo. And you can be the first to volunteer.'

'Who's Rectum Rosie?' I asked, looking at Ginger Hair.

'She's the Sister Tutor,' he replied. 'She gave us a few preliminary talks on the digestive system and the importance of opening your bowels regularly.'

'Och,' said Big Mac. 'Doesn't she mean 'avin a good shit every day?'

'That's about the strength of it,' replied Ginger Hair. 'By the way, my name's Knocker White, and this sheep shagger is Taff Hughes.'

Everyone shook hands.

'And what part of Liverpool are you from?' I asked Scouse.

'Kirkdale,' he replied, then with a laugh added, 'or if yer prefer it, Dodge City. Me names Dick Kilkenny, but needless to say everyone calls me Scouse.'

'Ted Burnside,' I replied shaking his hand. 'From Birkenhead.'

'One of the posh people from Cheshire, eh,' he said with a grin. 'I bet you lot 'ave inside heads?'(Naval term for toilets)

'That's right,' I answered, 'and real lavatory paper too.'

After a welcome dinner, Pinkie was waiting for us outside the staff quarters. The other lads who had come into the mess joined us. Pinkie looked flushed. He removed his cap and even though it was cold, appeared to be sweating.

'Had a good dinner, my loves?' said Pinkie wiping his brow with a handkerchief.

'He's been on the piss,' muttered Tinker from the side of his mouth.

'I wouldn't mind a bevy myself,' I answered in a whisper.

Pinkie put on his cap, placed one hand on his hip and gave

everyone a sickly smile. 'You've all got a make and mend,' he stammered. (A make and mend was an afternoon off duty ostensibly to repair clothes. Usually, men went ashore or got their heads down.) 'You will begin your ten week course tomorrow. Fall in here in the morning at eight o'clock,' still wearing a sickly smile, he added, 'and please don't be adrift.'

Spider who was standing next to me made an upward gesture with his hand. 'Have any letters arrived, PO?' he said anxiously.

'No mail has arrived dear boy,' replied Pinkie. 'Any that does is placed on the table in your mess.'

Spider didn't reply. He frowned and kicked the ground slightly with his foot.

'What about leave, PO?' asked Big Mac. 'We havna had a run ashore since we arrived in Pompey.'

For a second Pinkie looked flustered. 'Oh yes, I almost forgot,' he replied, quickly removing his hand from his hip. 'While you're under training, night leave expires at 2300 (eleven o'clock in the evening). Satisfied?'

'I will when I get a few drams doon me,' replied Big Mac with grin.

Back in the mess I asked Scouse about Pinkie. 'Is he, er...dodgy?'

'I'm not sure,' replied Scouse as he made up his hammock. 'But I wouldn't bend down in the showers when he's about!'

Scouse offered to show Big Mac and the other five around the hospital. Once outside I turned up the collar of my Burberry to protect against the bitterly cold wind and rain. The others did the same.

The gravel crunched under our shoes as we walked down a wide path towards a long three-storey building.

'That's A and B blocks,' said Scouse pointing to the buildings. 'All the blocks consist of double rows that connect with one another.' Scouse paused and lit a cigarette. 'Oh yes,' he went on, 'if we have an air raid, we've been told to go down to the cellars. The entrance to them are at the back of the staff quarters.'

'Cellars!' cried Buster. 'How about the patients?'

'During the Blitz, Haslar was a casualty clearing station. Most of the cases were sent to Winchester or Basingstoke hospitals. There still is an emergency operating room in the cellars.'

'How come after being here only a week you know so much?' asked Brum.

Scouse shrugged his shoulders and replied. 'Our DO, 'Dicky' Bird – he's a wardmaster sub lieutenant, gave us a lecture when we arrived. You lot'll meet him tomorrow.'

We passed several members of staff in white operating gowns. A chief petty officer stopped us and asked what we were doing.

'Just arrived, Chief,' said Scouse. 'Showin' 'em around like. Can't 'ave them gettin' lost can we?'

'Cheeky bugger,' snorted the chief and walked away.

We walked through an archway into a large open garden with a central pathway lined with trees. Another path ran across dividing the area into four squares.

'Over to your right is C and D Blocks,' said Scouse pointing to a similar building we passed earlier. 'There was a museum between the blocks but it got bombed.' With a laugh he added, 'Dicky Bird told us odd looking specimens were scattered around the place for weeks afterwards. It seems a nurse fainted one morning when she found a 'uman 'ead staring at her from a tree on her way to work!'

At the end of the central pathway I saw a red-bricked church with a small bell tower. Above the entrance was a round clock embedded in the masonry. Scouse saw me looking at it.

'That's St Luke's Church,' replied Scouse. 'It was built in 1762.'

'Och,' moaned Big Mac, 'Do we have ta attend the services?'

'Naw,' answered Scouse, 'But I'm told the communal wine isn't bad though.'

By this time everyone was soaking wet and we were glad to get some shelter. Scouse led us into a main arcade with a low, stone-barrelled roof.

'What are those?' asked Brum, pointing to a narrow set of

rails embedded in the cobbled floor stretching the length of the arcade.

'They've been there since Nelson's time,' replied Scouse. Wooden trucks ran on them to transport sick and wounded men from the ships. The rails used to stretch in a straight line past the main gate as far as a jetty. These have long since gone, but I was told you can catch a motor launch from the jetty to Pompey.'

'Handy for a run ashore, eh?' said Tinker.

On either side of the arcade a small ramp led up to a pair of swing doors. From one emerged a stout chief petty officer with a pale, wrinkled face and dark, deep-set eyes.

'What the 'ell's going on 'ere my 'andsome?' he snapped, looking at Scouse. He spoke in a rich West Country accent. 'A Cook's tour or summat?'

Scouse hurriedly explained who we were and what he was doing.

'Hmm… I see,' replied the chief eyeing us up. 'Then you'll be seeing a lot o' me. Me names Chief Petty Officer Pascoe and I'm one o' the training instructors.' He nodded towards a door behind where we were standing. 'If you go through yon door an' up the first flight o' stairs, you'll come to a lecture room. That's where you'll be spending the next ten weeks. Now bugger of the lot o' yer and don't be adrift tomorrow.' He turned away and with a slight limp walked up the ramp, opened a door and disappeared.

'Bloody hell!' exploded Buster. 'That's all we need – Long John Silver in person.'

'Pieces of Eight! Pieces of Eight!' cried Tinker walking with a limp. Everyone followed on behind doing a similar impersonation. By the time we reached the mess our sides were aching from laughing.

The next morning at 0800 we mustered in two lines of ten outside the mess. Pinkie, looking remarkably clean and smart stood next to a tall officer with a thin gold stripe on each sleeve.

'For the benefit of you newcomers,' said the officer in a thick, Hampshire accent, 'my name is Wardmaster Sub Lieutenant Bird and I am your divisional officer.' He paused, and with cold grey eyes looked along the front line. 'I am sure the others have told you about the hospital, so I won't do so again. Suffice to say, I expect you to apply yourselves and do your best.'

In a rather high falsetto voice, Pinkie then cried, 'Open order, March!'

The front line took one pace forward, the back line stepped one pace backwards.

The officer then walked slowly along each rank. When he came to me his steely grey eyes looked me up and down. He then passed on to Big Mac who was standing next to me.

'Where are you from?' I heard him say to Big Mac.

'Glasgow, sir,' replied Big Mac.

'Then get a hair cut,' replied the officer. 'You look as if you've spent the last year in the highlands.'

'He has, sir,' interrupted Buster, who was standing next to Big Mac. 'Shaggin' sheep.'

A ripple of laughter echoed along the ranks.

'Keep silence,' squeaked Pinkie.

'A comedian, eh?' snapped the officer glaring at Buster. He then turned to Pinkie. 'Make sure these two report to the chief cook after supper tonight. We'll see how funny they feel after doing an hour's washing up.'

As the officer turned and walked stiffly away, I overheard Big Mac utter under his breath, 'Bastard, I hope his balls fester and drop off.'

The lecture room was large and kept warm by the ubiquitous box fire. Four rows of five desks and chairs faced a blackboard. In front, by the side of a desk hung a skeleton hooked to a stand. Everyone sat down and with each shuffle of a chair, the skeleton appeared to rattle and move slightly.

'The soddin' thing's still alive,' whispered Tinker, whose desk was close to mine.

'Aye,' I replied, grinning at him. 'And it's looking at you!'

In one corner was a bed with a mattress on which rested blankets and sheets neatly folded. Nearby stood a trolley with an assortment of surgical instruments, bottles, dishes and bandages. Shelves were lined with various books and in a large wooden cabinet were more instruments.

A stout, matronly figure stood in front of us as we sat down; from under her cap hung a few strands of grey hair. Her blue and white uniform looked crisp and well starched and on her thick legs she wore black stockings and flat-soled shoes.

Scouse gave me a sly wink and mouthed 'Rectum Rosie.'

'My name is Sister Fanshaw,' she said with a forceful smile. 'I will be your tutor in medical and surgical nursing procedures while you are here. In front of you are two exercise books and pencils. There is also a blue book. This is the Manual of Instruction for the Sick Berth Branch. I strongly suggest you are to study it thoroughly.' She paused and opened a book on her desk. 'Today,' she went on, 'we will study the human skeleton. Then after Stand Easy (tea break in the morning and afternoons), we will examine the digestive system, or to give it its medical name, the Alimentary Canal.'

Scouse nudges me and grinned. 'What did I tell you?' he muttered, and opened his exercise book.

In the afternoon, Long John, as we nicknamed Chief Pascoe, took us for first aid, dispensing and ship's administration.

'Now, me 'andsomes,' said Long John, his wrinkled features breaking into a wide grin. 'The first thing you do when you give first aid is loosen all tight clothin.'

'What about if it's a girl, Chief?' asked Brum.

'Slip her a crippler first,' quipped Big Mac. 'That'll soon liven her up.'

This was met with a howl of laughter and a scowl from Long John.

'That's not very funny, my bird,' he said, pursing his lips. 'First aid can save lives. And I should know. I copped a piece of shrapnel at Dunkirk. If it hadn't been for the quick thinking of my killick, I'd have bled to death. So pay bloody attention.'

The last lecture of the day, given by Pinkie, was about contagious diseases. By this time the room was warm and clammy.

'If you turn to page two hundred and eighty-one,' said Pinkie, dabbing his face with his handkerchief, 'you will see the section on Rubella, or to give it its common name, German measles.' He stopped and placed one hand on his hip, then went on. 'Now. Have any of you had German measles?'

'I have, PO,' cried Brum, shooting his hand in the air. 'That was when I broke out in little swastikas!'

'Very funny, I must say,' replied Pinkie, removing his hand from his hip. 'Just for that, you can write out the whole passage for me by tomorrow.'

Brum grinned, looked sheepishly about, shrugged his shoulders and closed his book.

When we returned to the mess, mail was scattered on the table.

Everyone crowded around the table picking up letters hoping one was for them. A letter from Aunt Glad told me Shorty had been called up and was in the Cheshire Regiment. She also added, 'a girl called Iris sends her best. I've enclosed her address and she wants you to write to her.'

'There's one for you, mate,' said Taff Hughes, passing an envelope to Spider. His face lit up as he tore open the letter. As he read it a look of relief suddenly came over his face.

'Me missus, Anne, is all right!' he gasped, looking up at us with a relieved grin. 'She's due in the next week or so.'

'There, what did I tell you,' I said, patting him on the back. 'I told you everything would be all right.'

During the next two weeks we studied every disease in the sick berth manual. We practised everything from making beds to removing sutures after operations. We studied simple dispensing and even practised giving injections of sterile water to one another.

Once again the sight of a needle made Taff nervous!

'This won't hurt you, laddie,' said Big Mac, waving a metal syringe and needle in front of Taff's face. 'Watch me!'

Taff watched wide eyed as Big Mac injected the needle into the upper outer aspect of his thigh. 'See,' bragged Big Mac, 'there's nothin' to it.'

For once Taff didn't collapse. Instead he took hold of his syringe, closed his eyes and thrust the needle into Big Mac's thigh.

'Yeoww!' cried Big Ma, jumping away and clutching his

leg. 'Yer no supposed to ram it in like a bayonet.'

To everyone's surprise, Big Mac turned the colour of dishwater and slumped into a chair!

'Nothin' to it, is there?' said Taff with a smirk on his face.

One afternoon we were in class listening to a lecture on tropical diseases; suddenly the door opened and in came Dicky Bird, our DO.

'Excuse me, Sister,' he said in a subdued tone. 'May I take PSBA Webb?'

'Of course, Chief,' replied the sister. 'Nothing serious I hope?'

The officer didn't reply. Instead he looked at Spider and with a nod beckoned him forward.

All eyes suddenly focussed on Spider. He glanced around at everyone with a look of surprise, shrugged his shoulders and slowly stood up.

Spider didn't return to the class.

When lectures finished we returned to the mess; Spider was sitting alone at a table, holding his head with both hands; straight away everyone knew something was wrong.

Spider's eyes were red and swollen; it was obvious he had been crying. Suddenly his shoulder began to shake as he burst out sobbing.

'What's the matter, Spider?' I asked, 'is there anything we can do?'

Tinker took out a packet of Players from his pocket. 'Fancy a fag, mate?' he asked bending down close to Spider.

Spider shook his head, his face wet with tears. Big Mac drew up a chair and sat down beside him. The others and myself shot worrying glances at one another.

Big Mac placed an arm around Spider's shoulders. 'Come on laddie,' he said in an unusually quiet voice. 'Tell us what's the matter. Maybe we can help you.'

Spider stopped crying but continued to catch his breath. Big Mac lit a cigarette and gave it to him. With a trembling hand Spider accepted the cigarette and took a deep drag.

'They're…they're both… dead.' Spider's voice was almost inaudible, and as he spoke, he stared down at the table.

‘What do you mean?’ asked Big Mac, glancing anxiously up at the rest of us. ‘Who’s dead?’

‘Me…me missus… and the baby,’ replied Spider, allowing ash from his cigarette to fall on the table. ‘She… died giving birth. The kid was… stillborn.’ As he spoke the pain of his suffering fell across his face like a shadow. ‘Oh Christ!’ he gasped. ‘What am I to do?’

The silence suddenly that descended on the room was palpable. Nobody spoke. Looking at Spider made me remember how I felt when my mum and dad were killed. I knew what he was going through and felt helpless. You poor bugger, I thought feeling a sudden tightness in my throat.

As I watched Spider sobbing his heart out a wave of anger surged up inside me. This fuckin’ war! And those fuckin’ Germans! I almost cried out. Instead, as my eyes glazed over, I slowly sat down on my bunk and muttered, ‘Why God? Why?’

That evening after supper the noise in the mess, usually so boisterous, was subdued. Spider lay on his bunk, staring at the ceiling. Most of us wrote letters, or sat smoking or reading newspapers. The mood was sombre. Nobody even remembered to switch on the wireless to listen to Tommy Handley’s *Itma.*

Just after seven o’clock, Spider rose from his bunk and put on his uniform jacket and cap; all eyes followed him as he slowly walked to the mess door.

‘Where you going, mate?’ asked Brum, putting down his fountain pen. ‘Dye fancy some company?’

Spider didn’t answer. He opened the door and without saying a word left the mess.

Big Mac threw down his *Tit Bits* and heaved himself off his bunk.

‘Come on,’ he said, grabbing his jacket, cap and greatcoat, ‘let’s see where he’s going. It’s bloody cold outside and he no wearing his coat.’

Big Mac was right. Outside the bitter December air promised snow. As we buttoned our greatcoats our trousers flapped wildly around our ankles like sails from a windjammer. High above in a cloudless sky, a full moon bathed everything in a cold clear light.

The tall figure of Spider could be seen about a hundred yards away. We kept a respectable distance behind, and watched as he walked through the main gate. After passing HMS *Hornet,* he headed towards Pneumonia Bridge.

'D'you think he knows we're following him, Mac?' asked Brum, passing his cigarettes around.

'Quiet y' wee bugger,' hissed Big Mac. Vaporised breath streamed out of their mouths as they spoke. 'Maybe he wants to be alone. It might upset him if he hears us.'

Big Mac had a point. The last we wanted was to make things worse.

The cold seemed to keep everyone indoors; there wasn't a soul about and the MTB base was in complete darkness. The full moon cast an eerie glow across the murky waters of Haslar Creek, outlining the motor torpedo boats lying alongside a jetty. Across in Portsmouth harbour I could just make out the silhouettes of several warships and the dark shapes of houses.

We watched as Spider walked up Pneumonia Bridge. Suddenly, he stopped at the top and stared across the creek.

'Wait,' whispered Big Mac, placing an arm in front of us, 'I think he's gunna have a smoke, or something.'

'He must be bloody cold,' I said. 'He should have put a coat on.'

'The state of mind he's in,' replied Buster, 'he probably won't feel anything.'

We waited at the bottom of the bridge, anxiously looking up at the dark figure of Spider. He was slumped over a guardrail staring across the creek.

What happened next took a few seconds but seemed like hours.

Spider continued to stand still, gazing out into the darkness. Then, without warning, he suddenly heaved himself up onto edge of the railings.

'Christ almighty!' cried Big Mac. 'He's gunna jump!'

We immediately sprung forward. It was painfully apparent what he intended to do. For a fleeting second Spider stood still on the edge of the railings.

'*No, Spider! No Spider!*' shouted someone. '*For God's*

sake, don't do it!'

But it was too late. Keeping both arms by his sides Spider toppled forward. I felt the blood drain from my face as I watched him fall though the air. With a small splash he entered into the icy waters of Haslar Creek.

We reached the spot where Spider had been standing and looked down; alas there was nothing to see but a swirl of bubbles in the inky darkness.

However, some observant person in *Hornet* must have seen what had happened. I heard the jangle of a bell and in a matter of seconds a motor launch boat sped from a jetty towards the bridge. The engine was cut as two matelots, clad in sweaters, probed the waters with a hooked pole.

'What happened?' yelled one of them.

'He… he just jumped,' replied Big Mac.

We watched horrified as the sailors dragged the limp body of Spider out of the waters. One of the matelots looked up at us and gave the thumbs down.

'He's a goner!' shouted the matelot. 'You lot had best report to the Officer of the Watch and tell him what you saw.'

The Coroner at the inquest that followed a week later passed a verdict of 'Death while the balance of PSBA Webb's mind was disturbed'.

Spider's parents watched in silence. His father, a tall man with a military bearing, sat with his arm around his wife, a small, fair-haired lady who occasionally dabbed her eyes with a handkerchief.

Afterwards, Big Mac, the others and myself, tried to speak a few words of condolence to them. But it was no use. They were heartbroken; victims of a war that seemed endless.

A week later our class and the other trainees were granted twelve days leave covering Christmas and New Year. This would be my first festive season without mum and dad and I wasn't looking forward to neither. On Friday, 22 December, Big Mac, Buster, Tinker and myself had a farewell drink in the bar. The mood was cheerful and the beer plentiful.

'Here's to 1943!' cried Buster, raising his glass.

Big Mac chimed in. 'Aye,' he said. 'And here's hoping

we'll all be around to celebrate 1944!'

'Come on Ted,' said Scouse Kilkenny as we leant against the bar. 'Yer Aunt Glad will be over the moon to see yer. And besides, there's that tart, Iris you wrote to. She'll be only too eager to drop her drawers.'

The lads in the mess knew what happened to my parents. It was hard to keep a secret in such a close-knit community.

'I suppose so, Scouse,' I replied as I sipped my pint. 'Anyway, we'd best make the most of it. We take our finals when we return, and I'm gunna put in for a ship as soon as I can.'

'You sound determined to get into the war,' replied Scouse, downing his beer. With a laugh, he added, 'You want to watch it, mate, or you'll end up getting yer arse shot off. As fer me, I'll settle fer a cushy number in the hospital.'

Scouse was right.

Aunt Glad burst into tears when she saw me.

'Your room's made up and I've cooked a pan of Scouse for you.'

My mood improved at the sight of Shorty in his khaki battledress.

'I've even got me rifle with me at home,' he said, shaking my hand. 'I'm being posted to Salisbury Plain. There's a rumour of an invasion someplace, but God knows where.'

On Christmas Eve we took Iris and Janet to The Kingsland Dance Hall in Birkenhead. The place was crowded with servicemen and women including a few Americans wearing their smart uniforms and cocky smiles.

'Is it true,' said Shorty looking at a tall, American sergeant with Airborne flashes on his shoulder. 'That you Yanks are overpaid, over here and oversexed?'

The girls, Shorty and me were standing at the bar having a drink. Shorty had started drinking earlier than the rest of us. When he caught the American smiling at Janet, I sensed trouble. For a few moments I thought the American was going to take offence at Shorty's remark. Much to my relief the American looked up at Shorty's freckled face and grinned.

'It sure is feller,' he drawled in an accent reminiscent of

John Wayne. 'And you're undersexed, under paid and under Eisenhower!'

At that moment, a small, skinny lad in the RAF poked his head from behind the American. His collar was undone and his tie lay in a tangled mess around his neck.

'You're bloody-well right, Yank,' he slurred. He then held out his empty glass, gave a loud belch and added, 'and the next round's on you!'

Everyone, including Shorty and me burst out laughing.

'You bet, fly boy,' replied the American, and did the honours.

I didn't feel like dancing, but Iris insisted; she almost had to drag me onto the packed dance floor. I had to admit, she looked particularly inviting. She wore a low cut pink dress that did justice to her more than ample figure. As we moved around she looked up and said, 'Look Ted, I know how you feel. But try and enjoy yourself, after all, you only have less than a week before you go back.'

With a sigh I replied, 'I'll do my best, but it's hard to take my mind off things.'

I felt Iris grip my waist. She pulled me so close I could smell her perfume.

'Don't worry, love,' she said, placing her head against my chest. 'When you take me home, I'll make you forget.'

A few hours later as we crept into her parlour, the chimes of the clock echoed around the house.

'Bloody hell!' I said. 'That's loud enough to wake up the dead.'

'Quiet,' whispered Iris, placing a finger to her mouth. 'Dad's on nights and mum's a poor sleeper.'

The dim light from the lamp stand in the parlour bathed the room in a pale, yellow light. In next to no time we were lying on the sofa making love. Afterwards Iris lay back, her dress hanging around her waist with her firm breasts exposed. Both stockings lay in a wrinkled heap by her ankles.

'Mm…' muttered Iris, lighting a cigarette while and pulling on her black French knickers, 'that was lovely. When was the last time you…?'

'With you,' I replied, buttoning my flies and tucking my shirt into my trousers. 'Just before I joined up.'

'Oh yes,' replied Iris, watching my every move. 'In Birkenhead Park, I remember.'

Just as I fastened the last button she glanced at her wrist-watch, and with a gleam in her eyes, whispered, 'There's no need to hurry, love, Dad isn't due home for another two hours or so.'

The sight of her in such a sexy dishevelled state aroused me.

She threw her cigarette away in the fire grate. Using both hands she undid my flies. I felt her warm hand engulf my penis. Just then, she did something no girl had ever done. She covered me with her mouth. As she moved up and down, I could hear her breathing heavily. I lay back on the sofa, the blood pounding in my head. Excitement within me mounted. I felt her lips and tongue moved quicker…

Suddenly it was all over. Iris was good at her word. She certainly had taken my mind off things!

Iris, Janet, Shorty and me along with a few old pals from the St John's Ambulance Brigade, celebrated New Year's Eve in 'The Nag's Head'. After closing time we staggered back to Shorty's house and gathered around the piano while Shorty's mum played a medley of songs ranging from *White Cliffs of Dover,* to *Underneath the Arches.*

Much later Iris and I were hard at it again on her sofa when suddenly the parlour light came on. I looked up and to my horror, saw Iris's mother silhouetted in the doorway. She wore a dark dressing gown and a hairnet under which poked an array of metal curlers. In one hand she brandished a wooden walking stick.

'What's going on here, then?' she said in a tired voice. 'I thought I heard burglars.'

Quick as a flash, Iris pulled down her dress, patted her hair and stood up. I hurriedly pulled on my trousers.

It must have been painfully obvious to Iris's mother what was 'going on'. However, to her credit, she glared into the dimly lit room and turned around. As she stamped upstairs I heard her mutter, 'I don't know…young people today. You'd best get back to your ship or wherever you're going. This damn war…'

In January 1943 the Japanese began withdrawing from Guadalcanal; the 'Big Three' met at Casablanca and the Eight Army crossed into Tunisia in pursuit of Rommel's Afrika Corps. The American Air Force bombed the German cities of Emden and Wilhelmshaven. Meanwhile, in Los Angles, a jury of nine women and three men acquitted Errol Flynn of raping seventeen year-old Betty Hansen.

'That lecherous sod gets more fanny than a shit-house seat in the Wrens' quarters,' said Big Mac, reading his *Daily Mirror*. We were in the mess having returned from leave.

'"In like Flynn", that's what they say!' replied Buster. 'Jealousy will get yer nowhere.'

At the start of February our class began taking their final examinations. By the end of the first week we had taken written and oral tests in all subjects in our medical manual. These included advanced first aid, hospital administration and the grisly procedure of laying out the dead.

On the final day Big Mac emerged from an oral examination on medical nursing. With a beam he gave us the thumbs up, touched his backside and gave a little jump.

True to form, Rectum Rosie asked him and everyone else how to give an enema!

Two days later a list was posted on the main notice board. To our delight, all our class passed with flying colours. We were now Sick Berth Attendants and could sow on our scarlet crosses

'Now maybe you'll be sent to sea,' said Tinker, as we shook hands. 'And get your sodden head blown off.'

A few days later, I put in a request for sea duty.

Chief Petty Officer Milton looked up as I entered the regulating office. He was a pale, sharp-featured man with close-cropped grey hair and eyes to match.

'Any type of ship will do, Chief,' I said, handing him my slip of paper. 'I want to get into the war before it's over.'

'Determined bugger, aren't you,' he said, stamping my request. He then sat back in his chair, eyed me up and added, 'Believe you me. You'll get more than you bargained for before this lot's over.'

As a reward for passing our examinations, everyone was granted a long weekend.

'How about a few days in Smoke?' suggested Scouse Kilkenny.

We were in the bar having a celebratory drink.

'Good idea,' I replied, passing my cigarettes around. 'What ses you, Big Mac?'

Big Mac was leaning against the bar. He slowly drew himself up to his six-foot stature and grinned. 'Och, laddie,' he replied, before taking a slurp of beer. 'Sounds fine ta me.' He turned to Tinker. 'Tinker me laddo, you're from Lambeth. What's the partys like in dear old London toon?'

'Fabulous!' answered Tinker with a mischievous glint in his eyes. 'Especially at "The Windmill".'

'"The Windmill",' I repeated. 'What's that? A knockin' shop?'

Tinker looked at me and shook his head. 'You bloody northerners know nowt,' he said. '"The Windmill" is a show where all the partys stand around half naked – and it's open twenty-four hours a day.'

Big Mac's face broke into a wide grin. 'Och laddie!' he roared. 'That sounds like the place fer us.'

'Aye, but where could we stay?' asked Buster, finishing his drink, and like a typical Scotsman, added, 'it's pretty bloody expensive up the line.'

Tinker pursed his lips and said. 'We could stay at the "The Union Jack Club". I hear it's dirt cheap and the scran's great.'

'Where's that, Tinks?' piped up Brum, holding an empty glass.

'Waterloo,' replied Tinker. 'It's just outside the station. Don't worry. I'll show you.'

'Great!' replied Big Mac. 'That's settled then.' He waved his empty glass in front of Brum's face, and added, 'It's your round, wee man, and mine's a whisky.'

Little did I know the profound effect my first visit to London was to have on me, not only in the near future, but also in years to come.

CHAPTER FIVE

After buying half a dozen bottles of Nut Brown Ale in Portsmouth we caught the one o'clock train from Portsmouth, Harbour Station. During the two hour journey to London, Tinker explained how to get to 'The Windmill Theatre'.

'Take the tube to Piccadilly,' he said, downing a large swig from his bottle of beer. 'Turn right into Shaftesbury Avenue – that's where all the theatres are. Cross over the road and you'll come to Great Windmill Street. The theatre is at the top. You can't miss it.'

'Why do they call it "The Windmill", Tinks?' asked Brum. 'Is there a windmill there, or summat?'

Tinker finished the contents of his bottle, wiped his mouth then answered. 'Actually, you're not far wrong. When Charles II was king, a windmill stood there.' Using a bottle opener, Tinker helped himself to another beer. 'Now remember you lot,' he went on, 'you'll be in Soho so be careful, it's a den of vice. At least that's what me dad tells me!'

'Och away we ye!' exploded Big Mac, rubbing his hands together. 'It sounds just the place fer me.'

The rest of us grinned and nodded in agreement.

'It's been ages since I've 'add me leg over,' commented Scouse. 'Besides, who the fuck knows where we'll be this time next year.'

'Yea,' agreed Buster. 'Let's grab it while it's hot, I say.'

'Grab what while it's hot?' asked Brum, innocently.

'You'll find out,' I replied, passing my Woodbines around.

'But a word of advice,' went on Tinker, shooting a warning glance at Big Mac. 'Keep away from those Piccadilly Commandos. They're poxed up to the hilt. Ask any of the Yanks.'

'Piccadilly Commandos,' muttered Brum, glancing around

at us, 'what the 'ell are they?'

Big Mac rolled his dark brown eyes upwards and shook his head. The rest of us looked at one another and roared with laughter.

We arrived at Waterloo shortly after five o'clock. For a few moments I stopped and looked around. I had never seen so many people on the move.

Service personnel mingled with the crowds pouring out of the underground station. I recognised uniforms from as far a field as the Commonwealth, Poland, France and America. They hurried about seeking exits, or a warm drink from the dimly lit cafés; others clustered around numerous tea trolleys smoking and talking and at various intervals; the hidden voice of the announcer echoed around the station. The noise of shunting engines, the hissing of steam and the movement of people lent a touch of surrealism to the scene.

No doubt many were off to join ships, shore bases and regiments. But as I looked at some of the faces, I couldn't help but wonder how many would be alive when the war was over.

Outside an icy mist had descended on everything, frosting shop windows and those in a few parked cars. Men and women, their shoulders hunched against the cold, hurried past. As we made our way down the steps into the dusk of the evening, a blast of bitter wind hit me in the face making my eyes water.

My gas mask was slung over my shoulder and in one hand I carried a Pusser's canvas grip; I placed the grip on the ground and turned up the collar of my Burberry.

'How far away is this club, Tinks?' I asked. 'I'm freezing my bollocks off.'

'Aye,' added Big Mac, 'and when do the boozers open here? Train journeys make me thirsty!'

As we spoke dragon-like streams of vaporised breath poured from our mouths.

'Follow me, lads,' replied Tinker. 'It's just round the corner from the where we are.'

We followed Tinker down the steps and turned right into a busy road. Many people on bicycles, the lights from their lamps shaded, hurried towards a bridge that crossed the River Thames;

a few motorcars, their lights also partially covered, drove by. The white markings on the edges of the pavement, lampposts and trees stood out in the gloom. A newspaper vendor, stamping his feet, sold copies of *The Evening Standard* on a street corner. Next to him was a headline, which read *Last Pockets Of Germans In Stalingrad Surrender To The Russians!*

'That's Waterloo Bridge,' said Tinker pointing to his left. 'The blackout starts at six o'clock that's why everyone's in a panic to get home.'

Making our way through the crowds emerging from the station we found ourselves in a wide road busy with traffic. Across from where we were standing was an imposing, four storey building. At each corner and in the middle was a rounded turret; from each of these a Union Flag lay fluttered slightly in the evening air. Outside, many of the taped windows with metal balconies, overlooked the main road. A small flight of steps led up to an arched entrance.

'This is Waterloo Road,' said Tinker. 'And that place over there,' he paused and pointed across the road, 'is the Union Jack Club. I'm off home before the blackout. Just go in and tell the commissioner what you want. He's just inside the door.'

We thanked Tinker and arranged to meet him on platform four on Sunday afternoon.

'Come on lads,' said Buster, crossing the road, 'I don't know about you lot, but I'm bloody starving!'

The booking office was on our left inside the building. On either side of some carpeted steps stood a tall, exotic-looking vase containing shiny-leafed aspidistras. The clock on the wall above a short flight of stairs told us the time was half past five.

At the top of a flight of four stairs stood a commissioner in a blue uniform. Grey hairs matching his finely clipped military moustache sprouted either side of his well-lined face. He held himself upright and on his left breast were two rows of faded medals.

'And what can I do for you young lads, eh?' he said, peering over a pair of horn-rimmed spectacles. His dark brown eyes glared at us and for a moment I thought I was back in Victoria Barracks.

'We'd like a cabin each fer two nights,' said Big Mac, placing his grip on the highly polished linoleum floor.

'I see,' replied the commissioner. He then nodded towards the booking office. 'Then there's the place to report to.'

The head and shoulders of a small, elderly lady with short, grey hair barely visible behind the booking office counter, greeted us.

'That'll be three and sixpence each love,' she said with a cheerful smile. 'Your cabins are on the second floor.' She then passed each of us a key. 'Bathroom's at the end of the corridor.'

Once again, 'Old Dark Eyes' gave us the once over. 'The doors are locked after midnight,' he grunted. 'Ring the bell. And, remember, no women allowed inside.'

Big Mac suddenly put on his best innocent expression. 'Women!' he uttered, placing one hand on his hip and glancing at us. 'As if we would! Horrible creatures so they are!' He then picked up his grip, and added, 'Come on laddies. Time for tea,' and minced up the stairs.

Old Dark Eyes' mouth fell open. He glowered at us as we followed Big Mac.

'I shouldn't believe everything you hear,' said Scouse. As he passed the red-faced official, he smiled, fluttered his eyes and added, 'Ducks!'

I opened the door of my cabin, found the electric switch and looked around.

The bed was covered with a blue coverlet on which was embroidered a ship's anchor. Next to this was a small table on which rested a Gideon Bible. A stout oaken wardrobe was provided for clothes and in one corner close to a window, was a washbasin. A well-worn brown carpet almost covered the floor and on a wall was a framed photograph of the King and Queen. Just the job, I thought, closing the door, now all I need to find was the bar.

Big Mac and the other three had the same idea. Our cabins were next to one another and I could hear Scouse through the thin, wooden walls testing the springs on the bed; Big Mac in the other room was humming some strange Celtic tune.

I banged on the Big Mac's wall, and shouted. 'Let's find

out when the bar opens.'

'Bugger that,' I heard Scouse say. 'I want some scoff *and* a few bevies.'

The dining room was on the ground floor; it was a well-lit room with cafeteria service. Despite the continuation of rationing, (one egg, 3ozs cheese, 2ozs sugar, 4ozs bacon and 2ozs of butter, issued to each person weekly) like starving refuges we stuffed ourselves with steak and kidney pie, Pom, (powdered potato substitute) and vegetables, followed by apple pie and custard.

'By Christ!' exclaimed Scouse wiping his mouth with a serviette. 'For one and six, that was the best meal I've ever had.'

The bar was a spacious room next to the dining hall. As we entered a waft of hot, smoky air hit me in the face.

In the centre of the room was a round table surrounded by tables, comfortable-looking black-leathered Chesterfield chairs and sofas. Heavy, black curtains were drawn across the bay windows and the varnished floor was partially covered with a wide, well trodden carpet. Two bright chandeliers spread an even light around and above an open fire grate rested an ornamental silver clock; flanked on either side by a small union flag it told us the time was just after six thirty.

The room was quite crowded with servicemen sitting around, smoking, laughing and drinking. Three elderly waiters wearing white jackets, collected drinks from behind a bar and served them to those sitting down.

'This is the life fer me,' said Big Mac, flopping himself into a chair. 'Bring on the dancin' lassies!'

The other two ignored him and sat down. I remained standing admiring the clock. One of the waiters, a small man with thin, grey hair and a pale face, appeared next to me.

'Presented to the club just after the Boer War,' he said in a broad Cockney accent, 'by a lady called Violet Brook-Hunt.' He paused and adjusted a white tea towel draped over his arm; then with a toothy grin, added, 'When it chimes at ten o'clock, the shutters on the bar comes down. Now, what can I get you lads?'

'Bugger me, mon!' gasped Big Mac, looking up at him, 'it's service wee a smile, here.'

'Pipe down and get the bevy in,' chimed Scouse, relaxing back in his chair. 'Mine's a nice cool pint of bitter.'

'How much is the beer, mate?' Brum asked the waiter.

'Nine pence a pint, guv'nor,' (almost a pound in today's currency) replied the waiter, 'an' shorts is sixpence a shot.'

Since we started training I hadn't had much time to spend my pay of two pound ten shillings a fortnight. With over ten pounds in my money belt, (Five shillings in 1943 was worth approximately seven pounds today,) I felt like a 'Baron', (naval slang for someone who is well off).

'That's bloody marvellous,' said Buster, placing both hands behind his neck. 'I may spend the duration here.'

After a few pints of draught beer, Big Mac suggested we explore the place.

'Ye never know,' he said, standing up and stretching his arms above his head. 'One o' us might get pissed and loose his bearings.'

'Och aye,' replied Buster, winking at me, 'and we all know who that'll be.'

Along a corridor we entered a room with wall-to-wall cabinets containing leather-bound books. A wide, pastel-coloured lampshade allowed an even light and several small carpets covered the wooden floor. A few servicemen sat around smoking or reading newspapers and magazines; some sat at desks engrossed in writing letters. Soldiers and airmen, ties undone, jackets and battledress open, lounged around, no doubt sleeping off the previous nights booze.

'I hope you 'ave written 'ome, to that judy you told us about,' whispered Scouse glancing at me.

He was referring to Iris who had sent me a couple of letters. I glanced at him and gave a non-committal shrug of my shoulders.

Big Mac led us through a door into a room where two soldiers were playing billiards. One was small and stocky with ginger hair, the other tall with deep-set dark eyes. Ginger stood by the table, his cue-stick over his shoulder and a cigarette dangling from his mouth, and said, 'Any of youse fancy a game?'

'Next time, pal,' answered Scouse. 'We're off to "The Windmill", to get some real action!'

Dark Eyes potted a red and unbent himself. 'Get away with yer,' he said, lighting a cigarette. 'You'll all end up at Rainbow Corner.'

Big Mac shot the soldier a quizzical look. 'Where's that?'

'Bottom of Shaftesbury Avenue,' replied Ginger, chalking the end of his cue. 'Near the Rainbow Club where all the Yanks go.'

'Is that a fact, laddie,' murmured Big Mac, glancing lustfully at the rest of us. 'Come on lads, what are we waiting for.'

A bitterly cold February wind continued to blow downriver. A shaded, yellow light from a cyclist or a crawling taxi punctuated the darkness, and like a scene from a Boris Karloff film, huddled figures hurried past. High above, in the inky gloom I caught a glimpse of a barrage balloon, its shiny greyness exposed on the beam of a searchlight.

'Take the Bakerloo line to Piccadilly, mate,' said the ticket collector as we went through the barrier. 'Just after Charing Cross.'

We waited on a platform already crowded mainly with women, children and elderly men. In crumpled lines, they lay under blankets, old coats and eiderdowns. Nearby, rested flasks of warm drinks, boxes of food and a host of other items. Even though the Blitz was almost over, the Londoners were taking no chances.

A full moon, hanging in the cloudless sky, greeted us as we emerged from the underground at Piccadilly. This was known as a Bomber's Moon because its glow highlighted targets for the Luftwaffe – thankfully the air raid sirens remained silent.

Piccadilly presented a dismal sight. The statue of Eros I had seen on postcards was gone. In its place was an empty stone plinth covered with barbed wire. The Bovril and Guinness signs that once joined the glitter from the West End theatres were now absent. Instead of the hurly-burly of red buses, traffic hooting their horns, and masses of people, a palpable silence now reigned. I read somewhere Charles Dickens once called

Piccadilly, 'the centre of the universe'; looking around I wondered what he would think of it now.

We soon found Shaftsbury Avenue.

'Bloody hell!' cried Brum, rubbing his hands together. 'There's no danger of heat stroke tonight.'

The area was crowded with servicemen. The silhouettes of pork-pie hats and the nasal twang of voices reminding me of the films, told me many were American.

Girls, dressed in warm coats gathered in groups as if waiting for a bus; the glow from their cigarette ends pierced in the dim light, as did their high-pitched laughter.

'Jesus!' exclaimed Big Mac. 'Those pongos were right after all.'

'Keep it in yer trousers, Big Mac,' replied Scouse. 'You couldn't afford their lipstick.'

'Ha!' laughed Brum, glancing at Scouse. 'It ain't their lipstick he's after, is it?'

The soldiers, cigarettes glowing, loitered in the dark doorways. I watched as the girls slowly swayed past the Americans, pause, before striking matches close to their faces.

'Fancy a good time, Yank?' I heard one say. She and a sailor wearing a pork pie hat promptly disappeared into the darkness.

'Hey!' said Scouse, nudging Big Mac. 'Get an eyeful of one of those judies shining a light onto her legs. I bet she wears utility knickers, eh, big man?'

'What are those, Big Mac?' asked Brum.

Big Mac let out a loud laugh. 'One Yank and they're off!'

'Now you know what Piccadilly Commandos are, Brum,' said Buster.

'Aye,' muttered Big Mac. 'And some o' them are no bad either. I wonder how much they charge.'

'Too much fer you, big man,' uttered Buster, as we made our way down Great Windmill Street. 'Just keep it in yer trousers and remember that film on VD we saw in Vicky Barracks.'

'The Windmill' theatre, built of white masonry stood out in the gloom of the night. Sandbags were stacked either side of the entrance. A sign on the door read 'House Full. Next Performance at Eight o'clock'.

Groups of servicemen milled about waiting to go inside to see the show. American soldiers and sailors, in smart brown and blue uniforms, mingled with the red pom-poms berets of the Free French; badges of the famous Polish Eagle glinted in the moonlight; British soldiers and sailors in heavy greatcoats who, like ourselves, carried gas masks, rubbed shoulders with troops from the Commonwealth. As you might expect, female members of the armed forces were conspicuous by their absence.

'Blimey!' exploded Brum. 'It looks as if half the world is here. We'll never get in.'

'I agree with the wee feller,' replied Big Mac. 'Let's find a boozer and get pissed.'

'Bollocks,' I replied. 'Take a look at the sign high up above the name of the theatre. It says *We Are Never Closed.* And we've got plenty of time.'

'Fuck me!' gasped Scouse. 'Ted's right. We could spend the whole weekend here.'

'Yeah,' drooled Big Mac, 'wee all them naked lassies to keep us company, eh?'

A pub called 'The Red Lion' was close by. It too was packed but Big Mac managed to get a round of beers; he also produced a half bottle of whiskey.

'That must have set you back a few bob,' said Brum, taking a large gulp of ale.

'Aye, two quid,' replied Big Mac. 'Yon feller at the bar with the fancy trilby and black overcoat sold it ta me. It'll help keep out the cold.'

After a few pints Scouse suggested we try to get into the theatre. 'Come on,' he said, glancing at the clock behind the bar, 'it's ten to eight. We might just make it.'

We paid 1/6d each but could only find room standing at the back of the theatre.

The Windmill was surprisingly small with a single balcony; shaded lights allowed subdued lighting to reflect along the brown panelled walls. Scarlet curtains, shining in the dim, smoky light were drawn across a small stage and on either side of a cream-coloured pediment arose two Corinthian columns. In the narrow orchestra pit musicians sat down and lazily flicked through sheet music, while the crowd, boisterous and drunk waited eagerly, anticipating a feast of female flesh.

And they were not disappointed!

The four of us leant against a wooden partition. On my right stood an American sailor, his white, pork-pie cap casually balanced on the back of his head.

'Say, bud,' he drawled. 'Are there many joints like this in town?'

Big Mac, about to unscrew his bottle of Scotch overheard him. 'Noo, laddie,' he said. 'This is the only theatre open in the West End, a mate of ours who lives here told us.'

'Gee,' replied the American. 'You don't say. Them dames sure are a gutsy lot.'

Brum leant across to me, and dropping his voice, said, 'did he say gutsy or busty?'

Scouse passed his cigarette down the line. Big Mac, took a swig of whiskey, and handed the bottle to the rest of us.

At that moment, the musicians took their seats and struck up, *All The Nice Girls Love a Sailor.* The crowd immediately joined in and the mood was set.

The first act consisted of two jugglers dressed in silver tights. Then, in the middle of the performance, the backdrop curtains slowly opened to reveal three naked girls standing on podiums. One had a feather boar loosely draped around her midriff. The other two wore skimpy loincloths and held a vase in both hands. Their bodies glowed like porcelain in the bright stage lights. All three stood perfectly still; not one shapely, nipple-pointed breast quivered; each girl simply held a fixed smile and gazed directly into the audience.

The crowd went wild. Sailors threw their caps in the air. Others cupped their hands around their mouths and shouted. One American soldier stood up waving a fist full of dollars. 'A hundred bucks for the blonde!' he yelled.

The curtains closed to a tremendous ovation. Some sat and cheered; others stamped their feet while a few stood up and wildly applauded. Big Mac, Buster, Brum and myself accompanied the rest in a chorus of *'More! More! More!'* And once again we were not disappointed.

There followed a series of novelty acts, ranging from a performing monkey to a man standing on his head playing a violin. Like the rest, Big Mac and the others paid little attention to them. Our eyes were transfixed on the naked girls in the background.

The show ended with a chorus of men singing the national anthems of America, Britain and France. Once more the back curtains opened to reveal three girls, each completely naked, waving flags of the same three countries.

One man in a black evening suit wearing a red, white and blue sash sang *The Marseilles;* a few French sailors joined in, with obvious pride. Another man dressed like Uncle Sam then sang *The Stars and Stripes.* Many Americans, including the sailor next to me, stood and placed their right hand on their hearts. But the loudest singing was reserved for *God Save The King.* This was rendered with great gusto by a portly person in red, wearing a union jack waistcoat and a tall, blue stovepipe hat; to a man, everyone stood to attention and raised the roof with their voices.

After this we finished Big Mac's bottle of Scotch, and with almost hysterical enjoyment, clapped wildly, whistled and yelled.

'*I'm in love! I'm in love!*' cried Scouse. 'That blonde's got the most beautiful pubes I've ever seen!'

'I'll have the tall brunette!' yelled Big Mac.

'I'll have the lot!' chimed in Buster.

'And I don't care who I have,' added Brum. 'They're all fuckin' gorgeous!'

Brum was right.

The girls looked like a fantasy many men would take with them to the battlefront. For some, it might be the last time they saw such beauty before being killed.

As the curtains closed to end the show, those in the front stood up and left. As soon as this happened a hoard of men from the back leapt forward over seats to obtain a closer view of the next show. 'Fuck me!' exclaimed Scouse, 'it's like the bloody

Grand National.'

'You're right there, Jack,' said a soldier putting on his cap. 'I come here often. It's called the "Windmill Derby".'

We left the theatre and managed to have a few more pints in 'The Red Lon' before closing time. The sky had clouded over and a haze of fog had descended over the West End.

'I see the girls are still at it,' commented Scouse, as we made our way through crowds of servicemen. 'They all seem to waiting near that doorway.'

The doorway he was referring to was on the corner of Shaftsbury Avenue.

'That must be "The Rainbow Corner", that Pongo told us about,' said Buster.

'D'you think they're all wearing those utility knickers, Ted?' asked Brum.

I looked at one or two of the girls. A few had their coats slightly open, showing more than a glimpse of leg. For a moment I was tempted to speak to one of them, but thought better of it. A few quid, for a quick knee trembler down a dark alley, was not my way spending what little money I had left.

'I doubt if any one of 'em are wearing anything,' I laughed.

We stopped at the top of Piccadilly Tube Station; with the exception of many servicemen and women, the place was deserted.

Scouse took out a packet of Woodbines and handed them around.

Suddenly he cried, 'Hey! Where the 'ell's Big Mac?'

The three of us looked at each other, then turned and looked around. By this time the fog was a real peasouper, and visibility was poor.

'Mac! Mac!' I yelled, anxiously staring about.

Buster dodged through a crowd of drunken soldiers and stopped at the corner of Shaftesbury Avenue. 'Big Mac,' he cried several times. Buster turned and rejoined us. 'No sign of the bugger,' he said.

'Maybe he took a wrong turning,' said Brum, 'and he's wondering around, looking for us.'

'Stupid prick!' I cursed. 'Let's go back to the theatre. He

might be waiting there.'

We did this but it was no use; it seemed as if the ground had opened and swallowed him up.

'Christ Almighty!' said Scouse, with obvious concern in his voice. 'I 'ope the big streak of piss is OK.'

'Come on,' I said. 'He'll probably be waiting for us back in the club.'

But he wasn't. Big Mac's cabin door was locked and he couldn't be found anywhere.

Sometime during the night I was woken up by the sound of footsteps and the thud of a cabin door closing. I switched on the light; my watch told me it was shortly after four in the morning. I got out of bed and went into the corridor. To my surprise I met Buster, Scouse and Brum. They were barefooted, wearing only trousers and vests.

'Any sign of the sod?' asked Buster.

'Don't know,' I yawned. I then knocked on the door of Big Mac's cabin but got no answer.

'If he's not here by mornin',' whispered Scouse, 'we'd best report it to the cops.'

'Or the nearest morgue!' said Brum.

'Cheerful little bastard, aren't you,' I replied, giving him a gentle push.

'Less of the little,' replied Brum, hitching up his trousers. 'Anyways,' he went on, 'we're doing no good here. We might as well get turned in.'

Some time later the sound of Big Mac's door closing woke me up; the time was just after six in the morning. I had a head like Birkenhead and my bladder was bursting. As I relieved myself in the sink, I knocked on the wall and in a muted voice, said, 'Is that you, Mac?'

'Aye,' came a hoarse reply. I heard the springs of his bed creak, followed by a resounding fart and a muffled sigh.

I quickly left and went into his room; my head was till aching and I felt sick. The underpants I wore were scant protection against the coldness of the morning, and I began to shiver.

Big Mac was lying fully clothed on his bed. His tie was

missing and his shirt was undone.

'Where the fuck have you been?' I hissed. 'We've been searching high and low for you.'

Buster came into the room scratching his backside and yawning; his hair was a mess and he looked half asleep.

'Bloody hell, mon,' he said looking at Big Mac, 'you've got eyes like piss holes in snow.'

Scouse must have heard us talking and came in. Like Buster and myself he only wore underpants.

'We were gonna call the cops,' said Scouse, running a hand through his hair. 'We even thought of calling the morgue.'

'Just what the 'ell happened to you?' said Brum. 'We were up 'alf the bloomin' night lookin' for you.'

Big Mac blinked his eyes and propped himself up on his elbows. 'I…er, got lost in the fog,' he replied, avoiding our gaze. He sat up properly and lit a cigarette. 'Fell asleep on a bench somewhere,' then breathing out a stream of tobacco smoke, added, 'and here I am.'

'In this bloody weather?' said Scouse. 'Who d'yer think yer kidding. You've been on the nest with some judy. Anyway. I'm fuckin' freezin' See you lot in 'alf an 'our for breakfast.'

'Have you?' asked Brum, beginning to shiver.

'Have I what?' growled Big Mac.

'Been with a party?'

'Piss off,' answered Big Mac and closed his eyes. When we left him he was sound asleep. One arm hung over the side of his bed with a lighted cigarette dangling from his limp fingers. I gently removed the cigarette and closed the door.

'What do you mean, you're skint?' asked Scouse glaring suspiciously at Big Mac.

We were in the dining room eating breakfast; my stomach felt queasy and I wasn't hungry.

'I only had a shilling to pay for this lot,' said Big Mac, chewing a piece of bacon. 'It's like I said. I think I was robbed. All me money's gone.'

Scouse, glanced at Brum, Buster and me. 'Tell it to the marines,' said Scouse, his eyes narrowing. 'I still say you went with some friggin' bint.'

'Och, noo,' replied Big Mac, shaking his head. Looking innocently around he added, 'As if I'd do a thing like that…'

Later in the reading room each of us put a pound in the kitty and gave it to Big Mac.

'There, you miserable Scottish get,' I quipped, passing him the money. 'Now in future, keep it in your trousers.'

'Thanks lads,' muttered Big Mac, pocketing the money. 'But I told yer…'

Buster cut him short. 'Aye,' he said grinning, 'and I'm Adolf bloody Hitler!'

For a while we sat in the reading room catching up with news.

'Tripoli has been captured by Monty!' exclaimed Buster from behind his *Daily Express.* Then with a half-hearted laugh, added, 'And at home women are now doing men's jobs.'

'Great!' replied Scouse, 'When this lot's over me missus can carry on grafting and I'll retire.'

When the bar opened at twelve o'clock, Big Mac suggested we have a few pints and take a walk into the city.

'We canna not come to Smoke without seeing Buckingham Palace,' he said, rubbing his hands with glee.

'Are you sure you're not planning another trip to Piccadilly?' replied Brum, eyeing him cautiously.

Scouse and Buster looked at one another.

'Yeah,' said Scouse. 'An' remember that's all the money you've got.'

'Aye,' chimed in Buster. 'And it's all we've got too.'

I was still feeling under the weather and suggested they go on ahead and I would meet them in the bar at six o'clock.

They reluctantly agreed.

'Watch where you go, Ted,' snorted Scouse. 'We don't want *you* getting lost.'

After they left I crashed out on my bed for an hour. When I woke up I felt much better and ambled downstairs.

Old Dark Eyes, the commissioner, weighed me up and down as I entered the foyer.

'The other perverts 'ave gone out, I see,' he said stiffly.

'What's up with you?'

Smiling inwardly, I realised Big Mac was still leading him on. With a sigh, I rubbed my backside and said, 'Nothing much, but me bum's still sore from last night!'

Dark Eye's face reddened. He shook his head in disgust, turned his back and walked away.

In the Reading Room several servicemen sat around studying magazines or writing letters. After a quick squint at the *Daily Mirror* to see what Jane, the force's favourite strip cartoon, was up to, I made my way to the Games Room. As I opened the door I could hear the hollow click of billiard balls.

On one of the three tables two airmen were engrossed in a game of snooker. Nearby two soldiers with Polish flashes on each shoulder talked noisily while playing darts. Standing close by was a tall matelot with the physique of a middleweight boxer. His flaxen hair, parted on the left side gleamed with hair oil. In one hand he carried a billiard cue; as I entered the room he looked across at me.

'Fancy a game, Doc?' he said, indicating towards a spare table. The sharp edge in his voice indicated he was from Merseyside.

This was the first time I had been called, 'Doc'. Suddenly I felt rather self-conscious of the shiny new red cross. Like the two matelots I met on the train, he wore the insignia of a gunnery rating on the left arm of his uniform.

'Sorry, mate,' I replied, 'I can't play the game. I'm just havin' a look around.'

'Never mind,' he replied, placing his cue onto the empty table. As he spoke, his pale blue eyes wrinkled into a grin. 'The bar'll be open soon. D'you fancy a pint?'

The idea of a beer suddenly appealed to me.

'Aye, all right,' I replied.

'Me name's Harvey Rawlinson,' he said offering me a cigarette. 'I see you're a sick bay tiffy, eh?'

'Yes,' I replied, striking a match and lighting our cigarettes. 'I'm up here with a few oppo's from Haslar. My name's Ted Burnside.'

As we shook hands, Harvey's eyes lit up. 'Well I'll be

buggered,' he said. 'My judy's a VAD in Haslar. As a matter of fact I'm meeting her at Waterloo in just over an hour.'

The bar was open and the waiters were busy.

'Where are you from?' asked Harvey as we sat down. Before I had time to answer, he added, 'I'm from Chester. Susan, that's me judy, is from Ellsemere Port.'

I shook my head and laughed. 'I thought you were from somewhere near me,' I replied. 'I'm from Birkenhead.'

He grinned and ordered two pints of bitter. 'It's a small world, eh Ted?' he said. 'And this bloody war is making it smaller.'

We were both HO's. Harvey had been in the navy a year. His cap tally (the dark blue taffeta ribbon around a matelot's cap indicating which ship he is on.) had 'HM SHIPS', in gold lettering.

He told me Susan had been in Haslar for six months.

'We're hoping to get engaged soon,' said Harvey, sipping his pint. 'You might have seen her, she tells me she's on A 2 ward – something to do with dirty surgical.'

I explained I had only just qualified and hadn't had much experience of ward work.

'I've only spent a few days on the orthopaedic ward,' I said. 'I'll be assigned another when I get back.'

By the time we finished our beer and ordered another round, the bar was almost full. Loud conversation soon filled the smoke-ridden air. Just then someone switched on the wireless. Suddenly, the room fell silent. Men glanced at one another, glasses poised in hand, as the clear crisp voice of John Snagg read the one o'clock news.

'Last night, the RAF dropped nine hundred tons of bombs on the Rhur, the industrial heart of Germany', he said, pausing slightly before going on. *'And in Russia, the city of Kursk fell to the Red Army after a fierce tank battle'.*

This was met with loud cheering. 'Fuckin' great!' cried Harvey. 'Those Jerries are getting some of their own medicine at last.'

Everyone carried on drinking and the talk centred on the war and the continued arrival of American Forces in England.

'We've been doing lots of exercises with the Yanks,' said Harvey. 'There's something brewing. Mark my words.'

'What ship are you on, Harvey?' I asked.

Harvey looked at me and raised his eyebrows.

'Watch it, Ted lad,' he said, touching the tip of his nose with a forefinger. 'Careless talk an' all that.' He then bent forward, dropped his voice to a whisper and said, 'minesweepers.'

I told him about meeting Nobby and Pincher on the train.

'Ha! I know the two fellers you mean,' replied Harvey. 'They're on another "Mickey Mouse", the MMS (Motor Minesweeping Ship) 49. I'm on the MMS 50.'

'Mickey Mouse,' I replied with an air of curiosity. 'Why d'you call them that?'

Harvey grinned. 'MM... Mickey Mouse,' he replied, 'Savy?'

I laughed then added, 'I was told the minesweepers are called "The Suicide Squad". Why is that?'

The smile slowly faded from his weather-beaten, angular features and his blue eyes momentarily lost their sparkle. 'I hope you never find out, Ted,' he gravely replied.

His reply made me feel uncomfortable and for a few minutes we didn't speak.

Harvey sensed my unease and passed me a cigarette.

'Look Ted,' he said. 'Why don't you come with me and meet Susan. After all, you're both medics at Haslar and practically townies. We're staying with her cousin in Balham.' He paused and took a drag of his cigarette. 'We could have a drink together. What do you say?'

Why not, I thought. I wasn't due to meet Big Mac and the other two for some time and I had nothing better to do.

'Sound all right to me,' I replied, draining my glass.

'Great!' answered Harvey, 'but don't call her Sue, she hates it. We've just got time for another bevy before her train arrives.'

CHAPTER SIX

The concourse of Waterloo Station was crowded with service personnel; the sharp, throat-catching smell of steam, dust and tobacco smoke hung in the air like a miniature fog; groups of soldiers carrying kitbags and rifles, RAF personnel and matelots stood around lazily smoking, while others crowded in cafés drinking tea and reading newspapers. The hub of animated conversation blended with the loudspeaker announcing train information. At a glance it looked as if the whole of the armed forces had gathered in one place awaiting orders to move.

Harvey, carrying a grip, and I, waited near a ticket barrier. We watched as the train shunted into view hissing and bellowing steam. With a grind of brakes that set my teeth on edge, it slowly arrived at the platform. After a series of vaporous spurts, the train shuddered to a standstill.

The doors of various compartments opened allowing hordes of service men and women plus civilian commuters to pour onto the platform.

'There she is!' cried Harvey, waving frantically.

We moved towards the lines of people hustling through the ticket barrier.

I watched as a girl wearing a blue beret and naval greatcoat came into view. In front of her was a Wren struggling with a heavy suitcase. I smiled as a soldier offered her a helping hand.

Over one shoulder Harvey's girl carried a dust-coloured gas mask satchel and a blue handbag. One hand encased in a blue woollen glove steadied these. In the other, she held a small, brown Pusser's suitcase.

As she came closer I felt my stomach lurch and my heart rate increase. Suddenly, I was confronted by one of the most beautiful girls I had ever seen!

She stood a little over five feet; strands of hair hung loosely down either side of her blue beret, and except for a touch of mascara, there was very little make-up on her heart-shaped face. Natural dark eyelashes framed a pair of soft chocolate-coloured eyes, which, when she saw Harvey, lit up with a smile that would have melted an iceberg.

'Harvey! Harvey, love!' she cried arms outstretched.

I couldn't help but feel a tinge of envy as she dropped her case, and on tiptoe, threw her arms around Harvey. They then kissed, and for a moment seemed to be oblivious to everyone.

When they parted, Susan, her eyes moist with emotion, replied hoarsely, 'Oh Harv, I missed you so!'

'Me too, Susan,' replied Harvey.

It was then Harvey remembered I was standing next to them. He turned to me and said. 'This is Ted Burnside. H's a SBA in Haslar, and what's more he lives in Birkenhead, near you.'

'Nice to meet you, Ted, I'm Susan Hughes.' As she spoke the tip of her nose moved slightly up and down reminding me of Ingrid Bergman in *Casablanca.* 'So how long have you been in Haslar?'

As we shook hands I looked into her eyes. Suddenly, my mouth felt dry, and for a few seconds I couldn't speak.

'Er…not long,' I managed to reply.

I picked up Susan's case and noticed she wore a Portsmouth divisional insignia badge on the left shoulder of her greatcoat. As we left the station I told her I had just qualified as a SBA.

'He's still a bit green,' laughed Harvey, putting his arm around Susan's waist. 'But he'll soon learn.'

Harvey's remark made me feel a bit embarrassed.

'The way this war's going,' I replied, glancing at Harvey, 'I'll have plenty of time for that. I've already slapped in for a sea draft.'

'Well if you get one,' said Susan hugging Harvey, 'don't forget to come and see me on A1 ward. We can have a drink before you go.'

'Only a few wets, mind you,' laughed Harvey. 'I've heard about you Birkenhead Romeos.'

Susan tossed her head back and as she laughed her eyes sparkled. With her spare arm, she linked mine pulling me so close I could smell her perfume. My God, I thought, glancing at Harvey, you lucky bastard! Where on earth did you find such a girl?

The 'Wellington', on the corner of Sandell Street was a smoky, crowded pub. A quick glance around showed Waterloo had its own version of Piccadilly Commandos.

'Pity women aren't allowed in the UJ,' said Harvey as we sat down. 'The booze is a lot cheaper and the clientele's a bit better.'

One of the girls, a blowsy blonde, displayed a flash of white thigh as she slowly crossed her legs.

'Oh, I don't know,' I replied, thinking of Big Mac, 'there's a Scotsman I know who'd like it here.'

'You sailors are all the same,' said Susan smiling.

'All except me, love,' replied Harvey, placing his hand over hers. 'I'm a one man woman.'

For a few seconds I felt a pang of jealousy as Susan and Harvey stared into each other's eyes.

I gave a cough. 'Er… what'll you have,' I said, standing up.

'Oh, a pint of bitter,' replied Harvey without looking at me. 'And Susan'll have a port and lemon.'

When I arrived with the drinks they were both smoking. Susan's greatcoat hung over her chair along with her gas mask and handbag. Her uniform consisted of a white shirt and black tie, a navy blue skirt and single-breasted jacket with blue buttons; above a pocket on her left side was a Red Cross badge and the bulge of her jacket indicated a full, firm figure. Her well-shaped legs were encased in black stockings and on her small feet she wore matching flat-soled shoes. She removed her beret revealing a neat, chignon bun; after removing a few hairpins, a quick flick of her head allowed her chestnut-coloured hair to fall loosely around her shoulders. Like Harvey, I sat transfixed watching her every movement. She looked absolutely stunning and attracted more than a few admiring glances from a few soldiers sitting nearby.

'How long have you two known each other?' I said, trying

to make conversation.

'We met in the NAAFI in Pompey three months ago,' said Susan, 'didn't we, love?'

A thin line of smoke twirled lazily upwards from the cigarette she held between her long, tapered fingers. She had taken off her gloves and I noticed the red gloss of her nails matched her lipstick. 'You were on long weekend from Lowestoft. Oops! Sorry,' she said, hurriedly placing a hand over her mouth. 'Walls have ears…'

'Aye,' replied Harvey, taking a sip of beer, 'and if you remember, I stood on your toes!'

Susan gave a short laugh. 'That's right,' she replied, replacing her hand over his. 'I thought you were trying to do the hornpipe!'

Susan and Harvey finished their drinks.

'We'd best be off now Harv,' she said, standing up. 'It's a fair old bus ride to Balham.'

Harvey helped Susan on with her coat; she then picked up the rest of her gear.

'It was lovely meeting you, Ted,' said Susan. 'Now, remember what I said. If you do get that ship don't forget to come and see me before you go.'

'I'll do that,' I replied, handing her case to Harvey.

'Cheerio, Ted,' said Harvey, 'I hope we meet again.' His handshake was warm and firm; as he looked at me the expression in his eyes told me he meant what he said.

I watched as Harvey opened the door. Just before they left, Susan glanced around, flashed a smile and waved. After they had gone I looked at the lipstick marks on her glass and felt a strange emptiness inside.

'Fuck my tall hat!' exploded Scouse. 'She sounds like a cross between Betty Grable and Dorothy Lamour!'

The time was just after six. The other four and myself were in the bar; over a pint I told them about Susan and Harvey.

'And you say this feller called Harvey is off to sea?' asked Buster. 'You might be in there.'

'Not a chance,' I replied after taking a good gulp of beer.

'She's stuck on Harvey, and well, it wouldn't be....'

'Away wee yee, laddie,' interrupted Big Mac. 'Play yer cards right, and you'll be in like Flynn!'

'Whose Flynn?' asked Brum, glancing at us.

'Forget it Brum,' replied Buster, 'and get the beer in.'

That evening there was an air raid.

'The bastards are after the East End Docks again,' said one of the waiters. We were in the bar having a few pints prior to going into town. 'There can't be much left of them to bomb by now,' he added, placing four pints of beer on our table. As he walked away he muttered, 'The best place for you lads tonight is in 'ere.'

'I think 'e's right,' said Scouse. 'Besides, the booze is cheaper than in town.'

We took the waiter's advice and despite the distant sound of exploding bombs, succeeded in getting 'seven sheets to the wind' (naval term for getting drunk).

'You're back on orthopaedics, Burnside, my 'andsome,' said Chief Petty Officer Milton.

It was Monday morning. We were in the regulating office and all of us had hangovers. Brum was as pale as Stan Laurel; Big Mac and Buster looked like death warmed up and Scouse could hardly speak Only Tinker, who had been 'on the nest', as he called it, with his girl friend all weekend, appeared reasonably healthy.

Scouse and Tinker had been detailed off for duty on acute surgical. Big Mac and Buster were being sent to Zygomatics, (the infectious wards) while Brum, to his horror, was told to report to the operating theatre.

'But Chief!' moaned Brum, 'I don't know anything about OT work.'

'You don't have to know anything,' replied the chief, grinning like a Cheshire cat. 'All you'll have to do is scrub out and carry a few amputated arms and legs to the incinerator.'

That was obviously too much for Brum's delicate constitution. He bent forward, gripped his stomach and vomited a stream of brown liquid, splattering the chief's desk.

With a look of horror, the chief jumped up.

'You 'orrible little bastard!' cried the chief, staring down his front. 'You've ruined my uniform!'

Thick globules of carroty vomit dripped from his jacket. The handle of the telephone was a mess and the papers on his desk were saturated with yellowish fluid.

The chief looked across at Brum, his eyes blazing. 'I'll have yer guts fer garters…'

Before he had time to finish Pinkie Pinkerton, our esteemed Petty Officer from the training division, came in.

'Oh dear, Chief,' he said sniffing the air before turning a pale shade of grey. 'I'd have thought an old salt like you could have held his beer.' Then, with a toss of his head hurriedly closed the door.

'Fuck off, the lot of you!' bellowed the chief, using his hand to wipe away the vomit from his jacket. 'I'll have you horse-whipped, so I will!'

Brum, a line of spittle running from the side of his mouth, fell backwards.

'Jesus Christ!' exploded Big Mac, catching Brum as he fell. 'That smells bloody awful. What the hell were we drinking last night?'

Brum, his small frame supported by Big Mac, turned and in a weak voice, said, 'Sorry, Chief, I'll pay for any…'

Before the chief had time to reply, Big Mac and the rest of us ushered Brum out of the office.

'That wiped the smile of his face,' quipped Scouse when we were outside the building.

'Aye, that's as maybe,' I grinned. 'But I hope my request for a ship wasn't among those papers on his desk.'

As we entered the staff quarters Brum mumbled to himself, 'The chief wouldn't really have us horse-whipped, would he?'

Big Mac put a finger to his temple and shook his head. Once again, Brum's innocence provoked peels of laughter.

For the next month, although I was kept busy I couldn't get Susan out of my mind. I even made an excuse to visit her ward, but for some reason I always seemed to miss her.

My ward, B1, dealt with acute orthopaedic cases. It was

long, rectangular and heated by the ubiquitous box coal fire stoves. On either side ranged fifteen beds with metal lockers; shaded electric lighting hung from the high ceiling and curtained windows on either side were criss-crossed with tape; most of the beds were occupied, however, a few patients sat up in bed, their arms and shoulders encased in plaster of Paris. Many had protective cradles under bedding; some lay prostrate with small sandbags either side of their heads, while several, their legs resting on splints, had their limbs in traction.

One morning as I entered the ward a dank musky odour attacked my nostrils making me flinch. I looked around and saw Nurse Eldridge, a small, dark haired girl from Darlington, emerge from behind a bed surrounded by screens; she wore a white muslin mask and was carrying a tray covered with brown jaconet. With a sad expression she looked at me before hurrying down the ward towards the sluice, (ward bathroom).

Suddenly I heard the familiar voice of Slinger Wood, the killick of the ward, behind me. 'Gangrene!' he whispered out of earshot of the other patients. 'That's what the pong is, in case you wanted to know.'

Slinger was a stocky, fleshy-faced one badge leading hand. Like the others and myself, he wore a white operating gown. He nodded towards the screens.

'He came in last night,' said Slinger. 'The poor bugger is only a young lad. Shrapnel wound. He's havin' his leg amputated this morning. The smell's getting' through to everyone. The nurses have even started to use perfume on their masks to lessen it.'

Sister O'Malley, a small, slim woman from County Kildare, came from behind the screens. A pair of tired blue eyes peered at Slinger over her mask. The sleeves of her uniform were rolled up and were kept in place by ruffled bands. Using the back of her hand she wiped beads of perspiration from her brow and in the other hand was a stainless steel kidney dish and syringe.

'I've given him he's pre-medication, LSBA,' she said pulling her mask down. As she spoke she handed the kidney dish to Slinger. 'He'll go to A2 ward after the operation. Make sure his bed ticket is taken there.'

The mention of A2 immediately made me think of Susan.

'I'll take it there, Sister!' I said eagerly.

'Good,' she replied, 'I suggest you do so as soon as possible, then come back and help the others take the patient to the OT.'

'Well!' said Slinger. 'Don't stand there gawping. Do as the sister said.'

The name on the bed ticket read Able Seaman Jeffrey Donaldson. I glanced inside and saw he was nineteen, the same age as me.

A2 was in the opposite block to the orthopaedic section. Like B1, the ward appeared to be full, and staff were busy attending to various duties. I eagerly looked around but could not see Susan. A tall, harassed-looking sister with fair hair stood talking to an LSBA. She looked up and with a quick motion of her hand, beckoned me over.

'Is that bed ticket for me, SBA?' she asked crisply.

'Yes, sister,' I replied, handing her the document.

Without thanking me, she quickly took the bed ticket from me, glanced at it and gave it to the leading hand.

'Make sure everything's ready to receive this case,' she said. 'Tell the nurses to raise the end of the bed on blocks; ensure the electric blanket is switched on and there is a blood drip stand ready. And a special watch will be needed.' She then picked up a tray from a nearby table and walked down the ward to a patient's bedside.

'She seems in a bad mood,' I said to the LSBA.

'So would you be if you'd been on duty as long as she has,' he replied.

Just as I was about to turn and leave I saw Susan. For a second I didn't recognise her as she pushed a dressing trolley towards a patient's bedside. However, as she came closer I felt a surge of excitement. Dressed smartly in a pale grey uniform, a white cap and bib apron emblazoned with a red cross, she looked the personification of every man's idea of a nurse.

When she saw me her tired brown eyes creased into a smile.

'Ted,' she said, stopping the trolley. 'What a surprise!

Don't tell me you've got that ship you requested?'

'No,' I replied, feeling as if everyone in the ward was looking at me. 'Just delivering a bed ticket for someone being transferred to you. The poor bugger's havin' his leg amputated.'

With a pained expression, she replied, 'Not another one? That's the second in three days.'

'Any word from Harvey?' I asked.

'No,' she replied shaking her head. She dropped her voice and added, 'those little ships spend a lot of time away at sea, you know.'

The voice of the sister interrupted our conversation.

'Come along with that trolley, Nurse Hughes,' said the sister, frowning. 'The patient's stitches have to come out today. Not next week!'

'Coming sister,' replied Susan. As she pushed her trolley she looked at me, and said. 'I'm off at six. Meet me in the NAAFI around eight for a drink.'

Don't get too excited, I told myself on the way back to B1, she's probably missing Harvey and just wants someone to talk to. After all we do live near one another at home…

When I returned to B1, the screens around young Donaldson's bed had been removed. I saw a pale-faced lad with dark hair lying in bed wearing a cream-coloured operating gown. A bed cradle prevented his bedding from pressing on his lower limbs. Donaldson's eyes were half closed, but he kept blinking and trying to look down towards his feet. Then, like a man in a drunken stupor, he pushed himself up on his elbows.

'Can I just 'ave one last look sir,' he said in a whisper, 'before…' his voice then tailed off and he fell back into the pillow.

The sister removed the bed cradle.

'Lend a hand here, Ted,' said Slinger as two other SBA's, the sister and a doctor gently lifted Donaldson up. I placed both hands under the patient's warm body and together we lowered him onto a trolley. Donaldson's heavy eyes opened. He tried to force a smile but couldn't. Instead his head rolled to one side and he closed his eyes.

The sister, Slinger and two SBA's took Donaldson out of

the ward into a lift.

'Where's the operating theatre?' I asked.

'Down in the cellars,' replied Slinger. 'It was there during the heavy bombing last year. There are a few emergency wards as well. Empty now though.'

The cellar passageway was wide and painted white; a concrete pathway over cobbled stones allowed smooth progress to a set of swing doors. The atmosphere was warm, and the sharp smell of antiseptic played around my nostrils.

The first person I met as the doors opened was little Brum. Like the other OT staff, he wore a green gown and cap and white rubber boots. A green mask hung loosely around his neck like a cowboy's neckerchief.

'Didn't take you long to find this place, did it, Ted?' he quipped as he and two OT hands lifted Donaldson onto another trolley. Donaldson was then wheeled through another set of doors. Brum remained behind.

The sister left, followed by Slinger and the other two SBA's.

'Be with you in a minute,' I cried after them.

Brum looked up to me, his thin face paler than usual. 'Another leg for me to cart to the incinerator,' he moaned. 'I'm fuckin' fed up with this bloody place! And I mean *bloody.* If I stay here much longer, I'll go crazy!'

'Never mind, Brum,' I said, laughing. 'When the war's over, you and Buster could start up a butcher's shop.'

'Bollocks!' he cried, and stormed away through the swing doors of the OT.

However, Brum got his wish sooner than he expected.

A week later he burst into the mess, his normally pale face red with excitement.

'I'm going on draft! I'm going on draft!' he cried, his eyes almost popping out of his head. Big Mac, Tinker and me had a make-and-mend. Big Mac and Tinker were lying on their beds reading. I was sat writing a letter to Iris.

Big Mac and Tinker glanced up, a surprised look on their faces. 'For Chrissake, mon, calm down,' said Big Mac. 'Where the hell are you going?'

Brum came to the foot of Big Mac's bed. 'A cruiser, HMS *Belfast!*' he replied excitedly. 'I have to report on board in the morning. The ship's alongside in Pompey.'

I put down my fountain pen and shook my head. 'You lucky bugger,' I said. 'I wish I could get a ship. After what happened in the regulating office I think the Chief must have torn my request up.'

Tinker got out of bed. 'Tomorrow,' he said, throwing his book down. 'That's rather sudden, isn't it?'

'Yeah,' replied Brum, his face still flushed. 'The Chief said it was something called a "Pier Head Jump", whatever that is.'

A two badge SBA in the bed opposite glanced across at Brum. 'That's when you have to join a ship or base immediately without any warning. It happened to me in '40 when I was sent to the *Ark Royal.*'

That evening we helped Brum to pack his kit. Afterwards the five of us celebrated in the bar and got Brum drunk. The next morning we shook his hand, wondering when, or if, we would meet again.

A few days later I received a telephone call from the regulating office ordering me to report there immediately.

'What have you been up to now?' asked Slinger as I took off my ward gown. With a grin, he added, 'Maybe you're being sent to the OT in place of Brum.'

My heart pounded as I left the ward. What, I wondered could the chief possibly want?

Chief Milton sat behind his desk, flicking through some papers. I inwardly smiled noticing he wore a new uniform.

He looked up as I entered.

'Well, well,' he said, glaring at me. 'We've just got rid of that little bugger from Birmingham, now maybe it's your turn.'

'What d' you mean, Chief?' I asked. 'Am I going on draft?'

The chief narrowed his steely grey eyes. 'Not quite,' he replied. 'I've got a signal from Coastal Force HQ. They are asking for an SBA to look after a flotilla of minesweepers. Are you interested?'

Interested! I inwardly exclaimed. I most certainly was. This could be my big chance to get into the war. My heart began to pound. I suddenly remembered Harvey and the two men I met on the train. 'Am I ever!' I replied with mounting excitement. 'When do I leave?'

The chief looked at me again. 'Are you quite sure about this? It is a voluntary request, you know.'

'Yes, yes,' I replied eagerly.

'All right,' answered the chief sitting back in his chair. 'You leave for Lowestoft in a week.'

'Great!' I replied. 'Thanks a lot Chief.' Just as I reached the door to leave, I turned, 'By the way,' I asked, 'what happened to the SBA I am relieving?'

The chief raised his eyebrows and sighed. 'You won't be relieving anybody. SBA Bell was blown up when his ship hit a mine. There were no survivors!'

As I closed the door, I suddenly realised why men who served in the minesweepers were called 'The Suicide Squad'.

CHAPTER SEVEN

'Minesweepers!' cried Susan. 'Why, that's wonderful! You'll be with Harvey, won't you?'

Tinker, Big Mac and myself were in the NAAFI. Scouse and Buster had gone ashore. Several male and female members of staff sat around drinking tea or 'goffas', a naval term for soft drinks.

Susan was sitting at a table with another VAD. They both wore Burberrys over their uniform.

Susan introduced herself and her friend Jean, a pretty fair-haired girl, to everyone.

'Can I get all o'ye a cup o' something?' asked Big Mac leering at Jean.

'Tea, please,' replied Jean.

'Me too,' said Susan, smiling at me.

Big Mac stood up, winked at Jean and went to the counter.

'When are you leaving?' Susan asked me. 'Or is that classified information?'

'I suppose it is,' I replied, 'But it is very soon.'

Big Mac returned carrying four mugs of tea. He placed them on the table, took a sip of his then looked around in disgust. 'Do they no sell anything else but tea and "goffas", in this place?' he growled.

'I'm afraid not,' replied Jean. 'If you want a drink, you'll have to go to your bar. Pity we're not allowed in there.'

'Och aye,' replied Big Mac, giving Jean a cheeky grin. 'And I'd be the first one to ask yer in fer a wee dram, so I would.'

'Hark at Romeo, here,' said Tinker. 'Next thing you know he'll be asking you for a date.'

'That's no a bad idea at that,' replied Big Mac.

'In that case,' answered Jean, finishing her tea. 'I'll have another cuppa, please.'

'And so will I,' said Susan, pushing her cup across the table.

Straight away Big Mac got up and walked to the counter.

'I'll give him a hand with the tea,' said Jean, standing up.

'And I'm off to the heads,' added Tinker.

'Looks like your friend has found an admirer,' I said to Susan.

Susan turned and looked at me, her soft brown eyes twinkling with laughter. 'Now that those two have got fixed up, how about that date you promised me? Just as friends, of course.'

Bloody hell, I thought, avoiding her gaze, she remembered. For a second I didn't reply. My pulse rate increased and I felt my cheeks redden. I could hardly believe she was asking me for a date, albeit, on a friendly basis. After all, she and Harvey were practically engaged. Maybe it was my imagination, but as I looked up, the expression in her eyes seemed to convey a feeling more than friendship.

'OK,' I replied. 'I'm off duty at six tomorrow. I'll meet you at the main gate at seven.'

Just then Big Mac and Jean arrived carrying the tea. Tinker came back and sat down.

'Dinna you dare tell anyone I bought a round o' tea,' said Big Mac, 'it would be bad fer me reputation!'

'Don't worry,' replied Jean, laughing, 'your secret's safe with us.'

'She's a good looking party all right,' said Big Mac, 'but a date? I ask ye – didna you tell us she were spoken for?'

It was shortly after 1830 and we were in the mess.

'Yes,' I replied as I brushed my uniform, 'Harvey's a pal of mine and I'll be seeing him soon. What about you and Jean? Are you seeing her again?'

Big Mac screwed up his face. 'Och, no,' he replied, 'The lassie's courtin' one o' the doctors. I've no chance there.'

'Anyway,' I said, straightening my cap in the mirror, 'It's all innocent.'

'Innocent my eye,' said Scouse, throwing a shoe at me. 'Yer just a randy sod out t'get his leg over.'

'Lucky Bastard,' added Tinker. 'I wish it were me. Even though I am married.'

'Fuckin' perverts,' I said 'All you buggers think about is sex.'

But as I left the mess I had to admit, Scouse did have a point.

A warm May breeze ruffled the collar of my Burberry as I hurried towards the main gate. It was a mild evening with a full moon darting in and out of the heavy grey clouds. Although it was still quite light, curtains were drawn across every window in the hospital. A few pale lights glimmered from inside the colonnade: a prelude to the blackout shortly to begin.

At first I didn't see her. If she stood me up I had made up my mind to go ashore on my own rather that face Big Mac and the others.

I needn't have worried; as I walked past the policemen and guard I saw her waiting a little way down the road. She was in uniform and like myself carried a gas mask and steel helmet.

When she saw me, she gave a little wave and a smile.

'Sorry if I'm late,' I said.

'You're not,' she replied, 'I've only just arrived.'

With her free hand she linked her arm in mine. This took me by surprise. I could smell her perfume and the sudden closeness of her made me feel nervous.

By the time we walked over Pneumonia Bridge into Gosport, it was dark. The moonlight cast pale shadows over MTB Boats moored alongside a jetty in Haslar Creek. Across Portsmouth harbour the silhouette of ships' masts and housetops dominated the skyline. Suddenly, white beams of searchlights punctuated the darkness; while silently criss-crossing one another they occasionally produced a flickering, sliver sheen on several barrage balloons.

'Do you think they'll be a raid, Ted?' said Susan as we walked through a narrow passageway into Gosport High Street.

'Don't know,' I replied, looking up at the sky. 'We haven't

had one for some time now. Maybe Jerry's too busy stopping our bombers. I hear they bombed Berlin again last night.'

Except for an ARP (Air Raid Precaution) Warden and a few ghost-like pedestrians, the high street was deserted. A solitary motorcar slowly chugged passed as we entered a pub appropriately called 'The Ship'.

The atmosphere inside the pub was warm and thick with tobacco smoke. Two ratings were playing darts while a couple of the locals sat quietly sipping pints of beer. In a corner a matelot and a young girl snuggled up to one another oblivious to everyone. As we entered, the ratings paused and stared approvingly at Susan; she smiled at them and sat down while I went to the bar.

'And what can I get thee?' asked a round-faced barman with a beer belly any stoker would have been proud of.

I ordered a pint of bitter. Susan had asked for a gin and tonic.

'Those two over there look happy enough,' whispered Susan glancing at the matelot and his girl.

'Aye,' I replied, passing her a cigarette and lighting it. 'I suppose they'd best make hay while they can.'

We were sitting next to one another and I could feel the warmth of her thigh against mine.

'Yes,' replied Susan. 'I know what you mean.' She took a sip of her drink, paused and went on. 'I got a letter from Harvey today. He's asked me to marry him. He says we could be married in the registry office in Portsmouth.' As she spoke her eyes lit up. 'Isn't that wonderful, Ted?'

I suddenly felt my stomach contract. A pang of jealously ran through me like an electric shock. Although I had known she was almost engaged, I didn't think they would be married so soon. I told myself I was being foolish and tried to hide my feelings behind a forced smile.

'That's great!' I replied. 'What are you going to do?'

'Accept of course,' said Susan giving me a playful tap on the arm. 'But it's all a secret at present.'

I gave a half-heated laugh. 'My lips are sealed,' I said. 'Now, drink up and we'll have another.'

'Did you 'ear about that raid on them dams in Germany?' asked the barman as I ordered the drinks. 'It were on the news afore you come in.'

'No,' I replied. 'What raid was this. There's been so many lately.'

'On the Rhur, where all the Jerry industry is.' replied the barman passing me the drinks. 'They're calling it the Dam Busters raid. That'll be two and sixpence please.'

When I returned with the drinks, Susan was powdering her nose.

'By the way,' she said, putting her compact in her bag. 'I wrote to Harvey before I came out and told him we were going for a drink, *and* about your draft.'

'Won't that be censored?'

'It's all right,' replied Susan. 'I didn't put any details in the letter. Hope you don't mind?'

'Why should I mind,' I replied, sitting down. 'We're all good friends, aren't we?'

'Yes' she giggled, snuggling up to me. 'Very good friends.'

A crowd of matelots probably from HMS *Hornet* came in; one of then had a mouth organ. Susan and I joined in singing *Bless 'em All,* and other popular songs. However, it was when the matelot played *All The Nice Girls Love a Sailor,* Susan stood up and conducted the chorus while singing her head off. Even the sailor and his young girl joined in!

Shortly after ten o'clock as I shook hands with everyone. Susan gave each sailor a kiss on the cheek.

'You dirty lucky bugger!' one shouted as we left. 'Be bloody careful.'

'Aye,' said another, 'and if y'can't be careful, see the midwife.'

With our arms around one another we staggered along the road towards the hospital. When we reached the top of the bridge, Susan stopped and put her arms around my neck.

'Y'know, Ted,' she slurred, 'you're a lovely man. If it weren't for Harvey, I could fall for you.'

I laughed. Of course, I told myself, it was the drink talking. With a glazed expression in her eyes, she threw her arms around me and kissed me full on the lips; as her tongue found mine I couldn't help but respond. For a few seconds I let my hands slide down the sides of her Burberry onto her buttocks. Suddenly, I felt pangs of guilt. I raised my hands and gently pushed her away.

'No!' I gasped. 'This isn't right. I'll be on same ship as Harv, and...'

'Poor Teddy!' said Susan. Her cap was lopsided and she held me tightly around the waist. 'It's only a *friendly* kiss. No harm in that, is there?'

She looked so vulnerable standing against the bridge railings. Her eyes, sparkling like diamonds in the moonlight, looked up at me. For an instant I was tempted to take her in my arms, but yet again my conscience intervened.

'Come on, love,' I said, taking her hand. 'Let's get you back to the hospital before we both do something we'll regret.'

When we arrived outside her quarters, she unsteadily reached up and kissed me lightly on the lips. As she sank back on the ground I managed to catch her before she fell against the wall.

'Please take care of yourself,' she said with tears in her eyes. 'And look after Harvey for me, I'll be thinking of both of you.'

The night before I was due to leave I had a few drinks in the mess bar with Big Mac and the others. The bar was crowded with all ranks. On the wireless, *Itma* with Tommy Handley's voice cracking jokes, was barely audible over the noise of laughter and conversation.

'All the best, Ted,' said Scouse. 'Just think, this time next week you'll be bobbing up and down in the briny like a cork.'

'And spewing his bloody ring up,' added Tinker with a grin.

'Aye,' burbled Big Mac after downing his third pint, 'but what aboot that wee lassie you were oot with a few nights ago. Did you er...?'

I interrupted him. '*No* I didn't.' I quickly replied. 'I told you. She's engaged to a mate I know on the 'sweepers.'

'Och, so what,' quipped Buster. 'When the cat's away, an'

all that…'

Just then the door opened, and to our surprise in walked little Brum.

When he saw us his eyes lit up and he started to sway from side to side.

'Hello, you landlubbers,' he said. 'I thought I'd find you here.'

'Hey!' I replied, slapping him on the back, 'Watch who you're calling names. Just ask me who's being drafted to a minesweeper?'

'And the best of luck, Ted,' he replied as someone thrust a pint in his hand, 'Not enough guns for my liking. Not like the lovely *Belfast.'*

'When are you sailing?' asked Buster.

'Quiet,' interrupted Brum. 'Walls 'ave ears.' He stopped came closer and lowered his voice. 'Next week,' he whispered. At that moment his face lit up into a mischievous grin. 'Talking about guns, guess who's the chief GI on board us?' Without waiting for an answer, he said, 'Old Stormy Weather, the bastard from Vicky Barracks, who gave me extra rifle drill that time.'

'Did he recognise you, Brum?' asked Tinker.

'Recognise me!' exclaimed Brum with a satisfied smile. 'The bugger's caught the boat up, and twice a day I slowly syringe out his dick with pot permanganate. It's lovely to hear him yell in agony. You bet he recognised me!'

'Talking about catching the boat up,' said Scouse, giving Big Mac a suspicious look. 'What about that little wager we had with you, big man?'

'Yes,' said, Buster, 'as I remember, it was a ten bob bet, wasn't it?'

'Bollocks,' replied Big Mac, finishing his pint. 'D'you think I'd tell any of youse if I'd caught a dose. Now get the beer in and shut up.'

CHAPTER EIGHT

According to a pre-war booklet I found in the hospital library, Lowestoft was a fishing town in Suffolk, East Anglia. The name is said to have come from *toft,* a Viking word for 'homestead' and *Loth* or *Lowe,* a Viking male name; over a period of three centuries the original title was contracted to 'Lowestoft'.

So much for the history lesson!

My journey from Liverpool Street, London, to Lowestoft took over six hours. I arrived shortly after four in the afternoon and reported to the RTO office.

'So you're the new 'sweeper doc, eh?' said the Duty PO, a stout, round faced man with dark blue eyes and a cheerful grin. 'I hopes you're a good sailor,' he added, examining my draft order, ''cos them there minesweepers toss about like corks in a bottle, so they do. Tilly's outside. It'll take you to HMS *Europa.*' He then stamped my papers and handed them back to me. (A 'tilly' is an abbreviated word for utillicon, a blue naval van.)

A tall, gangly matelot wearing an RTO armband picked up my green Pusser's suitcase.

'Follow me. Doc,' he said in a heavy North Country accent. 'Me names Digger Barnes. I'm ship's company at the base.'(This meant he was on the base staff and not on board a ship.)

Outside the leaden sky threatened rain, and a cold, biting wind hit me in the face; in the distance the faint squawking of seagulls reminded me of happier times strolling along New Brighton promenade. Opening the rear door of the tilly, I couldn't help but wonder if I'd ever see the River Mersey again.

'What's this HMS *Europa?* Digger?' I asked, throwing my kitbag in the back of the van. 'I thought I was being sent to a ship.'

'That's the name of the patrol service shore base,' he

replied, starting the engine. 'You're lucky. You'll be billeted in the sick bay. The rest of us have to take pot luck and use the boarding houses in town. The stokers, cooks and stewards live in St Luke's Hospital. That's in town as well.'

I gave him a curious glance and asked, 'D'you mean to say there's no barracks at the base?'

'Only for the Captain and a few officers,' replied Digger. 'The ship's company have to report every morning for divisions. You'll see them pouring in from town. Some of 'em still pissed from the night before.'

'But where are the ships?' I asked feeling rather disappointed.

'Bloody hell!' replied Digger. 'You're a keen one, I must say. The harbour's not far away and afore you're finished I expect you'll 'ave 'ad yer fill of the ships, believe you me.'

'Is it always as cold as this?' I asked, turning up the collar of my Burberry.

Digger gave a sly chuckle. 'Ha!' he replied. 'It's only May, me old cocker. You wait till winter, then it really does blow a bastard.'

As drove down the main street I noticed several bombed buildings.

'Jesus!' I exclaimed. 'This place has taken a pasting, hasn't it?'

Digger shot me a quick glance. 'Lowestoft is the eastern most part of Britain facing France,' he said. 'I'm told the fuckin' Jerries use it as a navigation point. Consequently it's the most heavily bombed town in England. Last January there were sixty-nine men and women killed in one raid alone. They had to use the Odeon Picture House for a temporary mortuary.'

Blimey! I thought as we drove through the centre of town. No wonder my draft was for volunteers, nobody in their right mind would want to be stationed here. That was when I remembered something dad once said about never volunteering for anything…

A high wall topped with barbed wire surrounded the base. A matelot in white belt and gaiters stood at the main gate. After a cursory glance at my papers he waved us through.

'The new doc fer the 'sweepers, eh?' he said in a rich West Country accent. 'Good luck to yer my 'andsome. Welcome to the "Sparrows Nest".'

'Why do they call it the 'Sparrows Nest?' I asked Digger.

'Well, now,' he answered. 'The area was once the summer home of a Mister Robert Sparrow. He was a posh gent who lived in Worlingham Hall in Beccles, a village a few miles from here. The land was bought by Lowestoft Corporation, and in 1939 it were commandeered by the Royal Navy.'

At first glance the base resembled a large country park; wide gravel pathways led around well-trimmed lawns, and pink bougainvillea bushes blossomed in between oak and elm trees.

The sole indication that this was a naval establishment came when I saw a squat, rectangular building painted dull grey. Above an arched entrance a gold painted sign read HMS *Europa,* Commanding Officer, Headquarters, Royal Naval Patrol Service. Directly over the entrance was a balcony with windows criss-crossed with white tape; from the top of a flagstaff a white ensign flapped in the stiff breeze. Two officers wearing gold wavy-navy rings of the RNVR, (Royal Naval Volunteer Reserve) entered the building; they were engrossed in conversation and casually returned the salutes of ratings passing them. I noticed some ratings wore full blues others were clad in white, high-necked sweaters.

Opposite the headquarters was an oval-shaped parade ground; close by was a large imposing Victorian building. Half a dozen entrances with latticework doors and windows gave the impression of a stately country house.

'Who lives over there?' I asked, 'it looks like a posh hotel.'

Digger gave a hearty laugh. 'That's the concert hall,' he replied. 'It's used for admin offices and as an emergency billeting station. In the old days big acts like Elsie and Doris Waters, (Gert and Daisy, well known sister act during the war) played there. It's still used for dances.'

'Is there any Wrens here?' I asked with a grin.

'You bet,' replied Digger. 'Not here though,' he added with a sly grin. 'They're billeted away from the lecherous eyes of fellers like meself, in the Royal Hotel in town.'

As we drove further into the base I noticed the land swept upwards towards the crest of the town. Jutting into the air I saw a lighthouse, church spires, and roofs of houses. Numerous silver barrage balloons caught the rays of the sun peeking through the grey sky; moving further along we passed a few large Nissan huts.

'Them's the NAAFI and dining hall,' said Digger. 'The pay office and regulating offices are in the concert hall.' He then pointed to a red-bricked building directly ahead of us. 'That's the sick bay. It's next to the cells. Nice an' 'andy for the drunks to be examined by the duty doc.'

We stopped outside the sick bay. 'This is where I leave you,' said Digger, 'I'll no doubt see you around as I also drive the ambulance.'

Inside the sick bay I was immediately assailed by the familiar smell of antiseptic. Sitting at a desk was a stocky, pale-faced petty officer. He had black hair greying at the temples, three good conduct badges and a five o'clock shadow. He stood up as I entered.

'You must be Burnside,' he said, shaking my hand. 'I'm petty officer Dean. Dixie to you, me old cock sparrow.' His face broke into a wide grin. 'No pun intended. Good journey?'

'Yes,' I replied. 'I'm glad to be out of the bone-yard, PO,' I said, letting go of his hand, 'and in to the real navy.'

'You'll notice a helluva difference between the hospital discipline and the 'sweepers.'

'How d'you mean?' I asked with an air of curiosity.

'The crews are recruited from the trawlers,' replied the PO. 'Most are hardened fishermen and they don't take kindly to being ordered around. But they certainly know their job.'

'I see,' was my non-committal reply.

I wasn't sure what he meant, but I had a feeling I would soon find out.

Dixie introduced me to Smudge Smith, a small, overweight LSBA and another SBA, a lean looking lad with gaunt features appropriately nick-named Bogey Knight.

'We also have a nurse called Wanda Evans and Surgeon Lieutenant Jenkins,' said Dixie, 'but they are both helping out at

St Margret's, that's the hospital in town.'

'So the MO says,' grinned Bogey, displaying a row of yellow, uneven teeth. 'He's probably givin' young Busty one in some hotel.'

'I wouldn't mind shaftin' 'er,' replied Smudge offering me a cigarette. 'Come to think of it,' he added with an air of desperation, 'I wouldn't mind shaftin' anything.'

'What those two need is more bromide in their tea,' said Dixie showing me into a small mess. 'That's your bunk over there,' he said. 'It belonged to Harry Bell, your predecessor, the poor sod. By the way, Harry had a small caboose on the quay where the 'sweepers are berthed. He used it as a centre where men could report sick and be treated. It saved time and made less work for us.' He unhooked a rusty key from a board. 'You'll need this,' he added, handing it to me. 'It's a duplicate. The original was lost with Harry. He always kept it locked when he went to sea.'

Next to Harry's bunk was a chest of drawers. Inside one of the drawers I found a letter and a photograph. I picked it up and saw the eyes of a young girl staring at me; she wore a dark costume and a smile played around her mouth. Suddenly, I felt and affinity between her and myself; both of us had lost loved ones and although we would never meet I knew how she was feeling.

'Someone must have missed these,' I said handing the photograph and letter to Dixie.

I looked at the chest of drawers and made a mental note to take all my personal effects with me when I went to sea.

After stowing my gear, Smudge and Bogey took me to the dining hall for supper. My arrival was greeted by several ribald comments from a few men, who, I presumed were off the minesweepers. They sat at long wooden tables, laughing and talking; many were unshaven and a few sported beards of varying shades. Dressed like the others I had seen earlier in white sweaters, they looked a tough lot.

'I 'opes you can stitch better than the coxswain,' said a thickset sailor with arms like tree-trunks. 'When I cuts meself, he broke the needle twice.' He paused and held up his left hand and flexed his little finger. 'Look, I'm scared fer life!'

'Ah shut yer whining, Perky,' said a sailor sitting next to him. 'You can still 'old a pint, so stop worrying.'

'What did that sailor mean when he said the coxswain stitched him up?' I asked Smudge as we joined a queue for food.

Smudge grinned. 'If you're not around, the coxswain does the medical work.' He then looked across at a corpulent chef in a white apron who was serving food, and added, 'I'll have two baby's heads, (a small meat pie upon which the cook had imprinted a 'face') spuds and "train smash".'(Tinned tomatoes and fried egg)

It didn't sound very appetising, but not wanting to seem squeamish I had the same.

'When are we gunna get some fillet steak?' asked Bogey.

The chef glared at him. 'When Nelson gets his eye back,' he replied, flopping a large slice of Manchester Tart (jam topped up with blancmange) on Bogey's side plate. 'Now fuck off.'

Suddenly, I heard a loud voice from the back of the dining hall.

'Ted you bugger. When did you get here?'

I turned around and saw the unmistakable flaxen-haired figure of Harvey Rawlinson, the matelot I had met at the UJC. He came towards me waving his hands in the air and grinning like a Cheshire cat.

'Susan told me you'd been drafted to a minesweeper,' he said, as we shook hands, 'But she didn't say you'd be coming here.'

'How is she?' I asked trying to sound enthusiastic.

'Fine,' replied Harvey, his eyes lighting up. 'We're getting married in two weeks. Susan is arranging everything with the registry office in Pompey. Her mum's coming down. If you can get away you'll be more than welcome.'

Even though I always knew this would happen, news of their wedding came as a shock. Just as I was about to speak, an explosion rocked the room! I felt the ground shudder; plates, mugs along with an assortment of food went flying all over the place. Harvey grabbed me and dragged me under the nearest table. Another explosion some distance away, made me instinctively duck; the sound of ack-ack guns almost drowned out the moan of an air raid siren as ratings dived for cover.

'Don't panic!' shouted Harvey, huddling close me. 'It's another of Jerry's lightning raids. Their airfields in France aren't far away. You'll get used to it.'

The 'raid' was over in a matter of seconds. Bogey and Smudge along with some others slowly emerged from under the table. Much to my surprise, I saw the thick-set sailor with the injured finger eating his meal. He wore a steel helmet and was munching away as if nothing had happened.

'Fuckin' Krauts!' he mumbled, a stream of tomato juice running down the side of his mouth. 'Bloody pests, they are, bloody pests!'

Bogey looked at me and tapped the side of his head with his finger.

'Pay no attention to Perky Perratt,' said Harvey. 'He's the 50's cook, and a bit touched in the head like the rest of us. We're supposed to eat on board our ship, but we thought we'd scrounge a meal in the base.'

Harvey remained with us while we finished our meal.

'Great news about you and Susan,' I said, trying to sound convincing. 'I wouldn't miss it for anything.'

But even as I spoke my heat sank as a deep-seated feeling of jealousy erupted inside me.

'That's settled then,' replied Harvey, finishing his mug of tea. 'Come on down and I'll show you the 'sweepers. The harbour's only a ten minute walk away.'

His words immediately made me forget about Susan. My mood instantly changed from envy to excited anticipation; at long last I was about to see those minesweepers I had heard so much about.

'See you later, Ted,' said Bogey, 'Me and Smudge are off to the NAAFI for a pint.'

Harvey and I walked through the main gate along a narrow, cobbled-stoned roadway. Rows of fishermen's cottages, ships' chandlers and old warehouses lined the road on our right. Small houses swept inland and swirling threads of smoke poured from chimneys only to vanish into the grey sky.

Pointing to open fields on the left side, Harvey said, 'That's where the fishermen repair their nets. But there's not a lot of fishing done these days.'

At the end of the road, past a lifeboat station, the panoramic view of the North Sea, unfolded before me. Masses of white horses abounded, and in the distance the blurred line of the horizon separated the grey-green waters from the dark, cumulous-nimbus clouds. A biting cold wind whipped across my face leaving a sharp taste of salt on my lips; I turned up my collar and dug both hands into my pockets.

'Gets a bit nippy here,' said Harvey, holding on to his cap.

'I know,' I replied, hunching my shoulders. 'Digger, the tilly driver warned me.'

At the end of the road near a swing bridge that led into the town, the harbour came into view.

For a moment I stopped and surveyed the scene, then continued walking. Strong winds sent waves rippling along the surface of the green waters of the harbour. The sporadic squawking of seagulls filled the air. They hovered in the air like flocks of vultures, occasionally diving onto the decks of the ships, seeking food.

The harbour, surrounded on three sides by a covered quayside, was much bigger than I expected. Unlike a conventional dockyard, there was a conspicuous absence of cranes, creaking gantries and the clatter of dockside machinery. Tied up to the quayside were four ships no bigger than the Merseyside ferryboats. Each was painted a dull grey with their pennant numbers clearly marked on the side. At first glace they resembled up-market fishing vessels. Only a white ensign flying from the jack aft identified them as warships. Several sailors, wearing those ubiquitous sweaters, with their trousers tucked in sea boots, were busy hosing down decks.

'Are they the minesweepers, Harv?'

'That's them,' he replied. 'Welcome to "Harry Tate's Navy".' Then in a solemn voice added, 'there used to be five of 'em but…' his voice trailed away.

'Yes I know,' I quickly replied. Then after a slight pause, added, 'But who's this Harry Tate?'

'It's a nickname we give the Patrol Service,' replied Harvey grinning his head off. 'Harry Tate was a 1930's comedian. He was a Scot and his real name was Ronnie Hutchinson. In his act he used an old box Ford car that gradually fell to pieces on the stage. Some matelot from the "Sparrows Nest" yelled out, "just like our bloody ships!" and somehow the name stuck.'

At first glance they didn't look anything like warships. Each ship was approximately 300 feet long and about 30 feet wide. A sweeping deck ended sharply at the bow with a rounded stern; on either side ran, what I later learned, was a stretch of protective rubber called a rubbing strake. On every vessel a lifeboat, secured to a derrick rested inboard; as it swayed slightly in the wind I hoped it was big enough to take all the crew. The open bridge and superstructure of some were bigger than others; one or two were even designed differently. Some bridges were set further back on the superstructure; others appeared to be covered with canvas while a few had none at all. Each ship was armed with what I later discovered was a 20 mm Oerlikon on the fo'c'sle for'd of the mainmast, and a Hotchkiss gun aft.

For a moment I stood and listened to the squelching sound of each vessel rolling against their fenders protecting them from the harbour wall. I felt a wave of excitement run through me; suddenly I couldn't wait to get aboard them.

'What are those small ships tied up on the opposite quay?' I asked Harvey.

'Them's the fishing trawlers,' he replied. 'They only go out at night.'

'The river from the harbour seems to go right through the town,' I remarked.

'That's the River Waveney,' replied Harvey, 'It divides Lowestoft in two. The swing bridge allows passage to each section of the town.'

The cobbled quayside had concrete columns supporting a roof. At the end of the harbour a small section of the quayside lay in ruins, further evidence of Jerry's lightning raids.

'They're much smaller than I imagined,' I remarked.

'Don't worry, they're big enough,' replied Harvey with a touch of pride. 'Although they can be a bit cramped sometimes.'

'What are those bloody great drums on every quarterdeck?'

We stopped alongside one of the minesweepers.

'Oh them!' replied Harvey with a throaty laugh. 'They're used for magnetic sweeps. Wound around each drum are electric cables. The handles you see on each side of the drum have to be turned manually. This enables the cables to be paid out ready to sweep for magnetic mines. I'll tell you all about them later.'

'Magnetic mines!' I exclaimed staring across at him. 'What about the other mines? The ones with the spikes on?'

'When they are swept, they come to the surface. Then we use a 303 rifle and takes a pot shot at them and blow them sky high.'

'What happens if you miss?'

Harvey raised his eyebrows and shot me a cautious glance. 'I hope you never find out.' He paused, passed me a cigarette, took one himself and lit them. 'Remember this, Ted,' he said. 'A mine has no discrimination. The bugger just lies there. It kills and maims and cares nothin' for men, women and children, or even those who laid it.'

His words set me thinking.

'You mean if we lay mines, they can sink our own ships?'

'Aye,' replied Harvey, flicking his cigarette away. 'If a mine comes loose and floats close by, it can happen.'

We carried on walking along the quayside.

'Which ship is yours, Harv?'

'The MMS 50, the one at the end,' he replied, 'Best Mickey Mouse in the flotilla. Come on board and I'll introduce you to the lads.'

At the top of a narrow brow (gangway) a sailor sat on a chair reading a dog-eared copy of *Tit-Bits*. He wore a black oilskin and his trousers were tucked into a pair of sea boots. His cap was perched precariously on the back of his head under a mop of dark, curly hair. Near to where he was sitting was a Carley float secured to the bulkhead; behind him, a ladder led onto the top of the bridge and further aft the muzzle of a gun poked menacingly from under a canvas cover. As we walked on board a sudden breeze caught the numerous wires leading from the mainmast to various parts of the ship, making them rattle like the bones of a skeleton.

The sailor lowered his paper and glanced up. His weather-beaten face immediately broke into a toothy grin. 'Hello! Hello!' he said in a deep Yorkshire accent. 'Who 'ave we 'ear, then?'

'Wotcha, Jacko,' replied Harvey. 'This is Ted Burnside, the flotilla's new doc.'

The sailor stood up. ''Ow do, Doc,' he said, extending his hand. I winced as his vice-lie grip crushed my hand. 'I 'opes you've brought some Frenchies. I'm on a promise with a Wren tomorrow.'

'Chance would be a fine thing, Jacko,' commented Harvey. 'Who's on board?'

Jacko folded his paper and took out a packet of cigarettes. After giving one to Harvey and me, he lit up and sat down.

'The Skipper and the Jimmy are at a meeting with the Commodore,' replied Jacko. 'Jack Wrey's ashore,' he paused and took a drag of his cigarette, looked at me and added, 'he's the coxswain. Subby Eardley's Officer of the Watch and Jock Duthie is duty engineer.'

I followed Harvey aft down a hatchway into what surely must have been the most cramped living space in the navy.

As we entered the mess, a warm, claustrophobic smell of stale sweat, rum and tobacco mingled with diesel oil, made me wince. A grey blanket, draped over a rope, divided the room in two. From the oaken beams of a low-slung deck head hung a few shirts and underwear.

'What's the blanket for, Harv?' I asked.

Harvey gave a slight chuckle. 'That's where the chief engineer and coxswain sleep,' he said. 'They fart different to us rabble!'

Around a small wooden table sat four men. Half-smoked cigarettes dangled from their mouths as they played cards. One had a black beard speckled with grey; another, sitting opposite him, was man with thick ginger hair curling around the base of his neck; next to him was a sailor with a swarthy complexion. The fourth man was small, with a mop of fair hair. All four were stripped to the waist with overalls knotted around their waists. With the exception of Ginger, all had tattoos, ranging from dancing girls to images of birds, on arms and chests. Nearby, four chipped enamel mugs and an ashtray full of dog ends rested on the table.

Behind the card players, a fifth man with flaming red hair and a face like well-worn leather, sat on a bunk. His shirt hung out of his trousers and he was reading a book.

With hairy chests, unshaven faces plus the occasional beard, they looked more like a band of pirates than members of His Majesty's Navy!

As Harvey and I entered everyone glanced up.

'Be jeezus, Harvey,' said a matelot with flaming red hair, 'who's the poultice walloper?' Then with a sickly sneer, added, 'Another of yer oppos from the Nest scrounging rum?'

'No, Paddy, you miserable bugger,' was Harvey's laconic reply, 'He's our new doc.'

'Is he by God,' replied Paddy with a sarcastic grin. 'I hope he's luckier than the last one, so I do.'

A matelot with the black beard threw down his cards and glared across at Paddy.

'Why dinna you shit in it, you fuckin' bog-trotter,' he said in a strong Scottish accent. 'A lot o' good lads went down with the 43.'

Paddy stood up. He was over six feet tall and heavily built.

'Who the fuck are you calling a bogtrotter, you Scottish sheepshagger?' grunted Paddy.

'You, yer Irish get,' replied black beard, his dark eyes blazing.

I glanced at Harvey who quickly shook his head, as if to say, keep quiet.

'For fuck's sake, Jock!' yelled Ginger Hair, in a deep West Country accent. 'If you two want to start a fight again, bugger off ashore and give us some peace.'

Jock sprang to his feet. He was smaller than Paddy but built like a rugby scrum half. The veins in his muscular arms bulged as he clenched his fists. In one quick movement he moved towards Paddy and hit him on the side of the face. Paddy gave an ear-splitting cry and fell back against the blanket dragging it half off the rope.

'You Scots get!' yelled Paddy clutching his face. He

staggered to his feet and made a lunge at Jock. 'Wait till I get my hands on…'

At that moment an officer wearing a light brown duffel coat came into the mess. He was over six feet tall, young looking with a shock of fair hair protruding under his cap. Behind him standing next to Jacko was a small, grey-haired figure dressed in white overalls streaked with black diesel oil.

'Fuck me,' growled the grey-haired man, who, I later learned was the chief engineer. 'Don't tell me you two are at it again?'

'Just 'avin a friendly argument, Chief,' replied Paddy.

The chief raised both eyebrows and muttered, 'Well fix the soddin' blanket afore you turn in. Y'ken how the 'swain likes 'is privacy.' He then gave a contemptuous shrug of both shoulders and left the mess.

For a few seconds the officer stared at Jock and Paddy. 'What's the matter with you two?' he said, shaking his head. 'The Master-at-Arms had enough last week when you were both thrown out of the concert hall dance. Now what's the problem?'

The sailors who were sat down simply glanced at each other grinned, and carried on playing cards.

'To be sure,' said Paddy rubbing the side of his face. I noticed he didn't address the officer with a customary 'sir'. Instead he went on, 'We was only larking about, so we were.'

The officer pursed his lips then replied, 'A likely story. If there's anymore *larking* about you'll both end up in the rattle. Understood?' He then turned and looked at me. 'Who are you?' he asked.

Before I had time to answer, Harvey intervened. 'He's our new doc, just joined today.'

The officer's face wrinkled into a wide grin. 'I see,' he said, glancing across at Paddy. 'It looks like you've got your first customer!'

With a final glance around the mess, he then turned, climbed up the ladder and left the mess.

'That was Subby Eardley,' Jacko said, looking at me. 'The old man's due back anytime now. So I'd best get back on the brow.'

'Cheers Jacko,' I replied, 'I've got to check the medical post on the quayside.' I looked at Paddy and Jock then added, 'You never know when it might be needed.'

Paddy shot a withering glance at Jock and returned to his bunk. Jock, in turn, returned Paddy's stare and slowly sat down at the table.

Before I left Harvey introduced me to the man with ginger hair.

'Good to meet you, Doc, my bird,' said Ginger. His hand, when he grasped mine, felt as tough as teak. 'Harry Cornwall's the name, but Ginger'll do.'

Ginger was a leading seaman. I later learned he, like the others, was an ex-trawler man. He then glanced over at the swarthy man with untidy, greasy-brown hair and dark brooding eyes. 'This miserable looking-bugger is Joe Willoughby.'

''Owdo,' said Joe staring at his cards. He then glanced up at Harvey and muttered, 'You'd be miserable too if yer missus had pissed off with a Yank.'

'Cheer up,' replied Harvey, his handsome features breaking into a wide grin. 'Just think of all the money you can save when you stop her allotment.'

An allotment was a weekly amount of pay sent home to a wife or parent. Men could also make payments to naval tailors in order to buy a new uniform or 'rabbits', a naval term for presents for family and friends.

'What's the problem between Paddy and Jock?' I asked Harvey after we had left the mess. We were standing near the brow; Jacko was lounging against the bulkhead smoking.

'No bugger's quite sure,' replied Harvey, scratching his head. 'It all started a few months ago, something about a Wren from the base,' he paused and gave a throaty laugh. 'The funny thing is they're both married!'

'Talking about marriage,' I said. 'How long a leave have you got for yours?'

Harvey pursed his lips and shrugged his shoulders. 'Only a long weekend, mate,' he replied. 'We're gunna spend it in Southsea.'

'In bed you mean, you lucky bugger,' I answered.

'If I didn't know you better,' replied Harvey glancing at me, 'I'd think you were jealous.'

'Don't be daft,' I replied with a half-hearted laugh. '*Me jealous...?*'

As we spoke a staff car drove up alongside the bottom of the ship's gangway.

'Aye, aye,' snapped Jacko, 'here comes the old man.'

Harvey and I stood a few feet away from the top of the brow. We watched as two officers hurried on board. Both wore two gold rings on the cuffs of their uniforms signifying they were RNVR.

'Which one's the captain?' I asked Harvey almost in a whisper.

'The tall one in front,' replied Harvey from the side of his mouth, 'His name's Peter Reid. Amateur yachtsman in civvy street. Recently married a Wren officer. The Jimmy's the one behind him.'

'What's he like?'

'Nigel Partington. Good seaman,' answered Harvey. 'He was a solicitor before the war. He soon sorted out the lower deck lawyers when he joined the ship.'

As the officers stepped onto the deck I was able to have a closer look at them. The 'old man' looked about twenty-five and had deep-set brown eyes and a firm jaw. The first lieutenant was smaller, with broad shoulders and a fair complexion. Both officers had weather-beaten features, no doubt gained by many hours exposed to the elements on an open bridge.

'All quiet Jacko?' snapped the captain.

'No problems,' replied Jacko who didn't salute and held his cigarette close to his side.

'And who might you be?' asked the first lieutenant, his dark blue eyes staring directly at me.

'Burnside, sir,' I replied. 'The new flotilla SBA.'

'I see,' he replied. 'Draftee didn't waste much time sending Bell's relief, eh Peter?' he said glancing at the captain.

'Just as well, Nigel,' replied the captain, with a wry smile, 'we might need him sooner than you think.' The captain smiled and looked down at me. 'Welcome on board, Doc,' he said.

I promptly saluted, and replied, 'Thank you sir.'

The captain grinned and returned my salute. 'Don't forget to report to the flotilla commander, Lieutenant Commander Anderson in 51 as soon as possible.'

'Aye, aye, sir,' I replied in true nautical fashion. 'I'll do that as soon as I've finished my joining routine in the morning.'

The two officers turned away. 'Very Pusser, these young lads,' I overheard the captain say as they left. His reply was lost as the door closed.

'Going to the wardroom for a few pink guns, I expect,' remarked Jacko, taking a puff of his cigarette. 'I wouldn't say no to a nice warm tot meself.'

'I wonder what the captain meant when he said I might be needed sooner than I thought?' I asked Harvey as we walked to the brow.

'Search me, Ted,' replied Harvey shrugging his shoulders. 'Maybe it was something the commodore said at that meeting. Anyway, I expect we'll find out soon enough.'

The main offices of the base were situated in the concert hall. Therefore, completing my joining routine the next day took ten minutes.

'Harry Bell had a valise containing everything he would need in an emergency,' said Dixie. I was in the sick bay having a cuppa before going to inspect the medical post on the harbour wharf. 'I'm afraid it went down with his ship. However, I've managed to knock up another one for you. Smudge will give it to you before you leave.'

He then introduced me to the base doctor, an athletically built, good-looking surgeon lieutenant with dark brown, well-groomed hair.

'Good luck,' he said shaking my hand. 'Remember, you're on your own. If you get any serious injuries, your ship may not be able to return to base, so do what you can. I don't envy you your job.'

His advice made me think.

'What would I do if a case needed hospital treatment and we were at sea?' I asked with more than an air of concern.

'The safety of the ship and its crew is the captain's first

responsibility,' replied the doctor. 'It would be up to him to decide what to do.'

I also met Wanda, the nurse. The obvious bulge under her white apron showed me why she was called 'Busty'. She was about eighteen, small with fair hair and brown eyes. When we shook hands she looked at me and said, 'Pleased to meet you, Ted. We could do with some fresh blood around here.' Then with a flirtatious glance at the doctor, turned and with a swish of her starched uniform, left the room.

The valise Dixie made up was heavier than I thought. Made of strong canvas it contained everything including a copy of the sick berth manual, morphia, suturing equipment and medicines for general use. It was going to prove more useful in the days to come than I thought.

It was just after ten o'clock in the morning when I left the base; the early morning June sun felt warm on my back, and high in the clear blue sky the ubiquitous cry of seagulls rent the air.

The medical station on the wharf was small but contained shelves with bottles of everything, from so-called hangover cures to pungent-smelling antiseptics. There was an assortment of first field and shell dressing, plasters, slings and splints. Lying on a small table was a large leather-bound book; inside I found an alphabetical list of every member of each individual minesweeper. Alongside each name was the date every officer and rating was due his anti-tetanus, typhoid injections, smallpox vaccinations and routine medical examinations; I made a mental note to bring these up to date. As I locked the door, I said a silent 'thank you' to Harry Bell. He certainly knew his job.

Three minesweepers were tied up alongside the wharf for'd of MMS 51, the senior ship in the flotilla. Unlike the others the '51 had a slightly larger funnel, but was similarly armed with 20mm Oerlikon gun for'd and aft.

On the fo'c'sle of the 51 a group of ratings in blue overalls were busy washing the deck. One was hosing down the fo'c'sle while another followed on with a rubber squeegee. Two ratings, cigarettes hanging from their mouths, occupied themselves leisurely wiping the windows of what I later discovered was the wheelhouse. The head and shoulders of two officers poked over the open bridge; neither paid any attention to me as I walked up the gangway.

The duty quartermaster, a solid-looking able seaman wearing overalls, nodded, as I stepped over the brow onto the deck.

'OK to come on board?' I asked, saluting the quarterdeck.

The matelot grinned at me. 'No need for all the saluting Doc,' he said, 'This ain't the bleedin' *Rodney.'*

'Is the captain on board?' I asked. 'I've been told to make my mark with him.'

'Aye,' replied the matelot, 'He's around somewheres. Probably in the wardroom with the Jimmy.' He pointed to a door in the side of the bridge superstructure. 'Go through there and along the passageway.'

As I made my way along the deck, a voice with a Scouse accent attracted my attention.

'Well, well, well, look who's 'ere!' cried the voice.

I turned around and saw Pincher Martin, one of the matelots I met on the train. He was barefoot, and wore faded blue overalls rolled up at the ankles. He didn't wear a cap and strands of his dark hair, still parted in the middle, wavered in the breeze.

'I see you got your request granted, then,' I said shaking his wet hand.

'Yeah,' he replied, 'and so did Nobby. He's on board skiving somewhere. Will you be sailing with us?'

'I don't know yet,' I replied. 'It'll all depend on your captain. He's the flotilla leader.'

'Well if you do,' he said. 'You'll need to wear something warm. Wait here, and you can borrow one of me sweaters. I've got a few spare ones.'

Just then a sailor emerged from a hatchway. Straight away I recognised Nobby's smiling face and dark, curly hair. Like Pincher, he wore overalls but his trousers were tucked into a pair of sea boots.

'Are you following us?' he said shaking my hand.

'Good to see you, Nobby,' I replied. 'I don't know about following you, but I'll probably be sailing with you soon.'

'We shouldn't have told 'im about the hard-lying money, Nobby,' joked Pincher, aiming a jet of water at his mate.

'Piss off!' shouted Nobby ducking behind the Oerlikon gun.

Pincher gave a loud laugh and dropped his hose.

'I'll be back in a few shakes,' he said and disappeared down a hatch. In next to no time he re-appeared holding a sweater in his hand.

'Here,' he said, handing it to me. 'You can give me it back when you get yours from slops.'

'Cheers, Pincher,' I said feeling the thickness of the material in my hands. 'I'll leave it with the QM and pick it up when I go ashore.'

Nobby suddenly nudged Pincher. 'Watch it mate,' he said, 'here comes the skipper.'

As soon as he finished speaking an officer arrived.

The two and a half wavy gold rings around both cuffs, signified Lieutenant Commander Anderson was an RNVR officer. On his left breast was a row of medal ribbons, one of which was the purple and pale blue of the Distinguished Service Order. He was a medium-sized, sharp-featured man in his late thirties. Next to him stood a squat, pugnacious-looking chief petty officer. On each lapel wore the insignia of a coxswain. (A ship's wheel surrounded by a laurel wreath topped up with a crown.) Both had faces like leather parchment and wore their caps, minus its grommet, (a wire ring keeping the cap taut and in shape) at a rakish angle.

The captain's grey intelligent eyes focused on the red cross on my arm. 'Is someone injured?' he asked in a clear, distinct voice.

'No, sir,' replied the QM, 'This is the new doc.'

'I see.' The captain looked directly at me. 'Name?'

'Burnside, sir,' I replied, saluting. 'SBA Burnside.'

The captain casually returned my salute and turned to the Cox'n.

'Have we any room for him on board at present, 'swain?'

The chief face pursed his lips and slowly shook his head. 'Sorry, sir,' he replied in a deep Yorkshire accent. 'That last replacement got the remaining bunk.'

'Then,' said the captain, 'I'm afraid you'll have to find a berth elsewhere. But keep me informed of any problems.'

'Aye aye, sir,' I replied.

The captain then turned and walked through a doorway in the bridge superstructure.

'Be seeing you Doc,' said the coxswain giving me a quick wink before following the captain.

Meanwhile Pincher and Nobby had moved away and were standing on the fo'c'sle.

'It'll be stand easy soon,' said Nobby. 'Come down and 'ave sippers.'

In the mess I was introduced to five other ratings, including Knocker White, the cook. He was a portly, pale-faced man in his early forties.

'When yer come aboard,' he said shaking my hand. 'Y'can give always help me in the galley son.' As he spoke his double chins wobbled and his bright blue eyes broke into a smile.

'Aye,' added a sailor with a shaggy black beard. On his overalls he wore three propellers, the insignia of a stoker. He introduced himself as Bill Grundy. 'And' he added with a loud guffaw. 'If yer cut off anybody's leg, we can eat it. I'm gettin' fuckin' fed up with corn dog!'

Nobby handed me a small medicine bottle full of dark liquid.

'Here, Doc,' he said. 'Have a good swig o' this. It'll put hairs on yer chest.'

Not wanting to appear too green, I did as he asked. The liquid tasted harshly sweet. As the rum entered my stomach it felt as if my insides were on fire. I gave a gasp and handed the bottle back to Nobby.

'Th..that's strong!' I gasped. 'I…I thought you watered it down.'

'Not in this navy you don't,' replied Nobby screwing the bottle down. 'Anyway. We needs the water for washin' and things.'

'Speak fer yerself,' grunted Bill Grundy. 'It's been years afore I've shaved.'

'Or fuckin' washed,' added another rating. 'Judging by the

smell of yer.'

The others in the mess insisted in giving me a taste of their rum.

When I reached the fresh air of the upper deck, the sun seemed harsher and the wind cooler. Clutching Pincher's sweater I just about managed to return to the base. By the time I drew my tot my head was spinning.

After dinner I promptly fell asleep on my bunk and was woken up by Dixie shaking my shoulder. My head ached and I had a mouth like a vulture's crutch.

'You'd best wake up my son,' said Dixie. 'I've just been informed the 'sweepers are going to sea in the morning. And you're sailing on board the 50.'

CHAPTER NINE

'Ring on main engines, Chief, hands to sea stations.' I heard Lieutenant Peter Reid, the captain of MMS 50 order in a sharp, clear voice.

Suddenly I felt the dull throb of the engine vibrate under my feet as the ship swayed gently at her moorings. A surge of excitement suddenly ran through me making the palms of my hands sweat. It was then I remembered what happened to Harry Bell and his ship; instantly, the thrill of going to sea was tempered by the dangers that might be lurking outside the harbour.

Half an hour earlier at 0700 I took Dixie's advice and wore Pincher's warm sweater under overalls with woollen stockings tucked over my sea boots.

'Even in June it can get a might cold at sea, Ted,' he had said, handing me a duffel coat. 'And this'll come in handy too.'

Once on board, Harvey had taken me to the mess.

'That's your bunk there,' he said pointing to a bare, leather bench at the end of the mess, 'Not that you'll need it as we're returning to Lowestoft tonight. You can stow your gear in the locker above.' Just as Harvey was about to leave, he turned and added. 'Don't forget to wear your Mae West and put on an extra sweater.'

'Why the extra sweater?'

'They keep you warm in the water,' replied Harvey with a sly grin, 'and helps you float!'

'Cheers, mate!' I replied. Then mimicking *Itma's* Mrs Mop, moaned, *'It's being so cheerful that keeps you going!'*

Shortly afterwards, bulging with clothes under my Mae West, I stood holding the guardrail on the starboard side of the ship's open bridge. From here I had a perfect view of everything.

High above, the dark, cumulonimbus clouds raced across

the sky threatening rain. On the fo'c'sle, in front of the high mainmast stood the 20mm Oerlikon; on either side of the gun were winches and coils of wire rope. On the fo'c'sle stood Subby Eardsley. Close by were two ratings, one of whom stood on the wharf near a bollard, looking up at the bridge awaiting orders.

On the stern, the snap of the white ensign flapping from the gaff, echoed above the stiff morning breeze. Suspended outboard from two derricks was a cream-coloured object shaped like a torpedo. On its round snout was mounted a red duster attached to a tiny flagpole. This, I knew from my limited knowledge of minesweeping was a paravane.

'Cox'n on the wheel,' came a gruff voice from the wheelhouse.

I had met Jack Wrey, the coxswain, earlier that morning. He was a heavy-set man with rubicund features and a keen sense of humour. He was regular navy and judging by his campaign medals, had been in the navy for centuries.

'Good to 'ave you with us, Doc, my 'andsome,' he said shaking my hand. His strong, West Country accent sounded like marbles in a tin, and when he spoke his grey eyes sparkled. 'I bets your stitchin' is a might better than mine, eh?'

'I hope so, 'swain,' I replied with a laugh.

Now, as I felt the wind stiffen on my face, I took a deep breath. At last I was going to sea!

'Very good, 'swain,' I heard the captain reply down the voice pipe. I looked up and saw the captain's head and shoulders move to the starboard wing, his keen eyes scanning aft. 'Let go for'd,' he shouted down to Subby Eardsley. 'We'll swing out on the after spring.'

The young officer nodded to one of the ratings, who, jumped onto the wharf. The rating expertly removed the heavy-looking hemp ropes off the bollard and quickly returned on board to help haul in the lines.

'Let go aft!' cried the captain.

The ship slipped her moorings, rolled slightly and moved away from the wharf.

'Half ahead, starboard ten!' the captain shouted down the

voice pipe.

Once again I heard the coxswain repeat the order from the inside the wheelhouse.

The first lieutenant hurried past me binoculars swaying around the neck of his duffel coat; with surprising agility he climbed up a ladder leading onto the bridge.

'It'll be a short haul today, Nigel,' I heard the captain say.

'Pity we're canteen boat, Peter,' replied first lieutenant, slightly out of breath. 'I've a date with that popsy I met in the wardroom last night.'

The 'canteen boat' referred to by the first lieutenant, was the junior ship and was always last in and last out of harbour.

'Lucky bugger,' replied the captain with a short laugh. Then, in a stern voice ordered, 'Full ahead, starboard ten. Better close up all lookouts, Nigel.'

'Ten a starboard wheel on,' came the coxswain's reply.

Scattered around the sea, white horses unfurled themselves in foamy waves against the ship's side. As we left harbour, Lowestoft's houses, church spires and lighthouse gradually became smaller. The Norfolk coastline slowly faded away becoming a dark blur on the horizon.

Almost immediately the ship dipped and twisted as the North Sea swell hit us. The deck rose and fell forcing me to clutch hold of the guardrail. Suddenly, the wind increased becoming raw, stinging my face and making my eyes water.

Although I had visited MMS 51, the senior vessel, I hadn't had time to visit minesweepers 47 and 46. We were sailing in line ahead; from my vantage point I could see the masts and yardarms of the three ships in front swaying too and fro as the small flotilla cut their way through the rolling sea.

The first lieutenant piped. 'All lookouts close up.'

A few minutes later Harvey joined me, strands of his flaxen hair flaying in the breeze. His black oilskin was covered in beads of spray and he wore sea boots. Even though the sea was relatively calm, the bows bobbed up and down making me wish I had missed breakfast.

'Aye, aye, Ted,' said Harvey, scanning the horizon with his binoculars. 'Enjoying the cruise?'

'Funny bugger,' I replied, watching as the ships ahead spread out roughly two hundred yards apart in line abreast. 'It looks like we've got company,' I added, looking at the wake of a motor launch that had taken station behind the flotilla.

Harvey trained his binoculars aft. 'They lay the Danbouys after we've swept the channels. We also call them "coffin ships".'

'*Coffin ships!*' I blurted. 'What the hell are they?'

Harvey shot me a cautious glance. 'I hope you never find out,' he replied.

His comment made me pause for thought. The word *coffin,* had overtones I dared not think of. Instead, I asked, 'What'll happen now?'

'A convoy will be coming through soon and we'll sweep a channel for them.' Harvey lowered his binoculars and looked at me. 'Now for the Cook's tour! The Jimmy's told me to give you the low-down and to show you round the ship.'

'Sound good to me,' I replied. 'Judging by the size of her it shouldn't take long.'

The swell of the sea made the ship roll awkwardly; a stiff breeze billowed around my head flapping my trousers and battering my Mae West. Clutching the guardrail I followed Harvey aft; we came to the large metal drum I saw earlier. Around it were bound layers of thick rubber cables; I reached up and touched them; they were tightly wound together and felt surprisingly smooth.

'They're the magnetic sweep cables I told you about,' said Harvey. 'Two cables are trailed out from the stern; the shorter of the two cancels out any electric field from the ship. Both cables have a fifty-foot electrode at the end.' Harvey pointed to a large box-like structure aft of the bridge. 'Inside there is a generator that sends a three hundred amp pulse along the long one. Then *Whoosh!* Up goes the mine…hopefully.'

'Magnetic mines,' I said eyeing him curiously. 'I've never heard of them. What sets 'em off?'

Harvey tapped the side of the drum with his hand.

'All ships made of metal have an electric charge,' he paused, passed me a cigarette, put one in his mouth, and after cupping his hand against the wind lit up. 'The magnetic mines are attracted to the electricity and contain a hundredweight of explosives.' After exhaling a stream of tobacco smoke, he went on, 'And believe you me, when the buggers explode they can blow a ship in two.'

My heart missed a beat. I stopped, cigarette poised in the air.

'Christ almighty!' I exclaimed. 'There's metal on this ship. Does that mean…?'

Harvey handsome features broke into a wide grin.

'Take it easy, Ted,' he said interrupting me. 'All ships are de-gaussed. In other words the electric charge is removed.'

'Does that make the ships completely safe?'

'Not quite,' replied Harvey. 'Some merchant ships in particular might not have been properly de-gaussed or could have re-gained their electric charge.'

'What about our ships?'

'Mostly wood with brass fittings,' replied Harvey, flicking his dog-end into the sea, 'so don't worry.'

As we continued along the side of the ship, Harvey turned and said, 'Of course, there's always the acoustic mines.'

'Acoustic mines!' I exclaimed. 'What the fuck are they?'

'Calm down,' replied Harvey placing a hand on my shoulder. 'They explode by the sound of the ship's propellers, but we leave them to the big fleet 'sweepers.'

Suddenly I felt uncomfortable. Somewhere, I told myself, below that vast expanse of water lurked the kind of unseen danger that could end my life in a second. For all I knew one of those mines Harvey described might, at any moment, detonate and blow me into oblivion. By the time we arrived on the small quarterdeck I began to wonder what I had let myself in for.

'Are you all right?' asked Harvey. 'You look a little pale.'

'I'm OK Harv,' I replied, still holding onto the guardrail. 'Just finding my sea legs.'

I watched as Paddy and Jock, wearing leather gloves, lowered the paravane into the water. Like the other men they were bareheaded, clad only in well-scrubbed overalls and roll-necked sweaters.

'Those wires with serrated edges attached to the paravane are the cutters,' said Harvey. 'They could slice through a mine mooring cable like a knife going through cheese.'

'Mind she doesn't swing back,' shouted Subby Eardley, who was standing in the centre of the deck. 'And keep clear of the wires.'

With a clatter the wires were run out and splashed into the sea.

On the port side Ginger and Johnny Pue worked the handle of a large winch and paid out wire that slipped over the stern through a fairlead.

'What's that metal object on the wires for, Harv?'

'That's called a "kite" or "otter" as some call it,' he replied. 'Its purpose is to keep the wire at a certain depth. Once everything is in the water the ship will sail at an angle. This forces the wires away from the ship and they sink down deep "Oropesa Sweep", used in the First World War. OK so far?'

'Oh I see,' I replied, slowly nodding my head. 'The wires from the paravane and cutters have a kind of lasso effect like cowboys use.'

Harvey gave a short laugh. 'Something like that,' he replied.

'But what happens when the mine surfaces?'

'Oh, we just shoot it. May take ten minutes or half an hour. Then it either sinks or, explodes. Last time out we anchored, and a mine suddenly appeared and floated past us.'

'Bloody hell!' I exclaimed. 'What happened?'

'I pissed myself!' replied Harvey with a belly laugh.

When the 'sweep wires were paid out, the ship altered course. About two hundred yards away I watched the small foamy wake of the paravane's flag cutting through the sea; then I heard the captain's voice.

'Hoist signals,' he ordered.

Straight away Dicky Dickson, the bunting tosser, (signalman) raised three large black balls, wobbling in the wind, to the top of the mast.

'What are *they?*' I asked.

'Oh them,' said Harvey, looking upwards, 'they're to tell

other ships we are sweeping. The one on the port side tells which side we are working on.'

Once the 'sweep wires were out everyone relaxed and smoked cigarettes.

'Come on Ted, follow me,' said Harvey with a grin. 'When we sight a mine you'll hear all about it.'

Harvey led me down a hatch and along a narrow passageway. The acrid smell of warm air and diesel oil immediately assailed my nostrils.

'This is the for'd mess,' he said as we entered a room similar to the one aft. 'Eddy Gooding, and three seamen, bunk here. So do Stoker Ron Balshaw, Dicky Dickson, and Perky Perratt, who you've already met, Bungy Williams and Nobby Clark, the wardroom steward.'

'Bloody hell, Harv, Nelson's men had more room than this,' I remarked, looking around.

'You get used to it,' was Harvey's non-committal reply.

Next to the mess was a door leading to the cabin belonging to Subby Earley and the first lieutenant.

'Don't disturb either of them unless it's an emergency,' warned Harvey. 'They get little enough sleep as it is. The skipper's cabin is directly under the bridge. Better not go onto the bridge, it's always a bit crowded when we're sweeping.'

Then came the galley, with a few iron pots and pans swaying in unison above an electric stove. Wearing a white apron around his portly figure, Perky Perratt stood at a table chopping vegetables. Nearby pieces of meat freshly cut from a side of beef rested in a blood-soaked tray.

'Wocha matey!' he said in a distinct Cockney accent. Wiping his hands on the sides of his apron, he extended a hand, 'I think we met in the Nest.'

'Yes,' I replied accepting his podgy, damp hand, 'nice to meet you, Perky. How's the finger?'

'OK,' he answered waving it in the air. 'Welcome on board and before yer ask, we're on stew today.'

'Fuckin' well makes a change from corn dog,' replied Harvey.

'Piss off,' said Perky, picking up a small cleaver, 'afore I make mince meat outa yer.'

After leaving the galley we continued along a narrow passageway. Suddenly, from the deck on the port side a hatchway opened and out came the balding figure of Jock Duthie, the Chief Engineer. Beads of sweat trickled down the side of his face; from the trouser pocket of a pair of white overalls he took out a dirty handkerchief.

'Hello, Doc,' he said moping his brow, 'It's a wee bit warm doon there. I'm off for a breath of fresh air and a quick smoke.' He then climbed up a ladder and disappeared.

Then came the wardroom. It was very small. In one corner was a tiny bar built into the bulkhead. In the middle stood a table covered with green velvet and a few chairs screwed down to the deck.

Standing wiping glasses with a dishcloth was a thin-faced man with strands of dark hair plastered over an almost bald head. He wore a short, white jacket with brass buttons that looked out of place with his trousers tucked into a pair of sea boots.

'You're the new doc, aren't you,' he said. 'I overheard the Jimmy say you were on board.' He put the glasses on the table. 'Nobby Clark's the name,' he said, shaking hands. 'Not much room here if you want to use it as an operating room, eh?'

He was referring to the use of the wardroom, which, in small ships was used as an emergency operating theatre.

'There doesn't look much room for anything,' I said glancing around. 'The officers must take it in turns to eat.'

'Actually, they do,' replied Nobby. 'At sea, they hardly get time to eat especially when we're sweeping like now.'

In one corner six revolvers were locked in a small glass-faced cupboard. Next to this was a larger cupboard.

'What's kept in that one?' I asked, nodding towards the empty cupboard.

'303 rifles, matey,' replied Harvey. 'Subby Eardley has 'em on deck. You'll hear 'em when we sight a mine.'

This was confirmed by the sudden crack of gunfire.

'Come on, Ted!' cried Harvey, 'I think we've got a bugger.'

The sharp retort of small arms fire came closer as we made our along the passageway. When we arrived on the quarterdeck the scene was like that from a wild-west film. The stringent smell of gunpowder played under my nostrils before being carried away in the wind. Paddy, Jock, Ginger and a few others were kneeling down resting their rifles on the guardrail. With every volley a spent cartridge flew into the air accompanied by the sharp *click* of bolts being open and closed. Each shot produced a jerking movement of the barrel from which a tiny puff of black smoke emerged. Even Subby Eardley fancied his chances, firing from a standing position as if this was a training exercise.

My gaze followed the direction they were aiming. Suddenly, I felt my stomach inwardly contract! Bobbing up and down in the green water I caught sight of my first mine. Its rounded dark shape and evil-looking horns moved tantalisingly from side in the water. So this is what it's all about, I said to myself; for a second I stared at the object realising if one of its horns touched the ship I would be blown to bits. Suddenly, I was gripped with fear. I felt a trickle of sweat run down my back as I tightened my hold on the guardrail. Jesus Christ! I said to myself. If it comes any closer it'll hit the ship…

My thoughts were interrupted by excited shouts and yells as each man let off a round of bullets.

'You cross-eyed sod!' Paddy yelled across at Jock. 'You couldn't hit a barn door at ten paces.'

'If yer no careful, you Irish bugger,' replied Jock, taking careful aim. 'I'll put a bullet up yer arse.'

'What did you say?' yelled Paddy, pointing his rifle at Jock.

Bloody hell! I thought, they're going to shoot each other.

I breathed a sigh of relief as Subby Eardley intervened.

'That's enough, you two,' he barked. 'And point those rifles at the damn mine.'

Paddy and Jock glared at the officer, looked at each other, grinned and took aim at the mine.

'D'you fancy your chances, Doc?' asked the officer, handing me his rifle. 'An extra tot if you hit the blighter.'

At first I was reluctant to try. The last time I held a rifle was when Danny, my brother, showed me how to hold his when he was on leave. This one felt heavier and smelt of gunpowder.

'Go on, Doc,' yelled Ginger. 'Show us how the medics do it.'

'Aye,' added Jacko with a grin. 'But make sure you point the barrel away from us.'

Harvey showed me how to put in the clip of bullets.

'Keep the but firmly in yer shoulder,' said Harvey, standing next to me.

For a second I studied the distance from the ship to the rounded shape of the mine rolling in the sea.

Harvey went on, 'Just look through the sight, squeeze the trigger and remember that sod could sink a ship in seconds.'

Suddenly, I remembered mum and dad and felt I was fighting a personal war. I aimed and gently pulled the trigger. A sharp crack rent the air. As the rifle jerked heavily against my shoulder I dropped the weapon and fell backwards onto the deck. At that moment a tremendous explosion rocked the ship followed by a great cheer. I grabbed the rifle and staggered to my feet. A tall plume of black water hung over the spot where the mine once was.

'Bloody hell, Doc!' exclaimed Harvey, 'You must have hit the bastard.'

'Nice one, Doc,' yelled Paddy. 'I'll be round for sippers.'

I looked around. Most of the group were grinning at one another; it then occurred to me that they also were shooting at the mine!

'Did I really hit it, Harv?' I asked, observing the expressions on the faces of the men.

Harvey shrugged his shoulders. 'Of course you did, Ted.' he replied with an innocent look on his face. 'But you'd best give me that rifle, just in case…'

'Well I'll be buggered,' I muttered, 'and me a non-combatant.'

An expression of scepticism came into Harvey's eyes. 'There's no such thing as a non-combatant in this bloody war, Ted, believe you me,' he replied.

A series of watery explosions dotted the seascape as the

other three ships found their quarries. Using Harvey's binoculars I scanned the MMS 51; to my surprise I saw Nobby and Pincher on the quarterdeck. Like us they were busy shooting at mines. I gave them a wave but we were too far away for them to see me.

For the next few hours the flotilla cruised in line abreast. By late afternoon I estimated the ships had exploded or sunk half a dozen mines.

'What keeps the mines afloat, Harv?' I asked after we had drunk our tot.

Harvey was about to answer when Jock Duthie, the chief engineer, interrupted him.

Jock pulled back the curtain dividing the messes, and holding his tot glass full of amber liquid, proceeded to answer my question.

'Yer see, laddie,' he said, taking a good sip of rum. 'It's like this. A cable attached to a sinker drops the damn things. The cable adjusts itself and allows the mine to float at a certain level which is usually just below the surface.' The chief paused and took another steady swallow of rum, smacked his lips, and went on. 'Inside the sod is a buoyancy chamber and if the mine drifts, a special hydrostatic valve is inside to control the depth. The horns are made of lead and are attached to a detonator inside the iron casing. When they touch anything, up she goes!'

'Be Jebbas, Chief!' cried Paddy. 'Talking about getting blown up is putting me off me tot, so it is.'

'Ha!' exploded, Jock. 'That'll be the day,' and in one sumptuous swallow, knocked back his rum.

The run back to Lowestoft began quietly. The 'sweep gear was retrieved and everyone was relaxing. High above in the sky the fuselages of bombers glinted in the warm June sun accompanied by fighters. A few gave us a friendly roll of their wings.

'B 17's on their way to Germany, I bet,' said Harvey, shading his eyes against the sun's glare. 'They do the daylight raids and our lads bomb at night.'

Along with Ginger and a few others we were leaning on the guardrail having a smoke. 'I heard on the wireless Hamburg got a pasting last night.'

'Aye,' replied Ginger. 'And it said Leslie Howard got killed.'

'How did that happen?' I asked.

'He was in a civvy liner,' answered Ginger, 'and was shot down over the Bay of Biscay.'

'Och my missus fancied him,' said Jock, flicking his dog-end into the sea, 'She saw *Gone With The Wind,* three times.'

'From what I hear,' replied Paddy. 'Your missus fancied everyone.'

'And just what d'ye mean by that?' growled Paddy, standing upright and glaring at Jock.

Oh no, I thought, looking up them, not again

Tot time arrived and everyone went below. But as we entered the mess a sudden explosion rocked the ship. Glasses fell over spilling their contents over the table and running onto the deck. Someone caught the rum container, (a large aluminium pot euphemistically called a 'rum fanny') before it toppled over and an ashtray flew across the deck.

'What the fuck…' cried someone as we scrambled up the ladder.

'Some poor bugger's bought it!' shouted Harvey.

'Aye,' answered Jock grimly. 'But which poor bugger s it?'

We soon found out.

When I arrived on deck I couldn't believe my eyes. On our port quarter thick black cloud hung over the spot where one of the ships had been. More explosions sent jets of smoke, orange flame and debris billowing upwards.

'Christ Almighty!' gasped Ron Balshaw, a tall, wiry stoker, 'It's the 51. The poor sod's must have hit a mine.'

Nobody replied; everyone not on watch, including myself, stood by the guardrail too stunned to speak. The sickly smell of diesel oil hung in the air making me retch; suddenly, with a dull rumble, another explosion sent a hill of black, oily bubbles into the air. The bows of the ship reared up, and in an instant disappeared under the sea leaving behind a mass of wreckage. Pieces of the ship's superstructure mingled with a morass of debris floated about like matchwood. To my horror I saw two figures in overalls floating face down.

Suddenly, it was too much for me; without thinking I ran my hand down the sweater Pincher had lent me. I closed my eyes but all I could see was Pincher's face, his black hair parted in the middle, grinning at me.

'Everyone keep a sharp lookout!' came the voice of the first lieutenant. 'And that includes you, Doc. Look lively and get your medical bag.' Using his binoculars he scanned the wreckage. 'The poor souls,' he muttered, 'they must have hit a floater.'

A floater, as Harvey told me earlier, was a mine that had missed or broken free of its moorings and drifted aimlessly in the sea.

The sharpness in the first lieutenant's voice brought me to my senses. I dashed down into the after seaman's mess, grabbed my valise and returned on deck.

The ship increased speed and headed towards the pancake of swirling smoke where the 51 once lay. All eyes concentrated on bits of flotsam. I bit my lip hoping to see someone struggling in the sea. But to my horror, all I saw was a red-raw headless torso, an arm, a leg and bits of bloodstained clothing once worn by men I had, only a short while ago, shared a laugh and a tot of rum.

As the other ships approached the debris-covered area, I saw a limp figure in oil-soaked overalls being pulled on board the ML; for a fleeting second I thought someone had survived. My feelings were quickly dashed when an officer on board waved and shook his head.

During the next hour the three ships searched in vain for survivors before altering course for Lowestoft. For a while I stood in silence gripping the guardrail. I watched as the ML sped past our ship a sheet of brown canvas covering a body on its small quarterdeck. Suddenly my eyes clouded over and warm tears ran down my cheeks; I felt a hand on my shoulder, turned and saw Harvey.

'Now you know why they call it the coffin ship,' he said grimly, and slowly walked away.

CHAPTER TEN

'It's a pity you can't come to the wedding, Ted,' said Harvey.

A week had passed since the flotilla lost 51. During that time I had visited the other two 'sweepers. The Patrol Service and its personnel were a close community, and although nobody mentioned any of their comrades by name, the expression in their eyes as they looked across at the remaining two ships told its own story.

It was Thursday, June 17. A cool breeze blew across the harbour ruffling the white ensigns on the jacks of the three 'sweepers tied up alongside the wharf.

Harvey was standing on the top of the brow as I walked on board the 50. Ron Balshaw had invited us to the for'd seaman's mess for sippers. Johnny Pue was duty quartermaster. He was a big hulk of a man with fair hair and a face marinated by the weather. Unlike the rest, Johnny was a three badge-able seaman and in 1938, had served on board HMS *Nelson*; he was sat on a wooden box reading the *Daily Mirror*.

'I see the army have landed on some place in the Meddy called Pantelleria,' he said. 'Apparently it's an island between Tunisia and Sicily. I wonder where they'll land next?...' his voice tailed off and he carried on reading.

I left him engrossed in his newspaper and went below into the mess.

Harvey greeted me with a grin. 'You've timed it right,' he said, 'Tot's up in five minutes. How come you're on duty in the base sick bay on Saturday?'

The day before Harvey had asked me to be best man at his wedding. However, I had lied by telling him I was on duty; the truth was I just couldn't stand the sight of seeing him and Susan getting married. For the umpteenth time, I told myself this was ridiculous. Harvey was a good friend, but I couldn't help my feelings. The fact was I was jealous of Harvey, but felt it would have been wrong to let him see this.

The mess, housed eight men and was similar to the one aft. The smells were the same, as were the sight of underwear, white fronts and socks dangling from deck fixings.

'Here comes the rum rats from aft,' said Nobby Clark, the wardroom steward.

'Look who's talking,' replied Ron settling his large frame next to Nobby. 'At least they don't steal the skipper's gin then add water to make up the difference!'

As Harvey and I joined five other men at a table, the unmistakable spicy smell of rum filled the air.

'Come and get it,' cried Joe Steele, who entered the mess carrying the rum fanny. Joe was a diminutive able seaman with shoulders like an all-in wrestler. 'And don't forget to leave some for Johnny Pue on watch.'

One by one they dipped a brown Bakelite measure into the fanny and poured its contents into a glass.

'Here's to you and your judy,' said Eddy Gooding, handing Harvey his glass. Eddy was a fellow Scouser. Like Joe he was small but wiry with arms like tree trunks. 'Take a good wet, Harvey, lad,' he said, 'and may all yer troubles be little ones.'

Harvey and me accepted sippers from Taffy Jackson, a tall, wiry able seaman from Cardiff, Johnny Hutchins, a lanky wireman from Hull and Ron Norris, an overweight leading seaman from Barnsley.

'It's just as well we've got a make-and-mend,' slurred Harvey, 'I've got to pack me gear to-night.'

'I hope you've givin' 'im enough French letters fer the weekend, Doc,' said Eddy Gooding grinning his head off.

Johnny Hutchins joined the rest in raucous laughter. 'Go bareback, Harv,' he said. 'They like it better that way.'

A tinge of jealousy ran through as I imagined Harvey and Susan making love.

'Good luck, Harvey,' I forced myself to say, taking a sip of Ron's tot. The rum started to affect, and by the time I returned to my own mess aft I could hardly see straight.

Just after eleven next morning, I arrived on the wharf in

time to give Harvey a wave as he left in a tilly.

At the bottom of 50's brow I was joined by Jack Wrey, the ships coxswain and a few others.

'Oh well,' he sighed as we watched the tilly disappear towards town. 'One less for rum today.'

'And one less to be vaccinated,' I replied.

Earlier on I had pointed out to Dixie Dean in the base sick bay, that many of the minesweepers' crews were well overdue for injections and vaccinations.

'Not to mention their routine medical examinations,' I added, opening Harry Bell's book and showing Dixie the dates.

Dixie raised his eyebrows and gave me a curious look.

'Well, Ted,' he said. 'You'll have a job on your hands. Harry tried to do them but failed.'

'Why was that, Dixie?' I asked, closing the book.

'Harry Tate's navy, you see,' replied Dixie smiling. 'You'll find out.'

Now, with the early morning sun on my back, I began to find out what Dixie meant.

'Vaccinated!' exclaimed Jack Wrey his face becoming redder than usual.

I was standing on the brow talking to the 50's coxwain.

'Against what?'

'Smallpox, tetanus and typhoid,' I replied, patting my medical bag. 'I've got all the vaccines and needles in here.'

'Well,' blustered the coxswain, 'Check with the Jimmy first, but yer'll be lucky if you don't get thrown overboard.'

The first lieutenant was more forthcoming. 'I do appreciate that you are only doing your job, Doc,' he said with a sly smile. 'But we have a lot to do on board, and those shots of whatever might put many of the men out of action.' He paused and gave a short throaty cough. 'You see they're not used to such things.'

'What about the officers…sir?'

'Oh,' replied the first lieutenant, glancing at his wristwatch. 'We're far too busy,' and quickly walked away.

When I mentioned giving injections to Paddy and Jock, a look of horror came into their eyes.

'Och mon!' cried Jock, 'Yee can bugger off. Poor wee

Harry once chased me all around the ships we a needle and failed!'

'Aye,' said Paddy, giving Jock a friendly push. 'Only because you threatened the lad with an axe.'

The response from Jock Duthie was no better.

'Best forget it, laddie,' he said, offering me a sipper of rum from his bottle. 'Most o' these men are straight from civvy street and don't take too kindly to needles and such.'

It was the same on the other two ships.

The chief engineer on board the 46, a thickset Welshman with a red beard, really put me in the picture.

'You see it's like this, boyo,' he said, stroking his bead. 'Unless you can find a vaccination against mines, U-boats, E-boats and dive bombers, you're wasting your fuckin' time.'

So much for Harry Tate's Navy!

The first thing I thought of when I woke up on Saturday morning was the wedding. For a while I lay in bed wondering if Harvey and Susan had stuck to tradition and not seen each other before the ceremony. I closed my eyes and imagined Susan in a long white dress carrying a bouquet of roses. Harvey, no doubt hung over, would be wearing his number one suit with white tapes in place of the normal blue ones.

'Oh well!' I sighed, throwing back the bedclothes. 'Good luck to them. If this fuckin' war goes on much longer they'll probably need it.'

Later that morning after checking to see if anyone was waiting outside the medical room on the wharf, I strolled on board the 50; a few men were scrubbing the decks, one or two leisurely cleaned the Oerlikons while others made a brave attempt to polish the wheelhouse scuttles.

'The new flotilla CO has arrived with two replacements,' said Eddy Godding, wiping his brow with a piece of cotton waste. 'The Jimmy says he's comin' on board later on.'

The replacements Eddy referred to were the MMS's 43 and 44. Two *Mickey Mouse* 'sweepers similar to those lost.

'Waste of fuckin' time cleanin' these bloody guns!' cried Paddy, poking his head from behind the Oerlikon mounting. 'They'll only get covered in salt the minute we goes to sea.'

Johnny Pue and Jacko arrived. Both were barefoot with their overalls tied around their waists. Jocko carried a bucket full of water while Johnny held a scrubbing brush and a bar of Pusser's hard (soap).

'Would you believe it?' muttered Jacko. 'The skipper wants the bridge grating scrubbed.'

'Beats me,' said Johnny as they both walked away, 'The next thing he'll want his cabin cleaning!'

'I expect the new CO will want to see you, Doc,' said Paddy, lighting a cigarette.

'Aye,' added Eddy with a grin. 'He'll probably want some Frenchies.'

'Talking about Frenchies,' said Paddy. 'I wonder how Harvey is getting on. He'll be well and truly spliced by now.'

Eddy stopped his polishing and looked at us. 'Knowing our Harv,' he said, 'He'll be still on the job. What d'you think, Doc?'

I gave a half-hearted laugh. 'Yes,' I replied. 'You're probably right.'

Just before tot time Paddy and few others were in the after mess; the stocky figure of Joe Steele, who was duty QM, came in; he was slightly out of breath and appeared flustered.

'The new boss has just come on board with the skipper and Jimmy,' he said, 'and he asked if the doc were on board. I told him you were and he wants to see you, chop, chop.'

'Don't forget the Frenchies!' laughed Paddy as I left the mess.

After knocking on the captain's door, a voice told me to enter. The cabin was bigger than I imagined. The panelling was oak and on the deck head hung a solitary shaded electric bulb. On a small corner table an untidy pile of papers lay next to an open signal log. At the back of the table was a brass angle-poised lamp. Above, screwed to the bulkhead was a framed photograph of a pretty young Wren officer. Her tricorn corn cap was tucked neatly under one arm and she was smiling. The captain's cap, oilskin and leather gloves lay casually thrown onto a nearby bunk. A picture of the King and Queen hung next to an open scuttle. From a cigarette in an ashtray overflowing with dog-ends, a line of blue smoke trailed upwards.

Sitting in a chair next to the captain sat a stout, ruddy-faced officer. The two and a half wavy gold rings around each sleeve signified the rank of lieutenant commander, RNVR. His red beard and heavily lined tanned face made him look like the sailor on the front of Players cigarettes. The uniform he wore looked creased and well worn, and on his left breast was a row of faded campaign ribbons. Under thick bushy eyebrows a pair of deep-set blue eyes stared at me as I entered.

'Come in, Doc,' said our captain, Peter Reid, his craggy features breaking into a grin. 'Caught you before you had your tot, eh?'

'Yes, sir,' I replied with a grin.

'This is Lieutenant Commander Kennedy, our new boss,' he said.

Our 'new boss', didn't smile or offer his hand. Instead he stared at me and in a deep North Country accent, said, 'Your first ship, lad?'

'Yes, sir,' I replied.

'Volunteer?'

'Yes, sir,'

My reply to his last question brought a smile to his leathery features.

'Good man,' was his blustery reply. Then with a slight laugh, raised his eyebrows and added, 'One volunteer is worth three pressed men, eh what?'

Peter Reid retrieved his cigarette, took a puff and joined in his laughter. I simply smiled and stood wondering what they wanted.

I didn't have long to wait.

Lieutenant Commander Kennedy leant back in his chair and laced his fingers across his chest. 'I want you to do the following, young man,' he said. 'Firstly, issue every officer in the flotilla with one ampoule of morphia. I then want you to replenish all first aid boxes throughout the flotilla and ensure every coxswain has emergency stitching material. I would also like a first aid bag on every bridge,' he paused, undid his fingers and sat forward, 'As soon as possible. Is that clear?'

'Yes, sir,' I replied.

'Don't look so worried, Doc,' said Peter Reid, taking a long drag of his cigarette. 'We're not going to attack the *Scharnhorst* (a German battlecruiser). Carry on.'

When I returned to the sick bay I told Dixie about the meeting. He was sitting behind his desk reading *The Daily Express.*

'I heard your new two-and-a-half was merchant navy skipper before joining the 'sweepers,' said Dixie. 'I'm told he's been on several big convoys.'

'Oh yes,' I replied. 'He looks like an old salt,' I replied. 'With that red beard he'll certainly fit in nicely with the rest of the lads.'

'Anyway,' added Dixie, 'There's something in the wind,' he said. 'It says in the paper, troops have been seen practising landing on beaches in the south coast. And my missus in Pompey tells me a load of American BYMS's (Brooklyn Yard Mine Sweepers) and Algerines (Royal Navy fleet minesweepers) have arrived.'

'Do you think it could be the start of that second front Stalin's always on about?' I asked.

'Not really,' answered Dixie folding his newspaper, 'But it could another raid like Dieppe.'

'I hope not,' I replied. 'That was a bloody disaster.'

'*Bloody* is right!' said Dixie. 'That raid last August cost over two hundred and fifty Canadian and British lives. But I'm sure your new flotilla commander knows more than we do, so you'd better do as he says. Oh, and you'd best take a Neil Robertson stretcher, just in case.'

A Neil Robertson stretcher was a canvas structure re-enforced with bamboo cane. It opened out and a patient was strapped inside and could be carried using rope hand-grips.

'Right, Dixie,' I replied, making for the door. 'If you say so.'

'By the way,' said Dixie, folding his newspaper. 'Those ships your new boss was on were torpedoed and he survived, so he seems a lucky sod.'

'I only hope his luck holds out,' I answered before leaving.

On Saturday afternoon, even though I'd had my tot and dinner, I lay awake on my bunk thinking about Harvey and Susan. Whenever I closed my eyes I saw their naked bodies entwined around one another. Finally I fell into a dreamless sleep only to be woken up by Smudge standing over me with a mug of tea in his hand.

'Can't sleep here, Jack,' he said. 'Rise and shine. There's a dance on at the concert hall to-night.' He put the mug on my bunk table, placed a hand on his hip and in a high pitched voice, said, 'If you're lucky dear, you can have the first dance!'

My stomach was still in revolt and I didn't much feel like dancing; I kept on thinking about Harvey and Susan.

'Not for me, Smudge,' I replied, taking a sip of tea. 'I'm not in the mood for prancing about.'

'Come on,' urged Smudge, passing me a cigarette and lighting it. 'It'll do yer good. No point in hanging around here with nowt to do.'

Of course, he was right. A few hours later, Smudge, Bogey and myself, piled into the NAAFI for a few pints of 'Dutch Courage'.

As we entered the concert hall, the strains of a band playing *When the Red Red Robbin Comes Bob Bob Bonbin' Along* hit us like a tidal wave. Coloured bunting decorated the wall and the air was thick with tobacco smoke. Men and women in uniform plus civilian girls wearing pretty dresses moved around the dance floor. In one corner an American airman brought applause from onlookers as he tried valiantly to teach a Wren the art of the jitterbug.

Many of the 'sweeper crews were at the bar, leering at the talent as they swished by hoping to catch a glimpse of white thigh and suspenders.

A tall, plain-looking girl glided past in the arms of an American airman.

'Bloody hell!' remarked Bogey, slurping his pint. 'She's got to be the most doggo party here. Those Yanks'll fuck anything.'

'So what,' answered Smudge. 'So will I!'

A group of men from the 50 vectored in on us.

'Watch out, lads,' cried little Joe Steele,' Here comes the pill-pushers.'

'Be Jebbus,' said Paddy, holding a pint glass. 'I hopes you're not gunna wait until we're all pissed and give us those jabs against smallpox and all.'

Jock, who was standing next to him, threw his head back and gave a throaty laugh, 'It's na smallpox yer should be worried about,' he cried, spilling the beer from his glass, 'it's poxy gonorrhoea.'

'Who the hell cares,' interrupted Ron Balshaw. 'For all we know we could be fish bait in a week's time. Roll on my next good fuck, that's what I say.'

'And I'll second that,' burbled Digger Barnes. 'Who's round is it?'

Like the others he wore a small silver badge on the cuff of his left sleeve.

'What's the badge for, Digger?' I asked.

'That, my son,' he replied, glancing at the badge, 'is the emblem of the Sparrows.' He lifted his arm so I could have a closer look. 'That there,' he added, using his finger, 'is a shield covered with a net and represents the 'sweep. The shark by the side is the mine. Get it?'

'I see,' I replied. 'Does everyone get one?'

'Only after doing six months in the patrol service,' replied Digger.

'Aye,' interrupted Ginger. 'Your predecessor Harry Bell only had a few weeks to go before he got his. But I heard the CO sent one to his folks.'

'I see,' I quietly replied.

'Now that bit of information,' said Digger, holding his empty glass, 'will cost you a pint.'

The band, playing on a stage at the end of the hall, wore naval uniform. 'Good band,' I remarked. 'Are they from the base?'

'Aye.' replied Bogey. 'They're called the "Blue Jackets"; many were professionals before the war. The one playing the saxophone is Freddy Gardner. He's played with some of the leading orchestras.'

I bought a round of drinks and we surveyed the talent.

A very pretty blonde Wren, her arms fathoms around an American glided by.

'Wow!' exclaimed Bogey, leering at her open mouthed. 'She's a bit of all right. I could use her thighs for ear muffs.'

'Forget it, Bogey,' answered Smudge. 'She'd suck you in and blow you out in bubbles.'

'Yea,' sighed Bogey, 'but what a way to go!'

Just then I felt a tap on my shoulder. I turned around and saw Wanda. She was dressed in the dark blue serge jacket and skirt, white shirt, tie and sexy black stockings. On her left arm was the Red Cross insignia of a Wren SBA. For a second I didn't recognise her; the only time we met she wore her nurse's uniform.

'Hello, Wanda,' I said, stepping back and looking at her. 'You look different in your Wren's rig.'

'I hope you're not disappointed,' she replied flashing me a smile warm enough to melt an iceberg.

'No,' I answered almost spilling my beer. 'You look great.'

'Good,' she replied, at the same time taking my glass from me and handing it to Bogey. 'Then you can ask me to dance.'

'Aye, aye,' laughed Bogey. 'You'd best watch out for these Scousers, Wanda. They're all sex maniacs.'

'It'd make a change from sodding alcoholics with brewers' droop,' she replied taking my hand.

Luckily for me the band was playing a waltz.

'I'm not all that good at dancing,' I said as we began to move. 'So I'm sorry if I …'

'Don't worry,' she said, interrupting me. 'After dancing with some of those clodhoppers, you'll probably seem like Fred Astaire!'

With a smile she gently pulled me close to her.

'Relax, Ted,' she said, 'I'm not going to eat you. At least not yet.'

I placed my arm around her waist. Her body felt soft and firm. As we moved to the rhythm of the music I could feel her breasts pushing against my chest. Her perfume floated up under my nostrils adding to my excitement. She squeezed my hand and pressed herself closer. My obvious arousal made her look up and smile.

'Well,' she whispered in my ear. 'I'm glad to see someone hasn't got brewers' droop!'

Suddenly, over the sound of the music, a scream came from across the room; this was followed by the crash of glasses breaking. Like the other couples who were dancing, we looked across the room and saw two matelots rolling about on the floor; close by was an upturned table with bits of broken glass scattered about. A crowd, including many of the crew from the 50, quickly gathered around. The music of the band was almost drowned by men and women shouting.

'Come on.' I said to Wanda. 'Let's see what's up. You never know, we might be needed.'

'Oh let them fight it out,' replied Wanda. 'There's always a bit of bother at these things.'

Just then, I realised the two men were Paddy and Jock from the 50.

I watched as both men staggered to their feet, hair dishevelled, and panting for breath.

'Call me missus a Yank lover, eh?' yelled Paddy, his face red with anger. He then aimed a blow at Jock and missed.

'Och!' cried Jock, adopting a prizefighter's stance; 'I bet she drops 'em for anybody.'

Both men then charged at one another. A girl's scream rent the air as another table was knocked over spilling more glasses, only this time the drinks belonged to two Americans and their girls.

Straight away the two Americans stood up. One was a tall, broad-shouldered corporal, the other smaller with a swarthy, Latin complexion. The tall one attempted to pull Paddy and Jock apart.

'Hey, bud!' yelled the tall one, grabbing Jock. 'What was that you said about the Americans?'

The swarthy one then pushed Paddy on the shoulder. 'Yeah,' he drawled. 'We come over here to help you Limeys out, and all you do is insult us.'

At that point Ginger, Jacko and big Ron Balshaw moved

menacingly towards the Americans. 'Why don't you lot piss off,' snarled Ron. 'If they want to fight, let 'em fight. They're always at it.'

'Aye,' cried Jock, 'bugger off!'

'Begorra!' cried Paddy, pushing the swarthy in the chest. 'If we wanna have a scrap, it's no business of yours, so fuck off back to the States.' Paddy then hit the swarthy American square on the chin and sent him staggering back into the arms of a girl. She promptly dropped him and began screaming. At the same time Jock landed a blow on the tall one's nose. He immediately yelled and clutched his face as blood oozed through his fingers and down his jacket.

By this time the band had stopped playing.

'Please! Please!' shouted one of the bandsmen. 'If you lot don't pack it in I'll send for the patrol.'

'Come on,' said Wanda, 'Let's get away from here. The next thing you know we'll be giving the mad buggers first aid.'

She then tugged my arm and dragged me away from the crowd. As she did so, the last thing I remember was seeing the lads from the 50 grappling with the Americans in a wild melee in the middle of the dance floor. After collecting her cap from the cloakroom, we left just as a naval patrol, led by an angry-looking Master-at-Arms, passed us.

Outside the warm air was a pleasant change from the humidity of the hall; a full moon sent a glimmer of pale yellow light over the grounds, casting shadows amongst trees and hedges. Except for the occasional sound of seagulls the base seemed deserted.

'Where are we going?' I asked, feeling the gravelled path crunch under my shoes.

'I'll show you,' she whispered, putting her arm around my waist. She led me to a grassy verge protected above by a small hedge.

'Let's sit here,' said Wanda, taking off her cap and unbuttoning her jacket.

We sat down on the dry grass. Like Paul Henreid in the film *Now Voyager*, when he lit two cigarettes and passed one to Bettie Davies, I did the same.

'Thank you, kind sir,' she said.

She then took off her cap and gently shook her head allowing her short blonde hair to hang loose. Then, from her shoulder bag she produced a small bottle of Gordon's Gin.

'Bloody hell!' I muttered. 'Where did you get that?'

'A present from a certain surgeon lieutenant,' replied Wanda, unscrewing the top and passing it to me. 'Here, have a good swig.'

Gin wasn't my favourite bevy, but beggars couldn't be choosers and I did as she said.

The alcohol burned the back of my throat and set my stomach on fire.

'Whew!' I exclaimed, handing the bottle back to her. 'That stuff's pretty strong.'

'Good old mother's ruin,' she replied with a throaty laugh, and took a sip.

After another few good swigs my head began to spin.

With a glint in her eye, she took my cigarette from my hand, and along with hers, stubbed them out in the grass; she then gently pushed me back onto the grass and thrust he body against me. When we kissed her lips felt soft and warm; her tongue found mine and I felt her hand slide down onto my crutch…

'I think you'll need a little help,' she whispered, gently unfastening my flies.

However, as I felt her fumbling through my clothing she soon discovered how wrong she was!

'Hmm…' she cooed, caressing me, 'Hurry up Ted, the war might be over tomorrow.'

I reached up and nervously undid the buttons of her blouse; then, using both hands cupped her breasts. As I did so, I felt her nipples harden; she gave a throaty cry, and raised her hips; this allowed me to use one hand to slip her panties over her suspenders. Her legs immediately encircled my waist pulling me close.

'For God's sake be quick!' she cried, and guided me inside her.

For a while we made love as though the world was coming to an end. I cried out several times lost in my own thoughts, concerned only with self-gratification.

When it was over we lay in silence, staring at the mass of stars glittering like a million diamonds in the sky.

'Cigarette?' I asked.

'Yes,' she replied, adjusting her clothing. 'I'd love one.'

I lit a cigarette and passed it to her.

'Any more Gin left? I asked.'

She reached down and lifted up the bottle and shook her head. 'All gone,' she replied. She then glanced at her wristwatch. 'And I'd better be going, the bus to the hospital leaves in half an hour.'

When we arrived at the main gate several couples were huddled together around the coach. Groups of sailors staggered about arms around one another laughing and singing; I recognised Jock and Paddy, swaying about like a pair of dam buoys.

'Come on you lot, leave the girls alone,' cried the driver from inside, 'the coach leaves in five minutes.'

Wanda reached up and kissed me, leaving the sharp smell of Gin on my lips.

'Goodnight, Ted,' she said, touching the side of my face with her hand. Then, as she stepped up into the coach, she turned and with an with a half-heated laugh, said, 'And by the way – my name's Wanda, *not* Susan.'

CHAPTER ELEVEN

On Monday morning a few men were on the wharf waiting outside the medical room. Most suffered from hangovers; one had caught crabs; another, a short, chunky able seaman told me he was loosing his hair.

'Look Doc,' he said, removing a small toupee from his otherwise bald head, 'It's coming out in clusters!'

I laughed, suggested a hair tonic and told him to bugger off.

Earlier I had drawn extra monojects of morphia (small tubes of morphia easily injected into a person) from the sick bay for distribution among the ship's officers.

'And don't forget to get a signature for them,' said Dixie, 'even if you have to forge them yourself. No bugger's going to know the difference.'

During the rest of the morning I issued extra medical gear to the ships as ordered.

'Where can I stow the Neil Robertson, Chief?' I asked Jack Wrey, the 50's coxswain.

'I hope it doesn't take up too much space,' he replied. 'Better put it in the chain locker.'

At one point I was able to catch our first lieutenant in his cabin before he went ashore.

'Is there something up, sir?' I asked, handing him a monoject of morphia. 'Why the sudden request for extra medical stores?'

'You know as much as I do, Doc,' he said, signing my DDA (Dangerous Drug Act) form.

The coxswain of the 44, a medium-sized man with a wrinkled, weather-beaten face, was more forthright.

'I don't needs no proper stitching up gear,' he grinned, slinging the medical bag in a corner, 'I uses a needle and cotton from me housewife.' (A small rolled up pouch containing needles and cotton used for mending clothes.)

'Aye,' muttered a matelot who was cleaning a piece of brass work, 'And he uses his teeth to break off the thread!'

At tot time Harvey was welcomed back with the usual ritual of sippers and gulpers.

'How did everything go?' I asked him.

'Fine,' replied Harvey. For a man who had just been married, his manner seemed rather subdued. 'Everything was fine. Susan sends her love.'

I suppose that's something, I said to myself.

Harvey went on. 'Pompey was full of ships of all kinds, including merchant liners. We met some Bootnecks, (Royal Marines) in the pub after the wedding who said we were gunna invade Sardinia or some other place in the Meddy.'

'Och that'll suit me fine,' said Jock. 'I could do with a run ashore down the Gut in Malta.'

'Well I'll be banjacked!' cried Paddy reading his *Daily Sketch.* 'It says here, since rationing started two years ago, the average family spends seven pounds, ten bob a year on clothes compared with twenty quid before the war. How about that then?'

'Knowing your missus,' said Jock, stroking his black beard, 'She'll be gettin' nylons from the Yanks. And that ain't all…'

Paddy banged his newspaper on the table, stood up and glared at Jock.

'Are you two still at it,' interrupted Harvey, tossing back his tot. 'Pack it in and let's have some peace.' Then, shooting a smiling glance at Jock and Paddy, added. 'Besides. You're in the company of a respectable married man.'

Harvey's words seemed to work; Jock grinned and Paddy, albeit with a scowl on his face, sat down.

Jacko, who was rum bosun, passed around what remained after each had taken their tot (called *The Queens tot).* He told Harvey about the fight with the Americans. 'I noticed Ted and Wanda slinking away,' he said. Then glancing at me added, 'You dirty bugger, I bet you gave her one, eh?'

Harvey shot me a quizzical glance. 'I thought you said you were on duty, Ted?'

My brain went into overdrive. I felt my face redden. 'I

was,' I answered quickly, 'but Dixie relieved me around ten o'clock and I went to the dance.'

'And you got your end away,' he replied, then, in a manner surprisingly tinged with envy, added, 'you lucky sod.'

The next morning the flotilla left harbour for yet another channel sweep. The sky was dark and overcast. This was reflected in the shifting pattern of the sea that rose and fell like a rolling carpet of molten lead.

As soon as the ships cleared the harbour the captain exercised Action Stations.

I was on the quarterdeck watching Paddy and Jock winch out the paravane. When the claxon sounded they immediately stopped what they were doing and uncovered the Oerlikon. Paddy,who was ammunition feeder, stood by while Jock trained the 20mm gun around.

'I think I'll piss off to the bridge and check the first aid bag,' I said, 'see you lot later.'

I arrived on the bridge in time to see little Joe Steele clamp a Lewis gun to the port wing. It was similar to a rifle with a long barrel and a round ammunition holder clipped to the top. The Lewis gun fired 90 rounds a minute. (So I was later told.) Nearby, Eddy Gooding stood next to an open box ready to supply Joe with more ammunition.

'Port gun closed up,' yelled Joe.

Taffy Jackson and Ronnie Norris, two brawny ex trawler men from Whitby manning the starboard Lewis gun, gave a similar reply.

On the foc's'sle, Harvey and Johnny Pue manned the Oerlikon. Joe Willoughby, and Ginger Cornwall took their positions either side of the bridge as lookouts.

Much to my surprise nobody wore anti-flash gear, life jackets or steel helmets.

'Cox'n on the wheel,' came the gruff voice of Jack Wrey.

The captain glanced at his watch then at the first lieutenant.

'Not bad, Nigel,' he said, 'Test all guns and repeat the exercise in an hour's time. Keep the Lewis guns in position and leave the Oerlikons uncovered...just in case.'

As the captain finished I saw the excited figure of Johnny

Pue on the fo'c'sle. He had one hand cupped around his mouth.

'A floater's dead on the port side and it's heading directly for us,' he yelled pointing away to port.

Straight away the others and myself looked to our left; at first all I could see were white horses amidst the heavy swell of the sea. Then, to my horror I saw the black curve of a mine rolling gently with its spiky horns bobbing up and down. It was about fifty yards away and appeared to be moving towards us; suddenly, I remembered what had happened to the 51.

'The blighters going to hit us, number one!' I heard the captain say. 'Hard a starboard!'

I felt my stomach lurch and felt my bowels loosen; paralysed with fear I gripped the guardrail and watched as the mine slowly swayed towards the ship.

'It's no use!' cried the first lieutenant. 'We're not turning fast enough.'

'The damn thing's too near!' cried the captain. 'If we shoot it, we'll go up with the damn thing! Make to the others, "Floater close by. Keep well away".' Then, nervously licking his lips, he snapped. 'Clear the bridge Number One. Order everyone aft. We may have to abandon ship.'

Straight away Dicky Dickson, the signalman, using his Aldis lamp, flashed the message to the other ships.

Everyone except the captain and the first lieutenant hurriedly left the bridge; with speed of a gazelle I leapt down the ladder and made my way aft.

The quarterdeck was crowded with anxious faces leaning over the guardrail looking for'd.

'There it is!' cried someone. 'The bugger's coming down the port side. Christ all mighty, it's gunna hit us.'

What happened next took seconds but seemed like a lifetime.

Out of the corner of my eye I saw Paddy dash to the lifeboat. He grabbed an oar and in one quick movement dived onto the deck and thrust it outboard towards the oncoming mine.

'Holy Mother of God!' screamed Paddy, 'somebody hold me legs.'

In a flash Jock took a firm grip of Paddy's ankles while

others held his legs.

'Clear the quarterdeck!' yelled Subby Eardley.

He needn't have bothered with the order; most of the crew had already left the area.

I was too frightened to move – instead I gripped the guardrail. With my heart beating like a piston I watched Paddy push the end of the oar against the round, rusty surface of the mine. Like an enormous black hedgehog, it bobbled slightly and slowly moved away from the ship.

'Mind those fuckin' horns, you Irish bogtrotter!' yelled Jock.

'Just keep hold o'me, y' Scotch sheepshagger,' I heard Paddy scream above the wind. 'I'm no a good swimmer.'

'For fuck's sake, mon,' replied Jock. 'If that thing hits us, it won't matter if yer bloody Tarzan!'

As the mine continued to drift dangerously close, I felt the ship gradually veer to starboard. With a deep sigh of relief I watched as the gap between the mine and the ship increased.

I heard Paddy give a hoop of delight as he gave the mine a final prod sending it slowly rolling away.

A loud cheer rang around the ship as willing hands dragged Paddy inboard.

'You mad bastard!' cried Jock, helping Paddy to his feet. 'I suppose I'll have ta gee you a wet o' me tot, fer that.'

With rivulets of sweat streaming down his face and his red hair soaked with spray, Paddy thrust out his chest, and replied, 'It takes more than a Jerry mine to scare an Irishman!'

I turned and saw Harvey standing next to me.

'Are you all right, Ted?' he said. 'You look a little pale.'

It was then I became aware of cold sweat trickling down my spine and warm urine dribbling along the inside of my legs.

The flotilla arrived back in Lowestoft shortly after 1700.

'There's a couple of letters for you, Ted,' said Smudge, handing me a mug of tea. 'They arrived after you sailed this morning.'

I was in the sick bay drinking a mug of tea.

One was from Iris telling me she was joining the Wrens. 'Maybe if we meet up you can take me on board your ship', she wrote. Some hope, I laughed, the lads would have a field day. The second letter was from Aunt Agnes. Her opening paragraph sent a shock wave running through me. 'Sorry to have to tell you, Ted, but your pal Shorty is dead. I met his mum in the co-op queue and she told me she and Harry, her husband, received a telegram from the war office saying he had been killed in action. It didn't say where'.

Christ all mighty I inwardly screamed – first my parents, then the crew of the 51, now Shorty. Then I remembered the close call we had earlier with the mine, and wondered if it would be my turn next.

That evening I went to the NAAFI and got so drunk Ron Balshaw, Paddy and Joe Steele had to carry me back to the sick bay.

During the following week I went to sea on the 56, and the two replacement 'sweepers, 43 and 44. The weather was rough but by then I had gained my sea legs. The ships swept as far as North Foreland, just off Margate when the Algerine minesweepers took over.

'Thank God for that,' I overheard a matelot say as our flotilla turned for Lowestoft. 'The area between Margate and Beachy Head is known as "bomb alley". More ships 'ave been sunk there than anywhere else in the channel.'

Besides a few simple stitching cases, the only serious patient I saw was a rating on board the 56.

One morning I was in the galley helping Perky Perratt. Like so many of the 'sweeper men he had served in deep-sea fishing vessels before the war.

Just before stand easy, a tall able seaman with black curly hair named Bill Storey, came into the galley. Bill was from Barrow and had joined the ship shortly before we sailed. The first thing I noticed was his complexion; it was bright yellow, a sure sign of jaundice.

'I 'avent had a shit fer days and I'm not feeling too good, Doc,' he said in a whisper. 'Some o' the lads 'ave been taking the piss. They say I've got yellow jack. 'Ave yer got a few

Aspirins in yer bag?' (Yellow jack was a nickname for yellow fever, a disease prevalent in the tropics.)

'How long have you been like this?' I asked, wiping my hands on a dishcloth.

'Dunno,' he replied, shrugging his shoulders, 'fer a couple o'days I guess.'

Jaundice is caused by an obstruction of the bile duct; the bile passes into the blood giving the skin a yellowish tinge.

When I told him what I thought he was suffering from, he looked at me in disbelief.

'Fuckin' jaundice!' he cried. 'Could I 'ave caught it from some party?'

'Hardly likely,' I laughed.

However, when I told him I'd have to stop his tot as alcohol would make his condition worse, his face blanched.

'Oh, no, Doc,' he cried. 'Anything but that…'

'Sorry, mate,' I replied, 'I'm afraid it's hospital for orders when we get back to Lowestoft.'

As if that wasn't bad enough, when the word got around, his mates jokingly *hissed* him when he entered the mess. One even painted 'unclean', and 'slant eyes', on his locker!

A week later on June 20 all shore leave was suddenly cancelled.

'During the next two days,' came the captain's voice over the Tannoy. 'The flotilla will take on extra food and ammunition. We sail on the twenty-fourth in company with a destroyer, HMS *Javelin.* All mail is to be handed in to Sub Lieutenant Eardley by twelve hundred on the twenty-third. Do not mention we are sailing. That is all.'

Subby Eardley censored all mail before sending it ashore; anything he considered a breach of security was heavily scored out with black ink.

'*That is all!*' exclaimed Harvey standing next to me on the sweep deck. 'I should bloody-well hope it is.'

'Where d'you think we're going, Harv?' I asked.

'Search me,' he replied, lighting a cigarette, 'But maybe that bootneck I met in Pompey was right. Maybe we are off to the Meddy.'

None of the base staff in the sick bay knew either.

'Now you know why your new boss told you to check your stores,' said Dixie. 'Something's afoot believe me. But if I were you, I'd take plenty of tropical gear with me. You never know, you might end up in Italy.'

Wanda, who was sitting drinking a cup of tea, immediately looked up.

'Italians lovers,' she cooed, 'are no good. I read somewhere they're like plates of spaghetti, a few hours later you feel like another one.'

'Ha!' cried Dixie grinning at Wanda. 'There speaks the voice of experience.'

Wanda pulled her tongue out, turned her nose up and haughtily left the room.

Monday the 23 June was a warm day with the sun beating down from a cloudless blue sky. However, as the flotilla sailed out of Lowestoft the choppy sea and heavy swell made the ships pitch and toss like corks in a barrel.

Before we sailed I stowed my kitbag and small Pusser's brown case on board the 50. The day before I had ensured my medical bag plus extra stores were safely stored away in a spare mess locker.

'That's yours,' said Harvey, indicating a single bunk at the back of the mess. 'Nobody uses it.'

'Why is that, Harv?' I asked, placing my gear in the deck.

Harvey gave a wry smile, 'You'll find out,' he said as he left the mess.

That night I did find out.

My bunk was directly over the engine room. The vibration of the engines made the bunk shiver and shake.

'Och, you'll get used to it, laddie,' said Jock. 'Young Harry Bell said the movement gave him a hard on every night.'

'Is that a fact,' said Harvey frowning, 'Maybe I should change places with Ted.'

'It's all that fuckin' bromide Perky puts in tea, Harv,' said Jacko, 'not that it matters now. God knows how long we'll be at sea.'

Making a maximum speed of twelve knots, the small flotilla, sailing line ahead, bounded through the angry waters of the English Channel. The wind increased sending clouds of spray exploding over the ship's bows as we cut through the sea. I spent most of the time trying to avoid vomiting my heart out; luckily, as time passed my system regulated itself to the constant corkscrew motion of the ship.

So far the only sight of the enemy had been a Focke-Wolf Condor reconnaissance plane that lingered overhead before being chased away by a Spitfire.

'The bloody Jerries must be blind,' I said to Eddy Gooding, who, like me was standing on the sweep deck, having a smoke. 'The French coast isn't that far away, surely they can see us.'

'That's as maybe, Doc,' replied Eddy. 'But we're so low in the water it would be hard for them to hit us from where they are.'

As he spoke a huge green goffa, (naval slang for a wave) splashed over the side of the ship soaking Ron Balshaw.

'Bastard!' he gasped and disappeared down into the engine room.

'Will the weather get worse, Ed?'

Eddy flicked his dog end into the sea and grinned. 'Oh aye,' he replied. 'Luckily I expect we'll steer clear of the Goodwin Sands, but when we reach the Bay of Biscay it'll really get rough.'

'Where's the Goodwin Sands?' I asked.

'Just off the Kent coast,' he replied. 'I've sailed these waters plenty o' times, and them sands is always tricky. The old timers called them "the ship-swallower", or the "widow makers".' He paused and lit another cigarette. 'But if we avoid 'em, it'll mean going closer to the French coast.'

A few hours later as dusk was falling the flotilla altered course. I was standing on the port side of the bridge when I saw a series of flashes coming from the French coast. Muted explosions and jets of water erupted some distance away from the flotilla.

'Not very accurate, are they, Number One?' I heard the captain say. Like the first lieutenant and Subby Eardsley, he wore a duffel coat and towel tucked in around his neck to soak up the sea spray.

Just then a huge fountain of dark, cold water jettisoned in the air about twenty yards away. The wind carried the spray across the bridge drenching everybody.

'Maybe you spoke too soon, Peter,' replied the first lieutenant, wiping his face with the back of his hand.

'*Javelin's* 4.7 guns will take care of them,' replied the captain, training his binoculars towards the coast.

Sure enough, a few minutes later the flashes of the destroyer's guns momentarily lit up the gloom. It was impossible to see if they scored any hits on the enemy batteries, but all gunfire from the coast ceased almost immediately.

'No need for action stations,' said the captain, still looking through his binoculars, 'It must be time for their sour kraut!'

The next morning the first lieutenant ordered all guns tested.

I was on the starboard wing of the bridge watching Joe Steele firing his Lewis gun. Taffy Jackson stood nearby ready to pass him a pan of ammunition.

Below on the fo'c'sle Harvey and Johnny Pue manned the Oerlikon. The combined noise from them and the Oerlikon aft rattled in the air sending streaks of silver tracers arcing into infinity. The harsh smell of cordite permeated the air before being carried away by the wind.

'Here, Doc,' said Joe, 'Come and 'ave a go. The Jimmy won't mind, will you?' he added looking at the first lieutenant.

The officer glanced at the captain and grinned. 'Not at all, Joe' replied the first lieutenant. 'Providing he keeps the muzzle pointing seawards.'

'It's just like firing a rifle,' said Joe, showing me where to put the butt of the gun. 'Look through the sight, and squeeze the trigger.'

I aimed the gun up in the air and fired. The vibration made my body jerk and I fell backwards.

'Fine gunner you'd make!' laughed Joe, taking the weapon from me. 'I think you'd best stick to pill-pushing.'

That evening the flotilla entered the Bay of Biscay. The sun cast a glimmering sheen over the water as I watched, fascinated, as schools of shiny, dark-skinned porpoises darted around the ship in a flurry of phosphorescence.

Suddenly the weather deteriorated; the high wail of the wind echoed around like a crazy banshee; pellets of spray attacked my face; straight away I dashed inboard.

'Looks like being a bit rough,' I remarked, drying my face.

'Wouldn't surprise me in the least,' was Joe Steele's casual reply.

How right he was,

It was the worst night I had spent at sea so far; the ship began to roll and pitch heavily, so much so, I was thrown out of my bunk onto the deck.

'Best stay where you are, Doc,' said Jacko, throwing my blankets to me. 'It'll be a fuckin' sight more comfortable.'

The morning dawned grey with angry clouds racing across the sky. The warm wind whipped the sea into a charging mass of white horses as the bows rose and pitched like a thing possessed. The water slapped against the side of the ship with quick, sharp blows, before falling back, hissing and frothing like a massive bubble bath. Aft, beneath the 'sweep deck, the ship's screws sent up a turbulence of water leaving in its wake a fizzing trail of white foam.

I glanced across at the minesweepers. With their white ensigns fluttering wildly from their sterns and halyards rattling about, they looked so much smaller than our escort. Like us, the ships plunged in and out of the water, their decks awash under the high rolling swell. HMS *Javelin* fared no better; her fo'c'sle along with her two sets of 4.7 guns dipped in and out of the sea occasionally vanishing under torrents of watery spray before twisting herself upright.

'Never mind lads,' said Perky Perratt later on as he dished out the rum. 'We'll be safe and sound in dear old Gib this time tomorrow.'

'Aye,' growled Jock, grabbing his tot glass as it slithered across the table. 'Then maybe we'll find out where the hell we're going.'

The next day, 28 June, dawned clear with a warm, scented

wind blowing gently from North Africa. I climbed up onto the deck and for the first time saw the great Rock; shielding my eyes from the early morning sunlight, I gazed up at its raking summit shrouded in mist; silhouetted against a pale blue sky, this huge edifice dominated the port like some mythical giant. Rising from around its base, red terracotta buildings of the town glinted in the sun, while across a narrow stretch of waterway, bathed in a heat haze lay the port of Algeciras in neutral Spain.

'Christ all mighty!' exclaimed Harvey. Eddy Gooding, Harvey and I were standing near the port guardrail. Harvey stood by holding a fender as we came alongside a small tanker. I stood by ready to help if needed. 'The place is crawling with ships,' said Harvey. 'I've never seen so many Algerines, cruisers and battleships in me life. Look over there.' Harvey pointed across the harbour to where two civilian liners were berthed. 'They must be using civvy ships as troop carriers. And they're waving at us.'

'One of them's *The Reina del Pacifico!*' I excitedly exclaimed. 'I've seen her in Liverpool. She's a cruise ship'

'Well there's one thing for sure,' added Eddy. 'I bet those soldiers aren't going on any pleasure trip.'

The tall figure of Sub Lieutenant Eardley came and stood next to us. He carried his cap in his hand and his fair hair curled around his collar.

'Get ready with that fender, Rawlinson,' he said. 'We don't want to damage the paintwork, do we?'

'Any chance of a run ashore?' asked Harvey lowering the fender over the side. 'I can smell the beer on Main Street from here.'

'Ha!' added Eddy, his head jerking back with laughter. 'The whores from La Línea mores the like.'

'I'm afraid not,' replied the officer. 'Nobody will be landing at Ragged Staff Steps this trip. We'll be on our way as soon as we've finished re-fuelling.'

'Will there be any mail?' asked Harvey as he dropped the fender over the side of the ship.

'I doubt it,' replied the Sub. 'We won't be here long enough.'

Harvey looked at me, a pained expression in his eyes. 'I'd give the world to hear from Susan,' he said. Then, after a quick glance around, lowered his voice and went on. 'You know Ted, on our wedding night nothin' bloody-well happened.'

'What d'you mean, Harv?' I replied, raising my eyebrows in surprise.

'Between you and me, like,' he said almost in a whisper. 'It was the wrong time of the month.'

The sudden realisation Harvey and Susan hadn't consummated gave me a start. For a few seconds I inwardly felt elated and did my best to hide my feelings.

'You mean you and her have never...?'

Harvey bit his lip and looked down while shaking his head.

'No!' he answered hoarsely, 'we didn't er...'

'Never mind, mate,' I replied, nudging him with my elbow. 'You'll have plenty of time to make up it when we get home.'

Four hours later, in company with *Javelin,* we entered the Mediterranean Sea, Mussolini's *Mare Nostrum.*

'Next stop, Malta,' said Jacko. Jock, Paddy and me were on the 'sweep deck. Jock was cleaning part of the 'sweep wire while Paddy applied a fresh coat of white paint to a paravane.

'How long will that take?' I asked.

'A couple o' days,' replied Jacko, with a lecherous glint in is eyes, 'Maybe we'll get a run ashore down "The Gut".'

'I doubt it,' muttered Paddy, 'by the looks of that lot we left in Gib, there won't be much time for pissing up or baggin' off.'

I was just about to light a cigarette when a voice over the Tannoy cried, 'Unidentified aircraft approaching. Hands to Action Stations!'

Straight away Jacko whipped off the waterproof covering off the Oerlikon. Paddy dropped his paintbrush and pot and opened the ammunition locker.

I dashed to the mess, collected my medical valise and quickly made my way to the port side of the bridge. The captain, first lieutenant and lookouts had their binoculars trained skywards. Joe Steele was crouched behind his Lewis gun, one hand on the trigger the other supporting the but against his shoulder; the stocky figure of Jack Carroll stood by ready to supply ammunition.

The flotilla was sailing in line abreast. Each ship was roughly six cables (three-fifths of a mile) apart. *Javelin* led the way some distance ahead.

'They're ME 109's!' shouted Bill Storey, the starboard lookout.

At that moment two pale grey-coloured fighters, their black swastikas clearly visible under each wing, swooped overhead. The booming sound of *Javelin* opening up with her guns filled the air. The two aircraft soared up into the blue sky, turned and began another run on the flotilla.

'Signal from Commodore, all ships scatter,' cried Dicky Dickson.

'Port ten!' ordered the captain down the voice pipe, then snapped, 'Fire at will, Number One.'

As the ship heeled over, the sharp intermittent crack of Joe Steele's Lewis gun joined the cacophony made by the for'd Oerlikon. Suddenly the acrid smell of cordite was caught on the wind and stung my eyes.

The two fighters approached, cannon fire flickering angry flames from each wing; I instinctively ducked as they pulled up and roared overhead.

'Stand by with another pan of ammo, Jack,' yelled Joe, his shoulder jerking with each burst of fire. 'The bastards are comin' round again!'

The noise was deafening as all guns opened up following the two fighters in an arc as they attacked the flotilla.

The ME 109's came on again; one of them attacked the destroyer while the other concentrated on the 'sweepers. After strafing the ship opposite, the fighter turned and came directly at us; a line of splinters erupted along the fo'c'sle deck flying in the air like bits of matchwood.

Suddenly Jack Carroll collapsed against the outer side of the bridge wing clutching his left shoulder. A flood of blood immediately oozed through his blue shirt.

'The *bastards!*' cried Jack, blood trickling through his fingers.

A quick glance showed a large tear in his deltoid (the

muscle of the upper outer aspect of the shoulder). Straight away I applied two shell dressings over the wound.

'How is he?' shouted the captain his binoculars still trained on the fighters.

'Shoulder wound, he's lost a lot of blood,' I replied without looking up.

Jack's face began to pale as shock began to set in.

I gave him a shot of morphia, placed his arm in a sling and bound it to his chest. I then laid him flat and raised his legs on my medical valise.

Just as I finished, Joe yelled down, 'Quick, Doc, pass me a pan of ammo. The sods coming at us at sea level!'

Remembering the drill, I quickly picked up a round pan of ammunition from a metal box and clipped it onto the top of the gun.

With a wild glint in his eye and lines of sweat pouring down his face, Joe took careful aim.

'Come on you buggers!' I heard him yell.

His shoulder gave a series of sudden jerks as he let off intermittent bursts of fire. Stream of shells streaked towards the oncoming aircraft; for a fleeting second it seemed like a personal duel between Joe and the ME 109.

Suddenly there was a massive explosion. I instinctively ducked as the fighter burst into a mushroom of smoke and flames; pieces of metal flew in the air as the aircraft disintegrated and splashed into the sea.

'Gotcha yer fucka!' yelled Joe, throwing his hands in the air.

Everyone, including the officers cheered; Dicky Dickson slapped Joe on the back, even the captain shook Joe's hand. 'Well done Joe,' he said with a satisfied grin, 'that's one less sour kraut for tea when they get back in the mess.'

'Bloody marvellous, Joe,' cried Bill Storey, 'you'll probably get a gong for that.'

In fact, Joe was later awarded the Distinguished Service Medal. The inscription read, 'For valour in face of the enemy'.

Jack's wound was serious enough for me to suggest he be transferred to *Javelin.*

'She carries a doctor,' I said to the first lieutenant. 'He'll need proper rest and hospitalisation when we get to Malta.'

The captain glanced across at the first lieutenant. 'Looks like we've found a new ammo feeder, Nigel.'

The first lieutenant looked at me and grinned. 'Non-combatant or not, Doc. There's no passengers on this ship.'

The transfer was a tricky business. The destroyer slowed down as our ship came alongside; both vessels rolled badly; with fenders outboard, willing hands helped Jack across to the escort; normally a boat would have been lowered but time was at a premium and U-Boats were reported in the area.

The doctor and SBA on board the *Javelin* must have been kept busy, as two other wounded men from another 'sweeper were also taken on board the destroyer.

Two days later, on the evening of the 30 June, the yellow limestone cliffs of Malta hove into view.

'Christ Almighty!' cried Paddy. 'To be sure Valetta appears to be covered with those barrage balloons, so they do.'

The flotilla was sailing past the breakwater leading into Grand Harbour.

'I'm no surprised,' replied Jock. 'Look at the state of St Elmo's Point and Fort St Angelo. Like the rest of the island, they've been bombed to buggery.'

'Why can't we berth in Valetta?' I asked Paddy.

'Be Jebbus,' he replied, lighting a cigarette. 'That's only for the big buggers. We'll be dropping our hook in Sliema Creek with the rest o' the small ships.'

Sliema's wide, horseshoe-shaped harbour was full of destroyers, corvettes and minesweepers. Our flotilla berthed stern on to the long wharf close to the town.

'Holy Mother of God!' cried Paddy. 'There's certainly enough ships here to take on the whole of Jerry and Eyetie navy. And that's doesn't include those big buggers in Grand Harbour.'

'I bet we're gunna invade Italy,' said Jacko. 'I mean to say there's even a load of Yankee ships here.'

'That don't mean a thing,' replied Paddy.

'Yes it does,' chimed in Jock. 'Maybe they've done a deal with the Mafia to make old Mussolini surrender!'

'Fuck off, y'mad haggis yaffler,' replied Paddy tightening the rope around a derrick. 'You've been watching too many Humphrey Bogart films.'

Mail finally arrived; I received a solitary letter from Aunt Glad and a bundle of newspapers. Harvey's eyes lit up as he hurriedly grabbed several letters, which judging by his reaction, were from Susan. I couldn't help but feel envious as I watched him tear open each one.

'How's Susan?' I asked trying to sound uninterested.

'OK,' he replied. 'Her and another VAD are gunna go RA (Rationed Ashore) in Gosport. She hopes to have a flat or something by the time we get home,' as an afterthought he added, 'Oh, yes. She sends her best to you.'

Well, I thought opening my mail, at least she hasn't forgotten about me.

Subby Eardsley was right. We remained in Malta long enough to take on more fuel and ammunition. I never even had time to visit Jack Carroll after he was admitted to the Royal Naval Hospital at Bighi.

On 1 June as soon as we were clear of Malta, the captain addressed the crew.

'Here is the news you've all been waiting for,' he said in his usual calm, well-spoken voice. 'We are going to the invasion of Sicily.'

'Sicily!' exclaimed Eddy Gooding. 'That's half way across the bloody Meddy, for Chrissake!'

Along with those off watch I was in the for'd seaman's mess; the atmosphere, warm and clammy, was charged with tension

'Pipe down, Ed,' said Joe Willoughby, 'And listen to the old man.'

'The invasion, called "Operation Husky", will take place on July the tenth; the Americans will land on the western part of the island, and the Allies on the eastern section. Both landings will take place under cover of darkness at two forty-five am; an airborne drop will precede the landings. Our job, along with other 'sweepers will be to clear the pathway for the British thirteenth corps landing on the beaches around a place called

Avola. We will form part of section code-named Bark East, and will arrive two days before and will sweep twenty-four hours a day until D Day. During that time we can expect a hot reception from Jerry and the Italians.'

The first lieutenant then took over.

'Groups of 'sweepers from Milford Haven plus a flotilla of Algerines are ahead of us; by the time we arrive they will have begun sweeping the invasion channels. American 'sweepers will do the same in the western sector. The main convoys coming from as far away as America, North Africa and the UK will consist of over three thousand ships, so it should be some party. I will keep you informed.'

For a few seconds nobody in the mess spoke. Then Jacko slumped down into a chair and muttered, 'Some fuckin' party, I must say!'

Our flotilla arrived off Cape Passero on the evening of the 7 July. Under a full moon the sea glistened like a millpond with hardly a cloud in sight; a thin, yellow line of land barely visible some ten miles away, appeared lifeless.

On our starboard quarter about six cables away, groups of Mickey Mouses were sweeping in tandem; except for the lapping of the sea against the ship's hull, all was quiet. For the moment, our unseen enemy on land appeared oblivious to our presence.

'Where's the battlewagons and carriers, then?' said Jock almost in a whisper. 'We haven't got any air cover.'

'Don't be soft,' replied Paddy helping Jock to lower a paravane into the water. 'You heard what the old man said. The fuckin' invasion isn't for two days.'

'I don't like it,' said Johnny Pue, narrowing his eyes and looking landward. 'They're bound to see the Dan buoys and put two and two together.'

During the night the flotilla carried out Oropesa sweeps, working in pairs; at varying intervals rifle shots rang out followed by the inevitable explosive jets of water silhouetted ghostly white against the dark sea.

'The buggers are bound to know we're here now,' moaned

Joe Steele. 'If it weren't for the moonlight, we wouldn't be able to shoot the mines when they "re cut".'

'Isn't the 'sweeper in front in the most dangerous position, Joe?' I asked.

'It is that, son,' he replied. 'If they miss any loose mines, they could easy hit one of 'em.'

We were on the port side of the bridge. Those not involved in the sweep were closed up at defence stations.

Just as he finished speaking a white beam from a searchlight ashore penetrated the darkness; I caught my breath and watched as it moved in a slow arc illuminating the ships.

'Jesus!' cried someone. 'That's coming from Cape Passero. Now we're for it.'

Much to my relief, the searchlight suddenly went out leaving everyone wondering what had happened.

'Those Eyeties must be thick,' said Joe Steele. 'Surely the soft gets must have twigged on by now. What do they think we're doing out here. Fishin' for haddock?'

'I heard the Italians aren't too keen to go on fighting,' I said. 'In the newspapers I got from home, it said the Jerries didn't trust the Italians to fight anymore.'

'That's as maybe,' quipped Dicky Dickson. 'But wait until it gets daylight. It's not as if we can pull away out of range. The channels have got to be swept almost up to the beach – they won't need a searchlight then.'

Early next morning I felt someone shaking me; I opened my eyes and saw the chubby face of Leading Seaman Ronnie Norris. The time was shortly after five.

'You'd best come to the bridge, Doc,' he said. 'Someone on one of the 'sweepers has had an accident.'

Dawn was just breaking and a warm breeze fanned my face as I followed Ronnie along the deck; the sun, a small orange half disc on the horizon, had turned the calm sea into a carpet of rippling gold.

Except for a dim red light over the small chart table the bridge was in darkness. The duffel-coated figures of the first lieutenant, the captain and lookouts were barely visible.

'Just had a signal from the 46,' said the first lieutenant. 'A man has a serious head wound. The coxswain says it's too bad for him to deal with. We're going alongside, so get your gear and stand by to jump across.'

I quickly returned to the mess, gathered my valise, and after ensuring I had the necessary suture gear, went outside.

Leading Seaman Jack Cornwall and two others placed fenders outboard as the 46 came alongside. Luckily the sea was calm; as soon as I was safely on board, the 50 pulled away.

'This way, Doc,' said a tall officer as I landed on the deck. 'It's Able Seaman MacLeod. He slipped down a ladder and hurt his head.'

The layout of the ship looked the same as the 50. Even the smells and the men in the mess appeared similar. Lying on a side bunk was a man with a large, blood stained field dressing around his head; he had short fair hair with a heavily tanned face. From under thick eyebrows a pair of pale blue eyes sparkled at me.

'Och, it's nowt, Doc,' he said. 'I've 'add worse on Sauchiehall Street on a Sat'day nicht.'

The lights were on and everyone in the mess was awake. The coxswain, a stocky, ruddy-faced man with greying hair stood by the bunk.

Under a blood-soaked dressing was large gash on the left side of his forehead.

'Were you knocked out?' I said applying a fresh dressing over the old one.

'Och aye,' replied the man. 'I saw stars an' all fer a wee bit.'

Remembering my time on the accident ward in RNH Haslar, I asked for the lights to be turned out and examined his pupils. Luckily they reacted normally, an indication that he didn't have any fracture.

'I'll have to put a few stitches in you, Jock,' I said. I then glanced up at the coxswain. 'Maybe you could give him a shot of rum, 'swain.'

'Fuckin' great!' said someone. 'I have this sore foot, Doc. Can I have one as well?'

'Maybe we can all have one,' laughed another rating. 'I can't stand the sight of blood.'

'Piss off, you lot,' was the coxswain's curt reply.

I cleansed my hands with surgical spirit, then, using forceps, dabbed the area with cotton wool and Acraflavine (a reddish antiseptic).

Jock's eyes lit up when he saw the coxswain holding a tumbler full of rum.

He immediately reached out, took a large swig, and muttered, 'Pass it round Doc. If I'm gunna get pissed, so is yon buggers!'

Everyone laughed and accepted a quick swig. Everyone, that is, except me.

Using stitch-holding forceps, a curved needle and dark thread, I carefully inserted eight sutures into the wound. Each time I put one in, Jock would give me a toothy grin.

'Dig out, Doc,' he said at one point. 'Maybe yer can make me look like Tyrone Power!'

When I had finished, the coxswain appeared again with more rum. By the time I cleaned up, everyone, including Jock was merry.

'You can come here more often, mate,' said a huge sailor with a hairy chest and a set to match (a 'set' is a beard and moustache).

'Signal the 50,' I said to the coxswain, 'and tell them I'm going to stay here for the rest of the day. Just to make sure Jock's all right.'

The cook came in carrying a plate of bacon, powdered eggs and a mug of tea. I then sat on a chair close to Jock.

'If yer need anything, just sing out,' said a tall man who introduced himself as Bill Huntley, the killick of the mess.

I must have dozed off because someone shook me holding a mug of Kye. (Kye is hand sliced cocoa mixed with condensed milk, to which hot water is added. If made properly, it is so thick you could stand a spoon in it.)

'We took it in turns keeping an eye on Jock,' said Bill. 'You looked knackered.'

The time was just after twelve in the afternoon.

Jock was still asleep. Just as I stood up to stretch my arms, I heard a terrific explosion some distance away.

Jocks eyes opened. ‘What the fuck was that?’ he said, trying to sit up. ‘Don’t tell me we’re being bombed.’

I went up the hatchway onto the upper deck. A crowd of men had gathered on the ’sweep deck. One or two were pointing to a cloud of black smoke about two hundred yards away.

‘I think it’s the fifty,’ shouted one. ‘The poor bugger’s hit a floater!’

CHAPTER TWELVE

Suddenly, The picture of the 49 with its wreckage and loss of life flashed through my mind; a sense of desperation ran through me like an electric shock and I felt my stomach contract.

'*Christ, no!*' I yelled pushing my way to the guardrail. *'Not the fifty...'*

With my heart beating a cadence in my chest, I stared across at a pall of smoke and dust hanging in the early morning light liked a dark shroud. Thoughts of Harvey, Paddy, Jock and the rest sent a shiver of anxiety running through me. Then I remembered Susan. Sweet Jesus! I muttered to myself. What will I tell her?

I turned and slumped down on a bollard unable to look any longer. Then I heard another voice ring out. 'No, it's not the fifty. It's the 51.'

'Are you sure?' I cried, jumping up.

The rating shouted was a small stocky man with sparse fair hair.

'She was lead ship,' he shouted. 'I saw her pennant number as she went down.'

A wave of relief swept through me making me feel dizzy. I strained my eyes looking across at the swirling morass of oil and wreckage. However, my joy knowing the 50 was safe, was immediately tempered by the sadness of losing another twenty lives. Lieutenant Commander Kennedy's luck had finally run out; our captain, Peter Reid, was now senior officer and 50 would be in the van, (lead ship) when we swept.

Before I rejoined the 50, I told the coxswain how to remove Jock's stitches.

'They'll have to come out in a week,' I said. 'I'll leave you a pair of stitch scissors and forceps. Give him some rum and he won't feel a thing.'

On the evening of 9 July the weather deteriorated. High winds blowing from the northwest whipped up waves. Metallic grey skeins of dark clouds hovered above threatening rain; everyone donned oilskins, lifebelts and wrapped towels around their necks.

As I made my way to the for'd mess, the ship rolled and tossed about as if it had a life of its own. Huge bursts of spray broke over the fo'c'sle; the bows of the ship rose like a steeplechaser at Beeches Brook and rivulets of seawater gurgled along the scuppers as waves smashed hammer blows against the ship's side.

'This'll make it difficult for the landing craft,' said Ron Balshaw who had just come up from the engine room.

'Well now, maybe the landings will be postponed,' replied Paddy spilling half his tea down his oilskin. 'And we can all go home.'

'No chance,' interrupted Jock. 'Three thousand ships haven't come this far to turn back because of a drop of roughers.'

During the night of the 9 July the flotilla completed a final sweep. From my new action stations as ammunition loader, Joe Steele and I watched the dark shapes of Dakotas and Halifax's tow gliders over the island; this was the British sector's airborne assault.

'Better them than me, Doc,' was Joe's dry comment, as we looked skywards.

'Aye,' I replied, straining my eyes. 'It must take some guts to jump in the dark, especially with all their equipment.'

Just then, searchlights picking out the gliders suddenly pierced the darkness. Guns from shore batteries spat yellow, illuminating both sky and aircraft. We learned later many gliders were prematurely cast off from their tows; those lightly built landed in the sea resulting in great loss of life.

The next day the weather abated slightly; the wind dropped, the skies brighten up and the sea became calmer; everyone listened and watched as squadrons of bombers, escorted by Seafires and Martlets, converged on the coastal and inland defences. The dull thud of bombs exploding could easily heard and seen along the coastline as the sky became dotted with yellowish puffs of ack-ack smoke.

'But where the fuck are the big boys and the landing craft?' asked Jacko.

Eddy, Joe, Jock and a few others were on the 'sweep deck.

'Och, they'll be here all right,' said Jock gazing towards the horizon. 'Just you hold your horses.'

How right he was.

After everyone went to action stations shortly after midnight, the coastline became splattered with explosions, as bombs continued to rain down on enemy positions.

At 0200, just as if someone had waved a magic wand, an armada of ships appeared on the horizon.

'Christ Almighty!' exclaimed Dicky Dickson. 'I've never seen so many ships in me life.'

Even though it was still dark, the silhouettes of the armada could be seen clearly against the pale horizon.

'Look at 'em!' cried Joe Steele. 'There's civvy liners, battleships and bloody aircraft carriers. Old Winston certainly means business, don't he?'

Out of the dimness, lines of landing craft emerged, their foamy bow waves resembling a mass of white horses charging towards the shore.

'We are to take station ahead of the landing craft and lead them in,' came the captain's voice over the Tannoy. 'All gunners keep a close watch. Fire at anything you see as we approach the beach.'

'That means us, Doc, me old son,' grinned Joe, cocking the Lewis. 'Keep a level head and you might win a VC!'

I nervously opened the ammunition locker and lifted out a pan. 'Aye,' I replied, feeling my mouth go dry. 'Posthumously more's the like.'

I needn't have worried. As our flotilla led the way towards the beach, high explosive rockets, fired from behind the landing craft by LCTs (R) (Landing Craft Tank, Rockets), illuminated the night. I instinctively ducked as they streaked across the sky bursting in a ripple of orange explosions along the coast. This, Joe told me later, was called a creeping barrage, and was designed to support the assault troops.

Gun-flashes, explosions and smoke engulfed the beach; we were close enough to see masses of troops pour out of the landing craft and head inland; ahead of them detonations from the naval bombardment flashed over the landscape; added to the clamour was the rattle of gunfire as Seafires and Martlets from the carriers strafed and bombed enemy positions.

Suddenly, our ship veered away to port allowing more landing craft to proceed; as we did so I once again ducked as the *whoosh* of shells from the battleships whined overhead like the sound of express trains. The cacophony was deafening and also re-assuring; surely, I thought, nothing could survive this onslaught.

As dawn broke I recognised *The Reno del Pacifico,* and watched landing craft of all descriptions being lowered from her decks into the sea. I also saw the liners *Winchester Castle* and *Monarch of Bermuda,* both of which I had seen at various times in Liverpool. As well as destroyers, minesweepers and corvettes, there were battleships and aircraft carriers; I even saw two submarines that I suspected had been in the area long before anyone else.

The beach was crowded with landing craft of all types off-loading tanks, artillery and infantry; all opposition appeared to be overcome and troops were pushing inland.

'The army have taken the port of Syracuse,' echoed the first lieutenant's voice over the Tannoy. 'Our flotilla plus the *Seaham* have been ordered to sweep the channel and harbour to enable ships to enter. Hands will remain at defence stations. Grab a bite to eat whenever you can. It's going to be a long day.'

The early morning sun was high in the sky and the calm sea shrouded in a heat haze.

'Just be our luck to meet a bloody U-Boat,' I remarked ruefully.

'Maybe that why the *Seaham* is coming with us,' replied Joe, passing me a cigarette and lighting one. 'She's an anti-submarine 'sweeper and carries a couple of four point five guns.'

Syracuse, I was told by Dicky Dickson, who was standing close by, was about twenty miles away up north. *Seaham,* was now senior ship and led the way with the 50 and the other three close behind; with the invasion fleet roughly ten miles on our starboard beam, we kept a safe distance from the coastline.

I decided to go to the mess for a corn beef sandwich and a mug of tea.

'I won't be long, Joe,' I said. 'I'll bring you a sarnie and a wet when I come back.'

I had just entered the mess when a cry from the Tannoy startled me.

'Unidentified submarine surfaced dead ahead! Hands to Action Stations! Stand by to open fire!'

When I arrived on the bridge I saw the grey, cigar-shape of a submarine no fewer than two hundred yards away. Water was pouring from its conning tower and vents as a group of sailors clad in blue overalls manned the gun on her fo'c'sle.

'Stand by, Doc!' cried Joe, letting off a few bursts from the Lewis, 'The buggers carry a three point nine inch gun, and the sod's bloody powerful.'

At that moment the other three 'sweepers and *Seaham* began firing. Tall plumes of water exploded all around the submarine. Some of *Seaham's* 4.5 shells straddled the vessel and for a few seconds it was covered in clouds of spray. When this settled, several Italian sailors lay on the fo'c'sle. One or two of their comrades attempted to drag them inboard. Just then, someone appeared on the conning tower frantically waving a white sheet.

'Well I'll be buggered!' I heard Joe exclaim. 'We've captured our first sub.'

'Don't speak too soon,' said the captain ruefully. '*Seaham* is sending over a boarding party. I'll think she'll claim it for her own.'

We watched enviously as *Seaham* took the submarine in tow.

The captain then turned to the first lieutenant. 'Make to *Seaham*,' he said. '"Well done. I hope you regular navy chaps don't find the vino too strong!"'

The reply from *Seaham* came back, "Thanks for your help. Will save a few bottles for you!"

We later learned the submarine was an Italian called the *Bonzo*. Her captain and five of her crew had been killed, but remembering what had happened to the 51, nobody had much sympathy with them.

On 10 July the captain told us the port of Syracuse had been captured; however, resistance in the outskirts of the city was still heavy.

We swept all day and night. From my position on the starboard wing of the bridge, Joe Steele and I watched as troops from landing craft surged ashore and pushed inland. Gunfire from batteries inland sent fountains of water around the cluster of ships lying about five miles off the coast. Suddenly one ship burst into an inferno of smoke and flames; we later learned this was the hospital ship *Talamba* which was sunk with considerable loss of life.

As the flotilla approached the port the captain gave us another pep talk.

'From where we are, you can no doubt see the city has a large port with several docks. However, the harbour may be mined and it the job of the flotilla to clear them away.'

Just as he finished two enemy fighters attacked us. They came at us from out of the sun low and swift, spitting flame.

'*They're ME 109's!*' yelled Joe, cocking and aiming the Lewis. 'And they're coming in low. Stand by with more ammo, Doc.'

With trembling hands I took out a round of ammunition and waited as Joe opened fire.

The rattle of gunfire from the ship's armament joined in the cacophony; in an instant the sky was pockmarked with black explosions as the guns of the flotilla joined in. The noise was mind-bending. Tracer bullets like billiard balls, red, green orange and white burst into life. I stared transfixed with fright as the aircraft swooped over the ship firing as they did so; in a flash they zoomed away, leaving a line of small splashes close by the ship.

'That was too close for comfort,' said Joe, sweat pouring from his face while resting his arms over the gun.

I didn't reply. All I wanted to do was make a dash for the

nearest heads.

For the next two days the flotilla conducted Oropessa sweeps. We sunk several mines thus enabling warships and liners full of troops, including *Seaham* towing *Bonzo,* to enter the harbour and berth alongside the wharfs.

Two days later it also allowed us our first run ashore for weeks.

'A packet of fags!' exclaimed Harvey. 'Don't talk soft.'

We were in the mess putting on our number one uniforms; for the first time in weeks men pulled on their tight-fitting blue serge suits over white fronts. The atmosphere was charged with excitement and the air crackled with animated conversation.

'Bugger me!' cried Perky Perratt, pulling his top over his bulging stomach. 'I must 'ave put on a bit o' weight. This fuckin' thing used to fit me.'

'Can't think 'ow that's 'appened,' replied Eddy Gooding. 'The scran you've been givin' us wouldn't put meat on a donkey!'

With the exception of the coxswain, buffer and chief engineer, I was the only one wearing fore-and-aft rig, (a double breasted blue doeskin jacket and trousers, white shirt and black tie). The bellbottomed uniform worn by sailors was termed 'square rig'.

'I tell yer it's true, boyo,' said Taffy Jackson, studying himself in the shiny surface of a tickler tin, (tobacco tin). 'We won't need the lira we've been given. The women do a turn for a few fags. I heard it from the QM on the 48. He got it from a pongo on one of the liners.' He paused and turned his head from side to side, then continued, 'I don't know about youse lot, boyo, but I'm gunna take a few packets of Woodbines with me.'

'I heard they drop 'em for a bar of soap,' added Eddy, combing his hair. 'So take a few bars of Pusser's hard as well.'

Unlike the regular navy, the 'Squirrels', didn't fall in to be inspected before leaving the ship. Nevertheless everyone considered it important to look smart; after all, this could be the last run ashore for some time and we had to impress the ladies.

Syracuse is a port dating back to the thirteenth century BC.

According to Jock Duthie the Chief Engineer, Archimedes was born here in 227BC.

The harbour is crescent shaped with the town, a sprawling mass of buildings topped off with church spires, rising steeply from outside the dockyard wall. An ammunition ship had blown up at anchor few days previously and layers of black dust covered windows and the narrow, cobbled-stoned streets.

'Don't these buggers know there's a war on,' said Paddy. 'All the fuckin' lights in the town are on.'

It did seem odd, but the first lieutenant had told us the Sicilians weren't too keen on pursuing the war.

The first place we entered was so crowded with service personnel and girls; we couldn't see the bar.

'Bloody hell,' snorted Harvey, 'If they're all like this we'll never get a wet.'

'Ta'hell with the beer!' cried Jock. 'It's one o' them wee lassies I want'

'Shame on you, Jock,' I said. 'And you a married man.'

'They are the worst,' added Harvey, with a gleam in his eye.

And so it proved; the second bar we visited was not quite so busy. As soon as we entered we were surrounded by a bevy of females. A few were fat and frumpy but most were slim with typical dark, Latin looks. In one corner a few raven-haired beauties sat on soldiers' laps while sharing a bottle of red wine. A blue haze of tobacco smoke hovered in the air and, from a cracked record, the voice of an Italian tenor was almost inaudible over the sound of ribald laughter.

'This'll do me,' cried Paddy. Placing his ram around the waist of a young-looking bottle blonde, he added, 'ask 'em if they've got any good Irish whiskey.'

I disentangled myself from the arms of a very pretty brunette and pushed my way forward.

Behind the bar stood a fat, unshaven man with a bald head. A dirty grey apron was tied around his waist and his hands were filthy.

'Very good vino,' he said, giving me a toothless grin. His English was surprisingly good.

'Everything cheap for the Englisie. You 'ave cigarettes, yes?'

I flashed a packet of Senior Service, quickly replacing them in my pocket. His dark eyes immediately lit up like beacons in the night.

'Any whiskey?'

'No whiskey,' he replied with a pleading expression. 'You give me cigarettes, vino is all yours, yes?'

'Don't give him the packet,' interrupted a soldier. He had one arm around a fat woman's waist and a hand between her legs. 'Five 'll get you a couple of bottles. And that's not all mate, believe you me.'

I took his advice and slipped five cigarettes across the counter. With a scowl, baldy passed me a bottle of wine.

By the time I joined the others, each had their arms around a girl. Paddy's hand was squeezing the plump backside of a slim girl in a blue and white polka dotted dress; Taffy was staring up into the eyes of a peroxide blonde; Jock had one arm around a tall girl with uneven, yellow teeth while Harvey stared lustfully down the low cut blouse of a girl with red hair.

With uncouth eagerness each girl accepted a cigarette, placed it in a handbag and smiled benignly at us.

'You give another cigarette, big boy,' she said to me. 'I give you, this.' From the top of her dress she slowly removed a firm, milk white breast with a large cheery-pink nipple.

Needless to say this attracted all our attention.

Taffy eyes nearly popped out of his head. *'Whoopee!'* he cried, and made a quick grab. But he was too late.

With a shrieking laugh, the woman popped the breast back into her dress.

'Cente cigarettes,' she said coyly, 'then…'

Taff shot a lecherous glance at us and hurriedly gave her ten Woodbines. The woman immediately grabbed hold of Taffy's arm, and with the rest of us yelling obscenities, hauled him out of the bar.

After some quaint bargaining with their partners, Paddy, Harvey and Jock also left with their girls.

'See you domani, Doc!' shouted Jock as they made for the door.

'Hope you catch the boat up!' shouted someone.

'Be Jebbus, so what!' cried Paddy. 'We might be brown bread (slang, meaning "dead") tomorrow.'

After they left I noticed a young woman in a corner sitting next to a group of giggling girls.

She had long dark brown hair framed around her well-formed features; her high cheekbones and large, luminous eyes exaggerated her milk white complexion; she wore a yellow skirt and black blouse and around her neck hung a silver cross that dangled provocatively between her cleavage.

Her legs, half hidden by a table, were bare and on her feet was a pair of black leather sandals.

A drunken soldier was attempting to talk to her, but her angry reaction told me she wasn't interested.

Instead she took out a compact, flicked it open and with a bored expression powdered her nose.

She was strikingly beautiful and I couldn't help but wonder what desperate situation had forced such a woman to sell herself.

Taking a gulp of 'Dutch courage' I decided to find out.

I pushed through the crowd and stood looking down at her.

'Er…cigatetta?' I asked offering her an open packet of Players.

She looked up at me; her green eyes stared directly into mine and for a moment I thought she would refuse; to my surprise she smiled, replaced her compact and accepted a cigarette.

'Gratzi,' she said. As she did so, I noticed her fingernails were painted red and she wore a gold wedding ring.

'Vino?' I said, making a drinking gesture.

'Si,' she replied, 'per favour.'

I hurried to the bar and returned with a bottle of wine.

'Do you speak any English?' I ventured, handing her a half a glass of wine.

'A leetle,' she said, before taking a large sip.

She smiled at me and then finished the remains of the glass.

'Vino, per favore,' she said handing me her empty glass.

'You. More cigarettes. Si?' she said as I filled her glass.

'Yes… I mean, si,' I replied.

'Bene,' she replied.

She then drank her wine, smiled again, and said, 'We go, pronto.'

When she stood up her head came just above my shoulders. She took my hand and we walked to the door.

'Hope you've got plenty of fags, Doc,' yelled Eddy Gooding. 'That one looks as if she smokes cigars.'

'She can smoke me anytime!' sniggered Ron Balshaw, his arms fathoms around a tiny brunette.

Her flat was a few minutes walk away. It was sparsely furnished with a well-worn carpet, a sagging sofa, a table, two chairs and a small kitchenette; a shaded gaslight bathed the room in a pale yellow glow, and on a cluttered sideboard was a framed photograph of a man in uniform. From an open door I saw an unmade double bed; another door led into what I assumed to a bathroom.

'Your husband?' I said, pointing to the photograph.

Her eyes immediately softened and for a moment I thought she would cry. She picked up the photograph, held it to her chest and muttered, 'Si, mi marito, er…'usband. Hees name, Carlos.' With her hand she made an aeroplane gesture downwards. 'Carlos morto – caput.'

She was telling me her husband was a pilot and had crashed.

She then bent down and with a match, lit a small gas fire and stood up.

'Mio Gina,' she said pointing to herself, then, looking at me, added, 'you?'

'My name is Ted,' I replied. 'Englisie navy.'

'Ted,' she repeated. 'Englisie barka, er…sheep?'

'Si,' I replied.

She put her handbag on the table, and smiling, said, 'Cigarettas, per favore.'

'Oh yes,' I replied, and handed her a packet of twenty Players.

'Gratzi,' she said.

I watched as she walked across the room, knelt down and opened a cupboard drawer and placed the cigarettes inside. As she did so, I noticed the outline of her buttocks through the thin material of her dress. My God! I thought feeling a stirring in between my legs; she certainly is gorgeous.

Just then I heard the cry of a baby coming from the bedroom. The sound startled me and I felt my excitement subside.

'Oh,' said Gina, placing a hand over her mouth. 'Mi bambino, scusi,' and hurried into the bedroom. A few minutes later she returned carrying a small baby wrapped in a white woollen shawl. With loving care Gina showed me a chubby child with black curly hair and eyes like her mother. The tender expression in her eyes suddenly made me realise why she was sat in that bar. Loneliness, pain, poverty and war make strange bedfellows of us all.

'Mio bomba,' she said, kissing the baby on the forehead. ''Ees Carlos.'

Using one hand Gina unbuttoned her blouse. She then plucked out a breast from a black brassier and placed a dark red nipple into the baby's mouth. I watched as the child began to suck furiously. It seemed a natural thing for Gina to do, but made me feel embarrassed. I quickly looked away. Gina seemed to sense this, smiled, and walked back into the bedroom. I looked into the room and saw her place the baby in a cot, kiss its forehead and tuck it in.

Shortly afterwards she came back, into the room. With tantalisingly slowness she had removed her sweater and skirt and stood in a pair of black French knickers and bra. For a few seconds she stood, the pale light playing shadows on her porcelain white skin.

'Andiamo a letto,' she said with a smile. 'We go letto – to bed, yes?'

I felt my mouth go dry and didn't answer. Seeing the baby had somewhat dampened my ardour. However she led me into the bedroom and sat me on the bed; the soft touch of her fingers undoing my flies soon changed all that.

I woke up around five in the morning. Gina was lying on

her back, strands of hair strewn over her face. One arm lay across her naked breasts and she was quietly snoring. In a corner the baby made odd gurgling sounds but wasn't awake. I quickly dressed and placed my remaining two packets of Players plus a handful of lira in the baby's cot. Then, with a final glance at Gina, crept out.

Our next task was to sweep the approaches of Augusta. Unlike Syracuse, the Italians put up a considerable shore barrage; Savios, (Italian fighter bombers), Heinkels and ME 109's attacked the fleet, but were repulsed by RAF Spitfires from Malta.

'I thought the skipper said these buggers weren't too keen on fighting,' cried Joe Steele, letting off a stream of shells at an Italian fighter.

'This fuckin' place is a big Eyetie naval base,' shouted Dicky Dickson. 'That's why they're not too keen to surrender.'

I was at my action station nervously clutching a pan of ammunition ready to fit into the Lewis gun; whistling overhead, the shells from the monitor *Erebus* joined in the deafening noise of gunfire from the cruisers and destroyers. The dark shapes of fighters from the carriers swooped inland; slowly, a pall of black smoke settled over the port.

Close to our ship, plumes of water shot up as we cut adrift and exploded several mines. Shortly after 1000, on 13 July, the first lieutenant announced all resistance ceased and Augusta was in Allied hands.

'However,' he went on, 'I'm afraid there will be no shore leave. The Eighth Army is advancing along the coast. We have been ordered to sweep a channel so that units of Number 3 Commando can land at a place called Punta Murazzo, eight miles south of Catania.' The officer paused, cleared his throat then added, 'We can expect a warm welcome.'

'A welcome, he says!' moaned Joe Steele. 'What the fuck does he think we've been getting so far?'

A group of the crew and myself were on the 'sweep deck having a smoke; the blueness of the sky was blinding and the calm sea the colour of a peacock's wing. Beyond the sandy coastline the undulating plains of Catania stretched away like a lush, green carpet and in the distance, the majestic site of Mount Etna smouldering away reminded us that it wasn't just the enemy we should fear.

'Just think,' sighed Harvey. 'In peacetime Toffs used to sail past here in luxury liners sipping champagne.'

Seconds later 'Up Spirits' was piped.

'Bollocks!' came Paddy's curt reply. 'Give me my tot anytime.'

'I don't know about you lot,' said Harvey, flicking a dog end into the sea. 'But I'd settle for a few letters from home.'

Nobody disagreed, as we hadn't had mail since we left Malta.

Around 1900 we successfully completed our sweep. Using binoculars I watched the ramps of the landing craft disgorge the green bereted commandos; there appeared to be little opposition and they dug in on the beach. Spitfires provided cover, swooping along, firing at anything that moved; once again shells from the monitors and warships screeched overhead, sending up mountains of debris, flames and smoke from the shore.

But despite constant bombardment from the fleet, Catania was to prove difficult for the Allies to capture.

Once again, the captain brought us up to date.

'Monty's men are meeting stiff resistance,' he said. 'According to a signal I've received, the Germans have re-enforced their lines with paratroops, Panzer Grenadiers and the so-called elite Hermann Goering Division; all we can do is keep the channels clear while the fleet support the army by shelling the enemy from the sea. Meanwhile, General Patton's forces are fighting their way to Palermo.'

This news was greeted with general dismay.

'No soddin' runs ashore!' growled Eddy Gooding.

'No soddin' mail!' added Johnny Pue

'And no soddin' fanny!' moaned Ron Balshaw

Even though Catania was till in enemy hands, the flotilla was ordered to conduct a magnetic sweep as close to the harbour as possible. Harvey asked me to give him a hand to unwind the cable on the sweep drum.

'It'll give you something to do until tot time,' he said with a grin.

The three minesweepers formed up line abreast. Harvey and I stood on the port side of the sweep deck by the drum.

'It's important the three ships co-ordinate their electric pulses for the sweep to be effective,' said Harvey. 'When the cables are out those lights you see on the stern will flash to show the polarity of each pulse. As we are the senior ship the others will follow suit'

'How long are the cables, Harv,' I said, leaning against the drum handle.

'There are two of them,' replied Harvey. 'A short which one hundred and twenty five yards is attached to one that's five hundred odd yards in length. A fifty-foot electrode is at the end of the long cable. That's the one that sets the buggers off.'

'What's the short cable for?'

'To cancel out any magnetic fields caused by the ships itself,' answered Harvey. He then continued. 'In a minute you'll hear the throb of the generator, and Subby Eardsley will give the order to begin unwinding. The cables will be hauled through the fairleads and trailed behind and Bob's yer uncle.'

However, what happened next passed so quickly I hardly had time to breath.

'Unidentified aircraft approaching on the port beam!' yelled a voice from the Tannoy.

I was about to turn and look away to my left when Harvey dragged me down behind the drum. At the same time I heard the sound of the aircraft accompanied by sharp bursts of machine gun fire; suddenly, I felt the deck vibrating. This was followed by the staccato of splintery explosions. When the noise of the aircraft engine died away I suddenly became aware of Harvey's weight on top of me.

'Christ Almighty!' gasped as Harvey rolled off me. 'That was fuckin' close.'

For an instant I was too dazed to reply. Harvey helped me up. I shook my head and looked around; those on the sweep deck had scattered and were slowly emerging from the starboard side of the ship. Nobody appeared to be hurt.

'Jesus, Harvey!' I said accepting a cigarette. 'What happened?'

'An ME 109,' he replied. 'The sod must have come from an airfield ashore.'

Subby Eardsley checked the cable and found it undamaged. He reported this to the captain then ordered the sweep to proceed.

I took my position alongside Harvey and we both grasped the handle. That was when I noticed a line of machine gun bullet holes in the side of the drum, exactly where we had been standing when the fighter attacked us. The sudden realisation that Harvey had probably saved my life brought me out in a cold sweat.

'Looks like I owe you, Harv,' I said, nervously licking my lips.

Harvey gave a short laugh. 'Sippers will do, mate,' he said. 'And a pint when we get ashore.'

However, we both knew it was a defining moment in our friendship.

Monty's Eighth Army finally captured Catania on 5 August, and the first lieutenant told the crew Mussolini has been arrested and imprisoned.

'King Victor Emmanuel has now assumed command of the Italian forces,' said the officer, 'and Marshal Badaglio is now Prime Minister.'

'Thank fuck for that,' cried Harvey, 'maybe now we'll get some mail.'

And we did.

When the flotilla went alongside a wharf in Catania three sacks were delivered on board.

I noticed Harvey retreat into a corner of the mess clutching a small bundle of letters. For a while he sat quietly and read them; he then looked across at me, and said, 'Susan sends her best. She says her and a mate have finally got a flat in Gosport as Haslar is overcrowded.'

'Great,' I replied weakly. 'If we get to Pompey we can make up a foursome.'

I couldn't help but envy him; the only letters I received

were from Aunt Agnes telling me she had won at bingo, and two from Iris. In the first letter she wrote, 'As you can see I've joined the ATS. There are lots of Americans near where I am stationed, but I don't bother with them'. Not bloody much, I laughed and opened the other one. 'Thought I'd best tell you', she wrote, 'I've met a lovely American sergeant and we've become engaged!'

So much for Iris I thought and tore both letters up.

The headlines in the newspapers told us the Russians had defeated the Germans at Kursk in the biggest tank battle of the war so far. Also, Hamburg had been almost 'wiped off the map', by Allied bombing.

'Fuckin; good job too,' said Eddy Gooding. 'That'll serve the bastards right for what they did to Coventry.'

The harbour in Catania quickly filled up with ships of all descriptions; troops poured ashore from transports and warships, including ourselves took on fuel. When we went ashore crowds of children, dressed in rags and begging for food beleaguered us.

'Poor buggers,' said Harvey, as we handed them a few bars of chocolate. 'They look half starved. The sooner this bloody war's over, the better.'

Needless to say as in Augusta, anything could be obtained ashore for the price of a bar of soap. Everyone, I'm ashamed to say, including myself, took advantage of this.

In between runs ashore the flotilla plus some American minesweepers were kept busy doing magnetic sweeps northwards towards Messina.

One evening we were sat in the mess playing uckers. Ron Balshaw and Eddy Gooding were writing letters and Joe Steele lay on his bunk reading an old copy of *The Daily Mirror.*

'The sooner we cross the Straits to Italy,' said Harvey. 'The sooner we'll meet some of those dark eyed Italian beauties.'

'Can't you think of anything else but fanny,' said Ron Balshaw, glancing up from writing. 'And you a recently married man as well.'

'All fair in love and war,' replied Harvey, rolling a six. 'What the eyes don't see, the heart doesn't grieve.'

I said nothing, but was inwardly seething; how could he

behave like that with a girl like Susan waiting for him back home.

'What say you, Ted?' asked Harvey, nudging me with his elbow. 'You got your fare share in Augusta. Didn't you?'

'Yeah,' was my non-committal reply, 'I suppose I did.'

On 16 August the Americans entered Messina followed by elements of 40 Commando. The city had been shelled continually from enemy batteries on the Italian mainland. Harvey and I managed a quick run ashore. We needn't have bothered. The city was a complete ruin. Bomb craters had taken the place of streets and buildings. What people we saw, looked pale, haggard and half starved.

'No fanny here for you, Harv,' I said as we gave what cigarettes we had to an old lady.

'No booze either by the looks of things,' he replied.

In company with a flotilla of Algerine 'sweepers we began clearing channel in preparation for the Allies to cross the Straits of Messina.

Just after daylight on 1 September the two flotillas were in the middle of a magnetic sweep; Harvey and I were on the sweep deck standing by the handle; the whine of the generator feeding power to the cables echoed overhead. Suddenly, we heard the sound of enemy shells coming from the Italian coast; they screamed overhead making the deck vibrate. Mountains of water rose all around, rocking the ship and half lifting the cables out of the water.

'Bastards have got us in their sights!' yelled Harvey, 'You'd better take cover, Ted.'

At that moment, a great explosion sent a blast across the ship. I looked to starboard and saw a pall of smoke coming from one of the Algerine 'sweepers. This was quickly followed by another explosion as the ship disintegrated before my eyes. Her bow reared in the air like a wounded animal, and in a mass of oily bubbles, disappeared into the sea.

'Jesus!' gasped Harvey. 'That was the *Sentinel.* Nutty Slack, an old oppo of mine was on board her. The poor buggers never stood a chance.'

Nobody said anything. My mouth felt as dry as a bone as another salvo roared overhead; I instinctively ducked wondering if we would be next. However, after a few more salvos the barrage lifted. Once again I made a dash to the nearest heads!

On the morning of 3 September we watched an armada of landing craft cross into mainland Italy. High above, squadrons of fighters formed a protective umbrella, while a constant bombardment from cruisers and destroyers ensured the troops arrived unopposed.

The next day, having swept the harbour, our flotilla of three plus a squadron of Algerines, entered Reggio, a large port on the toe of Italy.

'Not much chance o' a run ashore here either,' muttered Jock, as he secured a heaving-line around a derrick. 'It looks as if the whole of the bloody Eighth Army's is being landed. They'll drink the bloody place dry!'

Jock was right. During the next forty-eight hours every piece of military impedimenta was unloaded from cargos ships onto the wharf. The only run ashore we had was a quick visit to a NAAFI canteen which arrived on the wharf – and all they served was tea.

On 5 September, after taking on oil and provisions, the flotilla put to sea.

Once outside the harbour, once again the captain addressed the crew over the Tannoy.

'The First Lieutenant and myself attended a meeting while we were in Reggio. The Americans and our troops are going to land at a place called Salerno; this is a town on the west coast of Italy. The object of the landing is to enable Naples to be taken quickly. The area is heavily guarded so we can expect a hot reception.'

The first lieutenant then took over.

'The invasion will consist of two attack forces, north and south; along with the Americans and Algerines, our job will be to sweep channels in the northern area. This will enable units of American Rangers, British commandos and two infantry divisions to land and capture the town of Salerno. The Americans will land in the southern region; hopefully both will meet up. We will be doing magnetic sweeps at night; the operation is called *Avalanche* and will coincide with landings at Taranto codenamed *Slapstick.* That is all.'

'Slapstick! Avalanche!' exclaimed Paddy. 'Be Jebbus! I wonder who the hell thinks up these stupid names. Sounds like we're all going to a Laurel and Hardy film.'

'I notice he didn't mention any destroyer support for us,' said Harvey. 'Maybe he thinks we'll be fuckin' invisible.'

'Och away we yee!' cried Jock slapping Paddy on the back. 'Providing the Jerries didn't go to night school maybe we will be.'

'Crazy haggis yaffler!' muttered Paddy.

'Watch it you soddin' bogtrotter!' answered Jock, glaring at his oppo.

'Save it you two,' interrupted Eddy. 'Tot's up in five minutes.'

Night sweeps were, by their very nature, hazardous.

I took my position on the starboard wing of the bridge; listening to the captain's orders it was obvious that keeping abreast of the other two 'sweepers was difficult. Luckily, the full moon helped this; it also helped the enemy spotters.

'This damn moonlight is devil disguised as an angel, Number One,' I overheard the captain say. 'Not only will it make us sitting ducks, but it'll do away with any element of surprise.'

We were about ten miles off the coast and could see the lights of Salerno twinkling in the distance. Every so often a burst of flame followed by a thudding detonation belched forth from batteries positioned above the town

'The buggers are at it again!' shouted Joe Steele as a deluge erupted close by the ship.

After each explosion I waited, praying silently and hoping we would survive the night.

Thankfully, my prayers were answered. When dawn broke our three Mickey Mouses remained intact. Unfortunately, an American 'sweeper and two Algerines were damaged and had to return to Reggio.

Just before dawn on 9 September the horizon was black with ships roughly five miles off shore. The news telling us German paratroopers had rescued Mussolini didn't serve to cheer us up.

'I suppose the fat bastard will get the Eyetie's to fight again,' muttered Joe Steele, polishing the barrel of his Lewis gun.

'I doubt it, Joe,' said the first lieutenant. 'The buzz is they've had enough.'

After marking the channels with Dan buoys our flotilla sheered away. As we closed in on the fleet, I saw soldiers clamber from transports down nets into landing craft. Red tail-lights on each one shone like glow-worms enabling each vessel to keep station. Behind them, sending up foamy bow waves, came more craft and amphibious trucks (DUKWS), carrying tanks, guns and artillery.

All at once, the sound of enemy shore batteries rent the air; lines of gun flashes sparkled from above the town; splashes soon dotted the sea around the landing craft and those in the rear. Allied warships immediately replied with a steady bombardment; rockets' fire and a blaze of fire from artillery turned a grey dawn into bright daylight.

As the dawn broke the coastline was obscured by smoke. All at once the sound of German fighters could be heard overhead. Diving vertically through a maelstrom of ack-ack, the unmistakable banshee whine of the Stukas echoed eerily in the air. Aircraft from the carriers tried desperately to intercept them; unfortunately they failed to stop the enemy pressing home their attack. The sky was pockmarked with hundreds of black explosions and the sea littered with splashes of debris, exploding bombs and flotsam from damaged ships.

'Look!' cried Joe Willoughby, one of the lookouts, 'The bastards are attacking the heavy ships.'

Even as he spoke, an explosion a mile or so away filled the air; we later learned the cruiser HMS *Uganda* and the battleship USS *Philadelphia* plus a hospital ship had been bombed.

'Full ahead!' ordered the captain. 'Stand by to rescue survivors.'

With the decks vibrating, we crashed through the sea at twelve knots; however, by the time we arrived, destroyers and lifeboats had picked up those who were in the water.

Later that same day, the first lieutenant who had kept us well informed of proceedings, informed the crew Mussolini had finally been deposed. With more than a hint of satisfaction, he added, 'The Italian fleet has also been interned in Malta.'

'Humf,' was Harvey's curt comment. 'Those Eyetie sailors will be getting their end away down the Gut, while we're stuck here. There's no fuckin' justice in this world.'

The fighting ashore raged on; the 5-inch guns of the battleships *Valiant* and *Warspite,* along with those of the British cruisers *Aurora* and *Penelope,* joined these. Attacks from the Lufwaffe and the barrage from German guns meant the fleet was under constant attack. The *Warspite* was bombed but remained afloat, but the American battleship USS *Savannah* was sunk with the loss of 200 officers and men.

During the first three days of the invasion, four transports, one heavy cruiser and seven landing craft were sunk.

'We have been told to stand by,' came the captain's voice over the Tannoy. 'According to the signal circulated around the fleet, the Americans and British forces ashore have failed to meet up and fighting is intense. We may have to go inshore to take off personnel.'

Joe and I were closed up on the Lewis. 'Bloody hell!' exploded Joe. 'I don't fancy that.' He then turned and yelled towards the captain and first lieutenant. 'What the fuck's goin' on?'

'Not sure,' said the captain. 'Just keep your eyes peeled for those ME 109's.'

During the next week we watched as formations of American B-25s, B-26s and B-17s blackened the area with bombs.

'Fuck me!' cried Dicky Dickson, 'surely nothin' could survive that lot.'

But it wasn't until 20 September that we were informed both forces had finally met up and were able to move inland. Much later we learned that the Allies had sustained more than

12,000 casualties. Of these, 2,000 were killed, 7,000 wounded and 3,500 missing.

On 1 October British troops entered Naples.

By then our small flotilla was on our way home.

CHAPTER THIRTEEN

The flotilla arrived back at Reggio on 28 September; the sky was overcast and the sea choppy. As we sailed into harbour I was on the ’sweep deck looking at a couple of young girls on the quayside. One had a tight-fitting black skirt and yellow sweater the other wore a pale blue dress. Both smiled and waved.

‘Give ’em a wave back, lads,’ said Jacko to Eddy Gooding and a few others who was busy securing hawsers around derricks. ‘You never know, we might be on there.’

Eddy grinned and waved his arms wildly in the air. The girl in pale blue lifted up her dress and revealed a length of shapely leg. Her friend blew a kiss, jumped up and down and waved. This immediately provoked a chorus of wolf whistles and catcalls from the crews on all three ships.

‘I hope we’re here long enough to sample some of that,’ said Harvey with a sigh.

‘Don’t you ever think about anything else, Harv?’ I asked.

‘Animal instincts, Ted,’ laughed Harvey. ‘One day you’ll understand.’

That night Harvey, Paddy, Jock and myself went ashore; Harvey was right; his ‘animal instincts’ did take over. I didn’t see him or the others until they crept on board the next morning. I was tempted to do the same; however, I got too drunk, vomited and staggered back on board.

The following morning during breakfast the captain’s voice came over the Tannoy.

‘I have some good news for you,’ he said in his usual calm, plumy voice. ‘The flotilla has been ordered home!’

Straight away, as if hypnotised, everyone in the mess stopped eating.

‘*Did yer ’ear that, lads?’* yelled Jacko, dropping half his meal down his overalls. *‘We’re going home!’*

'Shut up for fuck's sake,' said Harvey, holding his mug in the air. 'And let's hear what the skipper has to say.'

The captain carried on speaking. 'The flotilla will take on oil and provisions today and sail in company with the destroyer, *Brocklesby* for Gibraltar tomorrow. I'm afraid all leave is cancelled for security reasons.'

'*Fantastic!*' cried Harvey, throwing his arms around me. 'Wait till I write and tell Susan.'

'I shouldn't bother, mate,' said Paddy. 'It'll only be censored.'

At 0900 the next day, the three Mickey Mouses put to sea. The *Brocklesby,* her zig-zag camouflage shining in the morning sun, lay outside the harbour waiting for us; as we slowly pulled away, the two girls we saw when we arrived appeared on the quayside.

'*Arreverderci, Lolo!*' yelled Harvey waving frantically.

'*Cheerio Maria!*' shouted Jacko, blowing them a kiss.

This time both of them flashed their legs, blew kisses and waved. The rest of the crew whistled while performing a few obscene arm-bending gestures.

Later on I met the coxswain in passageway. 'When d'you suppose we'll get to Gib, Jack?' I asked.

His rubicund features broke into a wide grin. He took out his old meerschaum pipe, lit it and puffed a cloud of tobacco into the air. 'About five days,' he replied. 'Then, after re-fuelling and a rabbit run, it'll take about six days to reach UK.'

(A 'rabbit run', was naval slang for going ashore to buy presents.)

'Jesus,' I sighed. 'We've only been out here five months, but it seems like years.'

'Aye,' replied Jack, re-placing his pipe in his mouth. 'I know what you mean.'

We had been at sea for three days when Harvey stopped me outside the galley. I had been helping Perky Perratt, to cut up a few pieces of meat. The white apron I wore was splashed with blood and in one hand I held a large carving knife.

'I see your keeping your hand in Doc,' joked Nobby Clark,

the wardroom steward, as he hurried passed the galley.

Harvey shot a quick glance up and down the small corridor. Then, out of earshot of Perky, he whispered, 'Could I have a private word with you, Ted?'

Privacy was at a premium on board a small ship. However, after removing my apron, we managed to find a spot on the starboard side under the bridge.

Harvey's anxious expression told me something was bothering him.

'What's the problem then, Harv?' I asked as we leaned on the guardrail.

'I think I've caught a dose!' he said, avoiding my eyes.

His voice was almost inaudible against the harsh westerly wind.

'You what!' I exclaimed.

'I've a discharge,' said Harvey, 'and it burns when I piss.'

'When did this begin?'

'I noticed it yesterday,' he replied, staring out to sea.

The significance of what he said suddenly hit home. In ten days Harvey and Susan would be together again. If Harvey did have a venereal disease, it would be highly unlikely to clear up before then. The rest of the crew lived up north, so if they too had caught anything, they could be cured before going on leave.

'Are you sure?' I asked him.

Without looking at me, he nodded. 'Yeah,' he replied. 'I caught it once before in Liverpool. The quack in the hospital shoved a bloody great syringe down me dick. It hurt like hell.'

My mind raced; the only medicine for venereal disease I had in my valise was potassium bicarbonate; even if I had more medicines, it would be hard to treat him in a ship of this size without the crew knowing about it.

'Look Harv,' I said. 'I have some medicine that might help.'

Harvey turned and with a relieved expression looked at me.

'You have!' he cried grasping my shoulder. 'Thank Christ for that.'

'But I'm afraid you won't be able to have your tot,' I said. 'The alcohol will only aggravate the lining of your dick and make matters worse.'

A pained look immediately came into his eyes.

'Fuck me, Ted,' he replied. 'Everyone will catch on if I don't see my tot off.'

'Just say you've got a stomach complaint and you're on medicine.' I replied. 'I'll back you up. Besides. We'll be in Gib in two days. I can have you seen in the sick bay in HMS *Rooke.'*

HMS *Rooke* was the Royal Navy's shore base in Gibraltar.

Harvey gave a deep sigh, passed me a cigarette. He then asked me the question I had been dreading.

'Will it have cleared up by the time we get home?'

I didn't have the heart to tell him I didn't think it would; instead, I accepted a light for my cigarette, and replied, 'I'm not sure mate. We'll have to wait and see.'

Two days later, under the shadow of the rock, our small flotilla berthed alongside a jetty. No sooner had we done so than three matelots from the other two 'sweepers appeared in the mess; they also had the same problem as Harvey. The 'sick list' increased when Paddy and Jacko joined us complaining of symptoms similar to Harvey.

'Bloody secret weapons, those Eyetie floozies,' growled Paddy on our way to the base. 'Planted there by old Musso 'imself, I bet.'

'Isn't that against the Geneva Convention, Paddy?' asked Jacko.

'All's fair in love and war, isn't it Harvey?' I said as we entered the sick bay.

After the doctor examined each of them, he prescribed sulphonamide tablets and Potassium Citrate medicine.

'Make sure they drink plenty of water as the sulpha tablets may harm their kidneys,' he said writing up their case cards. 'And no shore leave until they are cleared in Portsmouth.'

Hmm, I thought to myself; stopping their leave might prove difficult.

When I told Harvey this, he was distraught. 'Christ all mighty, Ted,' he gasped. 'No leave! What the hell am I gunna tell Susan?'

Unkind as it was, I couldn't help feeling a smug sense of satisfaction. Harvey's 'animal instincts' had finally caught up with him.

That evening the crew had a final 'rabbit-run' in Gibraltar. I soon found out how pointless it was ordering the 'patients', to remain on board.

I was duty bound to inform the captain, and in the privacy of his cabin told him the problem.

'Well,' he said, pursing his lips. 'They won't take too kindly to it. If I do order them to stay on board and they break ship, it might make matters worse. The best thing to do is to rely on their common sense. After all, they're all old hands and they've been through a lot.'

The captain was right. The ones involved were non-too-pleased when I told them they should stay on board.

'To hell with that, Doc, me old son,' said Jacko. 'If the skipper does want to keep us on board, he'll have to clap us in irons.' He looked across at Paddy who was pulling on his uniform top. 'Ain't that right Paddy?'

'To be sure it is,' replied Paddy. 'An' even if that happens I'll dive overboard, so I will.'

'Well try and keep off the booze,' I said.

'That'll be the day,' remarked Eddy Gooding, who, like everyone else wasn't fooled by the 'stomach ailments' of Paddy, Jacko and Harvey.

That night I watched as everyone, including Harvey returned on board rip-roaring drunk; even the officers weren't too steady as they clambered up the gangway.

'Harry Tate's navy, you see, Doc,' muttered Eddy Gooding, who was QM. 'There's nowt y'can do about it.'

The next morning, in company with *Brocklesby,* we left Gibraltar. The following afternoon we entered the Bay of Biscay. The rig of the day was now in oilskins, duffel coats and sea boots. Three days later after a severe buffeting by howling winds and rain the flotilla entered the English Channel.

That's when the accident happened.

I was in the mess playing uckers with Ron Balshaw, Paddy and Eddy. With each roll of the ship, Eddy grabbed the board as it slid across the table.

'I can almost smell that good old English beer,' said Ron, throwing a four.

'Give me a drop o' Irish whiskey any day,' replied Paddy. Just as he was rattling the dice, Joe Willoughby came into the mess. His black oilskin gleamed with rain and droplets of water ran down his weather-beaten face.

'You'd better come pronto, Doc,' he said, catching his breath. 'Harvey's had a fall. He seems badly hurt.'

'Where is he?' I asked hastily donning my oilskin.

'On the deck, by the bridge,' replied Joe.

I grabbed my medical valise and followed Joe up onto the deck; the ship was darkened but the rain had stopped; as I hurried behind Joe the fierce north westerly wind bit against my face.

Harvey was lying on his back at the bottom of the ladder on the port side of the deck; his eyes were closed and he appeared to be unconscious. Dicky Dickson and the first lieutenant were kneeling beside him.

'Someone get an oilskin and a blanket and cover him up!' I yelled. 'What happened?'

'He slipped going down the ladder,' said Dicky. 'I was standing on the wings when he came up. Suddenly he fell backwards onto the deck. I reached out to get him but was too late.'

Jack Wrey arrived and covered Harvey up with an oilskin; the first lieutenant lifted Harvey's head and placed a rolled up blanket under his head; I checked Harvey's pulse – it was slow and weak. Just as I was doing this he opened his eyes; his mouth moved as he tried to speak but the screeching of the wind made it difficult to hear what he was saying, I bent closer to him.

'What happened?' I head him mutter.

'You fell arse over tit down the bridge ladder,' I said. 'Now, tell me Harv, where does it hurt. Can you move your legs?'

He tried to do so, and gave a gasp of pain.

'It's me arse, Ted,' he cried. 'It's all pins and needles and hurts if I move me legs.'

I had to think quickly. The ship was rolling badly and the rain had started again.

'Try not to move, Harv,' I said, 'I'm gunna give you a shot of morphia. That'll ease the pain.' I looked at the first lieutenant. 'We'll have to get him inside then I can try and find out how badly he's hurt.'

'Right,' came the officer's quick reply. 'Use the captain's cabin.'

The captain's cabin was below the bridge accessible through a door on the port side of the deck.

By this time everyone off watch had arrived, oilskins flapping about in the wind. The rain began to splatter down as the ship ploughed through the heavy, rolling sea.

'How are we gunna move him, Doc?' asked Dicky.

Suddenly, I remembered the Neil Robertson stretcher; I looked up, saw Jacko and told him where it was. I managed to roll up Harvey's oilskin, found his arm and gave him an injection of morphia; Nobby Clark lit a cigarette, covered it with his hand and held it to Harvey's mouth.

'Take it easy, matey,' said Nobby, 'Doc'll 'ave you fixed up in no time.'

Jacko, Eddy, Ron Balshaw and Paddy arrived.

'What d'yer want us to do, Doc?' said Ron, concern etched on his face.

I told two of them to kneel either side of Harvey and carefully feel underneath his back and legs. I then spread the stretcher alongside Harvey. We waited, and as the ship settled down after plunging into a trough, we gently lifted Harvey onto the stretcher.

Harvey gave a slight cry as I quickly strapped him up. Then, using the rope rings either side we lifted him up and carefully carried him into the captain's cabin.

The room was sparsely furnished with a small with a bunk, a table and chair screwed into the deck, and a shelf with official books; the deck head was a mass of pipes and the deck was covered with dark linoleum. A blue service coverlet covered the bunk and a voice pipe and bedside light rested on the bulkhead close to a pillow.

'How are you feeling, mate?' I asked, as we placed him on the bunk.

'Not too bad,' he replied, 'but it still fells numb around my waist and arse.'

With the help of Eddy and the others, we undid the straps and removed his oilskin. I then undid his trousers and gently felt around his hip. A small spread of blood on the front of his underpants indicated he had some kind of internal injury. .

'What have I done, Ted?' whispered Harvey, flicking his tongue over his lips.

'I'm not sure,' I replied covering him up.

I stood up and asked the first lieutenant to step outside.

I told him what I found. 'He's going to need proper medical treatment,' I said. 'How far are we away from England?'

The first lieutenant's face broke into a frown. 'If we go flat out we could reach Penzance by morning.'

Just then the captain climbed down from the bridge. A pair of binoculars hung around the neck of his duffel coat and droplets of water dripped from the peak of his cap.

'What's the problem, Nigel?' he asked.

The first lieutenant explained what had happened.

'I see,' said the captain. 'Get off a signal to the Commodore. Say we have a badly injured man and request an ambulance meet at Penzance. Give them our ETA. (Estimated Time of Arrival.) Also inform *Brocklesby* and the others we intend to leave the group. I'll share your cabin if need be.' He then turned to me. 'Keep me in formed, Doc,' and returned to the bridge.

I told Harvey what was happening.

'What about Susan?' he said wrinkling his brow. 'Who will tell her?'

'Don't worry about that, Harv,' I replied. 'You'll be all right. I'll take care of everything. Just you take it easy and rest; we'll have you tucked up in hospital in no time.'

I then held his head and gave him a drink of hot Kye. The bleeding appeared to have stopped and he seemed reasonably comfortable. On a signal pad I wrote the details of what had happened for the medical people ashore. I also mentioned he was under treatment for gonorrhoea. I found an envelope in a drawer and placed the note inside.

The first lieutenant made a pipe informing the crew about Harvey, ending with, 'I intend to make all speed, so ensure everything is secure.'

During the night every steel plate in the ship shuddered as we ploughed through the ocean. I remained with Harvey all night; at various intervals someone appeared with hot drinks; around 0200, Harvey woke up in great pain. I gave him another shot of morphia and as dawn broke he was sound asleep.

At 0600, the pipe, 'Hands stand by to come alongside,' was made.

The wind had dropped but it was still drizzling. The ship slowly cruised into the harbour. Looking outside the porthole, on the port side, I could just see the imposing edifice of St Michael's Mount and the tiny white cottages of Mousehole. For a while I looked at the green hills of Cornwall and remembered those lads on board the minesweepers and other warships who wouldn't be coming back. Nevertheless, it felt great to be home.

Harvey opened his eyes.

'Are we there Ted?'

'Yes,' I replied. 'The lads have packed your gear. They've put some nutty and ciggies in your small case,' and with a weak smile, added. 'You can bribe the nurses with 'em.'

Once alongside the wharf a tall, tired-looking civilian doctor and a male nurse appeared. Outside the captain's cabin I explained what happened and gave him the envelope. I said I thought he might have internal injuries. He stepped inside and after giving Harvey a brief examination, he looked at me.

'I think you may be right,' he said, 'but it's too early to say.' He then smiled at Harvey and in a more cheerful note, continued. 'Seems like you'll be laid up for a while, but try not to worry. We'll have you back on your feet in no time.'

The doctor then took out a notebook and wrote something down.

'This is the telephone number of Penzance General,' he said, tearing out the page and handing it to me. 'I expect his next of kin will find it useful.'

Harvey looked up at me. 'Have you told him about the other…?' his voice trailed away.

I gave him a re-assuring pat on the shoulder. 'Yes, Harv,' I replied. 'They'll soon fix that as well.'

'You saved my life, Ted,' said Harvey, looking up at me. 'Thanks mate.'

'That makes us even then, Harv,' I replied. 'Now pipe down and get some rest.'

All the crew waited as Paddy and the others carried Harvey off the ship. Without exception, all wore worried expressions. A few tried to make cheerful remarks ranging from 'take care of yourself, pal', to 'see you back at the Nest'.

As we carried Harvey off the ship, he reached out and touched me on the arm. 'You will let Susan know, won't you Ted?' he said almost in tears.

'Don't worry, Harv,' I replied as we placed him in the ambulance, 'I will.'

CHAPTER FOURTEEN

The MMS 50 arrived in Portsmouth at 0800 on 14 October 1943. As we sailed past HMS *Dolphin* I couldn't help but reflect upon what had happened since I joined the flotilla six months ago; during that time we had lost two minesweepers and forty men killed. This was almost fifty percent of the flotilla gone, with the war far from over. With a sigh I shook my head, wondering when it would all end.

The harbour was full of warships, many from the Commonwealth countries and America. While we were sailing down the Solent news came through telling of more losses in the Atlantic by U-Boats. The German battleship *Tirpitz* had been torpedoed by a midget submarine, and of special interest to me, a wonder drug called Penicillin would soon be in general use.

'Jesus, Mary and Joseph, Jacko!' cried Paddy. 'It's a pity Doc didn't have some of that in Gib.'

I was on the 'sweep deck standing close to Jacko and Paddy. They were busy securing lines to the two 'sweepers that had entered harbour before our departure to Penzance.

'Can't you get yer hands on some of it, Doc?' said Jacko.

'Not just yet,' I replied. 'But I expect it might be issued to the forces pretty soon. Not early enough to help you lot though.'

As soon as the ship's telephone was connected to shore I asked the captain if I could use his to call Penzance to find out how Harvey was. The captain was on the bridge talking to the first lieutenant.

'Of course, Doc,' he replied. Then, turning to his Number One, added. 'Perhaps you could write a letter to his wife, Nigel. Doc here could deliver it personally. Better than a telegram, don't you think?'

The first lieutenant nodded. 'Good idea, Peter,' he then

looked at me and said, 'And while you're at Haslar find out when the next refresher course for leading hand is. It's about time you became a killick.'

After a slight delay I finally got trough to Penzance General Hospital and spoke to the ward sister.

'Your man has suffered a fractures pelvis and a damaged bladder,' she said in a distinct, Cornish accent. 'His pelvis is pinned and his condition is quite stable.'

She went on to tell me it was hoped that Harvey would be fit enough to transfer to the Royal Naval Hospital at Plymouth in about two weeks.

The news of Harvey's condition soon spread around the ship.

'Just think,' said Jacko. 'Surrounded by gorgeous nurses, eating good grub and being waited on hand and foot. What a life, eh?'

'Makes you think it's worth while going sick,' replied Paddy.'

'You're already sick,' quipped Jock, and added, 'sick in the head.'

Directly after tot time I caught the routine Haslar ferry across the harbour. The masts of HMS *Victory* still remained proud in the grey sky, despite receiving a 15 feet hole in her port side during an air raid in 1941.

The first place I made for in the hospital was the regulating office. Inside, several ratings were sat behind desk doing clerical work. The office was partitioned of with glass panelling. Sitting behind a desk was the white-haired figure of Chief Milton. As I opened the door he looked up.

'Don't tell me they've kicked you offa those minesweepers?' he said. As he spoke his weather-beaten features broke scowl.

'No, Chief,' I replied.

After explaining why I was there the look on his face softened.

'I see,' he said, flicking through what appeared to be a duty roster. 'Nurse Rawlinson is on A2 ward. As for a refresher course,' he paused, opened a book and ran a finger down a page.

'Let's see now, today's Thursday.' He looked up at me and continued. 'The next course begins next Wednesday and lasts for three weeks. Write out a request now and I'll send a signal to your ship for you to be drafted in on Monday. Now go and see your VAD.'

A2 was a busy orthopaedic ward above the physiotherapy department; several patients lay in bed with their limbs in traction; others, with parts of their upper body encased in Plaster of Paris sat, propped up by a mountain of pillows, reading; some sat around in hospital dressing gowns, talking and smoking.

I immediately looked around for Susan. However, the first person I saw was the tall frame of Big Mac. He had just emerged from behind a set of screens holding a bedpan. When he saw me his face, framed by his black bushy eyebrows, broke into a wide grin.

'Great to see you Ted,' he said, glancing at the bedpan and pulling a face. 'I'll be back in a minute.' As he hurried towards the heads at the end of the ward, Susan appeared from behind some screens carrying a tray. She wore her VAD's white uniform with its distinctive red cross on the front; when she saw me her lovely brown eyes lit up.

'Ted!' she cried hurrying up to me. 'Ted, it's so good to see you. How's Harvey?'

Just then the sister, a tall, dark-haired, no nonsense woman with a hint of a moustache arrived. 'What's all this fuss?' she snapped, glaring at me. 'And who are you, may I ask?'

I introduced myself and said I had a message about Susan's husband; straight away both women sensed something was wrong.

Susan's face suddenly blanched and she almost dropped the tray; her hand shot up to her face. 'Oh my God,' she gasped, 'he's not…?'

'No,' I quickly replied. 'He's had an accident.'

'What *kind* of accident?' cried Susan.

I was about to answer when Big Mac arrived. Glancing at Susan's expression he realised my visit wasn't social.

An air of silence descended on the ward as our behaviour attracted the attention of patients and staff.

Looking at Susan, the sister said, 'You two need some privacy. Use my cabin.'

This was a small room set aside for the sister and doctor to discuss patients. Glancing up at Big Mac, she added, 'Take Nurse Rawlinson's tray away then organise some tea for them.'

The sister ushered us into the cabin.

'If you need anything,' she said, 'just let me know,' closed the door and left.

I gave Susan the first lieutenant's letter.

She sat down at the sister's desk and ripped it open.

After reading its contents, she looked up at me, tears in her eyes. 'My God!' she gasped 'He sounds badly hurt. I must try and go to him.'

A knock came at the door and Big Mac appeared with two cups of tea on a tray.

'Not bad news I hope?' he said, placing the tray on the table.

'Bad enough,' I replied. 'Susan's husband's been injured.'

'Sorry, to hear it, love,' said Big Mac. Then glancing at me, added, 'see you later Ted.'

He was about to close the door when sister appeared.

'Is there anything I can do?' she quietly asked.

'Yes, sister,' I replied, 'I think there is.' I told her where Harvey was.

'Right,' she said, straightening her shoulders. 'I'll 'phone the regulating chief and arrange for you to take a long weekend and travel to Penzance first thing in the morning. Go and report to him now.' She then picked up the telephone from her desk.

Big Mac and a few members of staff were waiting outside the ward.

'Sorry to hear about your hubby, Susan,' said a pretty blonde nurse, 'do you need anything?'

'Thanks, Jean,' replied Susan, dabbing her eyes. 'I've been given a long weekend. I'll see you and the others when I come back.'

While Susan collected her cape from outside, I had a quick word with Big Mac.

'I'll meet you in the "The Nelson" Saturday night at eight, OK?'

The 'Nelson', was popular pub just off Gosport High Street.

'Aye,' replied Big Mac, 'And the first pint's on me.'

'Oh Ted!' said Susan as we walked up the colonnade, 'I do hope Harvey's all right. Exactly how did he hurt himself?'

After I told her, she began to cry. 'It must have been awful for you,' she said, 'I do hope he's all right.'

'Don't worry,' I replied, trying my best to re-assure her, 'He will be. Mark my words.'

By the time we arrived at the regulating office Susan was composed.

'Be back here by eight o'clock on Monday morning,' said Chief Milton, handing Susan a travel warrant and leave pass. 'And I hope you're your husband is OK. If you need an extension, ring me here.'

On the way back to the ward Susan told me she was sharing a flat in Gosport with another VAD.

'Her name's Janet,' said Susan. 'We did our training together. She's going on draft to Malta soon and is on two weeks' foreign-service leave.'

Before saying goodbye, I told her about the refresher course.

'That's wonderful. Ted,' she replied. 'Come and see me and I'll let you know how everything is. And thanks for all you did for Harvey.'

The 'Nelson' was crowded with men and women from the three services. A thick blur of blue tobacco smoke hung in the air and from a wireless, the sound of Bing Crosby singing *Moonlight Becomes You* was barely audible over raucous conversation and laughter.

Big Mac was standing at the bar talking to a sailor.

'It really is good ta see you, mon,' he said shaking my hand. 'What'll ye have?'

During the next few hours we talked of old times. Tinker Taylor and Scouse Kilkenny were in the Royal Naval Hospital, Bighi, Malta; Brum was still on board *Belfast* and Buster Brown had been drafted to a destroyer.

I told him about the invasion of Sicily and how Harvey was injured.

'Tough luck on Susan,' he said, sipping his pint. 'They've only just got married so I heard.'

I remembered what Harvey said about the non-consummation on wedding night. 'Yes,' I replied. 'Not much of a coming home present for her.'

Before we parted, much worse for wear at ten thirty, Big Mac said, 'Ye won't need yer hammock when ye join on Wednesday. We have bunks now. There's a spare one above me in two mess. That's at the bottom of the hall. Me name's on me locker so yer can't miss it.'

Before leaving the ship on Monday morning I said farewell to the lads.

'Three bloody weeks in Haslar, mon!' said Jock. 'It'll be like a holiday camp after being here.'

'Aye,' chimed in Ron Balshaw, 'With hot and cold running nurses.'

Although I was only going away for a few weeks, I was overcome by a deep feeling of sadness. I looked around at the faces of Ron Balshaw, Eddy Gooding, Paddy, Jock and the others. These were some of the men with whom I had shared the dangers of war. They were the kind of men who you could trust with your life, but not your girl friend or wife; as I shook their hands, I suddenly realised how much I would miss them.

'See you lot in a fortnight,' I said to Johnny Pue as I walked over the gangway. 'And tell Jacko to keep taking those tablets the MO gave you both.'

Little did I know I would never see him or the others again.

I arrived at Haslar shortly after noon on Monday. After stowing my gear I hurried to see Susan. I found her in the galley outside the ward; she and an SBA were washing the dinner dishes. Strands of chestnut coloured hair curled down from under her cap; her face was drawn and she looked tired. Even so, she looked as beautiful as ever. When she saw me, she wiped her brow with the back of her hand and smiled. Before she had time to speak, I asked, 'How is he?'

'Harvey's doing fine.' replied Susan, drying her hands on a towel. 'He seemed cheerful enough but I could tell he was in pain. He'll remain in bed for at least a fortnight, then we'll have to wait and see.'

'Perhaps he'll be transferred here,' I said.

'I hope so,' answered Susan. 'It's been so long…' her voice tailed off.

Before I left she wrote down her address.

'The door to the flat is next to the newspaper shop on Gosport High Street. You can't miss it, it's bright red,' she said, pressing the note into my hand. 'Come on Wednesday about six. Just ring the bell. I'll have a nice meal prepared for you. It's the least I can do for way you looked after Harvey.'

I gave a start. Suddenly, the thought of being alone with her sent my pulse racing. She then leant up and kissed me on the cheek.

'See you on Wednesday,' she said and walked into the ward.

'Refresher course, eh?' said Petty Officer Pinkerton, his florid features breaking into a sly grin. 'You can't keep away from us, can you?'

I was in the main office of the training division.

'Bollocks!' I replied.

Pinkie laughed. 'Mixing with those hairy-arsed matelots hasn't improved your manners, I see.'

Pinky went to outline the refresher course. 'It is basically the same as your sick berth attendants' course, except you have to get a higher mark,' he said. 'And after sailing the seven seas, I'm sure you'll manage that.'

Later on in the bar I told Big Mac about my date with Susan.

'Watch yer step there, laddie,' he said, before taking a sip of beer. 'Don't go shittin' on yer own doorstep.'

'Don't be daft,' I replied. 'Harvey saved my life. I couldn't do anything like that.'

'Och aye!' answered Big Mac, 'But she might have other ideas. And remember. Your dick'll drag you further than dynamite 'll blow yer.'

Walking over Pneumonia Bridge to Gosport brought back memories of Spider Webb's suicide. So much had happened to me since then. I had seen men and ships blown to bits – strong men reduced to tears and quiet men perform brave deeds. I stopped for a few seconds and gazed across the darkened harbour; how long can this bloody war last I fumed, and carried on walking.

Very few people were about. The blackout was still in progress and Gosport was in darkness. The door to the flat was next to a narrow street just off the main street. After ringing the bell, I heard the sound footsteps and the door opened.

Susan wore a dark green skirt and brown sweater and her hair hung loosely around her shoulders.

'Hello, Ted,' she said, flashing me a smile. 'You're right on time, come in, it's this way.'

I followed her watching how her hips gently swayed as she climbed a small flight of stairs. The seams of her stockings rose from black high-heeled shoes making my pulse race and my palms sweat.

'Well!' said Susan, twirling around with her hands open. 'Here it is.'

As I entered the flat the mouth watering smell of roast meat attacked my nostrils.

'Mmm…' I said. 'Something smells good.'

'Lamb chops,' replied Susan. 'That's all I could get.'

'Lamb chops sounds great,' I said.

The flat was bigger than I expected. The living room, done in cream and pale green, and kitchen were combined. On the right as I entered, heavy dark brown curtains were drawn across a window. A patterned carpet covered the floor and in the centre was a comfortable-looking brown sofa with two matching armchairs. A small clock encased in a wooden frame rested on a mantelpiece under which glowed an electric fire and on a sideboard, next to a wireless, was a framed photograph of Harvey in uniform. Prints of Devon countryside hung on the wall and shaded electric lighting gave the room a quiet, intimate atmosphere.

'That's my bedroom,' said Susan pointing to one of three doors. 'The other one belongs to Janet. She'll be back from leave in ten days. The small door is the bathroom. It's nice and cosy here, no snoopy neighbours.'

Being alone with Susan suddenly made me feel nervous; I half expected Harvey to walk in any minute.

'Er…very nice,' I remarked, looking around.

'Take off your Burberry and sit down,' she said, pouring me a glass of beer. Then with a smile, added, 'I'm not going to bite you. Relax. Tell me, Ted, what did you do before the war?'

'I worked for the Mersey Docks and Harbour Board in Liverpool,' I replied.

'Did you like it?'

With a casual shrug of my shoulders, I replied, 'It was all right, I suppose.'

I went on to tell her about the St John's Ambulance Brigade.

'Do you think you'll go back to your old job when the war's over?'

I pursed my lips. 'I might, that's if I survive. What about you?'

Susan gave a short laugh. 'I was a typist for an accountant in Chester,' she said. 'In my spare time I joined the Red Cross. That's how I ended up a VAD.'

Over the meal I told her about the invasion of Sicily and Italy.

'It must have been terribly dangerous,' said Susan, topping up my glass with beer. Then with a gleam in her eyes, added, 'But tell me, what did you and Harvey get up to when you went ashore?'

'Not much,' I replied, lying through my teeth, 'Harvey hardly left the ship.'

She turned her head to one side, and gave me a disbelieving look. 'And you?' she asked, 'What did you get up to? Did you meet any of those Italian girls?'

'I did meet one,' I replied.

'*Really!*' she cried. 'You must tell me about her. Finish your beer. I've got a bottle of gin in the cupboard. Go and sit on the couch; I want to hear all about your escapades.'

She stood up and brought a bottle from the sideboard, poured out two large glasses of gin and placed the bottle on a small table. I finished my beer and moved to the couch.

The provocative whisper made by her stockings as she slowly crossed her legs made every nerve in my body tingle with excitement – so much so, I nearly dropped my glass.

'What was your Italian girl like?' said Susan, moving close to me. The smell of her perfume was intoxicating and I could feel the warmth of her thigh against mine.

'Was she, er... sexy?' she added. As she spoke I detected more than a hint of excitement in her voice.

She took a good swallow of gin, licked her lips then finished the contents of the glass. She then leant back into the sofa; as she did so the hem of her dress slid over her knees. For a few seconds I became hypnotised by the sight of her thighs. When I looked up I saw her staring at me, her eyes glazed and dark.

'Er...maybe, I can't remember,' I replied, before taking a quick gulp of gin.

'I don't believe you,' replied Susan coyly. 'Tell me. What was her name?' She was beginning to slur her words and her cheeks had turned a deep red.

I cleared my throat and replied. 'Gina.'

'Mmm,' said Susan. 'That's a nice name. Did you, er...you know what?'

I felt myself blush and took another swig of gin.

Susan slowly tucked her legs under her then gave my thigh a playful pat.

'Come now, don't be shy,' she murmured. 'I want to know everything.'

My mouth felt dry; I shrugged my shoulders and answered, 'Yes, I suppose we did.'

Susan threw back her head and laughed. 'You *suppose!*' she cried, squeezing my thigh. 'Either you did or you didn't.'

Her touch was like an electric current running into my groin. I instantly felt myself harden; my pulse started to race and a trickle of sweat ran down my back. With one gulp I finished my drink and placed the empty glass on the table.

'W…well,' I stuttered. 'We did.'

Susan removed her hand from my thigh and re-filled both our glasses. Our eyes met as she passed me the drink. A smile played around the corners of her mouth as she leant her head on my shoulder.

'Tell me more,' she said almost in a whisper.

My God, I told myself; clearly, she's had too much to drink. Why else would she be behaving like this? After all, she's married to a man who once saved my life.

She leant forward and passed my drink to me. 'Come on, Ted' she said, 'Did you take her clothes off?'

By this time my heart was beating a constant barrage against my rib cage. My mouth, despite the gin, felt like parchment. Once again I felt her warm hand on my thigh; a dull ache of desire ran through me and for a moment, I thought I would explode.

'Why do you want to know all this?' I asked, running my tongue over my lips.

Susan saw off her drink and with a glazed expression in her eyes, cried, 'Ha! Ha!' she cried, 'that's for me to know, and you to find out. Besides, it's been such a long time since I…' She paused, then, asked, 'well, *did* you take her clothes off?'

The catch in her voice told me she was excited.

'Yes,' I replied. 'We were both naked.'

She gave a short gasp. As her hand moved higher I suddenly realised what I was getting myself into. A picture of Harvey lying in a hospital bed flashed through my mind. Suddenly, I stood up.

'I need the heads,' I said covering up the aching bulge in my trousers, and hurried into the bathroom.

'Don't be too long,' I heard her say as I closed the door.

I slumped down on the toilet seat with beads of sweat pouring down my face; the sight of black underwear and stockings hanging from a makeshift clothesline didn't help my state of mind.

I lit a cigarette and tried to think straight. How often, I told myself, had I fantasised about a moment like this. I told myself what might happen was wrong. Especially when it affected the relationship of two people who were close friends.

The sound of Susan knocking on the door suddenly interrupted my thoughts.

'Are you all right, Ted?' Her voice sounded a decibel higher than normal and was slurred.

'Yes,' I replied, standing up and pulling the chain. 'Just had too much to drink, that's all.'

I took a deep breath, pulled the chain and opened the door. Susan stood facing me, a full glass of gin in her hand and a smile on her face. 'Thought you might need this,' she said offering me the drink.

'No thanks, love,' I replied. 'I think I'd best be going. I want to keep a clear head for this course I'm on.' It was a feeble lie but the only one I could think of.

'Oh,' replied Susan with an air of disappointment. 'If you must...'

'Thanks for the meal,' I said, putting on my Burberry and cap. 'It beats navy cooking any day. Harvey's a lucky man.'

Susan looked up at me and frowned. 'Harvey,' she murmured, toying with her empty glass. 'Yes, but not in a hospital bed.' She swayed against me and almost in a whisper, added, 'I'm off at the weekend. Why don't you come over on Saturday about six o'clock. I'll do something nice for you.'

I hesitated before answering. 'I may be on duty myself,' I lied. 'I'll ring you on the ward on Friday. If you don't hear from me by twelve, you know I'll be there.'

'What about one for the road, as the Yanks say?' she said, waving her empty glass in front of me.

'No thanks, love,' I replied. 'Tara for now, and thanks again.'

She then reached up and gave me a quick kiss; her lips felt soft and warm. That electric feeling in my groin returned and for a moment I was tempted to stay.

'There, 'she said, 'Every sailor should always have a goodnight kiss.'

I grinned sheepishly and muttered, 'Goodnight, and thanks again.'

Outside a stiff breeze blew in my face. I took a deep breath, crossed the road turned, and saw her silhouetted in the doorway. She stood still and waved. Suddenly I felt ashamed but deep inside I knew my fantasy would inevitably become a reality.

The next day, along with six other SBA's, we began the refresher course. Much to my delight, the matronly figure of, 'Rectum Rosie', Sister Fanshaw, greeted us. Her moustache appeared to have grown, as had her girth.

'I see we have a few familiar faces amongst us,' she said eyeing me with a smug smile. 'I hope you have all come prepared to work. I'm told more warships are being built and they're going to need every available SBA.'

That evening I decided to discuss my dilemma with Big Mac. The staff bar had just opened and we were having a quiet drink.

Big Mac gave a snort of derision. 'Och laddie!' he said, 'Yer playin' we fire. If her old man ever finds out you've fucked his missus, he'll kill you. Besides. It's a lousy thing to do, especially to a pal.'

'I haven't touched her yet,' I replied, lighting a cigarette and passing him one.

'Aye,' he replied, shoving his empty glass across to me. '*Yet,* is the operative word. Now get 'em in.'

That night I lay awake wracked with guilt; Big Mac was right: it would be a lousy thing to do. I cursed myself because I knew I didn't have the willpower to stay away from her; every time I closed my eyes I saw her soft brown eyes staring at me; I could even smell her perfume and feel her body close to mine. As the night wore on I realised I was fighting a losing battle with myself, and what's more, I had a feeling Susan knew it also.

I didn't telephone her.

As I left the mess just after 1730 on Saturday, Big Mac, who was lying on his bunk reading, shook his head. 'Be bloody careful,' he said putting down his dog-eared copy of *Lilliput.* 'In more ways than one, d'yer hear now?'

'Yes, I know,' I replied, with a sigh. 'But…' I didn't finish. Instead I put on my Burberry and left the mess.

When Susan opened the door a smile, warm enough to melt

snow, spread across her face.

She was dressed in a plain, button-down blue dress. A white belt accentuated her narrow waist. Her legs were bare and she wore a pair of slippers.

'Come in, Ted,' she said, her eyes sparkling. 'I'm glad you could make it. When you didn't 'phone, I hoped you'd be here.'

This time there was no preliminary drinks or small talk. The emotive expression in her eyes told me we both knew what was going to happen. For a few seconds we stood in silence and looked at one another. Then, as if by magnetism our arms went around each other. The next thing I felt her warm lips on mine kissing me with a passion I never knew existed; even though I still had my uniform on, I could feel her soft body pressing against mine.

'Oh Ted!' she gasped, placing her head on my chest. 'Your arms feel so good around me. It's been so long since I felt this way.' She then looked up at me and murmured, 'Kiss me again!'

My head was pounding and I thought my heart would burst; suddenly, all thoughts of Harvey were forgotten; with mounting excitement, I felt Susan's hands undo my Burberry, and jacket. I hardly noticed as they fell in a heap on the floor.

Then, while kissing her I fumbled with her belt and buttons. She stepped back allowing her dress to fall open. I gave a hollow gasp; all she had on was a pair of white silk knickers and matching brassier.

'Jesus Christ, Susan!' I cried, 'You look bloody gorgeous!'

She looked directly at me, her eyes dark with passion. 'As gorgeous as Gina?' she replied in a throaty voice.

I didn't reply.

With frantic movements she removed my shirt and unbuckled my belt. As she did so, I cupped her breasts with both hands. They felt hard and firm. In an instant we were both naked.

Clinging to each other we fell backwards onto the sofa; her body felt warm, soft and smooth as silk.

Our lovemaking was quick, frenzied and over all too quickly. Afterwards we lay bathed in each other's sweat, panting like marathon runners.

'God!' gasped Susan, 'That was wonderful.' She slowly unwound herself from me and stood up; a thin line of sweat ran tantalisingly between her breasts onto her stomach. 'Come on Ted,' she said extending her hand. 'Let's go to bed.'

A few hours later I woke up; Susan was asleep with her backside cocooned into my lap. I had one arm around her resting across her breasts and watched as they gently rose and fell with her breathing. I gently caressed a breast and heard her murmur something incoherent; she slowly turned around, smiled and kissed me gently.

'Cigarette?' she asked.

I nodded and removed my hand. She then twisted about and reached across to the bedside table. Her breasts with nipples, dark and taut, moved slightly as she passed me a Craven 'A'.

'I hope you don't think too badly of me, Ted,' she said. 'I wouldn't blame you if you did.'

At that moment, however, I didn't feel any sense of guilt whatsoever; instead I looked at Susan and wished time would standstill.

'No, love, I don't,' trying to sound noble. 'I haven't stopped thinking about you since we met in London. I tried to stay away, but I couldn't. So if anyone's to blame it's me.'

She turned away from me, exhaled a steam of tobacco smoke into the air, and said, 'There is something I must tell you.'

'What's that, then?' I replied.

'You may not believe me,' she said, avoiding my gaze, 'and I realise this may sound awful after…' her voice momentarily faltered. 'But I'm still in love with Harvey. It's…it's just been so long since I…' Once more she hesitated. After quickly taking a deep puff of her cigarette, she went on to tell me what Harvey had said about their wedding night. 'I had my monthlies, you see, and the night was a disaster for both of us.'

Naturally I didn't mention that Harvey had already told me what had happened.

'I see,' I replied, allowing flakes of ash to fall onto the bedclothes. 'I suppose you'd rather not see me again, then?'

'No, no, Ted!' she cried, looking at me. 'I do. I'm really

attracted to you. I...I just couldn't have done this with anyone. Please believe me' Tears welled up in her eyes as she spoke. 'This *bloody war!*' she sobbed. 'It's got us all mixed up.'

'Yes,' I sighed. 'But there is something you should know also.'

'What's that?' she asked. She stubbed her cigarette in an ashtray on the bedside table. She then propped herself up on one elbow. Her chestnut coloured hair was a mess and what little eye make-up she wore was smudged.

'Harvey saved my life,' I said quietly.

'My God!' exclaimed Susan. 'He never mentioned anything like that to me. What happened?'

I told her about the incident on board the MMS 50 when we were suddenly attacked. I paused and put my cigarette out. 'Ironic, isn't it. If it hadn't been for his quick thinking I wouldn't be here now.'

'But don't forget, Ted,' said Susan, cuddling down against me. 'You helped to save his life as well. He told me all about that so don't feel guilty. We're both to blame.'

Over the next week, we saw each other every night. My early arrival in the mess every morning provoked several sarcastic comments.

'Lucky bastard!' said one SBA climbing out of his bunk. 'Wish I were getting grippos (naval slang for any rating invited into someone's home). She must be givin' you stacks.'

'Who's the unlucky party, then, Ted?' asked someone else.

'A feller, mores the like, darling,' quipped another lad on the way to the heads.

From the bunk below me, Big Mac muttered, 'Dirty wee waster. I hope yer dick drops off!'

One evening, Susan and I were in the kitchen eating a meal listening to the wireless. The strident voice of Alvin Adell, the BBC newsreader, told of fierce fighting by allied armies at Monte Cassino, Italy; sixty U-Boats had been sunk in the last three months and the Americans had captured the Gilbert Islands in the Pacific.

'Things seem to be bucking up,' I said, sipping a cup of tea.

Susan ignored my comment. Instead she took out a letter from her handbag and placed it on the table. In a quiet voice, she said, 'Harvey tells me he is being transferred to the naval hospital Plymouth in two days.'

'I see,' I replied, pursing my lips. 'That means he'll arrive there on the second of November. Sounds like he's on the mend.'

'And Janet will be coming back off leave in four days.'

I shot her an inquisitive glance. 'How long will she be here?' I asked. 'You told me she was going on draft.'

'She'll be gone in two days.'

'Then we'd best make the most of what time we've left,' I said.

On Monday 15 October, five days before the course and examinations were due to finish, Susan received a letter from Harvey saying he had been given ten days' sick leave. As soon as Susan opened the door she avoided my eyes. I instinctively knew something was worrying her.

'Harvey arrives this Wednesday,' she said once we were inside the flat. 'He wants to stay here for a few days then go back to Penzance. Apparently he met someone in the hospital who owns a hotel there. They've invited us to stay.'

'What are you going to do?' I asked, passing her a cigarette and lighting it.

'I've got some leave due to me,' she replied, 'so we'll do as he suggests.'

As she spoke, our eyes met; we both knew something like this was bound to happen sooner or later and for a few seconds, neither of us spoke.

Finally, I said, 'Well, that's that. Let's face it, we couldn't go on like this forever. What with Janet coming back and now this.'

Suddenly she started crying; I sat down and put my arms around her. 'No need for tears, love,' I said. 'At least we've been honest with each other. Now, the most important thing is for you and Harvey to be as happy as this soddin' war will let you.'

I didn't stay the night.

'Thank you for everything, Ted,' she whispered before I left. 'You've kept me from going insane these past few weeks.'

As I slowly returned to the hospital the thought of never holding Susan in my arms again made me depressed. Walking over Pneumonia Bridge I felt a deep emptiness in the pit of my stomach. Even the full moon shining on the harbour waters didn't seem as bright as normal.

However, just when I thought things couldn't get worse…they did.

The next morning while shaving I felt a sudden sharp pain in my right side. I dropped my razor and held on to the washbasin.

'Are you all right?' said Big Mac who was standing next to me. 'Why are you doubled up like that?'

'It's my guts!' I cried. 'I've a terrible pain…' The pain increased and I vomited into the basin. I felt my legs go weak; the bathroom began to spin and I everything went blank. When I opened my eyes I was lying on a bed. The pain in my side was still there and the face of a young man with fair hair was bending over me.

'What happened?' I gasped. .

'You fainted,' said the young man. 'How are you feeling?'

'This bloody pain,' I said, placing a hand over my right side, 'is killing me.'

The young man was wearing the uniform of a surgeon lieutenant. Behind him stood Big Mac and a few other members of staff.

A gentle prod by the doctor's hand over the painful area made me cry out in agony.

'Looks like you may have appendicitis, old boy,' said the doctor.

'Bloody hell!' I moaned. 'That's all I need.'

As I was placed on a stretcher I looked up at Big Mac, and said, 'Get word to Susan. Tell her what's happened. I'll be in A 2 ward.'

'Don't worry, Ted,' quipped Big Mac, 'The surgeon's hand may slip and cut yer balls off. That would solve all you worries!'

A more detailed examination on the ward confirmed the

doctor's diagnosis. A few hours later I was operated on.

I woke up some hours later; my mouth was dry and my lower abdomen swathed in bandages.

During the next twelve hours I drifted in and out of sleep. When I finally woke up the pain in my side had subsided and I felt much better. The next morning I received a visit from the grey haired figure of Chief Petty Officer Milton.

'I'm afraid we've had to draft another SBA to the minesweepers,' he said. 'You won't be fit for some time and the ships need medical coverage.'

This news really upset me as I had shared some harrowing moments on board the Mickey Mouses and would miss the men.

'Bastard!' I replied venomously. 'Is there no chance of me returning when I'm OK?'

'I'm afraid not,' replied the chief. 'However, your marks so far on your course have been so good, I expect the SRA (Surgeon Rear Admiral) will approve your promotion to leading hand.'

'Well,' I replied, trying to sound cheerful,' I suppose that's something.'

On Saturday afternoon I received another surprise.

The ward gradually filled up with visitors; I was propped up with pillows and about to doze off. Quite abruptly, I was awakened by a familiar voice.

'Loafing bugger,' said the speaker with a laugh.

I opened my eyes and saw Harvey. His blue eyes had dark rings around them and he looked tired. Standing just behind him was Susan. She was in uniform and as usual looked fabulous.

'Bloody hell, Harv!' I exclaimed, sitting slightly forward and blinking. 'What a surprise! How are you, mate?'

As we shook hands I glanced at Susan. She was smiling but there was a hint of sadness in her eyes.

'How am I?' laughed Harvey. 'It's how you are that's important.'

Harvey had lost weight. His uniform no longer fitted his athletic frame like a second skin and his chiselled feature appeared thinner.

'Oh, I'll be as right as rain in a week or so,' I replied.

Although I already knew, I asked him what him and Susan would be doing.

He told me about the invitation to Penzance. While doing so he put his arm around Susan's shoulders and gave her a hug. 'After all,' he said, 'we didn't have much of a honeymoon did we love?'

Susan looked at Harvey and smiled weakly. 'Not really,' she replied.

'That's great,' I answered, trying my best to sound cheerful. 'When will you return?'

'I'll be back on my own in a week,' replied Susan, 'Harvey here, will travel to Plymouth.'

'That's right,' replied Harvey. 'Then with a bit of luck, I'll join the old MMS 50.'

An SBA provided chairs and we talked about the lads and the ship.

I also told Harvey I wouldn't be returning to the flotilla.

'I'm sorry to hear that,' said Harvey, 'Joe and the rest will be as well.'

After an hour, the sister asked them to leave.

'Visiting time is restricted,' she said, pumping up my pillows. 'Even though he is a member of staff.'

Before they left Harvey shook my hand. 'Thanks for everything mate,' he said. 'I won't forget what you did.' He glanced at Susan and with a grin, added, 'If we ever have a son, we'll name him after you.'

My God, I thought; if he ever found out about Susan and me he'd kill me. As Susan bent down and kissed me on the cheek, I felt my face redden. The smell of her perfume made me feel ashamed of myself.

CHAPTER FIFTEEN

Two weeks later, on Wednesday 14 December, I was discharged on seven days' sick leave.

Three days before this, however, Susan came into the ward on some pretext or other. I was sitting reading the paper in a dressing gown and slippers. It was shortly after 1400 and the ward was relatively quiet. She looked tired and as she came close to where I was sitting, a frown appeared on her brow. I immediately sensed something was wrong.

'How are you, Ted?' she said without smiling.

'Much better after seeing you' I replied. 'How was your trip to Penzance?'

'Oh,' she replied, glancing at the floor. 'Not bad.' She then looked at me and said, 'When are you being discharged?'

'After rounds this morning, the MO said I could go on sick leave,' I replied.

'For how long?'

I told her.

Susan glanced warily at two patients sitting nearby talking. Suddenly a worried look came in her eyes.

'Look Ted,' she said, 'I must speak to you, privately. Before you go on leave could you come and see me?'

'Is there anything wrong?'

'I'll tell you when I see you.'

I decided not to go home. After all, there was nothing there for me. Shorty was dead, Iris was engaged and most of the lads I knew in the St John's had been called up.

'I'll stay in the mess,' I told Chief Milton in the regulating office. 'At least the beer bar will be handy.'

On Wednesday afternoon I went to see Susan. Screens were around several bed spaces and the staff were busy. Susan and another nurse were making beds. When she saw me she stopped what she was doing and came over to me.

'When are you going home?' she said.

I told her I was staying in the hospital.

Her eyes lit up. 'Good,' she said, 'Jean, the girl who took Janet's place is on night duty. She leaves the flat at seven each night. Can you come round on Saturday about eight?'

'But what is it you want to see me for?' I asked.

Two SBA's came out of the ward carrying trays of water carafes and tumblers.

'Aye! Aye!' grinned one of them. 'No time for courting here y' know.'

Susan shot them a smile. Then, turning to me, she reached across and touched my arm. 'I can't speak here please come on Saturday.'

What on earth did she want to see me about I wondered? Harvey was recovering all right and would soon be drafted to Portsmouth. What could possibly be wrong?

When I told Big Mac he rolled up his eyes and sat down on his bed.

'Y' stupid bugger,' he exploded. 'Did yer use any jonnies when you were with her?'

I hesitated before replying. 'Er...of course, I bought some from the chemist in Gosport High Street.'

Big Mac lit a cigarette. 'Well I hope they didn't burst on yer,' he said. 'Maybe she's told her husband and he wants a divorce!'

'Don't be daft,' I replied. 'They've only been married a dog-watch.'

Nevertheless, Big Mac remark gave me food for thought; if she had told Harvey I'm sure he would have confronted me – even if it meant not returning to Plymouth. However, one thing I was sure of – I was in love with Susan and had been since the first time we met. If she and Harvey were about to split up I would jump at the chance of marrying her. Then I remembered what she had said about being in love with Harvey. Whatever happened, I was determined not to get involved with her again; Harvey had been so glad to see me, while all I felt was a constant feeling of guilt. Walking over Pneumonia Bridge on

Saturday evening I wondered what problems awaited me in Gosport.

'Impotent!' I exclaimed. 'How could he be impotent?'

Susan and I were sitting on her sofa; I still had my Burberry on. Susan was dressed in a plain dark skirt and white blouse. She sat, tears in her eyes, twisting a handkerchief with her fingers.

'It was the injury,' she said, catching her breath. 'Some nerves were damaged. It affected his…penis. He can't do anything.'

'But surely it's not permanent?' I replied. 'Surely the doctors can help him?'

Susan dried the corners of her eyes. 'Yes, but they don't know how long it'll take. It may be years before he can…'

'So you still haven't?'

She shot me a tearful glance and shook her head. 'Oh Ted,' she cried, resting her head on my chest. 'What are we to do?'

I wasn't sure what she meant.

'You mean Harvey and you?'

'Yes,' she replied.

'Wait and hope everything will be OK, I suppose.'

She sat back and dried her eyes and smiled. 'You're right, of course,' she said flatly. 'Harvey told me he can't wait to go back to his ship. What with all the talk of a second front, who knows what will happen….' Her voice tailed away as she finished her beer.

I reminded her about my not re-joining the MMS 50.

'That's a shame,' replied Susan, touching my hand. 'Anyway, maybe it's for the best. Now, take your Burberry off and we'll have another drink.'

As I crawled from the flat early next morning I told myself it was the effect of the booze that caused us to end up in her bed again. Of course, I was lying to myself. When she kissed me my all my good intentions vanished. My willpower disintegrated as quickly as we shed our clothes.

'I hope my operation incision doesn't open up,' I gasped after a particularly passionate session.

'What are you worried about, love,' replied Susan grinning.

'I'm a nurse. I'll stitch you up again if it does!'

Three days later, even though Susan started her periods, we stayed together. However, our trysts came to an abrupt halt over Christmas.

'Harvey and I have got Christmas and New Year at home. We're going up to Ellesmere Port to stay with my mum and dad, then on to Chester,' said Susan one evening. 'If you're home, why not come and see us. Birkenhead's only a few miles away.'

The thought of seeing Harvey and Susan together again suddenly gave me a start.

'No thanks,' I replied. 'I'm taking New Year's leave, so I'll miss Christmas. Anyway, it might be a bit awkward…'

'Yes,' replied Susan, biting her lip. 'I see what you mean.'

Leave over the Festive Season was split into two. Half of the staff had a week at home over Christmas. Scots took seven days that included New Year. I was sent to A2, the ward I was operated in. Any patient who could walk was sent home leaving the ward fairly quiet except for emergencies. When those on first leave returned, Big Mac and I packed our bags and made for the nearest pub.

'Your best bet, laddie,' said Big Mac downing his third pint. 'Is to try and forget about yon lassie. It can only lead to heartache fer both of yer.'

'Maybe you're right, Mac,' I replied sullenly.

But on the journey up north I couldn't get her out of my mind.

New Year passed in an alcoholic haze. At times I was tempted to go to Ellesmere Port but quickly put it out of my mind; the truth was I didn't have the courage to face Harvey. On the train back to Portsmouth I became determined to stop seeing Susan. I tried to sleep, but every time I closed my eyes the sight of her naked body flashed before me. By the time I arrived in Portsmouth I knew I was fighting a loosing battle.

However, I was in for another surprise.

No sooner had I reported for duty then I was received a telephone call ordering me to report to the regulating office.

As I entered the office, Chief Milton's leathery features broke into a grin. 'Ah yes,' he said, 'our hero from the minesweepers.'

I didn't laugh.

'What's up, Chief?' I said.

'You're going on draft again,' he said, sitting back in his chair. 'To HMS *Falcon.*'

'HMS *Falcon!'* I exploded. 'What the fuck's that? A ship?'

'No,' replied the chief. He then sat forwards and laughed. 'It's a naval air station in Malta.'

'Malta! But, Chief,' I pleaded. 'I've only just come off the 'sweepers.'

The chief shook his head. 'Don't blame me,' he replied, 'it's draftee's fault, not mine.'

Christ Almighty! I thought, wait till Susan hears this.

'When?' I asked.

'In a week's time,' replied the chief. 'You and SBA MacDonald will be flying out in a Dakota from Lee-on-Solent on Monday the twelfth of February.'

'A week's time,' I repeated. 'Bloody hell, Chief, that doesn't give us much time. Does Big Mac know yet?'

'No,' replied the chief shaking his head. 'I've just sent for him.

Just then the bulky frame of Big Mac appeared in the office.

'You sent for me, Chief?' he said, shooting me a quizzical glance.

When the chief told him he was leaving, his face lit up like a log fire.

'Bloody marvellous!' he said, banging me on the shoulder, 'All that vino and gorgeous Maltese girls. When do we get issued with our tropical gear?'

The chief handed us a signed form. 'Report to slops (naval clothing stores,) in *Dolphin* tomorrow.'

'Any chance of a few days' Foreign Service leave, Chief?' asked Big Mac

The chief gave him a look of distain, shook his head and said, 'Bugger off!'

'We'll have a bloody good time there,' said Big Mac after we left the office. 'Duty free booze and all that sunshine.'

Suddenly, all thoughts of Susan suddenly left me. Big Mac was right. At one time, Malta had been the most bombed island in the world. Recently, Eisenhower had visited the island to pay tribute to its inhabitants. In North Africa, the Allies had beaten Rommel and Sicily had fallen and the Royal Navy had greater command of the Mediterranean. Germany's last battleship the *Scharnhorst* had been sunk and Berlin was being bombed constantly.

'And besides,' I replied. 'Scouse and Tinker are in Bighi, they'll put us in the picture.'

'Well, laddie,' said Big Mac as we walked out of the office. 'This 'll solve all yer problems. Just as well too if yer ask me.'

I decided to go and see Susan.

Everyone in her ward was very busy. Trolleys and stretchers lay in the middle of the ward and staff moved behind beds surrounded by screens. Susan appeared carrying a tray of blood soaked bandages. Strands of hair hung down from under her cap, her sleeves were rolled up and beads of sweat trickled down her face. When she saw me she took a deep breath and smiled.

'Bad time to talk, Ted,' she said, coming up to me. 'We've just admitted two RTA's (Road Traffic Accidents). One's just died.'

'There's something important I have to tell you,' I said.

'Come to the flat to-night,' she replied, 'Must go, the sister's on the warpath.' She then turned and hurried towards the treatment area.

I arrived at the flat shortly after eight. She opened the door; except for her cap, she was still in her uniform and looked tired. I sat down on the sofa and she poured me a glass of beer. She then sat down and passed me a cigarette and lit it.

'Now what was it you wanted to tell me?' she asked.

I took a gulp of beer and exhaled a long stream of tobacco smoke.

'I'm going on draft to Malta!' I blurted.

Susan looked at me in amazement. Her mouth dropped open and her eyes widened.

'You can't be serious!' she gasped. *'You've not long been*

in the hospital.'

'That's what I told the Chief,' I replied. 'Big Mac's coming with me. We're going to some naval air base called HMS *Falcon.'*

Tears welled up in her eyes. 'When?' she muttered.

Before answering, I drained the glass and took another drag. 'Next Monday,' I replied.

Susan's face blanched. 'My God,' she replied in a whisper. 'That soon.'

'At least that gives us six days,' I answered, 'I suppose that's something.'

Susan stood up, placed her cigarette in an ash try, and walked to the sideboard. She took out half a bottle of gin and poured some in two glasses.

'No it doesn't,' she said, handing me a glass, 'Harvey's coming on Friday for a long weekend.'

'How is, er…everything?' I asked. 'Is he still…?'

'Yes,' replied Susan looking down into her glass. 'Nothing's changed.'

She stood looking down at me. Her eyes glistened with tears and she looked pale. With an air of resignation, she sighed. 'I suppose we both knew this couldn't last. Deep down I was expecting something like this to happen, but not quite so soon.'

I put my glass on a nearby table, stubbed out my cigarette and gently pulled her down.

'But I've not gone yet,' I said putting my arms around her.

'No Ted,' she whispered, 'Not now, later. Just hold me.'

The next day Big Mac and I went to HMS *Dolphin,* and drew two sets of Number tens, (white tropical shorts, shirts, socks and shoes,) and Number Sixes (tropical jacket and trousers).

'Och, mon!' laughed Big Mac, on the way back to the hospital, 'Wearing these, I'll put Mountbatten 'imsel ta shame.'

'Aye,' I replied. 'All you need is a few dozen medals to go with them.'

'There's still time,' he replied. 'I saw a crowd of Yanks in the "Nelson" the other night and they had loads of 'em. And the bugger's have only just arrived here.'

'Well, if Winston gives Stalin his second front,' I said. 'They might have a few more.'

'What do we care, anyway,' said Big Mac as we entered the mess. 'We'll be well and truly out of it.'

Throwing my gear on my bed, I replied, 'In that case you won't get any fuckin' medals.'

Susan had prepared lamb chops, vegetables and potatoes – the same meal she had made on our first night. As we ate in silence the tension in the air became palpable. Each mouthful stuck in my throat and even though I was hungry my stomach felt empty. We both knew this would be our last meal together and the ticking of the clock on the mantelpiece reminded us time was passing all too quickly.

'Harvey asks in his letter if you will come around on Saturday evening for a drink,' said Susan, toying with her food.

I took a deep swallow of beer. 'No,' I replied, glancing around, 'Not here. I'll meet you both in the "Nelson" around eight.'

Susan didn't answer. Instead, she pushed her plate away, and said, 'Come on, Ted, let's get pissed!'

I saw Harvey and Susan as soon as I entered the smoke-filled bar of the 'Nelson'. They were sitting at a table in a corner. Harvey was laughing while Susan sat smoking a cigarette. The place was crowded with service personnel including many Americans. Nobody appeared to be drunk, however it was shortly after eight but with over two hours left before closing time a lot of drinking time lay ahead.

When Harvey saw me his eyes lit up. He immediately stood up and came towards me. Susan looked at me and smiled; suddenly, she bit her lip and looked down at the table.

'Great to see you, Ted!' said Harvey shaking my hand. His flaxen hair looked groomed and his face had filled out. 'Susan tells me you're off to "you know where",' he added.

'Yeah, 'I replied. 'The bastards have got me again.'

While I sat down Harvey went to the bar to order drinks.

'How are you Susan?' I asked, 'Harvey's looking well.'

‘Yes,’ she replied, avoiding my gaze. ‘He’s being sent to RNB (Royal Naval Barracks) in Pompey next week. P7R.’(Medical non-drafting category.)

‘I see,’ I said, ‘Looks like you’ll be seeing a lot of one another then?’

Harvey arrived with the drinks. Susan picked up her port and lemon and quickly finished it.

For the next two hours we sat and talked about our times on board the MMS 50. Susan didn’t say much, instead she sat quietly drinking and doing her best to look interested. At 2215, the bell rang for last orders.

‘Well, good luck, to you, Ted,’ said Harvey raising his glass. ‘Take care of yourself, and when this bloody war is over, here’s hoping we meet again.’

Tears ran down Susan’s cheeks as she drained her glass of gin and lemonade.

‘Bloody hell, Ted!’ cried Harvey, passing Susan a handkerchief. ‘You must be well in, mate. She never cries when I go away.’

Suddenly I couldn’t get away quick enough.

Outside in the dimness of the blackout, servicemen and women, arms around one another staggered down the road. Strains of drunken laughter filled the air along with renderings of *Roll Out the Barrel,* and *Run Rabbit Run.*

I shook Harvey’s hand and said goodbye.

‘Drop us a line,’ he said, ‘and let us know how you are.’

‘Yes,’ I replied, knowing full well I wouldn’t.

Susan then reached up and kissed me on the cheek; I felt her fingers dig into my arm.

‘Goodbye Ted,’ she whispered, ‘Take good care of yourself. I do hope we meet again.’

The moonlight seemed to dance in her eyes as she looked up at me. My throat seemed to seize up and for a few seconds I couldn’t speak.

Finally, I muttered, ‘Yes. Me too,’ and turned away.

HMS *Falcon* was a large naval air station at Hal Far Malta. Situated a few miles inland from Valetta, the base was fully operational throughout and after the war; every type of aircraft from Spitfires to large American and British bombers used the station.

Big Mac and I met up with Scouse Kilkenny and Buster Brown again and enjoyed a few runs ashore down the Gut. We even downed a few bottles of Blue Label with little Brum when HMS *Belfast* arrived in Grand Harbour.

We celebrated in the mess on VE (Victory in Europe) Day. However, the pilots and grounds staff knew the war in the Far East was far from won. Following the dropping of the Atomic bombs on Hiroshima and Nagasaki in August 1945 Japan surrendered.

On VJ (Victory in Japan) night, Big Mac, Scouse, Buster and myself met in the 'Vernon Club' in Valetta. The city went wild with delight; bands played, people danced in the streets and bunting flew from every building; even the whores down the Gut were overgenerous with their favours.

Clutching a few bottles of 'Blue' we staggered out of a bar and wandered into Barraka Gardens. From a balcony overlooking Grand Harbour we watched as a destroyer cruised out to sea. Suddenly I gave a start! Behind came a squadron of Mickey Mouses. I strained my eyes to see if the MMS 50 was among them, but they were too far away.

'You used to be with that lot, didn't you Ted?' asked Buster. 'Too bloody small if you ask me.'

I watched as the minesweepers, dipping and rolling, sailed past the breakwater into the calm blue Mediterranean Sea. For the first time in ages I thought of Harvey and Susan. I closed my eyes and saw the faces of Eddy Godding, Joe Steele Ron Balshaw and the other lads from the MMS 50.

'They were big enough,' I replied with more than a hint of nostalgia. 'Believe you me they were – Harry Tate's Navy, you see.'

EPILOGUE

The first thing I noticed when I entered the club was a wide reception desk done in what looked like Swedish pine. Above the desk rows of naval and military crests served to remind everyone the club was primarily for service personnel past and present. Behind the counter two attractive girls, one blonde, the other black, attended to a group of people. On my left sitting behind another desk was another young man also wearing a blue shirt; he had dark hair and oriental features.

'Are you booked in, sir?' he asked.

Yes,' I replied. I then showed him my discharge papers. His eyes ran down a list. 'Ah yes, Mr Burnside. There's a message for you. A Mr Rawlinson says he will meet you in the lounge at five o'clock. Please check in at the desk.'

Good old Harvey, I said to myself, he probably thought I'd forget.

While I waited while the group in front of me were attended to, I looked around. On the right side was a lounge with comfortable-looking Chesterfield sofas and armchairs; to my left another smaller lounge with more crests on the walls was similarly furnished; on the floor immaculately polished cream tiles reflected the light from wide, dimmed glass windows. Studded lighting from a high ceiling bathed everything in a pale light producing a relaxed atmosphere of warmth and comfort.

It certainly was a far cry from the Union Jack Club I knew in 1943.

The black girl gave me lovely smile and asked me my name.

'One night, sir, with television, shower and bathroom,' she said, 'that'll be fifty pounds, fifty pence.'

I laughed and handed her my credit card. 'When I stayed at the old Union Jack in 1943 it was only one and six!'

She looked at her blonde colleague and grinned. 'Room three hundred and twenty-four, sir, on the nineteenth floor,' she replied. 'Have a good stay. The lifts are down the hall on your left.'

I thanked her and picked up my suitcase. I paused to admire the same memorial to Ethel McCaul, the founder of the club, I saw when I first came here. Underneath the glass case in which her bust rested was a plaque on which was written: 'In Gratitude For a few Scraps of Comfort'. As I read the words, I wondered what scraps of comfort awaited me inside.

To my surprise and great interest I saw that the walls on my left were full of framed photographs of men from Britain and the Commonwealth awarded the Victoria Cross.

Opposite embossed in gold lettering on oak panels were names of those similarly honoured. For a while I stood and examined the list, half-hoping to find a familiar name – wishful thinking I thought, and moved on.

Queen Victoria inaugurated the award in 1857. Since then one thousand, three hundred medals, made from the cannons captured in Crimean War had been struck. Looking around I was certain they were all represented here. It was a magnificent display and one that made me feel humble as well as proud.

At the top of the steps were three lifts, all of which were in use. Close by were two public telephone kiosks. I decided to call Edna. She sounded relieved when I spoke to her.

'Are you sure you're all right, dear?' she asked. 'Remember to wrap up well. And take your tablets.'

I smiled inwardly, told her I hadn't seen Harvey yet and not to worry. 'I'll see you tomorrow, love,' I said, and hung up.

My room, containing a single bed, wardrobe, tea-making facilities, desk and chair was small but very clean and comfortable. It reminded me of the cabin I had in Haslar when I was promoted to petty officer. However, the view was worth its weight in gold.

Under a grey sky, Waterloo Bridge with its busy pedestrians and buses stretched across the River Thames to the Embankment. The colourful glass structure of The Imax cinema loomed at the base of the bridge looking like a miniature coliseum.

Away to my right, dominating the skyline, I could see the all glass structure nicknamed by the Londoners, the 'Gherkin', dwarfing the dome of St Paul's Cathedral; on the left of the bridge was famous Savoy Hotel. Then came the rounded roofs of Charing Cross Station and further along the unmistakable gothic spires of the Houses of Parliament and Big Ben. By craning my neck to the right, I was able to see part of the National Theatre complex and the London Eye with its oval-shaped, glass pods moving imperceptibly around.

I smiled remembering Big Mac, Scouse Kilkenny and Buster and our visit to the 'Windmill Theatre'. I sighed and turned away. My God! I thought, was it really over sixty years since I was here?

By then time I had unpacked, had a nice soak in the bath to help ease the ache in my hip, the time was half past four. I made myself a cup of tea, took two painkillers and sat on the bed. Perhaps Edna would be right. Maybe Harvey and I wouldn't recognise one another; I smiled wondering what would happen then. I took a sip of tea and laughed out aloud; it would be quite hilarious if, after travelling all this way we simply sat and stared at one another, wondering who was who. Outside the window the dull rumble of trains leaving Waterloo Station brought me to my senses. My watch said 1655; to hell with it, I muttered, finishing my tea, let's see what the mystery is all about.

I took the lift to the ground floor and walked into the bar. An attractive young girl with dark hair stood behind the counter drying glasses. At one end a group of men in blue dungarees and shirts stood talking in French; another man sat perched on a stool sipping a drink.

I hurried into the lounge. It was deserted except for a white haired man sitting in a chair reading a copy of the *Evening Standard.* He was wearing a blue suit, white shirt and coloured tie; for a moment I stopped and stared at him. When he looked up I immediately recognised Harvey's face and pale blue eyes. Even though his once finely chiselled features had fattened out he hadn't changed much. Resting on the side of his chair I saw a wooden walking stick.

He took hold of the walking stick and pushed himself up. 'Ted, you old bugger!' he yelled across the room, 'Great to see you!' Walking with a limp he made his way around the glass-topped tables and leather armchairs, and grabbed my hand. 'Thanks for coming mate,' he added, his eyes moistening as he spoke. The Australian inflexion in his voice was a far cry from the Cheshire accent I remembered.

'What's with the stick, Harv?' I asked feeling my feet glide over the fine, blue-patterned carpet. 'The war?'

Harvey gave out a loud guffaw. 'No, Ted,' he replied. 'Bloody osteoarthritis of both me knees.'

'I know what you mean,' I replied, feeling my left hip. 'It's old age catching up with us. You know, I didn't think we'd recognise one another after all these years.'

He gave a grin and patted his paunch. 'We've both changed a bit but I'd recognise your ugly mug anywhere. Come on, let's sit down and have a drink.'

Although still over six feet tall, his athletic frame had spread out and his tanned features were heavily lined. His once broad shoulders were rounded and like myself he walked with a slight stoop.

We made our way to a table and two chairs. As we did so I glanced around the room. A large chandelier hung from a high ceiling and around the walls coloured etchings of eighteenth century warships were displayed in subdued lighting. In a far corner stood a model of an eighteen-gun brigantine in a glass case. One side of the wall consisted of a wide, dimmed window flanked by heavy curtains through which could be seen a leafy-green garden.

'That looks familiar,' I said, staring at a tall clock resting on a plinth above an electric piano. 'I'm sure it's the same one that was in the bar in the old club.'

'Could be,' replied Harvey. 'Can't say I remember.'

The waitress, a young girl with short dark hair and a pleasant smile, came from behind the bar carrying a tray. The nametag on her blouse read 'Marazina'. Can I get you anything, sir,' she said, looking at Harvey. Her accent was foreign but her English was very good.

'Yes, love,' replied Harvey. 'You sound foreign. Where a' you from?'

The waitress smiled and replied. 'I am from Poland, sir.'

'Stone the crows!' replied Harvey, glancing across at me. 'I met a lot of your people in the old UJ Club during the war, bloody good men too.' He then gave her a ten-pound note. 'I'll have a pint of your best bitter, and keep the change.' He paused and looked at me, 'What about you, Ted?'

'I'll have a small whisky, no ice just a drop of water, thank you,' I replied. I had a feeling I would need more than one of them before the day was much older.

The girl flashed another smile, said a polite 'thank you sir', and left.

'There seems to be a lot of people from abroad working here,' I remarked.

'Aye,' replied Harvey. 'Apparently they employ a lot of students and also have a contract with the French for the tunnel workers. Families, single women in the services are allowed in.'

I gave a short laugh. 'A far cry from the old days, eh, Harv?'

A wide grin spread across his face. 'It sure is,' he said, he then sat back in his chair. 'Well' he added with a sigh, 'here we are after all these years. I must say you look in good nick, Ted.'

'You don't look too bad yourself,' I replied, 'But tell me, how's Susan. Is she with you?'

Suddenly, his expression changed. Deep creases became etched on his and he looked down at the table.

'No, Ted,' he replied almost in a whisper. 'She's not.' He paused and continued staring at the table. 'She passed away a year ago. Heart attack.'

For a while I was I was too stunned to speak. A picture of a young, vibrant woman with a radiant smile and soft brown eyes appeared in my head. How could she possibly be dead? The thought made my stomach churn and I felt the blood drain from my face. I tried to swallow but my mouth had suddenly gone dry.

'My God, Harv!' I finally managed to say. 'That's terrible. How have you...?'

'She'd been ill for some time,' he said, interrupting me. 'Even so, it came as a shock. We came out to Oz in '48. I was a carpenter before the war and tradesmen were badly needed. I made good money and we had a good life together.' His voice faltered, 'I miss her like hell.'

The waitress arrived with the drinks. I downed mine in one swallow. Harvey took a deep gulp, and said, 'Same again, love.'

Harvey sniffed, wiped his eyes with a handkerchief and looked at me. 'Y' know, Ted,' he said with a sad, half-heated laugh, 'She once told me she thought she was in love with you. Did you know that?'

My head was still spinning. Now I knew why he didn't want to discus Susan over the telephone; I shook my head and muttered, 'No, I didn't.'

'We, er…never had kids,' he said, finishing his drink. 'You remember that injury I got coming back from Sicily?'

'Yes,' I replied, nodding my head.

'Well, it affected my John Thomas.'

The drinks arrived and I paid the waitress.

A man and woman with two young boys came into the room. They sat at one of the leather sofas that surrounded the edge of the room. The boys started to laugh and joke and were told by the man in no uncertain manner to be quiet.

Harvey glanced across at them and continued. 'I couldn't raise a bloody hard on for a year or so,' he said in a whisper. 'But after a few visits to the MO and trick cyclist (psychiatrist), things improved. But the damage was done. From then on I fired blanks.'

'I'm sorry, Harvey,' I replied. 'I didn't know.'

Harvey looked at me with a curious expression in his eyes. At that moment I realised he knew about Susan and me. My pulse rate increased and my heart thumped like a gong in my chest – so this is why he wanted to see me; I felt my face redden and wondered what he would do next.

Harvey sat forward, and with a wry smile, said, 'Susan told me all about you and her a long time ago. So take that guilty look off your face.'

I took a deep breath. 'I don't know what to say,' I replied, avoiding his gaze.

Harvey lifted his glass and took a deep swallow; I reached for my whisky and did the same. This time the liquid burnt my throat and sent a welcome glow deep inside me.

'Nothin' much to say, mate,' was Harvey's candid reply. He then stared directly at me. 'But there is something else you should know. Susan knew she didn't have long; it was her idea for me to try and find you.'

I craned forward in my chair, intrigued at Harvey's words.

'What d' you mean, Harv?' I said. 'I don't understand.'

Harvey glanced at his watch, 'You will in a few minutes,' he replied.

Just then I heard a voice with a distinct Australian accent behind me. 'The bloody tube was jam packed; I had to stand all the way from Knightsbridge.'

I turned and saw a tall man. He looked in his late fifties with dark brown hair greying at the temples. He wore a blue sports jacket, light trousers a white shirt and a loud blue and red spotted tie. In each hand he held a bulging yellow bag marked Selfridges. As I stared at him I caught my breath. The person looking down at me was the spitting image of myself at his age. He had the same swarthy complexion, brown eyes and straight nose. The only differences were his size and heavily set shoulders. With his dark, good looks he looked nothing like Harvey. He looked at Harvey and said, 'Hi Dad, the bloody traffic in this city is a crime!'

Harvey grinned and turned to me. 'I'd like you to meet Ted,' said Harvey. 'We call him Big Ted.'

Big Ted placed the bags on the floor. With more than a hint of dampness in his eyes, he extended his hand. 'I can't tell you how pleased I am to meet you at long last,' he said.

I stood up and shook his hand. I then stared down at Harvey. 'I thought you said…'

Harvey, raised a hand and interrupted me. 'I'll explain in a minute.'

Big Ted grinned at me. 'You look as if you've seen a ghost,' he said.

'I think I have,' I managed to reply.

'Ted is your son,' said Harvey looking at me. 'He's known about you since he was twelve,' he paused and looked up, 'Haven't you Big Ted?'

'Yes,' he replied. 'Mum told me all about you and her.'

'Jesus!' I exclaimed. 'You mean to tell me all these years I've had a son I never knew about?'

'That's about the size of it,' replied Harvey.

'Bloody hell!' I exclaimed, slumping into my chair.

What happened next really knocked me sideways. From his wallet Big Ted took out a coloured photograph. He passed it to me. The photograph showed a dark haired woman and Ted. On either side of them stood a grown up girl, each of whom held a baby in their arms. I felt my heart sink; one of the girls bore a remarkable resemblance to Susan.

'The woman next to me is Janet my wife,' said Big Ted bending down and pointing with his finger. 'The two girls are Susan, named after mum, and Irene. Peter and Jack are their respective sons.'

'*Jesus!*' I cried, 'you mean to tell me I'm not only a father, but a grandfather as well? I can't believe it!'

'Keep the photos,' said Big Ted. 'The names, addresses and phone numbers are on the back so you can keep in touch.'

Big Ted picked up his two bags. 'Just a few things for Janet and the family,' he said, grinning at me. 'I'll just take them upstairs. Get me in a pint. I'll be back in a jiff.'

I watched his tall frame swaying slightly as he left the lounge.

After Big Ted left, I say back in my chair, my heart pounding like a drum in my chest. 'He's a fine man,' I said to Harvey. 'I can't get over what you and Susan have done. All these years you've nurtured him as if he were your own. That's really something Harv. I feel so, so…'

Harvey reached across and covered my hand with his. 'Don't upset yourself, Ted,' he said. 'Susan and I wanted it this way.'

'You must be very proud of him.' I replied. 'What does he do?'

'He's an architect,' replied Harvey. 'He's helped to design

parts of Perth in Western Australia, where we settled down.'

'You must have thought I was a right bastard when you found out,' I said with a sigh.

'Yeah,' he replied, 'I guess I did. At first I could have killed you. I nearly walked out on her. But it was when Susan told me she still loved me I had second thoughts. I reckoned if she could put up with me and my injury problem, I should be able to forgive her. After all the war was far from over and I could have easily been killed.' He paused and took a deep breath. 'Besides, I really did love her. It was the wisest thing I ever did. Will you tell your missus?'

'Not straight away,' I replied. 'It was such a long time ago.' I paused. 'It's ironic really. Edna and I always wanted kids but an operation years ago prevented that. Now, to find out all these years later I have a son and grandchildren might be too much for her.' I toyed with my glass and added, 'In a way I've been punished for what I did, and I hope you'll forgive me, Harv.'

He shook his head and sighed. 'That war, like all fuckin' wars caused a lot of heartache, and as you've just said, it was a long time ago.'

The bar was filling up; a group of white-haired men in blue blazers were laughing and joking; they were all about the same age as Harvey and me.

'Looks like there's a bit of a re-union going on there.' I said. 'I wouldn't mind meeting the crew of the old MMS 50 again, wouldn't you?'

Harvey slowly nodded and a far away look came into his eyes. 'Aye,' he replied. 'I sure as hell would. They were the finest men I ever knew.'

I raised my glass and said, 'Here's to Susan. God Bless her.'

Harvey did the same, and added, 'and the lads of the MMS 50. I wonder where they are now?'

As we looked at one another, a lump came into my throat. 'At least we know where two of 'em are,' I said and clinked glasses.

Memorial of the R.N. Patrol Service – Lowestoft.

Burial at sea.

A typical 'Mickey Mouse'.

Me!

Another 'Mickey Mouse'. A trawler converted into a 'sweeper.

Another 'Mickey Mouse'. A trawler converted into a 'sweeper.

Me again!